EMMA DARCY

is the award-winning Australian author of over 80 Modern Romance™ novels. Her compelling, sexy, intensely emotional stories have gripped the imagination of readers around the globe. She's sold nearly 60 million books worldwide and Mills & Boon® are delighted to bring you:

Kings *of the* Outback

—three masterful brothers and the women who tame them!

Dear Reader

Last year I chartered a plane to fly me from Broome, the pearling capital of the world, right across the Kimberly region of the great Australian outback. The vast plains are home to huge cattle stations, the earth holds rich minerals, and the outposts of civilisation are few and far between. I wondered how people coped, living in such isolated communities.

'They breed them big up here,' my pilot said. 'It's no place for narrow minds, mean hearts or weak spirits. You take it on and make it work.' He grinned at me. 'And you fly. Can't do without a plane to cover the distances.'

Yes, I thought. Big men. Kings of the outback. Making it work for them. And so the King family started to take shape in my mind – one brother mastering the land, running a legendary cattle station; one who mastered the outback with flight, providing an air charter service; and one who mined its riches – pearls, gold, diamonds – selling them to the world.

Such men needed special women. Who would be their queens? I wondered. They have come to me, one by one – women who match these men, women who bring love into their lives, soulmates in every sense.

I now invite you to share the journeys of the heart for these Kings of the Outback. Firstly is Nathan and Miranda's story. Tom's will follow. Then Jared's. Three romances encompassing the timeless, primitive challenge of the Australian outback, and a touch of what the Aboriginals call 'The Dreamtime'.

With love –

Emma Darcy

Kings *of the* Outback

THE CATTLE KING'S MISTRESS

THE PLAYBOY KING'S WIFE

THE PLEASURE KING'S BRIDE

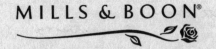

MILLS & BOON®

*All the characters in this book have no existence outside the imagination
of the author, and have no relation whatsoever to anyone bearing the
same name or names. They are not even distantly inspired by any
individual known or unknown to the author, and all the incidents are
pure invention.*

*First published in Great Britain as a collection 2004
Harlequin Mills & Boon Limited,
Eton House, 18-24 Paradise Road,
Richmond, Surrey, TW9 1SR*

KINGS OF THE OUTBACK © Harlequin Enterprises II B.V., 2004

The publisher acknowledges the copyright holder of the
individual works as follows:

The Cattle King's Mistress © Emma Darcy 2000
The Playboy King's Wife © Emma Darcy 2000
The Pleasure King's Bride © Emma Darcy 2000

ISBN 0 263 84094 8

108-0404

*Printed and bound in Spain
by Litografia Rosés S.A., Barcelona*

*Look out for Emma Darcy's exciting new trilogy
that starts this month in Modern Romance !*

OUTBACK KNIGHTS

Once they were Outback bad boys.

*Now they're rich, powerful men...and marriage
is their mission!*

April – THE OUTBACK MARRIAGE RANSOM

June – THE OUTBACK WEDDING TAKEOVER

November – THE OUTBACK BRIDAL RESCUE

THE CATTLE KING'S MISTRESS

CHAPTER ONE

MISTRESS to a married man…no way!

Miranda realised she was gritting her teeth again and consciously relaxed her jaw. She'd end up grinding her teeth right down if she kept thinking of Bobby Hewson and his blithe assumption they could continue as lovers, his forthcoming marriage being no barrier whatsoever to what *they shared!*

Well, he could find someone else to warm his bed next time he flew into Sydney. Adultery was not her scene. She might have been a fool to have let Bobby play her along with promises for three years, but she was not going to be *used* for his extra-marital pleasure. She'd seen what that second-string kind of relationship had done to her mother. Never, never, never would she go down the same demeaning and destructive path!

"Miss Wade, your gin and tonic."

Miranda wrenched her mind off burning thoughts and looked up at the smiling airline hostess who proceeded to lay a serviette on the small metal drinks tray, which extended from the wide armrest of the first-class seat. A little bottle of gin, a can of tonic water and a glass with ice cubes were set down.

Nice to be treated to first-class service by her new employers, Miranda thought, and hoped the drink might help relax her. "Thank you," she said, returning the smile.

The hostess's eyes glowed with interest as she remarked, "I just noticed the book in your lap, *King's Eden*. Are you heading there?"

It was the book Elizabeth King had given her for background information, once Miranda had signed the two-year contract that tied her to managing the wilderness resort. A history of the place and the family who owned it might be dry reading, but mandatory in the circumstances, and the best use of these hours in flight to Darwin. Miranda sternly told herself it was time she concentrated on her future course and put the past in the past.

"Yes, I am," she answered, deciding to plumb the interest being displayed. "Do you know it?"

"I've been there," came the obviously enthusiastic reply. "It's what you might call a legendary place in the Kimberly, owned and run by the cattle Kings. Now that they've opened up the wilderness park for tourists and built a resort to cater for them, it's a very popular outback destination."

"Did you stay at the resort?"

"Not at the homestead." An expressive eye-roll. "Too expensive. A group of us stayed three days in the tented cabins at Granny Gorge."

Tented cabins, camping sites, bungalows and homestead suites—four levels of accommodation to be managed, Miranda reminded herself—a far cry from a five-star hotel. Was she mad to take it on...two years in the wilderness?

"Did you think it was worth the trip?" she asked the hostess.

"Oh, yes! Well worth it! I've never seen so many

butterflies. The trees around there were filled with them. And we swam in a gorgeous turquoise waterhole fed by waterfalls off the cliffs. Great way to have a shower.''

"So you'd definitely recommend it.''

"To anyone,'' the hostess confirmed. "Don't miss the Aboriginal carvings in the caves if you go to the Gorge.''

"I won't. Thank you.''

Well, King's Eden had appealed to at least one person, Miranda noted as the hostess moved off. Its only appeal to her at the present moment, was the chance it offered to live her life on her own terms.

If she'd stayed with the Regency hotel chain, she might have moved from assistant manager in Sydney to an overseas posting, an ambition she'd once nursed, but it would have only happened now if she'd also stayed sweet with Bobby. He'd made that clear, offering steps up the managerial ladder as a persuader to win her compliance with his marriage, which, he'd argued, was only for the purpose of cementing an alliance between two great international hotel chains.

Another lie!

The photograph of his French fiancée in the newspaper was more than enough proof to Miranda that Bobby would find his honeymoon no hardship at all.

He'd obviously been lying to her all along—three years of lies. The only thing she'd ended up believing was his threat to stop her getting a decent position anywhere else if she walked out on him. It was sickeningly clear he'd do and say anything to get his own way.

King's Eden offered her the perfect escape from that

kind of victimisation. It was a one-off resort complex, not linked to anything or anyone that Bobby Hewson could touch or influence.

She smiled grimly as she recalled one of the questions Elizabeth King had asked at the interview.

"You are...unattached?"

*De*tached, Miranda had almost answered, barely swallowing her bitterness over Bobby's sleazy propositions and manipulations. "I am completely free, Mrs King," she had stated. "My life is very much my own."

And that was how it was going to be at King's Eden, Miranda vowed. Her own life run by herself. She didn't care how different the environment was, what problems she'd have to cope with. Her strong sense of self-worth demanded she make good on her own abilities...not by being a playboy's mistress!

She opened the book on her lap, determined on focusing her mind on the future. A map on the first page showed the Kimberly region—three hundred and twenty thousand square kilometres, stretching from the seaport of Broome on the high west coast of Australia to the border of the Northern Territory. Blocked out in green was King's Eden—a big chunk of outback country that would be the last place on earth Bobby Hewson would look for her.

It might not be the Garden of Eden, but at least it had no serpent in it. With that blessed assurance in her mind, Miranda turned the page and began reading, acutely aware of having turned a page in her life and there was only one way to go...forward.

CHAPTER TWO

"Just tell me one thing, Mother. Why choose a woman?"

Because you need one.

And with Susan Butler finally out of your life, you might look for more than a convenient mistress.

Elizabeth King hid these thoughts as she assessed the depth of her eldest son's annoyance at the decision she'd made. The irritable note in his voice and the V creased between his brows, plus the tense impatience of his actions since he'd entered the sitting-room, did not promise an encouraging start between Nathan and Miranda Wade, whom he was about to meet.

Running the resort was part of Tommy's business. Running the cattle station was his, and he drew a firm line between the two enterprises. For the most part, Nathan kept his world to himself, but to Elizabeth's mind, that had to change.

He was thirty-five years old. Time for him to get married. Time for him to have children. Passing that particular buck to his younger brothers wouldn't wash. It was Nathan who had inherited the major share of Lachlan's genes and Elizabeth didn't want to see them wasted.

"I chose the person with the best qualifications to manage the resort," she answered, raising a quizzical eyebrow at the man who was so very much his father's son. "I wasn't aware you held any prejudice against women taking on responsible positions, Nathan."

He threw her a mocking look from the leather armchair he'd made his, since it was the only one big enough to accommodate his length and breadth comfortably. "Not even you could stick it out here all year around."

That old argument wouldn't wash, either. "I had other interests to look after, as you very well know."

His eyes remained sceptical. "The point is, we all agreed a married couple was the best choice."

"Fine, if the marriage is stable," Elizabeth retorted, a pointed reminder that the last manager had left under threat of divorce by his wife. "And who is to judge how good a relationship is, on an interview where everyone puts their best foot forward? We've been down that track."

"Then I would have thought a single man would cope with the location better than a single woman," he argued.

Elizabeth shrugged. "I wasn't impressed with the men who applied. A bit too soft for my liking."

"So what have we got? A woman of steel?" His mouth thinned. "She'd better be, because I will not be at her beck and call to clean up any mess she makes of it. If she needs someone to hold her hand, Tommy can do it."

"I'm sure you can make that clear to her, Nathan." Elizabeth could not repress a satisfied little smile as she added, "If you wish to."

Nathan's black eyebrows beetled down. "What's that supposed to mean?"

"I doubt Miranda Wade would be inclined to cling to any man's hand." *And that, my son, may well set a sexual challenge you'll find hard to resist.*

"Just what we need—a raging feminist to play charming hostess to the resort guests who expect to be pampered," he commented derisively.

"Oh, I think someone who's been in the hospitality trade for twelve years knows how to manage guests," Elizabeth drawled. "But judge for yourself, Nathan. That sounds like Tommy's vehicle arriving now. I trust you'll make an effort to be welcoming."

He rolled his eyes and muttered, "I'm sure Tommy will be in good form. He'll undoubtedly cover any lapse on my part."

True, Elizabeth thought. Her highly extroverted middle son was probably flirting his head off with Miranda Wade right now. It was second nature to Tommy to spark a response in women. He liked to be liked. But the cool blonde she'd interviewed would let his charm wash over her like water off a duck's back. Those green eyes of hers had burned with a need to prove something to herself. They were focused inwardly, not outwardly.

It would be interesting to see if Nathan drew a flicker of awareness from her, Nathan who was what he was and you could like him or not as you pleased. He was a challenge, too. A challenge most women gave up on. Elizabeth didn't think Miranda Wade was the giving-up type. Even so, the equation still needed the right chemistry, and no one could make that happen.

Such a capricious element—sexual chemistry—but vital. She could only hope…

Miranda had seen it from the air this morning—the area comprising the resort and the layout of the cattle station. She hadn't realised the buildings relating to each business would be entirely separate, the "homestead" at the resort having no connection whatsoever to the family homestead. The former was of very modern design and construction. The latter, as it was approached at ground level, gathered an allure that touched an empty place in her life.

Deep roots had been put down here, the kind of roots she had never known. Nothing had been fixed or solid in her mother's life and Miranda had been glad to get out of it, knowing she was an unwelcome reminder of her mother's mistake, a reminder of her age, too, as well as a resented distraction to the men who'd kept her.

As soon as she was sixteen, she'd left and had been in live-in hotel positions ever since, not really letting her surroundings touch her. They were simply places that put a roof over her head. She had no sense of *home,* no sense of family tradition, no sense of belonging to anything except herself.

It felt strange, coming face-to-face with something so different to her own experience. No modern landscaping here. The trees that had been planted for both shade and ornament were old, the girth of their trunks and the breadth of their branches proclaiming the growth of more years than any one person's lifetime. The intense entanglement of the multicoloured bougainvillea hedge surrounding the house indicated longevity, as well.

Like all the buildings on the cattle station, the homestead was white, set off by an expanse of green lawns. However, it sat alone, on a rise above the river, and the verandahs with their ornamentation of cast-iron balustrading and frieze panels, topped by the symmetrical peaks of its roof gave it the appearance of a shining crown on top of all the land it overlooked.

As Tommy King drove his Jeep up to the front steps, she was prompted by the sheer scale of the house to ask, "When was this built?"

"Oh, coming up ninety years ago," he answered with one of his sparkling grins. "One of the first King brothers here—Gerald it was—saw some government official's home in Queensland and was so impressed with it, he copied the design and had all the materials shipped to Wyndham."

Cost no object, Miranda thought, recalling from the book she'd read that the first pioneering King brothers had mined a fortune in gold at Kalgoorlie before taking up this land.

"It's very impressive," she murmured, thinking houses simply weren't built to such huge proportions any more. Certainly not in suburbia, she amended, smiling ruefully at her limited knowledge.

"It used to serve many purposes in the old days," Tommy cheerfully explained. "Everyone lived in and travellers passing through stopped by for days to rest up. Hospitality has always been big in the outback."

"I guess it broke the sense of isolation," Miranda remarked.

"Well, taking to the air fixes that now," he answered, his handsome face beaming pleasure in the accessibility he provided.

She'd learnt he owned and ran an airline company from Kununurra, small plane and helicopter charters making up the bulk of his business, much of which was connected to the resort. Tommy King was a go-getter entrepreneur, with the confidence, likeable personality and gift of the gab that could sell anything. Most of all himself.

Miranda wasn't about to buy. The charm came too easily, and while he might be a shrewd businessman and definitely no lightweight for a man only in his early thirties, he had playboy looks; a riot of black curly hair that bobbed endearingly over his forehead, dark dancing eyes inviting flirtatious fun, a face as handsome as sin, and a lean, athletic body exuding charismatic energy and sex appeal.

She'd been in his company since he'd collected her from Kununurra airport this morning and as an informative guide he was excellent, but she was determined on keeping a very firm personal distance between them. The likes of Tommy King could not tempt her into mixing business with pleasure. She hoped he was getting that message because she certainly didn't want an awkward situation developing between them.

"This place is getting to be like a white elephant now," he commented as he brought the Jeep to a halt. "Wasted…" He shook his head over the wicked shame of it. "Guests would probably give their eye-teeth to stay here, but Nathan just won't hear of it." He grimaced, though his dark eyes twinkled cheerfully at her as he added, "Like a brick wall, my brother."

Nathan…oldest son of Elizabeth and Lachlan. Just as well she had studied the family tree in the book on

King's Eden. The people she'd met so far assumed she knew these details about the Kings as well as they did.

"It's understandable that he prefers privacy for his family," Miranda said, thinking some things came ahead of turning everything into dollars.

"If he ever got himself married and had a family, I'd agree," Tommy shot back at her. "As it is, he's here by himself most of the time, and that doesn't look like changing."

He alighted from the Jeep, quickly striding around it to open Miranda's door for her. She had little time to digest this new information. The invitation to dine with the family at the old homestead tonight had seemed to encompass more than the actual reality of one man. Two, counting Tommy.

"I thought Mrs King lived here, too," she said as she stepped out of the Jeep.

"Not on any regular basis. Mum's fairly tied up in Broome, managing the pearl farm…"

Pearls…

He grinned. "…but she flew in yesterday to be on hand to greet you and make sure everything is to your satisfaction."

Her inner tension eased. She wouldn't be the only woman at the dinner table. Elizabeth King would undoubtedly direct the conversation tonight and provide a comfort zone. Miranda smiled. "How kind of her!"

Tommy laughed. "Mum is a diplomat from way back."

They proceeded up the steps, Miranda wondering just how different the two brothers were and how much their mother had to work at welding their separate interests into a reasonably harmonious unit. "Isn't there a third son?" she asked tentatively, her mind seeing three names listed in print—Nathan, Thomas, Jared.

But the book on King's Eden had been written some years ago. She had assumed marriages would have taken place since then. Having been wrong on that score with Tommy and Nathan, and with no mention being made of a younger brother from Tommy, she wondered if something had happened to the third son.

"Oh, Jared flits around the mining operations and oversees what's done with the pearls. He's hardly ever here," came the offhand reply. "You'll probably meet him some time or other but not tonight. I think he's in Hong Kong at the moment."

Mining operations...

Miranda did a very quick mental readjustment about the King family. What she was meeting here was very serious wealth, on a similar scale, if not higher, than the Hewson family. All three of the King brothers would be used to getting what they wanted, just as Bobby was. When they married, it would undoubtedly be into a family who had connections to their business interests and could probably broaden and enhance them. That was the way their kind of world worked.

She was an outsider, an employee who had her uses. Miranda resolved to keep those *uses* strictly defined. No blurred lines. However attractive any of the King men were, they were out of bounds in any personal sense.

She would never allow herself to be flattered by Tommy's show of interest. If Nathan had a brick wall around him, it could stay totally intact, as far as she was concerned. Jared was more or less out of the picture so she didn't have the problem of proximity with him.

Best to concentrate completely on Elizabeth King tonight.

With this decision firmly settled in her mind, Miranda's attention turned to observing features of the house she was entering. Leadlight windows surrounded the solid cedar door Tommy opened for her. As she stepped into the main entrance hall, she realised it ran right through to the back of the house and actually formed a gallery of framed photographs. A collection of King's Eden history, she wondered, but didn't have the opportunity to look.

Tommy walked straight to the first door off the hallway and ushered her into a sitting room so full of riches, she was momentarily dazed by all there was to see. Much of the decor had an Asian influence, yet there seemed be an eclectic range of styles that somehow melded together into a fascinating collection.

Her skating gaze was halted—joltingly—by the man rising from a large leather armchair, a man whose length seemed to climb up like a mountain, blocking everything else out. He had to be well over six foot, broad-shouldered, broad-chested, one of the biggest men Miranda had ever met, and all of him emitting hard muscular strength that gave way to nothing.

Unaccountably a convulsive little shiver ran down her spine. His sheer physical presence had an impact that seemed to hit her whole nervous system, leaving her with an odd tremulous feeling that was deeply disturbing. He wasn't threatening her. He stood out of courtesy. She had no cause to feel...vulnerable.

With a sense of self-determination, Miranda made eye contact with him and plastered a polite little smile on her face. *His* face could have been carved out of brown granite—all hard, sharp planes. Even the curves of his mouth seemed carved, defined emphatically, as though to deny any softness. Absolutely nothing "pretty-playboy" about Nathan King.

His thick black hair was straight. His black brows were straight. And cutting straight across the room at her were laser-sharp blue eyes, the vivid intensity of their colour made all the more stunning by his darkly tanned skin. Miranda felt utterly pinned by them, unable to break their captivating power...until Elizabeth King spoke.

"Welcome to King's Eden..."

Miranda jerked her head towards the distinctive, familiar voice. The woman who had hired her sat on an ornately carved armchair, its rich scarlet and gold silk upholstery forming a striking frame for her white hair and white pantsuit. And the beautiful pearls around her neck.

"It's both a pleasure and a privilege to be here, Mrs King," Miranda managed to reply with creditable aplomb. "Thank you for inviting me."

The older woman was smiling, her dark eyes warm with some private satisfaction. She waved attention back to her son. "This is Nathan, who has the controlling hand on the station. Miranda Wade, Nathan, our new resort manager."

He remained precisely where he was, sizing her up,

silent, formidable, daunting, challenging. For a moment, Miranda remained pinned, but the long years of training for greeting people urged her forward. Taking the initiative always broke the ice. She had to associate with this man, when business required his co-operation. Some kind of reasonable footing with him had to be developed.

Yet all the stern reasoning in her mind had no strengthening effect on her legs. They were alarmingly shaky as she stepped forward to offer her hand to Nathan King. This was a man who would dominate everything he touched...and she was about to touch him.

CHAPTER THREE

NATHAN was stunned. He'd seen many beautiful women but none quite as striking as this one. From head to foot she was something else...built on a scale that accentuated every womanly asset. And she certainly had them all!

She almost matched Tommy in height, which had to put her close to six feet tall and she wasn't wearing high heels. Her hair was an instant tactile temptation, a softly curved fall to her shoulders, gleaming with a fascinating blend of blonde shades from silver to strawberry.

The classical perfection of her face was made even more intriguing by the slight cleft at the centre of her chinline, and the long neck below it promised an alluring suppleness. Her honey-gold skin glowed—face, arms, legs—all bare, and her limbs were as perfectly proportioned as her face.

She wore a rather high-necked, sleeveless dress that skimmed her lushly curved figure, the skirt flaring to just above her knees, a modest dress but boldly coloured in an abstract floral pattern on black. Splotches of lemon, orange, lime green, turquoise, royal blue seemed to leap off the black background, a dazzling kaleidoscope of colour. On her feet were strappy lemon sandals.

A very confident woman, Nathan thought, prepared

to stand out rather than blend in. A strong individual. Certainly no shy violet or clinging vine. A long dormant excitement began to stir in him. This might be a woman worth knowing...an experience worth having.

The visual pleasure of her was too enticing to give up. He stayed where he stood, letting her move forward to formalise his mother's introduction. Lovely, almond-shaped, green eyes, as uniquely distinctive as the rest of her. Honey-brown lashes and brows. Was the hair-colour natural?

"I'm delighted to meet you, Mr King," she said with cool deliberation as she held out her hand.

Establishing impersonal distance.

Nathan barely stopped himself from grinning at the implicit challenge as he gripped her hand, enfolding it in his own, liking the soft, silky warmth of it. His smile was controlled into a mere expression of friendly acknowledgement. Playing the stand-offish game suited him just as well, while he took her measure.

"Even the children on the station call me Nathan, so please feel comfortable with it," he assured her. "And since the resort also operates on a first name basis, I trust I may call you Miranda."

"Of course," she answered smoothly, starting to extract her hand.

Nathan did not resist the movement, finding it interesting she felt the need to break the physical link with him so quickly. It wasn't exactly a rude rejection of contact, more a discomfort with it. Did she sense what she was stirring in him? Was she stirred herself? Her eyes reflected no more than the obliging interest of an employee to an employer, not so much as a hint of speculation on a woman to man basis.

His mother's words came back to him... *I doubt Miranda Wade would be inclined to cling to any man's hand.*

"What would you like to drink?" he asked, wondering if she was a raging feminist. "My mother's having champagne..."

"A glass of water would be fine," she quickly interposed.

Keeping a cool head, Nathan thought as he nodded and disconnected himself from her by turning to his brother. "A beer for you, Tommy?"

"Thanks, Nathan," came the ready agreement.

He left them to sort out seating while he got the drinks from the bar in the adjoining billiard room. Miranda Wade was not a woman to be rushed. That much was obvious. He had the impression there were many layers to her, not an easy woman to tag in any sense.

He wondered how Tommy was faring with her. His brother had spent most of the day in her company. Had he managed to draw any sparks of interest? Resolving to simply sit and watch the interplay between them, Nathan returned with the drinks, ironically amused at the way this meeting was turning out. His annoyance with his mother's decision had winked out the moment Miranda Wade had appeared in person.

She'd chosen to sit in an armchair close to his mother, right across the room from where he'd been seated. Tommy bridged the gap, having dropped onto a sofa that could have invited sharing, but that option had not been taken up by the fair Miranda. She nodded to a drink coaster on the small table beside her as Nathan approached and gave him a flashing smile of acknowledgement when he set the glass down where she'd indicated.

"Thank you," she said, breaking briefly from her conversation with his mother, then instantly resuming it.

Done with grace, but holding him at a very firm distance, Nathan observed. He didn't linger, didn't attempt to draw her attention. A two-year contract gave him plenty of time to make her acquaintance. He strolled over to Tommy and handed him the beer.

"Happy with the choice?" he asked quietly, watching for any reservation in his brother's expressive eyes.

"Are you?" Tommy retorted, mischief dancing.

Nathan shrugged. "Your business, Tommy."

"An asset, I think." Definitely male appreciation in the gaze he slanted at Miranda. However his mouth made a wry little moue as he added, "Mind very focused on the job."

"Glad to hear it," Nathan murmured and moved back to his chair, content with the confirmation that his brother's charm had failed to evoke the usual response.

This now promised to be a most interesting evening. Didn't feminists preach wanting men, not needing them? Sexual freedom? Taking as they pleased? What if Miranda Wade wanted what he wanted?

Miranda was grateful the meal had been easy to eat—prawns cooked with coconut and served with a mango sauce, followed by barramundi, and now a melt-in-the-mouth passion-fruit mousse. Dining with the Kings was certainly a testing experience, but she thought she'd managed the evening reasonably well, given the unnerving presence of the man at the head of the table.

Nathan had barely said a word during the dinner conversation, but she was acutely aware of him listening to everything she said, the turn of his head towards her, the silent force of his concentrated attention. She sensed he was cataloguing her questions, her responses, her opinions, building up a picture of the kind of person she was while giving nothing of himself away.

The worst of it was, she kept remembering how his hand had felt, wrapped around hers. Maybe it was because he was the cattle King, but the impression he had left was one of branding her with his imprint. She wished he wasn't quite so big, so overwhelmingly *male*. It made her ridiculously conscious of being female, disconcertingly so since not even Bobby Hewson had triggered such a disturbingly pervasive effect on her.

Fortunately, both Tommy, sitting across the table from her, and Elizabeth King at the foot of it, had been very relaxed in their manner towards her, friendly, helpful, informative. And the dining room itself was a fascinating distraction from the man who dominated too much of it.

All the furniture here was of beautiful, polished mahogany. China cabinets held a magnificent array of treasures. The paintings on the walls were of birds and executed in splendid detail. Everything looked in mint condition and Miranda wondered about the household staff. Dinner had been served by a middle-aged woman, introduced as Nancy, but there had to be several people looking after this amazing place.

Elizabeth King casually remarked, "I think it would be a good idea for Miranda to do the regular tourist trips before the season really gets underway at the resort. She should know at firsthand what she's recommending to guests."

Tommy frowned. "Sam's still laid up with a sprained ankle…"

Miranda had already met Samantha Connelly, the resident helicopter pilot at the resort, a generally pleasant young woman, though bluntly terse in response to Tommy's teasing over her temporary handicap.

"I'm flying down to the Bungle Bungle Range, day after tomorrow. Miranda can come with me if she likes."

The words were spoken offhandedly, yet coming so unexpectedly from Nathan, they had the effect of a thunderbolt cracking through the air, jolting the rest of the company.

Tommy's head swivelled towards his older brother. *"You?"*

The astonishment in his voice heightened the weird panic attacking Miranda's stomach. She had to force herself to glance at the man who was offering her his company on a one-to-one basis. It felt as though her whole body was screaming danger. Yet there was nothing on his face to indicate any special interest in her.

He raised an eyebrow at Tommy as though his brother was over-reacting to a perfectly natural suggestion. "Some problem?" he asked.

"And never the twain shall meet except during the

June muster,'' Tommy drily taunted. ''Here it is only March, Nathan, and you're offering to help with resort business?''

''Hardly business,'' he retorted just as drily. ''I'm making the trip anyway. It's an opportunity going begging if Miranda wants to take it up.''

His gaze swung to her inquiringly.

Trapped in a small plane or helicopter with *him?* Her mind scurried to find some excuse not to accept.

''What are you going for?'' Tommy asked, giving her more time.

The mesmerising blue eyes released her as they targeted his brother again. ''The head park ranger wants to borrow the Sarah King diaries on the local Aboriginal tribes. Background reading. I said I'd drop them in to him.''

''Well, that fixes one trip for you, Miranda,'' Elizabeth King said brightly, her face beaming satisfaction.

''But, Mrs King, the day after tomorrow...'' Miranda frowned. ''I see this week as very busy, getting myself familiarised with the workings of the resort and checking the intake of staff for the season. Much as I appreciate the offer, Nathan—'' she quickly constructed a look of apologetic appeal ''—I have barely arrived and...''

''Best to go while you can, Miranda,'' Elizabeth King interjected firmly. ''Besides, it won't be taking up Samantha's time or using one of Tommy's pilots. This is much the more economical arrangement.''

Which neatly whipped the mat out from under

Miranda's feet, since insistence on some other time would cost the resort money.

"A dawn trip, Nathan?" his mother went on, having dispensed with any further protest from Miranda.

"Oh, I daresay we can catch the sunrise," he answered.

Miranda sat seething as they settled the arrangements between them, totally ignoring whether what was being decided suited her or not. The arrogance of wealth, she thought, moving people around like pawns to their will. She barely quelled the urge to make a stand against them. The problem was she wasn't familiar with the outback and firsthand experience of it probably was important in handling her job well.

And, in fact, she wouldn't be objecting at all if it wasn't Nathan she had to accompany. He rattled her. She didn't feel in control with him. *Get a grip on yourself, Miranda,* she sternly berated herself. Like it or not, she had to deal with Nathan King, and maybe getting to know him better was the best way. He might lose his attraction on closer acquaintance.

"I'll have you back at the resort by noon," he assured her.

Six hours close to him. "Thank you," she said, her heart fluttering in agitation.

"What do you think of it?"

"Pardon?" What was he referring to?

His eyes glinted with amused mockery, making her even more nervous. Did he sense how she felt about him?

"The resort. Since you've always held a city position, I wondered how it looked to you. I presume Tommy took you on a tour of it this afternoon.''

"The accommodation sectors are exceptionally well planned,'' she could answer with confidence. ''The homestead is brilliantly located, and the decor very attractive. Everything looks top class.''

One eyebrow rose challengingly. "No sinking heart feeling? No uneasy twang of, What have I done?''

She laughed and shook her head. ''More, How marvellous! I'm really looking forward to taking over and making the best of it.''

"A new world for you.''

"Yes.''

"Most people hang onto the world they know.''

"I guess I'm not most people.''

"An adventuress? Looking for something different?''

"More satisfying a need for something different.''

"Then I hope all your needs are satisfied here.''

"That would indeed be Eden.''

He laughed, his whole face springing alive so strikingly, Miranda was totally captivated by it. Her mind was zinging from the quick repartee between them and her body was pumping adrenaline so fast, every part of her felt highly invigorated.

His eyes literally danced with pleasure, shooting tingles of it into her bloodstream as he remarked, ''I tend to think Eden is what we fashion for ourselves. It seems to me that's what our choices are about…aiming for what will give us a happy situation.''

She was suddenly hit by a shockwave of intimacy that had to be turned back. Common sense insisted on

ringing down a warning that life wasn't quite as easy
as that. "Unfortunately we can't control the choices
other people make," she replied, her eyes trying to cool
the warmth in his. "And that can create a hell for us."

"You can always walk away."

"But will they respect that?"

"Make them."

"I'm not quite as big as you, Nathan," she retorted
lightly.

He smiled. "But you do have a mind of your own,
Miranda. And very interesting it is."

"Thank you."

"Oh, I should be thanking you. I'm sure you will
take any boredom out of our trip together."

Miranda's breath caught in her throat. He didn't
mean the flight to the Bungle Bungle Range. She knew
he didn't. He meant the continuing journey of a close
acquaintance spreading over the two years she was going to be here. And that was going to be very, very
dangerous to any peace of mind.

"Well, don't forget to be a tour guide, as well,
Nathan," Tommy drawled. "This is resort business."

Was there a touch of resentment in his voice. A flash
of sibling rivalry? Miranda quickly switched her attention to the man whose interests she would be looking
after. "I'll make the most of the trip, Tommy," she
assured him. "I know how essential it is that I do."
She mustn't—not for one moment—forget her place.

He nodded.

"I'm sure you'll find it an amazing experience,"
Elizabeth King put in with an approving smile.

Miranda hoped so. She would need every amazing
distraction she could get to keep holding Nathan King
at a distance.

CHAPTER FOUR

NEEDING to push Nathan King out of her mind and gain a sense of control over her immediate environment, Miranda filled her first morning at King's Eden with a staff meeting. Since the resort was only open from the beginning of April to the end of November, the full complement of employees was not yet in residence, but the maintenance crew and those in charge of each accommodation level and amenities rolled up to meet and assess their new manager.

Miranda was very aware of not having the firsthand knowledge of this area, while those facing her did. She'd had no experience of the Big Wet, the monsoonal rains that made much of the Top End of Australia inaccessible by road during the summer months, but the oppressive heat outside was enough to convince her the December to March period was not a good time to travel to this part of the outback for sightseeing, even by air. She blessed the fact the resort homestead was air-conditioned, or she'd be wilting in front of these people.

They had spread themselves around the large living area, which had been designed for the pleasure and comfort of top-paying guests. The slate floor in blue-green hues looked invitingly cool and the cane furniture with its brightly patterned cushions lent a relaxing, tropical feel to the room. Aboriginal artefacts and paintings were reminders of how close visitors were to an ancient heritage. A wall of glass gave a view of the resort pool and some of the outdoors chairs had been brought inside to accommodate everyone.

Miranda had deliberately chosen this normally exclusive leisure room as the gathering place, wanting to set the tone of a top team getting together. The resort restaurant was used for staff meetings when business was in full swing, but this was only the key group who would be answering directly to her and she needed to get them onside.

They all wore casual clothes, shorts and T-shirts, a different vision of staff for her, accustomed as she was to more formal uniforms. Miranda had donned a lime-green sleeveless shift, wanting the effect of both dignity and simplicity, and she'd wound her hair up for a look of neat efficiency, but she quickly decided that tailored safari shorts and shirt were more the style for this resort. Stupid to look out of place.

Apart from a couple of men on the maintenance crew, everyone else was younger than she was, very young in terms of managerial positions. Understandable in such a location, she quickly reasoned. A spirit of adventure had probably brought them here, wanting the outback experience while they were still footloose and fancy free, or at least not tied down with families.

She spent most of the meeting asking questions, listening to reports, inviting suggestions for resolving problems, which were raised, keeping discussions open while she absorbed the easy camaraderie amongst the staff and made notes on the practicalities of getting things done in time for the beginning of the season.

Over and over again, mention was made of problems caused by cancelling the regular time-off for the transient service staff. They went stir-crazy, becoming careless and rude to guests. Breaks away from the isolation of the resort restored their good humour. It only raised trouble if too many bookings required the postponing of leave.

Miranda took on board that everyone was keen for her to understand this. Isolation was a very real social problem. Her mind drifted to the King family…a hundred years of living in isolation…Nathan running the cattle station…alone, unmarried. Did he ever feel stir-crazy? Would she, here at King's Eden?

Paradise or hell?

Too late to change her decision to take this job on, Miranda sternly reminded herself. Whatever its difficulties, she *would* see it through. Nathan had been subtly challenging her on that last night. Her jaw tightened as she recalled his amused mockery. She would show him!

Having collected all the information she wanted from her staff, Miranda brought the meeting to a close with a personal policy statement, emphasising that good hospitality depended on good communication and she didn't want any breakdowns in that area. Anticipation of guest requirements was her other main point and she would be instituting checks that would help to ensure this.

The response was nods and smiles of satisfaction. Having memorised names throughout the morning,

Miranda made a point of using them as the dispersing staff made friendly parting comments. Samantha Connelly, the injured helicopter pilot, stayed behind, her sprained ankle propped on a footstool.

"Do you need help?" Miranda asked with a sympathetic smile.

"I'm here to help you," was the dry reply. "Until I can throw away these wretched crutches."

She leaned over the side of the armchair to pick up the resented aids to her disability. Sensing a fierce independence Miranda made no move to do it for her. She admired the head of burnished copper curls as it bobbed down and noticed the well-defined musculature in the young woman's arms. Samantha Connelly was built on a smaller and more slender scale than Miranda herself, but she was certainly lithe and strong.

"I hate being hobbled," she muttered as her face came up, though her expression was one of wry resignation as she added, "Stuck in an office instead of flying high."

"I didn't realise you did office work, as well," Miranda said in surprise.

"Oh, I fill in, taking the resort bookings at the Kununurra Headquarters during the Wet. Not so much charter business then. I've loaded all the facts and figures into your computer here, so if you need a hand with anything until your clerical assistant clocks on…"

"I'd appreciate it," Miranda said warmly.

"No problem." Samantha slid her leg off the footstool and heaved herself out of the armchair.

Miranda had the impression of a pride that would always deny personal problems and minimise others as much as possible. The young pilot had a rather narrow, gamine face, her fair skin liberally freckled, yet an innate strength of character seemed to shine through its finely boned structure and her sky-blue eyes would undoubtedly scorn any suggestion of cuteness.

"How did you get into flying?" Miranda asked, as they set off towards the wide hallway that bisected the homestead and led to the administration and accommodation wings.

"I was born to it," came the dismissive reply. "Since I'm currently grounded, I guess Tommy jumped in and offered to fly you around the regular tours." She slanted Miranda a derisive look. "Only too eager to show you the sights, I'll bet."

Caution was instantly pricked. "Why should he be eager, Samantha?"

"Call me Sam. Everyone else does." Another derisive look. "And if you didn't notice Tommy's tongue hanging out yesterday, I sure did. To put it bluntly, Miranda, you're stacked in all the right places and gorgeous to boot. So don't tell me he didn't give you the rush."

Jealousy? The acid little thread in Sam's tone alerted Miranda to very sensitive ground here. "Well, I guess the rush got diverted," she answered dryly. "In any event I'm not interested in a personal relationship with Tommy King."

"You're not?" Sam stopped, eyeing Miranda with sheer astonishment. "Most women fall for him like ninepins."

She shrugged. "You can chalk up a miss as far as I'm concerned."

A gleeful grin lit up Sam's face. "I've never known Tommy strike out. What a lovely dent in his ego!"

"Do you know him very well?"

"Too well." The grin turned into a grimace. "Like I'm the kid sister he never had. I've been working for the Kings for years, mustering cattle, even before the resort was built."

Which explained the familiarity between Sam and Tommy, the teasing and her disrespectful responses yesterday. "Then you must know Nathan well, too." The words slipped out before Miranda could bite on her tongue. She didn't want to reveal any curiosity about him. She didn't even want to think about him.

"I know all of them well," Sam replied with feeling, sounding exasperated by them or their family attitudes.

She set off down the hall again and Miranda kept pace with her, grateful the subject was apparently dropped.

"Come to think of it," Sam muttered. "It's not like Tommy to give up." She frowned at Miranda. "Didn't he even line up one trip with you?"

Miranda stifled a sigh. No point in hiding what would soon be common knowledge. "Nathan is flying me to the Bungle Bungle Range tomorrow," she stated flatly.

"Nathan?" Another dead halt as Sam stared wide-eyed at her. "Nathan's taking you?"

"He's going anyway," Miranda explained, trying to keep a terse note out of her voice. "He plans to take some old diaries about the Aboriginal tribes to the park ranger there."

Sam's mouth twitched. Her eyes danced with inner hilarity. "Nothing to do with you, of course."

"Just a ready opportunity," Miranda said dismissively.

Sam laughed out loud. "Oh, I wish I could have seen Tommy's face when Nathan beat him to the draw."

She chuckled on and off, little bursts of private amusement, all the way to the main administration office. Miranda hid her vexation behind silence, disdaining any comment, yet the memory of Tommy's face at the dinner table last night kept playing through her mind.

She hoped the two King brothers were not going to make her the meat in their sandwich. Would they respect her choice not to get personally involved with either of them? It could become very unpleasant if they didn't.

Miranda's stomach was churning by the time she and Sam finally settled in the office, both of them in chairs, facing the computer on her desk. She needed to get her thoughts focused on business again. Tomorrow morning she would face what she had to with Nathan King. Until then...

"He's free," Sam said with a sidelong look at her.

"I beg your pardon?" Miranda answered distractedly, watching the monitor screen as the computer went through its start procedure.

"Nathan...he's unattached right now. The woman he was seeing got married. He hasn't started up with anyone else yet."

"Well, I guess he's feeling rejected," Miranda commented, hoping she sounded careless, though she was amazed that Nathan King had been turned down for some other man.

"Oh, she didn't reject him. It wasn't that kind of relationship. Just casual lovers, really, though it did go on for a few years."

Miranda gritted her teeth as anger blazed through her. *Casual lovers!* More like a convenient mistress who finally wised up and got herself a man who really loved her. If Nathan King was harbouring the idea that *she* could now fall into that convenient slot, he could think again. One way or another she would make her position very clear to him tomorrow.

"Shall we get down to business?" she said coldly, drawing a startled glance from Sam.

"Sure! Just thought you might like to know about Nathan."

"I know all I need to know, Sam. He's a member of the King family. Okay?"

Wide blue eyes met green ice and curiosity was instantly quenched. "Fine!" Sam's gaze snapped to the monitor screen. "The bookings are listed in time sequence and…"

Finally…business!

Miranda savagely recalled Tommy King saying Nathan was a brick wall. She vowed that the cattle King would meet a steel wall tomorrow, with barbed wire on top to deter any attempt at scaling it.

CHAPTER FIVE

MIRANDA was already at the resort helipad when Nathan pulled up in his Jeep. She had arrived five minutes before the arranged time of meeting, driving one of the luggage buggies, which she'd commandeered for her use. Being early made her feel more prepared, more on top of the situation.

Even so, Nathan swung himself out of the Jeep and Miranda's breath caught in her throat. Regardless of her mental shields, his physical impact got to her, a big blast of strong maleness that instantly set everything female in her aquiver. Like herself, he was dressed in shorts, shirt, walking boots, a hat in one hand, a backpack dangling from his shoulder, but he emanated purposeful vitality while she felt hopelessly paralysed.

"Good morning," he said, shooting a smile at her that jump-started her heart again. "We've struck it lucky with a cloudless sky. A clear sunrise makes the colours more vivid."

"Yes, it is a good morning," she agreed, though it promised a hot, hot day to come. In more ways than one, given her instinctive response to him.

He waved her towards the helicopter on the pad and she fell into step beside him, concentrating on injecting more steel into her spine.

"Have you read anything about the Bungle Bungle Range?" he asked.

"Only what was in the tour pamphlet."

"Well, seeing says it all."

Clearly he was not interested in lecturing or showing off his local knowledge, but his interest in her was twinkling from his eyes and playing havoc with Miranda's nerves.

"Having trouble sleeping?" he asked.

"No," she instantly denied, wondering if she looked tired from last night's tossing and turning over this meeting. "Why should I?" she challenged, wanting to pin-point the reason for his speculation.

"Oh, the quiet sometimes gets to city people. They miss the background noise, and other things they're used to."

Like sex?

Miranda found her jaw clenching and mentally berated herself for being ultra-sensitive. On the surface his comment was perfectly reasonable. On the surface he wasn't saying or doing anything she could take objection to. But under the surface she felt the buzz of possibilities that were far from innocent.

"The last two days have been so busy, I guess the quiet hasn't impressed itself on me yet," she answered.

"It will," he said matter-of-factly. "You'll come to like it or hate it. One thing can be said definitively about the outback. It very quickly sorts out the visitors and the stayers."

"So I understand. I've been told there can be a stir-crazy problem with some of the staff if they don't get regular leave." That moved the conversation to a more impersonal level!

"Not just with staff," he returned drily. "Most women I've known."

He slanted her a look that seemed to be weighing if she had the grit to be a stayer. It set Miranda wondering about the woman who'd chosen to marry someone else...a woman who didn't want to spend her life on a cattle station? But why would Nathan King keep the relationship going for years if it hadn't suited him?

"There must be women who were born and bred to the outback like you," she said pertinently. "Like Sam Connelly."

"Ah, Sam," he said in a tone of fond indulgence. He slid her an ironic look. "There aren't many like Sam, believe me, and she only has eyes for Tommy. One of these days he might stop chasing glitter and see the gold right under his nose."

Was that true about Sam? Miranda tucked the information away for future reference and targeted the man who was criticising his brother. "Perhaps he's not inclined to look. Some men don't want real commitment to a woman."

"Is that personal experience speaking?"

Bitterly personal. Miranda barely stemmed a burning rush of blood as she fought those memories, determined not to reveal her humiliation to a man who'd spent two years pleasuring himself with a woman he must have considered *unsuitable* for marriage. Why else would he have let her go to another man? With cool deliberation Miranda turned the question back on him.

"I was just wondering why *you* haven't found gold somewhere in this vast Kimberly region."

His mouth quirked, drawing her attention to its sensual promise. "Funny thing about gold. It has certain chemical properties. If they're missing it's just fool's gold."

"Maybe they're missing for Tommy," she argued, all too aware of the chemistry Nathan tapped in her.

"No. He covers it with teasing. Sam covers it with aggression. And Tommy's damned fool ego gets in the way. He'd add you to his pride list if he could."

They'd crossed the ground to the helicopter. Nathan opened the door for her. Miranda didn't immediately step up to the passenger seat. She stood stockstill, her mind whirling back over her evening with the Kings...Nathan, stand-offish, watching, only inserting himself when Tommy was considering taking her on tour trips. Had she got Nathan's purpose with her entirely wrong? Nothing to do with sexual attraction?

She eyed him directly. "Is this what today is about, Nathan? Putting yourself between me and Tommy to save Sam's feelings?"

He returned a look that simmered with appreciative warmth, liking her bluntness. "From what I observed, you're not particularly drawn to him, Miranda. But Tommy doesn't give up easily..."

Sam's words!

"...and as time goes on, you might find yourself getting bored enough to play with his interest. Proximity and availability tend to overcome other shortcomings."

"I see. You're warning me off."

"No. It's your choice. I don't believe in interfering with people's choices. I'd be sorry to see Sam hurt, though. It's one thing knowing Tommy drifts in and out of affairs, quite another watching one at close quarters.''

''I take your point,'' she conceded, knowing she wasn't interested in getting involved with Tommy King anyway.

Nathan nodded, then suddenly grinned at her, his blue eyes dancing with more than appreciation. ''Besides, I'd much prefer you to relieve your boredom with me.''

''What?'' Her mouth fell open and stayed open in surprise at the abrupt switch from do-gooding friend of Sam to man making a move on her.

Miranda barely had time to register his words, let alone his intent as he stepped closer, cupped her cheek, tilted her chin, and with his eyes blazing into hers, wickedly inviting, teasing, wanting, he murmured, ''Let's try it, shall we?''

Then he was *kissing* her, soft, seductive pressures that kept her shocked in stillness. She hadn't been expecting it, wasn't prepared for it, and his very gentleness was both confusing and tantalising. It was a take, but there was nothing really offensive about…about the way his mouth was loving hers. Yet he really had no right to just do it like this. She should stop it. Where would it lead? Where *could* it lead?

She lifted her hands. They clamped onto his chest, but instead of pushing, they found a magnetic attraction to the heat and muscle behind his shirt, and somehow they couldn't stop sliding up to the big, broad shoulders that were on a higher level than hers, which was a new experience…reaching up to a man…and it sparked a swarm of previously thwarted female feelings…a man whose physique more than complemented her own too generous body length.

The temptation to feel what it was like with such a man as Nathan King—just this once—dissolved all the reasons why she shouldn't. It was only a kiss, which he was delicately deepening, inviting her active partic- ipation, promising a pleasurable exploration that would satisfy her curiosity. No force involved. No danger at- tached to it. She could back out any time she liked, dismissing the impulse to taste as inconsequential.

He knew how to kiss. He was very good at it. So distractingly good she was barely aware of his hands sliding around her waist, though her whole body was instantly and acutely conscious of his when he hauled her against him. But by then that was what she wanted, to feel more of him, revelling in the dominant maleness he emitted and incredibly excited by it.

Hungry, urgent kisses, a gathering passion for them, and her hands climbing, clutching his head, pulling him down to her, her body arching into his, pinned there by his hands, engulfed by a sweet storm of sensation, riding with it until the growing hardness of his wanting sparked some shred of sanity in her mind, and the shock of her susceptibility to Nathan King's attraction took hold.

She grabbed his ears and forced his head up. He stared at her, his eyes hot and glazed, steaming with rampant desire. She stared back, panic clutching her stomach where he was pressed so explicitly against her, panic screeching through her mind at having let this…this foolish experiment…go so far.

"You're right," he muttered gruffly. "Not the time or place."

Before she had wits to make any reply, he collected himself and moved, scooping her off her feet and lifting her onto the passenger seat of the helicopter as effortlessly as though she were some lightweight doll.

"Throw your hat and bag on the back seat," he instructed, and closed the door, sealing her into position.

Miranda was a trembling mess, her mind stuck in a maze of incredulity...unanswerable questions about herself and her totally inappropriate and shamingly intimate response to a man she barely knew and didn't want to know. Even now, her body was in revolt at having been deprived of what it had wanted from him.

Chemistry!

How did one switch it off?

One solution zipped through her squirming confusion. Get out of the helicopter! She didn't have to go with him or even be with him. She found the handle to open the door. Then a surge of pride insisted running away was not the most effective move to deal with this.

She had a choice to make here and she had to make Nathan King respect her choice. Her contract at King's Eden ran two years and there was no way of avoiding him for two years. A stand had to be taken. Words said. He had to be convinced there was never going to be a *right* time or place for what he wanted from her. No way was she going to fall into the Bobby Hewson trap again.

She'd barely remembered to toss her hat and bag onto the back seat before Nathan King hauled himself into the space beside her, triggering an awful sense of vulnerability. She fastened her seat-belt and did her utmost to ignore his impact on her senses as he settled himself.

"Have to get moving if we're to catch the sunrise," he said, handing her a set of headphones and linking up the electronics.

Thankfully he switched on the ignition and busied himself with getting them off the ground. Miranda donned the headphones, which drowned out the noise and allowed her to speak to him but decided any talking was best done later. After she had calmed down. When she could choose her words carefully, not in heat. And when being in the wretchedly small space of this helicopter didn't make her feel so *crowded* by him.

Determined on shutting him out for the duration of the flight, Miranda resolved to keep her gaze trained strictly on the view. Which was what she was here for…firsthand knowledge of tourist territory…and which she proceeded to do, once they were in the air.

All the same, even as she watched a seemingly endless vista of beige grass dotted by the grey-green foliage of the universally small outback trees, her nerves were strung taut, waiting for Nathan to say something. As time dragged by, she began to hate the thought he was simply sitting tight, congratulating himself on having sparked a positive response from her, and anticipating more of the same.

"You'll miss the approach if you keep looking out of the side window, Miranda."

The advice boomed into her ears, jolting her out of her dark brooding.

"That's the start of the Bungle Bungle Range straight ahead of us.''

Relief poured through her at his matter-of-fact tone, and the moment she looked where he directed, his domination of her thoughts faded, her mind filling with the wonder of what lay before her.

She had seen photographs of Ayer's Rock, a huge monolith rising with stunning effect from a vista of flat land as far as the eye could see. The Bungle Bungle Range gave the same weird sense of not belonging to the general landscape, but it was much more than a monumental rock. It looked like some ancient remnant of a lost civilisation, embodying mysteries that no one knew the answers to any more.

The photographs in the pamphlet hadn't captured what she was seeing, couldn't capture the size and fascination of it. It seemed to rise out of nowhere, unconnected to anything else, a huge amalgamation of massive beehive structures, horizontally striped in orange and black. The rising sun vividly illuminated the orange sections and made the black more stark.

Miranda knew there were geological explanations for the colours—layers of silica and lichen—and the shapes. She'd read them in the pamphlet. Yet the stripes seemed so evenly spaced, as though to some deliberate, artistic plan, and the striations in the rock of some of the massive domes on the outskirts of the range gave her the impression of buildings built of bricks, like pyramids with the sharp edges having crumbled away over thousands and thousands of years.

She knew it was fanciful to ignore expert knowledge—this was all solid sandstone, and the formation was actually dated back three hundred and fifty million years—but she couldn't help envisaging ancient rulers being buried inside those time-worn domes.

"Had enough or do you want to see more?" Nathan asked evenly, not pushing either way.

"More, please," she answered, not grudging those words to him.

He flew the helicopter over the range in a criss-cross pattern, giving her every aspect of it. The narrow canyons or gorges had been carved by water, so she'd read, yet the rock-face it had carved was so smooth and sheer in places, the impression of narrow streets running deep down beside blocks of petrified, windowless skyscrapers kept flowing through Miranda's mind. If this was the work of nature, it had been wrought in incredible patterns.

"Time we landed if we're to keep our schedule," Nathan informed her.

"Okay," she conceded, realising he'd seen all this before and had been pandering to her interest, probably indulging her so she would be more ready to indulge him. And on the ground she would be more accessible to whatever he had in mind.

He set the helicopter down close to a group of buildings beyond the massif, presumably the park rangers' headquarters. Intensely wary of his intentions, Miranda swiftly unfastened her seat-belt, whipped off her headphones, opened the door on her side and was out before Nathan could *help* her, thereby avoiding any macho familiarity he might take, being bigger and stronger than she was.

"Forgot your hat and bag," he said, handing her the items as he joined her on the ground.

"Thanks," she mumbled, deeply vexed she hadn't thought of them in her hurry to get out. The omission revealed her distracted state of mind. "That was so fantastic from the air, I'm eager to see more of it from ground level," she rolled out as an excuse, not wanting him to think *he* was the cause of her haste.

"Worth catching the sunrise?" he remarked, his blue eyes glinting with amused mockery.

"Very much so."

"Sorry if I offended your dignity by bundling you into the helicopter back at the resort, but we were running short of time. Nature doesn't wait on anything. If we want it working for us we have to follow its dictates."

Which was a double-edged excuse if she'd ever heard one! If he thought she was going to take sexual dictation from nature, he could think again.

"I didn't ask for a delay to our departure, Nathan," she said pointedly.

"True!" He had the gall to grin. "But I didn't hear or feel any protest for quite some time. Which leaves us with a promising area to explore, doesn't it?"

"Only if the wish is there to explore it," she flashed back at him with a look that should have shrivelled his confidence.

It merely raised a quizzical eyebrow. "No problem on my side. Is there one on yours?"

She fixed some mockery of her own directly on him. "Just where do you see this exploration leading to?"

He made a playful frown. "Well, the start of it suggested we're onto something special together. And now you're throwing in some mystery. No doubt about a strong dash of excitement. Who can tell what will come out of it?''

He was laughing at her, making light of any possible reservations she might have about an open-ended future. Except it wasn't open-ended to her. She saw a very inevitable end.

''That sounds quite romantic. Except you know and I know there won't be any romance involved. I bet right now you're figuring on a two-year convenient affair. And I tell you right now—'' her voice hardened as she delivered the bottom line ''—I won't play.''

CHAPTER SIX

"PLAY?"

Nathan King's incredulous repetition of her word gave Miranda a queasy moment of doubt. Had she let her own fears paint a crass picture of what he intended?

She watched, with galloping trepidation, while his expression underwent several changes...disbelief shifting to reassessment, then distaste.

He couldn't have had anything serious in mind with her, she fiercely told herself. He just didn't like having his motives baldly laid out. Probably no other woman had ever knocked him back quite so bluntly or abruptly. New experience for him!

Just as his eyes took on a laser-like probe, a greeting rang out. They both turned to see a lean bearded man strolling towards them. The interruption was silently welcomed by Miranda. It broke the imminent threat of further confrontation with Nathan King and gave her the chance to regroup her defences.

The newcomer looked to be only in his early thirties and he viewed Miranda with speculative interest as Nathan introduced them. "Jim Hoskins, head park ranger, Miranda Wade, the new resort manager at King's Eden."

They shook hands but there was no opportunity for any conversation between them. Nathan claimed Jim's attention, withdrawing a parcel of books from his bag. "The diaries. Take good care of them, won't you?"

Jim took the parcel, handling it with reverential care. "I'm much obliged, Nathan. I'll treat them with the utmost respect. Hard to get any history on this area."

"Personal diaries aren't exact historical fact," Nathan drily warned. "My great-grandmother might have been fed tall tales by the Aborigines of the time. Generally white people weren't let into tribal secrets."

"Well, I'm sure I'll find them interesting anyway."

Miranda thought she would, too, but she could hardly ask for a loan of old family diaries from a man she was intent on rejecting.

"Come along," Jim invited, waving to the building. "I'll put tea or coffee on for you." He smiled at Miranda as she and Nathan fell into step with him. "Your first time here?"

"Yes. This is an amazing place."

"Unfortunately we're short of time, Jim," Nathan interjected.

Miranda tensed. Was that true, or was he impatient to get her to himself again?

"I promised to show Miranda Cathedral Gorge and have her back at the resort at noon," he explained. "I know she's eager to get on with the sight-seeing, so we'll pass up the coffee, if you don't mind. I've got some packed."

Which neatly cut the park ranger out of the agenda, using her own excuse for hurrying out of the helicopter. It was clear Nathan was not going to allow her to use Jim Hoskins as a buffer between them. Not even for a short time. Though to be fair, she didn't know how long it took to get to Cathedral Gorge.

Jim shrugged, accepting the argument without question. "Pity you're so rushed." He pointed to a heavy duty four-wheel-drive vehicle parked beside the road. "The Land Cruiser's ready to go. Keys in the ignition."

"Thanks, Jim. We'll be off then."

"No problem."

He parted company with them with a cheery wave and Miranda resigned herself to being alone with Nathan again.

They headed straight for the Land Cruiser, neither of them offering conversation. Miranda didn't look at Nathan but she was extremely conscious of purposeful energy radiating from him and knew he was going to contest her "no play" decision. But if he kept it to only words, she would cope, and she didn't have to be more than polite in her replies. Let him think whatever he liked. The only important thing was to maintain a safe distance.

He opened the passenger door for her. She stepped past him with a cool "Thank you," and heaved herself into the high cabin, noting that he didn't attempt to assist. Her independent exit from the helicopter had at least made that point.

He didn't speak even when they were on the road. In fact they travelled a considerable distance, the silence in the Land Cruiser growing more and more nerve-racking as the track they were taking got rougher and rougher, the four-wheel drive ploughing through deep sand, bumping over corrugations, traversing a rocky creek bed where running water could have made the crossing more perilous if he hadn't known which way to go.

There was no sign of anyone else now, no trace of any humanity in the ancient land around them. The clumps of spinifex and the high conical termite mounds added to the sense of life reduced to a minimal state. It was a far different world from the one she'd known all her life and she began to sense she was with a very different kind of man, too…a man who made his own rules.

She wasn't running this game.

He was.

At his own pace and on his own terms.

And that realisation sent a chill down Miranda's spine. His patient silence at the dinner table that first night, his patient silence in the helicopter, now in this Land Cruiser, waiting…waiting for what?

"You're right," Nathan said abruptly. "I'm not offering romance. I've been there, done that, and come out empty every time. Fool's gold."

The edge of contempt in his voice startled her into looking at him. He sliced her a hard, challenging glance, searing in its intensity. "Look around you," he directed, turning his gaze back to the hazardous track. "My life is bound up in this land. It comes down to basic needs and that is pervasive if you live here long enough. I have a great respect for basic needs. And sharing them makes sense to me."

Miranda frowned, realising he was talking of a stark reality he faced day after day. If basic needs weren't respected—and shared—survival could very well be at risk. She'd read stories of people who had perished in the outback, not appreciating all that could go wrong, nor comprehending the sheer isolation of great, empty distances—no ready help to call upon.

"Now I'd say there's something very basic between us that we could answer for each other," he went on.

One could survive without *sex,* Miranda silently argued, gritting her teeth against saying so, determined not to invite or encourage any conversation on that subject.

"A sharing. Not a taking," he emphasised.

Miranda remained stubbornly silent, her gaze trained out the side window, but she felt the hot, penetrating blast of his eyes on her and couldn't stop her muscles from tensing against it.

"I'm not interested in the games men and women play in the world you come from," he continued with a relentless beat that seemed to drum on her mind and heart. "I don't make promises I can't or won't keep. I'll say how it is for me. I want you, yes."

She didn't actually need that blunt honesty, having no doubts herself on that score.

"And you want me, Miranda."

That stung her into whipping her head around. "Oh, no, I don't!" she shot at him.

His eyes instantly and sharply derided her contention. "Deny it as much as you like, for whatever reasons you have, but it's not going to go away."

"Is that how you argued your last mistress into bed with you?"

"Mistress?"

His incredulity and the subsequent shake of his head

left Miranda furious with herself at having let those words slip. She snapped her gaze back to the road, willing him not to pick up on them, to simply let the whole matter drop.

No such luck!

"I don't know where you're coming from, Miranda," he said tersely, "but I am *not* married, and if I had a wife, I certainly wouldn't be seeking a mistress."

Mistress...lover...what was the difference when the arrangement was for sex on tap?

"The relationships I've had with women were all mutually desired and not one of them was an adulterous affair," he went on, his voice gathering an acid bite. "I happen to respect the commitment of marriage. A pity you don't."

"I beg your pardon!" Miranda hurled at him in bitter resentment of his judgement of her.

"So what happened?" he threw back at her. "The guy wouldn't leave his wife for you? Is that why you took the job at King's Eden, burning your boats?"

It was so close to the truth, a wave of humiliating heat scorched up Miranda's neck.

Nathan didn't miss it. He turned on more heat. "Or maybe you threw down the gauntlet and you're hoping he'll follow you up here. Which explains the no-go with me."

"This is none of your business!" she seethed.

"Well, I take exception to being coupled with a sleaze-bag who plays a game of deceit with the women in his life."

"Then please accept my apology." She managed to

get frost into her voice even though her face was still flaming.

"And it most certainly is Tommy's business if you're counting on breaking the two-year contract, should your lover toe your line."

"I have no intention of breaking it," she grated out. "And I do not appreciate all this supposition on your part."

"You opened the door, Miranda."

"And I'd take it kindly if you'd respect my choice to close it."

Blue eyes clashed with green in an electric exchange that sizzled the air between them. Miranda's heart thumped erratically. She could hear it in her ears, feel the strong throb of it in her temples. Goose-bumps rose on her skin.

"It's not a choice I can respect, but so be it," he said tersely, and broke the connection with her.

The ensuing silence was incredibly oppressive. Miranda felt totally drained of energy and miserable over the impression she'd left him with by not correcting his assumptions. Not that he had any right to make them!

Okay, she shouldn't have used the word, *mistress,* but it had been what Bobby had wanted of her, not what she had been. As for Nathan King, maybe she'd let her experience with Bobby Hewson colour her reading of his last relationship. On the other hand, he wasn't promising anything other than sex, which was all a mistress got from a man.

If there was one thing Miranda had learnt, it was she wanted to be valued for more than a roll in the hay. A roll with Nathan King might be…an interesting experience. Even special, she grudgingly conceded. But that wasn't enough for her. Especially not after Bobby Hewson. She wanted the kind of sharing that encompassed everything, the kind that led to marriage because no one else could fulfil that very special equation of wanting to be with each other. Exclusively! Which was hardly a likely prospect with Nathan King of the legendary King family.

Miranda was still brooding over this when the Land Cruiser came to a halt in an open camping area on the outskirts of the Bungle Bungle Range. A four-wheel-drive wagon was parked close to four tents but they all seemed abandoned, no one in view anywhere.

"We hike in from here," Nathan stated. "The camping amenities block is kept clean. If you want to use it before we set out…"

"Yes, I will. Thank you."

She didn't wait for him to open her door. As she strode away from the Land Cruiser, she thought he probably hadn't intended to extend that courtesy to her anyway. A woman who didn't care about committing adultery didn't deserve his respect. Except she did care, and she hated having him think that of her.

No use telling herself it didn't matter, so long as it kept him away from her. It was a point of pride. And reputation. Though it went deeper than that, right down to her sense of self-worth.

She was not like her mother.

She was never going to be like her mother.

She needed to live her life on her own terms and somehow she had to make Nathan King understand that. And respect it.

CHAPTER SEVEN

MISTRESS!

Nathan brooded over his misconception of Miranda Wade as he waited for her to be ready for the trek into the gorge. Far from being a feminist, she was right at the other end of the scale, pleasuring married men. Of course, a woman with her looks would naturally attract wealthy targets whose egos were fed by having a mistress with such spectacular physical assets. And no doubt she'd profited by it. The dress she'd worn to dinner that first night undoubtedly had a designer label.

Was she turning the screws on some guy, putting herself out of easy reach by this shift to King's Eden? Or maybe she saw the resort homestead as a fertile hunting ground. The few select suites for guests there cost almost a thousand dollars a night. Anyone who could afford to stay for several days was in the millionaire class, and the managerial position put her in close proximity with them, hostessing dinner each night. It was a much more intimate footing than she'd get, managing a city hotel.

Nevertheless, despite whatever cool calculations went on in her mind, she had slipped up this morning. There *was* strong chemistry between them, however much she might want to dismiss it. Obviously he didn't have what she wanted out of life, so he was a waste of her time.

And, face it, man! She was a waste of his.

However frustrated he might feel about her ice beating the fire of this morning, pursuing the instincts still raging through him would only lead to more frustration. Best to let go right now. The last thing he needed was to be screwed up by a woman who was practised in deceit. Especially adulterous deceit.

The click of a door opening alerted him to her imminent return to his side. He half turned to watch her. She'd crammed her hat on her head so it came halfway down her forehead, shadowing her eyes. The rest of her still had the kick of a mule, but he was not going to be drawn by her lush femininity again. Let her sell it to the highest bidder. He was well out of that game.

He was looking at her as though she had crawled out from under some rock. Miranda instinctively stiffened her spine but her stomach was in a sickening knot. She cursed herself again for having allowed this man past her guard. Now here he was, standing in judgement on her, so formidable and forbidding she hated her vulnerability to what he thought of her. She shouldn't have to defend herself.

And she wouldn't.

She had apologised for misinterpreting his last relationship. Nothing more need be said on any personal score. She glanced at her watch as she neared where he stood waiting for her. It was almost eight o'clock. Only four more hours to get through with him.

"This way," he said, barely waiting for her to fall into step beside him before setting off.

Miranda kept her mouth firmly shut. The route into

the gorge was signposted. She didn't really need his guidance. In fact, she would have been better without it. He set such a brisk pace, she was so busy watching her footing over the rough ground, determined not to stumble or fall, there was little time for gazing around.

The beehive domes gradually amalgamated into a gorge whose walls rose higher and higher. As the walking track narrowed and the terrain became more difficult, Nathan took the lead with a muttered, ''Best to follow where I tread.''

As much as she bridled against his high-handed manner, there was nothing to be gained from disobeying. The sun had gathered heat and there was no shelter from it anywhere. Nathan unerringly chose the safest way over rocks and past tricky little chasms. A couple of times he paused to check if she needed a hand to negotiate an awkward ascent or descent but Miranda was proudly determined on not accepting any assistance.

Nevertheless, she reviewed her opinion about not needing a guide. The walk would have been much more hazardous and longer, picking her own way. As it was, she ended up misjudging her footing on a loose section of gravel at the top of a stony ridge, and as she took a steep step down to the next secure place, her back foot skidded out from under her, catapulting her straight towards the solid mass of Nathan King, who'd instantly swung at her yelp of distress.

She thumped into him, her hands automatically grabbing his arms to save her from falling in a heap at his feet. Not that she needed to worry about that. He reacted so fast, she found herself clamped to him, then hauled up his body until her feet found steady ground...between the legs he'd spread to anchor himself. But he didn't let her go...and she didn't let him go.

Her breasts were squashed against his chest and it felt as though their hearts were thundering in unison. Her pelvis and his seemed locked together, the key to his manhood fitting sensationally into the apex of her thighs. Her hands were wrapped around his biceps, loving their tensile strength. His vibrant heat and the sheer power of the man seemed to flood through her, holding her transfixed with a melting flow of insidious excitement.

She wasn't even aware that her hat had been knocked off. Her mind was abuzz with sexual signals that short-circuited all warning buttons. Her head tilted back, instinctively seeking more direct contact with him. The naked blast of desire in his eyes tore through the wanton glaze that had blinded her to what was happening. She sucked in a quick sobering breath through lips she realised were invitingly parted.

She saw his mouth compress, his jaw tighten and a savage mockery wiped the blaze of wanting from his eyes. He set her firmly apart from him, swept up her hat from where it had fallen and presented it to her.

"Better watch yourself more carefully, Miranda," he advised acidly. "Another slip like that...who knows what might get broken?"

Like her credibility in insisting she didn't want him.

"Thanks for saving me," she managed to mutter, cramming her hat back on to hide her burning face.

"Tommy needs you operational," he slung at her

before turning a broad, brick wall back and setting off again.

Miranda's legs felt like jelly. She forced them to work as they should, willing more energy into them. It wasn't fair, she thought, staring resentfully at the pumped-out strength of his stride. She'd gone weak from that treacherous embrace and he'd gained power. Nothing was fair where sex was concerned, she grimly concluded.

Twice now she'd succumbed to his attraction. He seemed to have some inbuilt magnet that got to her, overriding all common sense. She found herself eyeing the taut action of his buttocks and wrenched her gaze away. Somehow she had to switch off this *physical* thing with him, get her mind focused on her job again. Nathan King was not the object of this sight-seeing trip.

The rock edifice on either side of them was not striped as the domes were. The colours were still striking, a mixture of red and orange, yellow ochre, beige and black. Miranda was wondering why this was called Cathedral Gorge, when she heard the sound, a deep haunting throb that seemed to vibrate off the cliff walls in a weird unearthly rhythm. She stopped dead, absorbed with listening to it.

Nathan moved on a few steps, then turned, aware of her failure to follow. He frowned at her stillness, emitting impatience. He was about to voice it when she whipped up a hand to stop him.

"Don't you hear it?" she queried in an urgent whisper.

He nodded, his eyes glinting with ironic amusement at her enthrallment.

It goaded her into asking, "What is it?"

"A didgeridoo being played against the cavern wall. Come on. You'll see it around the next bend. Albert must have decided to give the tourists a demonstration."

Albert?

A didgeridoo was an Aboriginal instrument. Did one of the tribes still live here?

Miranda sped after Nathan, eager to experience more of what she was hearing. And suddenly it came into view...the end of the gorge...a fantastic open cavern, the side walls towering up in incredibly sheer sheets of rock, the back one curved inward, sheltering a pool of mysterious black water surrounded by sand.

Behind the pool a group of six people sat on a jumble of flat rocks, watching an Aboriginal man blowing into a long hollow pole, the end of it resting on the ground as his hands moved over the holes in the wood, controlling the emissions of sound.

The eerie notes boomed up with all the power of a pipe organ in a cathedral, filling the cavern, echoing out like some primitive call that had passed through aeons of time, as though summoning the heartbeat of the earth itself so that those who heard it would feel its underlying rhythm and be in harmony with it.

It couldn't be called a song. There was no melody. Yet the interplay of sounds touched some deep soul chord that suddenly reminded Miranda of what Nathan had said earlier about his life being bound up in this land—ancient land—where survival reduced everything to basic needs.

She hadn't comprehended the full context of what he was saying but she had a glimmering of it now...the stark simplicity of choices laid out by nature, a cycle to be followed...birth, growth, mating, reproducing, death...an endless replenishment as long as the earth kept feeding it.

No romantic gloss.

Just life as it really was, underneath all the trimmings that civilisation had manufactured to sweeten it.

The playing ended on a long, deep, mournful note, which seemed to reverberate through Miranda, making her tingle in a shivery way. The Aboriginal man shouldered his didgeridoo. The group of six applauded, their enthusiastic clapping sounding totally wrong to Miranda, somehow trivialising an experience that should have been savoured in silence.

She was frowning over it when Nathan turned to look at her, his eyes hard and cynical. "The performance not worth your applause?"

She stared at him, feeling his contempt for the lack of understanding that connected what they'd just heard to a *performance* to be clapped. "Not everyone has your background, Nathan," she excused.

He raised an eyebrow. "You're not going to show some mark of appreciation?"

She struggled to express what she'd felt. "To me it was a communication, not a concert."

"Oh? And what did it communicate to you?"

His eyes were a pitiless blue, scorning any sensitivity from her. His challenge was a deliberate ploy to confirm the place he'd put her in—a woman without soul, a woman who cared only for herself, disregarding the hurt she might give to others.

Miranda's gaze bored straight back at him, resentment goading her into flouting his superficial and insulting reading of her character. "It gave me an insight into your life. And the life of those who have inhabited this land. How it must have always demanded they be attuned to its heartbeat."

Her reply visibly jolted him. His chin butted up as though hit by a punch of disbelief. His eyes flared as though she'd done serious violence to his feelings. For a few nerve-shaking moments, she felt caught in a fiercely questing force that tore at everything she was. Then just as suddenly it was withdrawn, Nathan turning away and walking on.

Denial? Frustration?

Feeling as though she'd been pulped and tossed aside, Miranda had to recollect herself *again* before following. The deep drifts of sand made walking heavy going, but clearly the cavern was their destination so there wasn't far to go now, and at least she wouldn't be *alone* with Nathan here.

Having consoled herself with this thought, she was dismayed to see the group of six getting to their feet and gathering up their bags. They trailed after the Aboriginal man who was skirting the pool and heading towards her and Nathan. Then she realised he was dressed in a tour guide uniform and had obviously been hired by these people to give them the benefit of his specialised knowledge.

"G'day, Nathan," he greeted familiarly, his face wreathed in a welcoming grin.

"G'day to you, Albert," came the warm reply, a tone of voice Miranda hadn't heard for some time. "You'll be haunting the tourists if you keep laying that on them."

The Aboriginal laughed as though it was a great joke. He patted his didgeridoo. "Only calling up good spirits." He flicked a twinkling glance at Miranda before adding, "Maybe you need them."

"Maybe I do," Nathan said with a nod of appreciation. "This is Miranda Wade. She's taken over management of Tommy's resort. Albert's a tribal elder around these parts, Miranda."

She offered her hand. "Thank you for playing. That was quite magical."

He shook it, his dark eyes shining happily at her comment. "Always good magic, Miss Wade. You staying on for a while?"

"Yes."

He released her hand and tipped his hat to Nathan. "Could be the right spirit for you, oldfella."

He strolled off, chuckling to himself. Nathan threw her a look that simmered with scepticism, then trudged on towards the pool. The sand firmed as they neared it, much to Miranda's relief. Albert's group passed them, breaking their conversation to say "Hi!" Miranda smiled and returned their greetings. Nathan merely nodded, though Miranda noted he drew long appraising looks from the women in the group.

Physically he'd have an impact on any woman, she thought, though he probably wouldn't expend his energy on many. An extremely self-contained man, she decided, watching him stride forward around the pool to the flat rocks which would undoubtedly serve as their resting place for refreshment. Everything about him seemed to shout *elemental male,* and it was true what he'd said, she couldn't deny his effect on her.

In a primitive society, he'd be the prize mate to get. No denying that, either. She had no doubt he could and would endure anything from this land, and still make it work for him. In some quintessential way, he belonged to it…as hard as these rocks, and just as unforgiving.

Maybe she was a fool to pass up an intimate involvement with him. Not that he was likely to give her a second chance after this morning's contretemps.

Might it have developed into something very special? Some wanton core in her pulsed yes and it was difficult to argue away. Nevertheless, she worked hard at it.

Sexual attraction was no assurance of anything working out well. And why should she believe what Nathan King said about himself and his relationships with other women? He'd undoubtedly bedded the woman who'd chosen to marry another man. What did that say about him?

He dropped his bag onto a large flat rock. Miranda settled for one about a metre short of his. Since the cavern shaded them from the sun, she took off her hat, welcoming the cooler air here. In an attempt to ignore the tension of having to share some inactive time with Nathan, she emptied her bag, placing the plastic container of melon, which she'd sliced into finger-size pieces on the rock between them, then taking a long drink from the bottle of mineral water everyone had told her to take, warning of dehydration.

"I have a thermos of coffee. Would you like some?" he asked.

"Yes. Please."

He used the same "table" rock to set out mugs and fill them, then produced two plastic containers of sandwiches. "Bacon, lettuce, tomato and cheese," he informed her. "You'll need something more substantial than melon. Help yourself."

"You, too," she invited.

They sat, munching and drinking in a loaded silence.

Eventually Miranda decided to settle a harmless point of curiosity. "Why did Albert call you 'oldfella'? I wouldn't call you old."

"It relates to my family having been linked to this area for more years than Albert has lived. Longevity is counted in generations. Five generations here makes all of the Kings 'oldfellas.'"

"I see," she murmured, mentally kicking herself for even momentarily regretting her earlier rejection of him. A member of the King family would never seriously link himself with her, any more than a member of the Hewson family would, as Bobby had finally spelled out to her.

"What do you see, Miranda?"

She shrugged, meeting the searing question in his eyes with the inescapable fact she'd known from the beginning. "That I don't belong and you do."

"Where do you belong?" he asked.

She broke into laughter, shaking her head over the

emptiness of that question. "Nowhere. That's part of why I'm here. It doesn't matter where I am." She flashed him an ironic look. "I guess you could say I belong to myself."

He frowned and turned his gaze down to the pool below them. A dark, dark pool, Miranda thought, like her family background. Not that it could actually be called family, just her and her mother whose men had never offered a wedding ring…the whole sorry misery of it coming to a lonely end years ago. It was hardly the kind of history the King family would want attached to them in any shape or form.

"So you don't care about breaking up anyone else's sense of belonging."

The harsh remark was one too many for Miranda. "You have no right to probe into my personal life. I am here on a professional basis," she stated icily.

"You might have fooled my mother…"

She leapt to her feet, snapping with anger. "That's enough! I have never been a married man's mistress. Nor would I ever put myself in such a demeaning situation."

"Then what was all that mistress stuff about?" he shot back at her.

"It was about a man like you, wanting to put me in that position, and he had the power to mess up all I'd worked for. Just as you have the power to mess up my contracted time at King's Eden."

He was suddenly on his feet, a towering figure of proud indignation. "That's a hell of a thing to think of me!"

"Like the things you've being thinking about me,

huh? Treating me like dirt because I said *no play!*''
Her eyes raked his arrogant pride into meaningless tatters. ''Well, let me tell you I'm not about to take the
chance you're any different from him. I don't care how
sexy you are. I...won't...play!''

Her whole body was shaking with the vehemence of
that denial and her last three words boomed around the
cavern, echoing, echoing...out of her control. She'd let
him drive her out of control.

Desperate to grab some shreds of it back, she shoved
her drink bottle into her bag. Her hands fumbled over
the lid of the melon container. A hand clamped around
her wrist, stilling the agitated action.

''I promise you...I swear to you...your position at
King's Eden is safe from any interference from me.''

Her heart was pounding so hard she couldn't bring
herself to speak at all. She stared down at the strong
brown fingers wrapped around her wrist, imprisoning
it.

''And please...accept my apology for making you
feel at risk. That was not my intention.''

His voice seemed to throb with sincerity. She
couldn't look at him, couldn't tear her gaze from the
hold he had on her, his flesh imprinting itself on hers,
fingers pressing on her pulse, his energy zipping into
her bloodstream, imparting an indelible sense of joining that wasn't true. It couldn't be true.

''As for what I thought of you...I'm glad I was
wrong. And I apologise for that, too. Believe me
now...you are safe with me, Miranda. Okay?''

She nodded, too choked by a tumult of emotion to
do anything else. He released her and began repacking

his bag. Miranda concentrated hard on finishing with hers.

Her mind thrummed with the knowledge that she didn't feel *safe* with Nathan King and never would. He was more than Bobby Hewson. Much more. And even if he left her alone, as he promised, she would not stop being acutely aware of him and the power he had to reach into her.

Neither of them said anything throughout the hours it took to journey back to the resort. There was no touching, physical or verbal. Miranda did her utmost to block him out of her personal space but he kept infiltrating it just by the sheer force of his presence.

For all her practised professionalism, she found herself hopelessly tongue-tied when she finally had to face him on the helipad at King's Eden. She forced her gaze to meet his and almost flinched at the intense blue of his eyes as they probed hers.

"Thank you," she blurted out, barely stopping herself from backing away from him.

"Miranda, I have nothing to do with the resort and Tommy would certainly not welcome any interference from me in his business," he stated emphatically. "It's entirely up to you to make good your position here."

She nodded, her throat too constricted to speak.

"You want time to feel settled into your job...fine!" he went on. "But I don't see myself forgetting what there is between us. And I don't think you will, either."

She did not answer, feeling the threat to her peace of mind and not knowing what to do about it.

"I'll see you again sometime," he added, and took his leave of her.

She watched him get into his Jeep and drive away. Only when he was out of sight did she begin to breathe easily. Two years at King's Eden, she thought. Of course she would see him again…sometime. And what then?

What then?

CHAPTER EIGHT

IT WAS good to see Jared again. Nathan reflected that he always had enjoyed his youngest brother's company. Tommy had a competitive streak, wanting to score points on everything, while Jared was simply content to be himself, not in contest with either brother. Maybe it was because he'd moved himself into their mother's world, away from King's Eden. Or maybe it was simply his nature.

They sat in the breakfast room, idling over morning tea, Jared and their mother relaxing after their flight from Broome, Nathan catching up on their recent activities. Tommy would fly in this afternoon and would inevitably draw Jared's attention to himself, but for the moment, it was very pleasant listening to his youngest brother's plans to extend the pearl business from wholesale into retail, as well.

"So how goes it with you, Nathan?" he asked, the conversation having lulled after he and their mother had filled him in on their news.

"Oh, nothing really changes here," he drawled, except he only had half his mind concentrated on station business. Miranda Wade occupied the other half, but he wasn't about to lay out that very private issue.

In fact, he was thinking this family get-together on the station—the first this year—may very well provide the opportunity to get him close to Miranda again, in a non-threatening social situation, which would surely ease her fears.

"Mum tells me we have a new manager at the resort," Jared prompted. "A woman."

"Yes." A woman who haunted his nights and wouldn't get out of his head even during the day.

"So how is she working out?"

"I have no idea." Which was really a lie. He'd envisaged her a thousand times, burning with utter commitment to getting everything right at the resort, shutting out everything else from her mind. Including him. Especially him. Though he didn't believe she could be any more successful than he was at setting aside the strong attraction they'd experienced. All the same, the need to know wouldn't wait much longer.

"Don't you have some impression, Nathan?" his mother asked, frowning at him.

"Why should I? I don't stick my nose into Tommy's business any more than I stick it into Jared's."

His mother's gaze sharpened on him. "You did take Miranda on a sight-seeing trip, didn't you?"

"Six weeks ago," he answered with a shrug. "I haven't seen her since."

His mother sighed, looking extremely vexed.

"I'm sure Tommy will fill you in when he arrives this afternoon." Nathan smiled at her, seeing a way to use her frustration. "You can grill him to your heart's content," he added casually.

It earned an exasperated glare. "I wanted another point of view."

"Then why not ask Miranda over to dinner tonight, satisfy yourself about her? Satisfy Jared's curiosity, too. You could ask Sam, as well. Get her opinion. Make a party of it.''

''Yes,'' his mother snapped, looking at him as though she wanted to box his ears. ''I shall do that, Nathan. I'll get some answers for myself since I can't count on either you or Tommy to be sensible about women.''

Her eyes glittered bitter disapproval.

He thought fleetingly of Susan, aware his mother had considered her a waste of his time. But mothers didn't know everything. All the same, he was glad that door was shut now because another door had opened and it had a stronger lure than any he had ever known.

''Well, it's lucky you can count on Jared to be sensible,'' he tossed out, then slanted a teasing grin at his brother. ''Been a good boy, have you?''

He laughed and they moved onto a lighter vein of conversation, which suited Nathan just fine since he only had to give half his mind to it.

Tonight, he thought with deep satisfaction.

Tonight he would find out more about the woman he wanted.

As was her custom, Miranda was ready to welcome back the homestead guests as they returned from their day's activities. She waited on the verandah, watching the fishing party unload themselves from the Jeep Sam always commandeered, and thinking they looked well satisfied with what they had chosen to do.

''Look at these great barramundi!'' John Trumbell crowed, holding up his catch for her to admire as he led the others up the path.

Miranda laughed at his glee. "Biggest I've seen this season, John."

Robyn, his wife, asked. "Can we give them to the chef to cook for our dinner tonight?"

"Of course. Should make a great feast for you."

"It was a marvellous day," Robyn enthused. "I've never gone fishing in a helicopter before." She swung around to Sam who was trailing after them. "Thanks for the ride."

"Couldn't get you to that part of the river any other way," Sam informed her.

Robyn sighed happily, turning to the other couple who had accompanied her and her husband. "Don't you just love the outback? It was like fishing in a world of our own."

The others made equally enthusiastic comments as they passed Miranda. Sam sidled up to her and remarked sotto voce, "Wonderful, when you've got money to burn."

She grinned. It was true the guests who took homestead suites never seemed to count the cost of anything. Nevertheless, in the month since the resort opened, she'd found that even the campers loved being here, just exploring the gorges, swimming in waterholes, enjoying the unique wildlife.

"So what's on for tomorrow?" Sam asked, rolling her eyes.

"For them the Bungle Bungle Range."

"Got Albert lined up to take them in after I've landed them?"

"Of course."

Miranda's mind flinched away from the memory of

her morning with Nathan. It still haunted her, even after six weeks of seeing nothing of him. It seemed he had decided to respect her choice not to play. The problem was, in the lonely hours of the night, she was tormented by the question of what might have been if she'd chosen differently.

"Someone coming," Sam remarked, squinting past Miranda at a Jeep, which was fast approaching. "Looks like Tommy. Must be coming from the station homestead. Are you expecting him?"

"No, I'm not." She was puzzled by this unheralded visit. "He dropped in on Tuesday to check through everything with me."

Sam gave her a crooked smile. "Well, it's Saturday. Maybe he's without a date tonight and hopes you'll fill in."

"Then he'll be out of luck."

Sam shook her head in bemusement. "It's an education, watching you block him out. Mind if I stay to watch the fun?"

"As you like."

She didn't find Tommy's flirtatiousness fun, and didn't really see what fun Sam could get out of watching them together. Apparently it amused her, yet Miranda kept remembering what Nathan had said about Sam's feelings for Tommy, and she couldn't help thinking it was masochistic to want to watch. Or maybe it was a case of not being able to help herself. If he was like a magnet to her...

A convulsive little shiver ran down Miranda's spine. It had certainly been easier, throwing herself into her job and getting on top of it with Nathan out of sight, if not completely out of mind. Tommy was not a problem to her. His irrepressible personality seemed to bounce around her personal sidesteps and he never pushed beyond the boundaries she set. Getting the business right came first with him and he wasn't about to upset that applecart.

"How's it going?" he called cheerily as he came up the path.

"Fine!" Miranda answered.

He stopped short of the verandah, looking up at them with a quizzical little smile. "Mum and Jared have flown in for the weekend. You are commanded to come to dinner at the station homestead tonight."

She frowned. "Commanded?"

Her heart started skittering. Nathan had *commanded?*

"Invited," Tommy corrected wryly. "But take it from me, there's no ducking out of my mother's invitations."

His mother, not Nathan.

Her mind started skittering.

Did Tommy think she ducked out of *his* invitations? Why couldn't he simply accept her disinterest? Was he behind this *command?* Was Nathan? Was it simply Elizabeth King dictating her own desire to check the situation at the resort?

Why couldn't they simply let her be? She was doing a good job. Yet she felt an irresistible tug at the thought of meeting Nathan again...what it might mean...

It would be safe, she reasoned. Had to be safe with Elizabeth King there, and the other brother, Jared. It might even dispose of the wanton thoughts that plagued her lonely nights…show her beyond question how foolish any involvement with him would be.

"What about our guests here?" she prevaricated, feeling hopelessly at odds with a desire she *knew* could lead nowhere good.

"Spend Happy Hour with them," Tommy promptly replied. "Settle them at the table, and leave them to their own devices. They know each other from last night, don't they?"

He'd checked the bookings earlier in the week and all four couples in the homestead suites overlapped this weekend. "I won't be able to leave here until after seven," she pointed out.

"That's understood. We'll be dining at eight." He slid Sam a teasing look. "Mum said for you to come, too, squirt. Balance the table."

"Oh, sure! I can just hear Elizabeth saying that," she scorned.

"Well, I told her you probably didn't have a dress to wear."

"I'll put one on especially for Jared." She cocked her head on one side. "Or maybe I'll make a play for Nathan, now that Susan's out of the picture."

Susan…Miranda found her hands clenching and consciously relaxed them. Susan might not have been Nathan's *mistress,* but he hadn't married her. *Don't forget that!*

Tommy laughed and bounded up the steps, ruffling Sam's copper curls as he passed. "Go get him, Red!" Then to Miranda, "I'll just have a word with Roberto. He can come out of his kitchen between courses and wax lyrical about what he's cooked for the guests. Keep them happy.''

They watched him head off inside, mission accomplished as far as they were concerned.

''One of these days I'm going to kick him in the shins,'' Sam muttered.

It drew an instant wave of sympathy. Both of them fools over men. ''You have beautiful hair,'' Miranda quietly assured her. ''If you ask me, Tommy couldn't resist touching it.''

She heaved a rueful sigh. ''I bet no man has ever ruffled your hair, Miranda.''

''I haven't had the easy-going kind of friendships you've made. I rather envy you that.''

It drew a speculative look that Miranda instantly shied away from, not wanting to answer questions about her life. She glanced at her watch. ''Better get moving. Are you going to accompany me to the commanded dinner or go over earlier by yourself?''

''I'll wait for you. I'll get one of the resort Jeeps and have it out here at seven-fifteen. Okay?''

''Yes. Thanks, Sam.''

''You'll like Jared,'' she remarked, still with that speculative look.

''We'll see,'' Miranda returned non-committally.

It wasn't Jared on her mind as she headed off to get ready for tonight. It wasn't Jared or Tommy or Elizabeth King playing havoc with her pulse rate and tying knots in her stomach.

Nathan…his name was like a drumbeat on her heart.

Tonight she would see him again.

And she wanted it to be right.

But how could it be?

It was mad to think it…mad to want it…yet despite every bit of hard, common sense reasoning…there was no denying what she felt.

CHAPTER NINE

IT WAS Tommy, not Nathan, who greeted them at the
door and ushered them inside. As they moved towards
the lounge room, the usual snippy repartee went on
between him and Sam but it floated over Miranda's
head. Every nerve in her body was screwed tight, waiting with an excruciating awareness of her own helpless
fever-pitch anticipation, to feel whatever she would
feel when she came face-to-face with Nathan King
again.

Then they entered the room where he had to be…and
he wasn't there. The big black leather armchair where
he'd been sitting that first night was unoccupied.
Elizabeth King was sitting in *her* chair. A tall young
man—the third brother?—had risen from the nearby
chesterfield and was holding his arms out in welcome.
No one else was in the room!

Sam rushed forward and into Jared's offered embrace with all the gusto of an excited puppy, delighted
to see a much-missed loved one. While she was being
whirled around, admired and kissed, a strange, blank
feeling descended on Miranda, stilling all the wild agitation this visit had set in motion.

She wasn't aware of having come to a dead halt,
wasn't aware of Tommy lingering at her side, wasn't
aware of Elizabeth King watching her. For several
empty moments, she didn't know what she was doing

here. The whole focus of her coming was lost. Nathan wasn't even present.

Then Tommy nudged her elbow, and her mind clicked into a different alert phase. It was Elizabeth King who had commanded her presence and there was another brother to meet. It took a giant effort to recollect herself, to smile at Nathan's mother, to move forward for the introduction Tommy obviously wanted to make. The older woman, dressed in a pale green shift tonight, and the pearls she seemingly always wore, dipped her head in a gracious acknowledgement.

Miranda had chosen to wear white, wanting Sam to feel she outshone her, which Sam did in a bright blue clingy dress that enhanced the colour of her eyes. Whether Sam's glamorised appearance had the desired effect on Tommy, Miranda neither knew nor cared at the moment. His voice seemed to boom in her ears, accentuating the hollowness inside her.

"Jared, if you wouldn't mind freeing yourself from the sex-kitten clinging onto you..."

The man with Sam grinned at him. "Jealous, Tommy?"

"Wait for the claws, little brother. That kitten can deliver lethal scratches."

"Oh, there are some guys who can make me purr," Sam tossed at him, purring so exaggeratedly it made both men laugh.

Miranda managed to keep a smile pasted on her face and tried to inject interest into her eyes as Tommy proceeded to present her to his brother.

"This is my resort manager, Miranda Wade. And Sam's victim for the night is my brother, Jared, the jet setter, who has deigned to touch down with us this weekend.''

"Now, Tommy, you know you wear the title of King of the Air. I'm merely a passenger," Jared remarked good-humouredly as he offered his hand to Miranda, smiling into her eyes. "I'm delighted to meet you."

"Thank you. It's a pleasure to meet you, too, Jared."

She forced her mind to gather impressions. Of the three sons, he most favoured his mother in looks, the same deep brown eyes, high cheekbones, straight aristocratic nose. His thick black hair dipped over his forehead in an attractive wave, softening what was a rather lean face. He was slightly taller than Tommy, not as tall as Nathan, and his slim physique seemed to carry a whip-chord strength rather than solidly built muscle.

"I hope it will be," he said, projecting warm friendliness. "Some people find our family a bit daunting en masse. Sam is used to us—" he withdrew his hand and put his arm around her shoulders, giving her a smile and a hug "—virtually grew up with us…"

En masse? The phrase jolted Miranda. Would Nathan be joining them?

Unaccountably her skin began prickling. Her attention drifted from what Jared was saying. As though tugged by some invisible force, her head turned…and he was there, bringing with him a current of energy that blasted everyone else out of Miranda's consciousness.

Her body instantly reacted to how big he was, how male he was, and a shock wave of memory supplied how he'd felt pressed close to her…the power and the strength of the man tapping on instincts that responded in full flood. An aching weakness spread through her, threatening every bit of composure she'd managed to harness.

She watched his approach with a sense of helpless vulnerability, belatedly realising he was carrying a tray of drinks from an adjoining room and not really targeting her.

"Champagne cocktails for everyone," he announced, drawing enthusiastic replies from the rest of the party.

Miranda stood dumbly, feeling his deep voice thrum into her bloodstream, kicking her heart into a wild gallop. He made good-humoured comments to everyone as he offered the tray, first to his mother, then to her and Sam. Miranda took a glass before caution could whisper she shouldn't consume anything so potent as a champagne cocktail. The men took their drinks and Nathan made a toast.

"To a happy evening together."

Tommy and Jared kept topping that toast in a stream of witty repartee. Sam and Elizabeth King laughed at them. Nathan casually moved aside, placing himself directly in front of Miranda.

"Would you prefer iced water?" he asked. "I've just remembered…"

"No, this is fine, thank you," she rushed out so fast her voice sounded breathless. Her gaze was stuck at the gleaming V of brown flesh revealed by his open-necked shirt. She had to force it up, feeling dreadfully unprotected as the force of his dangerously discerning gaze hit hers. "Drinking a toast with iced water isn't quite the same, is it?'' she said in a more moderate tone.

He smiled. ''The choice is yours.''

Her mind seized on his seemingly deliberate use of the word, *choice.* His smile was inviting, encouraging, or was she so giddy from trying to control her own desires she was misreading his intention?

''This will do for now,'' she said, sipping the cocktail gingerly.

''Good! Is the resort working out as you wanted?''

''Everything is running very smoothly at the moment.''

His smile took on an ironic curl. ''My mother was extremely vexed I knew nothing to tell her. Tommy, incidentally, gave a glowing report.''

''I'm glad he's pleased with my management.''

''No question about that,'' he assured her, though his eyes seemed to burn with questions.

Miranda could feel herself flushing. Did he think she had Tommy dangling on a string? ''I like my work,'' she said defensively.

''My mother will be glad to hear it. She likes to check things for herself.''

Was he excusing himself from having anything to do with this command invitation? Letting her know she was still *safe* from him? Subtly directing her to where she should be *right now!*

Her gaze shot to Elizabeth King and her cheeks grew hotter at the realisation that the older woman was keenly observing her. Distracted by Nathan, Miranda had ignored her hostess, and was probably being judged wanting in good manners. It was all the more embarrassing, with Nathan actually hinting where her place was.

"Please excuse me," she gabbled, and made a bee-line for Elizabeth King, concentrating fiercely on how to minimise her gaffe.

She was graciously welcomed to the seat beside Elizabeth and remained there, doing her utmost to redeem herself in the older woman's eyes until dinner was called. Not that she was subjected to a cross-examination of business angles. The conversation seemed more directed towards her feelings about King's Eden, apparently determining how settled or unsettled she was in her new location. Miranda hoped her replies gave satisfaction. It was impossible to stop the dreadful churning in her stomach.

When they moved into the dining room, she was expecting to be placed next to Elizabeth. It was disconcerting—the purpose of her being here thrown out of kilter again—when she and Sam were directed to flank Nathan at the end of the table with Tommy and Jared on either side of their mother.

A balanced table... Tommy's comment flitted through Miranda's mind, yet it didn't feel right to her. The three King brothers and Sam shared a long familiarity. She was the outsider, placed in their midst but not a part of them, and that feeling deepened as dinner progressed and the others talked of people and events she had no knowledge of.

This was a world that was closed to her, she kept thinking, and she would never belong to it. Somehow she would have to stifle the feelings Nathan stirred in her. As it was, being seated so close to him was a nagging torment. Every movement he made, every word he said, burned more brightly on her consciousness than anything else.

When Jared started asking questions about her experience in the hospitality business in the city, compared to the situation she was handling now, she responded eagerly to his interest, welcoming a conversation that took her mind off Nathan. Tommy moved the topic onto tourism, and Sam brought up comments from her parents who were currently touring Argentina.

"What about your family, Miranda?" Nathan suddenly inserted, making her heart leap and her head jerk towards him.

He offered a sympathetic smile. "You're in the midst of ours. Sam's been rattling on about hers. I guess it's made you feel a bit homesick for yours."

"Not at all," she denied, confusion whirling through her mind again. Why was he asking? She'd told him she didn't belong anywhere. Despite the smile, his eyes seemed to be gleaming with purpose.

"Well, no doubt they'll be coming to visit you," Jared suggested.

Shaken by Nathan's unexpected and forceful focus on her, Miranda was slow to respond to his brother.

Sam leapt in. "Have you got any scrumptious bachelor brothers that might drop in?" she asked, picking up the ball she'd been playing against Tommy all night.

"No," Miranda answered with what she hoped was discouraging brevity.

"Sensational sisters?" Tommy countered.

"I have no family," she stated bluntly, cornered into revealing that much.

Sam goggled at her. "You were an orphan?"

How could she stop this rolling inquisition? "I wasn't as a child. I simply have no family now," she said with emphatic finality.

"You mean they were all wiped out in some terrible accident?"

"Sam," Nathan cut in tersely, his frown chastising her for avid curiosity, which might lead into painful areas.

"Sorry!" She grimaced an apology. "Guess I've drunk too much champagne." Her eyes appealed to Miranda. "It's just you've been such a mystery, never mentioning anything personal in your past."

The comment focused even more interest on her and Miranda realised it would linger if it went unanswered, casting an awkward mood for the rest of the evening. Besides, what did it really matter? What point was there in hiding the fact she had no family pedigree whatsoever, nothing at all to recommend her to this company, apart from the business connection?

"There's no great mystery, Sam," she said with a casual shrug. "Unlike you and everyone else here, I have no family history going back generations. My mother was an orphan. I was her only child. She wasn't married and never did marry. I wasn't told who my father was and my mother died some years ago. So you see, I have very little to talk about."

An appalled silence followed this little speech. Miranda found it so unnerving, she felt a compelling urge to fill it in with more talk, minimising the great black hole in her life they were probably all envisaging.

"Family is not a factor in my life, but it's been very enlightening listening to all your news and the long connections between the Connellys and the Kings. It's very different from what I've known myself."

She tore her gaze from the miserable embarrassment on Sam's face and steeled herself to look straight at Nathan who'd started this spotlight on her, digging under her skin again. She might as well hammer home the point that she was an unsuitable match for a King, and knew it too well to imagine any personal relationship between them could be viable.

"The framed photographs along your hallway here…such a history must be fascinating to have…to look back on…to feel a part of…"

"Yes," he agreed, his eyes burning back a relentless challenge. "And most remarkable are the women who chose to follow their men here and make a life with them on this land. Like Sarah, who ran a brothel in Kalgoorlie, before throwing her lot in with Gerard."

"Sarah? Who wrote the diaries?" Miranda couldn't believe it.

"Yes. You might find them interesting to read sometime."

It must be true, Miranda thought dazedly.

"Then there was Dorothy, a governess on one of the cattle stations in The Territory," he went on. "One of nine children whose family was so poor she was virtually sold into slave labour. One less mouth to feed."

He paused to let that information sink in, his eyes mocking any sense of grandeur about his family.

"Irene was the wife of a stockman who was thrown from his horse and died of a broken neck. She had nowhere to go. No one to turn to. She stayed here and married Henry King."

"But that was in the old pioneering days," Miranda finally found wits enough to protest. "I daresay there weren't so many women then who would want to cope with such a life."

"Not so many women now, either," Nathan snapped back at her.

"I'm sure you're wrong. The status is very different now." She swung her gaze pointedly to Elizabeth King whose necklace of pearls was probably worth a fortune. "Wouldn't you agree?"

"It's true there are many long-established families in the Kimberly, which give them a kind of status rating over relative newcomers," she said consideringly. "But our population is so small...what is it, Nathan? Thirty thousand people in an area that covers over three hundred thousand square kilometres?"

"And that clustered mostly around the six major towns," he said in affirmation.

"For the most part, the outback rule still holds," Elizabeth King went on. "It's not so much who you are or where you come from, but what you accomplish *here* that earns respect and status."

For the most part...Miranda silently noted that reservation.

"In fact," Tommy chimed in, "there are so many people with checkered pasts in the Kimberly, it's wiser to accept them at face value than to inquire too closely."

"The last outpost of civilisation," Jared said with a grin.

"Full of colourful characters," Tommy tagged on.

"But it does take time to earn respect and status," Miranda said, cutting to the heart of the matter. "The King family has an investment of a hundred years here. And I understand the pearl farms in Broome have been held by the same families for a similar length of time."

"And have been through as many ups and downs as those working the land," Elizabeth replied with a wry smile. "When I married Lachlan, all pearling activity in Broome had been virtually dead for years. Mother-of-pearl shell had been the main source of income and that had been undercut by the introduction of the plastic button. It wasn't until the advent of the cultured pearl that the farms built into the multimillion dollar business they are today. In marrying me, Lachlan got...only me."

Her gaze moved to Nathan, the dark brown eyes boring straight at her eldest son. "My life was with your father. He was where I wanted to be. It wasn't until after he died that I returned to Broome and involved myself in the pearl farming. You were old enough to take over from him, Nathan. You know you were. And that was what I couldn't bear...not King's Eden... King's Eden without Lachlan."

She paused, as though waiting for some critical comment from him. The sense of some running issue between mother and son was very strong. Miranda's mind spun with possibilities. Had Nathan judged his mother harshly for leaving? Had her departure triggered a mistrust in any woman being content to stay here, since not even his mother would? Was that why he had affairs rather than attempt a serious relationship?

She risked a covert glance at him. His face was like granite, revealing nothing. His eyes were narrowed, their expression veiled by lowered lashes, but his gaze was fixed on his mother. The silence was filling up with tension when he finally spoke.

"You did what you wanted to do," he said quietly. "I have no quarrel with that." He paused a moment, then added, "Trying to make people do what they don't want...is a fool's game...don't you think? It never gets the result we'd like."

Miranda felt the words, as though they were directed at her, reinforcing his claim that he would never manipulate a pressure situation to get what he wanted from her. She darted a glance at him but his gaze remained trained on his mother...a silent clash of wills that probably had nothing to do with her at all.

"Choices are always influenced by other things," came Elizabeth's pointed reply. "Which is why the *other things* need re-examining at times."

"On that I am in total agreement with you."

His gaze slid to Miranda, and the knowledge thumped into her heart that he was aware of the effect of his words on her, and every one of them was designed to reshape her view of him.

"I get the impression you're applying to us the kind of value system that operates in a more sophisticated society than we have here," he said with an ironic little smile. "Is that so, Miranda?"

Was he implying that wealth and power didn't count in their lives, in the associations they made?

"You can hardly say your name doesn't carry weight in the Kimberly," she asserted, unconvinced that such status was meaningless to this family, despite the examples they had cited.

His eyes mocked her reading of their situation. "It carries the weight of survival...which is what is most valued here."

"That's true," his mother cut in, swinging attention back to her. "The Kings, the Connellys, and my own family are survivors. It takes a certain breed of people—those I'd call of gritty character—to hold on in the Kimberly...to ride the good with the bad. There's no red carpet, Miranda. If I'd thought you were a red carpet person at heart, I would not have hired you for King's Eden."

"I see," she murmured, relief seeping through her at the realisation she wasn't viewed as an outsider by Elizabeth King, but as someone with the capability of being an insider. "I shall take that as a compliment."

"I might add that none of what we have now will survive unless there's a next generation." Her dark eyes glittered at Nathan and then moved to Tommy. "What will all your work and enterprise be worth then?"

"We're not exactly old men," Tommy protested jokingly.

"Time doesn't wait," his mother warned. "People always think there's plenty of time. Take it from me, Tommy, time runs out and what has been postponed never happens."

"Ah, now we're getting back to choice," Nathan

drawled. "Do we seize the day or plan for the future? What do you think, Miranda?"

He was zeroing in on her now, pouring out a current of energy that wound around her and tugged on the desire to pursue whatever might develop between them. Her pulse rate accelerated so quickly she felt dizzy. It was decision time. She could turn him off with her reply or open the door. Denial or risk?

His mother's words drummed through her mind... *time running out...opportunities lost...* She didn't know what her life was moving towards, didn't know if Nathan King could become an important part of it. All she knew was she no longer wanted to deny the chance that he might.

"I think I would like to read Sarah's diaries," she said, playing the safest line she could while inviting more contact with him.

For a moment it seemed she'd startled him. Then his eyes started dancing in amusement and his mouth widened into a grin. "I think you'll find your interest rewarded. I'll bring them over to you as soon as Jim Hoskins returns them."

"Thank you. I'd appreciate it."

He laughed, a ripple of joyous warmth that was far more intoxicating than a champagne cocktail.

Whether it was triggered by pleasure or triumph or simply amusement at the way she had answered him, Miranda couldn't tell. He was stunningly handsome when he laughed, his face alive with magnetic vitality, and it shot a wild zing of elation through her.

He *was* special.

She couldn't be feeling like this if he wasn't.

And right at this moment, she didn't care what the cost might be of knowing more of him.

CHAPTER TEN

DAY after day Miranda reminded herself she could not expect to see Nathan until Jim Hoskins returned Sarah's diaries, yet no amount of reasoning lessened the anticipation zinging through her mind, the excitement that fluttered through her every time she thought of being with him, and each day she felt a twinge of disappointment that he hadn't come.

When she lay in bed at night, she mentally replayed every minute of the dinner party at the station homestead, interpreting and re-interpreting Nathan's every word and action.

There was no doubt in her mind he had meant to push for another chance to move into her life, and when she'd given it, he was wise enough, or clever enough, not to capitalise on it too much, too soon. In fact, after he'd won what he wanted, he'd turned the dinner conversation back to general topics until they all rose from the table to have coffee and liqueurs back in the lounge room.

Then had come his casual offer to give her a personal tour of the photographs in the hallway. He'd pointed out the people he'd spoken of, giving a quick potted history of their lives on the cattle station, told a few amusing stories about them, and answered Miranda's questions without once attempting to seize any advantage with her.

There was no physical touching. Nevertheless, every time their eyes met, it felt as though he was reaching into her, stamping himself more and more irrevocably on *her* life and drawing her into his. The power of it was both exhilarating and frightening. Even when she and Sam left, she could feel it following her...desire that somehow tunnelled deeper than any desire she'd known before.

To Miranda's secret relief, Sam hadn't noticed anything *special* occurring with Nathan, or she was reserving comment on it. Neither Tommy nor Jared had shown any awareness that a shift had taken place between their brother and the new resort manager. Even Elizabeth King had seemed content with the evening at the end of it.

Of course, this *privacy* wouldn't last...couldn't once Nathan made his next move. This was a small community. People were going to notice and talk. But at least Nathan wasn't directly involved with the resort business, and the way he'd kept away from her so far proved there would be no unpleasantness at work, should a relationship between them not go well. Though she couldn't help hoping it would be something special. Really special.

As it happened, no amount of thinking prepared her for the circumstances that hit her on Thursday afternoon, just five days after she'd opened an invitational door to Nathan King. She'd done the rounds of the resort, checking that all accommodations levels were up to standard for the heavily booked weekend ahead, and supplies were more than adequate to meet demand. It was just past four o'clock when she entered her administration office, and without warning, the new world she'd begun to believe was free from her past, was suddenly attacked by it.

Val Warren, her clerical assistant, greeted her with a happy grin. "That cancellation we had on one of the homestead suites for this weekend…it's been taken up. We've got a full house again."

"Great! Short notice, though."

"I guess people who stay here can afford to be spontaneous," Val reasoned.

"Lucky for us! I'll have to check with Roberto that he's got enough gourmet food for the extra guests. What are their names?"

Val looked back at her monitor screen. "Married couple, currently staying at the Ayer's Rock resort, chartering a plane to fly directly here tomorrow, expected arrival time three o'clock…and their names are Celine and Bobby Hewson."

Miranda could feel the blood draining from her face. "Right!" she said weakly, and spun out of the office before Val saw the shock she'd delivered.

For several moments she leaned back against the closed door, fighting to recover some equilibrium. Maybe it was another Bobby Hewson whose wife just happened to be named Celine. They weren't uncommon names. Ayer's Rock, where they were currently staying, was like an Australian Mecca for tourists…the ancient red heart of the continent…but she couldn't imagine the Bobby she knew wanting to go there. But what about his wife? If she had accompanied him to Sydney…a honeymoon sight-seeing trip…

Wife… Miranda shook her head. Surely they weren't

even married yet. The engagement had only been announced three months ago. Shouldn't it take longer than that to arrange a big society wedding? It had to be some other couple. Had to be…

There was one way of settling any uncertainty. Galvanised into action, Miranda strode down the hall to her live-in quarters, intent on putting through a private call to the manager of the Ayer's Rock resort. The Bobby Hewson she knew would not be an unobtrusive guest. He would demand the best suite, the best service, and would let the manager know precisely who he was and what he stood for.

Once inside her self-contained apartment, Miranda moved straight to the telephone on her bedside table. She reached for the receiver, saw that her hand was trembling and sat down on the bed to compose herself, taking several deep breaths before proceeding to make the needed contact. A few minutes later she was connected to the man who could give her the critical information.

''This is Miranda Wade, manager of the King's Eden Resort.''

''Hi, there! What can I do for you?''

''Today we took a booking for a Mr and Mrs Bobby Hewson…''

''Ah yes, made it for him myself. He and his wife had planned to fly on to Broome. Another couple we have staying here—you'll remember them—John and Robyn Trumbell—apparently raved on about King's Eden and they decided to take in a weekend there. Lucky you could accommodate them.''

"Yes. Would that be the Bobby Hewson of the Regent Hotel chain?"

"Certainly is," came the dry reply.

Miranda's heart dropped like a stone.

"And his wife is a member of the Parmentier family who owns the Soleil Levant chain," the manager ran on, confirming their identities beyond any possible doubt. "It's her first trip to Australia. Keen to see the sights."

Coincidence…sheer rotten coincidence that they had connected with the Trumbells! And finding available accommodation here! Miranda felt too sick to speak.

"Mr Hewson mentioned that you'd been trained up to a managerial position at the Regent in Sydney. Sounded as though he was interested in finding out how you're dealing with an outback resort."

Bobby *knew* she was here! It wasn't just a trick of fate. He *knew*. John or Robyn Trumbell must have spoken of her. And that was why he was breaking his trip to Broome to come to King's Eden. Nothing to do with *the sights,* though he'd probably played that line to his wife. Bobby Hewson, Miranda knew with stomach-churning certainty, had *her* in his sights!

"I thought it might be him," she forced herself to say through the bitter taste of bile. "Thank you for filling me in."

"Well, I guess you now know what to expect."

"Yes. I do. Thank you again."

She hung up, her mind crawling with scenarios of what she could expect, and every one of them was a nightmare from hell. Tears started welling, tears of miserable frustration at not having escaped the punishment

Bobby Hewson would inevitably deal out to her for having flouted his plans. She remembered only too well her last meeting with him, her eyes cleared of the gullible scales that had blinded her to the man he really was...seeing the totally selfish ego behind his smiling charm.

He had expected her to give in to him.

She'd walked away. Flown away.

And now he was going to catch up with her.

The tears overflowed and trickled down her cheeks. She bent over, pulled off her shoes and socks, then curled up on the bed, hugging a pillow for comfort. She was facing a totally wretched situation. He'd arrive tomorrow, then all day Saturday, all day Sunday, three nights...and he'd be getting at her every chance he had. She knew he would.

Regrets for ever having fallen in love with him savaged her as she wept into the pillow. It hadn't been a real love. More a prolonged affair, sugared and peppered by the excitement and glamour Bobby always brought with him on his flying trips to Sydney. He'd swept in and out of her life, dazzling her with his charm, seducing her with honeyed words, always leaving with the promise of having more time with her on his next visit, making her feel important to him, necessary to him.

She'd fitted in with what he'd wanted. He hadn't cared about her needs. Didn't care about them now, either. He was coming here to satisfy himself, and he'd be scoring off her any way he could...subtle little digs in front of his wife, then seeking her out privately, maybe even trying to get into her bed again. He would see that as a triumph over her bid to put him out of her life. And if she didn't *oblige* him… Miranda shuddered, every instinct telling her no one frustrated Bobby Hewson and got away with it.

A knock on her door broke into the train of misery. She swiped at her tear-sodden face and looked at her watch. It jolted her to see it was a few minutes past five. The current homestead guests were probably back from their day trips and she hadn't been on hand to deal with any requests or problems. The knock meant someone was looking for her.

She scrambled off the bed, grabbed some tissues, rubbed her eyes and cheeks, shoved her feet into sandals, finger smoothed her hair back behind her ears. The knock came again as she struggled to calm herself enough to answer it. Probably Val, she thought, wanting to pass some message on before leaving for the day.

She opened the door and shock hit her again.

Nathan!

"Ah! You're here." He smiled, his eyes warm with pleasure.

Having steeled herself to face responsibility, Miranda was totally undone by Nathan's smile. The steel collapsed and her whole body turned to jelly.

"I was looking for you to give you Sarah's diaries," he went on, holding out the package he was carrying. "Just as well you are here in your private quarters. Makes it easy to put them in a safe place."

Somehow she lifted her hands to take the package. Her gaze dropped to it as her mind tried to change gears, adjusting to Nathan's presence and recalling what she had anticipated...hoped...from it. Except it all felt unreal now, shaky, without substance. She stared down at the diaries—Sarah's diaries—of a life that was in the past.

"Miranda?"

She heard the query but it seemed to come from a long distance. Her past was all too alive, threatening to mess her up again and she didn't know when or where that would stop, now that Bobby had access to her.

"Is there something wrong?"

Wrong...the awful sense of wrongness was so twisted up inside her... Nathan here at the wrong time... Bobby coming to do more wrong...another wave of tears swam into her eyes. She shook her head, too choked to say anything.

"You did say you wanted to read them." The edge in his voice seemed to slice into her heart. "If you've changed your mind..."

She swallowed hard, fighting to order her mind to come up with something that might cover her failure to welcome his company. "I'm sorry, Nathan. I'm not..." Her voice was wobbling. She scooped in a quick breath and forced herself on. "This is bad timing. But thank you for..."

Her chin was forcibly tilted up. The swift action halted her erratic little speech. She was startled into looking at him, though the moisture in her eyes blurred her vision, preventing any clear view of his reaction to her all too obvious distress.

"You've got a problem. Best you use me to talk it over with, Miranda," he stated firmly.

Before she could raise a protest or deter him from

his purpose, he pushed her door wide-open and was steering her around, his arm hugging her shoulders as he walked her to the closest armchair in her sitting area. He set her down in it, retrieved the diaries from her hold, placed them on the bench that divided off the kitchenette, then closed her door, sealing their privacy.

"Now tell me what's upset you."

She shook her head, knowing he had no control over this situation. "It doesn't have anything to do with you, Nathan."

"If it's resort business, Tommy would want me to help, Miranda," he asserted strongly.

Hopelessly agitated by his insistence on getting involved, she pushed herself out of the chair to plead for him to leave her. "It's personal. You can't help. Please…"

"Try me!"

He stood there, a strong mountain of a man, emitting immovable purpose, and Miranda could feel her own will crumpling under his. She didn't know what to do, couldn't see a way of resolving anything. She wasn't aware of her hands fretting at each other, wasn't even aware that her tear ducts were betraying her inner distress again.

Then he was coming at her and suddenly she was enveloped in a warm embrace, her head was pressed onto a broad shoulder, and a hand was stroking her hair.

"It's okay," he murmured comfortingly. "We'll sort it out. A problem is always better shared."

"No, it's not," she cried, even as she passively accepted his physical support, inwardly craving more.

"Trust me." It was more of a command than an appeal. "Sooner or later you'll have to learn to trust me, Miranda. You might as well start now."

She wanted to, but the thought of explaining everything was so daunting, her heart cringed from it. And what if he misunderstood her position? He hadn't lived in Bobby Hewson's world.

"It's not good," she blurted out.

"So what? Who's perfect?"

Anguish splintered her mind. She could no longer find the point of arguing. "It's the man I told you about," she confided in a fearful rush. "Bobby Hewson. He's coming tomorrow. With his wife. And he knows I'm here. He knows."

CHAPTER ELEVEN

TENSION! Being pressed so close to Nathan, Miranda instantly felt it whipping through him, transmitting a stiffening jolt to her shredded nerves. The firm wall of his chest expanded. The hand stroking her hair clenched. The muscular thighs supporting hers tautened to rock-hardness. It seemed for several seconds, he didn't breathe at all. And neither did she!

Sheer panic threw her mind into chaos. What had she done by spilling that information? He'd wanted to know. He'd asked her to trust him. But words spoken couldn't be taken back. If he was thinking badly of her again…

A primitive savagery seized Nathan's mind. *I will not let him have her. I will not let him hurt her. He's a dead man if he so much as touches her!* Then some spark of rationality pulled him back from that violent edge and argued that he had to handle this situation with some finesse. Miranda was not his and only God knew what she felt for the scum who didn't have the decency to leave her alone.

His breath whooshed out, making her scalp tingle with apprehension. The feeling that she was poised on the edge of an abyss with her whole life in the balance made her heart clench with fear. A surge of adrenaline spurred a need to fight for what she wanted. Though she didn't know how she was going to go about it, she lifted her head, ready to face whatever she had to.

"Right!" he snapped, easing away from her, his hands grasping her upper arms to hold her steady.

She braved meeting his eyes, her own completely dry now, and was stunned by the blue blaze of purpose burning from them.

"So he's the cause of your stress. What are you expecting him to do and why, Miranda? Spell it out to me. I'll be able to help you better if I'm aware of all the nuances to this situation."

Relief! Nathan wasn't judging. He was going to listen…to help. Dizzy from the wrangle of emotions still seizing her brain, Miranda took a deep breath to feed some oxygen into her bloodstream, and tried to focus her mind on delivering the salient facts.

Her mouth was dry. She worked some moisture into it and started to outline the problem, her eyes begging his understanding. "The Hewson family own the Regent Hotel chain. They're…they're very rich, influential. I didn't want to continue any kind of relationship with Bobby once I heard he was committed to marrying Celine Parmentier. Her family owns the Soleil Levant hotels. The marriage was going to give Bobby more power. He said I could ride up the ladder with him or…"

The bitter disillusionment of that scene rushed in on her again, the terms Bobby had laid out, ringing with the kind of corrupt promises that had taken her mother down a road that had emptied her heart of all love.

"Or?" Nathan prompted.

She sighed away the dark, grievous memory and pushed on with the deal Bobby had pressed, the revulsion she'd felt reflected in her voice. "If I didn't see sense, I might find my career on shaky ground. If I sought a position elsewhere, a good reference could be withheld."

Nathan frowned. "But it wasn't. My mother said your references were excellent."

"Bobby didn't expect me to leave. He thought he had me. So he didn't bother instructing the manager to withhold the truth about my capabilities, or cast any slur on them."

"So you left without telling him you were going."

"I told no one about applying for this job or getting it. Once I was notified I had it, I packed up my possessions, handed in my resignation and walked out of the Sydney Regent the same day. To all intents and purposes, I disappeared."

"Drastic action," he mused, as though measuring all it meant.

Sensing some criticism of her decisions, and discomforted by it, Miranda broke out of his hold and paced around the two armchairs that faced the television set before turning to confront him again, her hands gesticulating the urgency she'd felt to escape any rebound effect from walking out on Bobby Hewson.

"I wanted a clean break. King's Eden offered me that. It was out of his reach, not connected to people or places he knew. I thought he couldn't get at me here or do me any damage by bad-mouthing me because this was outside the normal hotel trade."

''Get at you?'' Nathan picked up sharply, his eyes searing hers with questions.

She flushed, hating the admission she had to make. Her arms instinctively hugged her midriff, holding in the awful vulnerability she felt. ''We were together for three years. You don't just forget all that intimate knowledge, Nathan. And he'll use it. I know he will.''

The muscles in his face tightened. A wave of disapproval seemed to come at her and it instantly struck a fierce well of resentment. What about him and his two years with Susan? At least she had thought of marriage with Bobby.

''Do you still want him?'' he shot at her.

''No!'' she flared, throwing out her hands in exasperated denial. ''What do you think this is all about? I don't want anything more to do with him. Can't you see that?''

''I see how upset you are by his coming, which suggests to me the relationship is not dead for you. If it were dead, he couldn't get at you, Miranda,'' he argued tersely.

''You miss the point,'' she fiercely retorted. ''It's not dead for him. And if you think he's going to leave it alone on my say-so...'' She shook her head. ''My exit from his life told him I wanted out and he's ignoring it. He's deliberately pursuing me, breaking the other plans he'd made the moment he heard where I was. I didn't invite him.''

''No, but that doesn't mean you won't want him when he's with you again.''

''He's with *his wife!*''

''Miranda, you can say no in your mind.'' He

walked slowly towards her, his eyes boring into hers. "You said it to me. And you can mean it in your mind, bolstering the no with any number of reasons. I'm not questioning that."

"Then what are you questioning?" she gabbled, feeling the strong male force of him increase as he stepped closer and closer, encompassing her, sending her nerves haywire, stirring all the wild desires she had nursed in the darkness of the nights. It was Nathan she wanted. Not Bobby. And her heart wept that he should think otherwise.

"I think you're worried about what you'll *feel* when he's here...when you're faced with him. Feelings aren't something we can easily govern. What if he draws you into his arms..."

He followed the words with the action, slowly gathering Miranda close to him, but behind the seemingly controlled deliberation in his eyes, she saw the flicker of something that wasn't controlled at all, and it ignited a wild, wanton recklessness in her. Or perhaps the pressure of his body did, the sexuality that seemed to brood from it and clutch at her.

"When you kissed me back, that morning beside the helicopter...were you missing him, Miranda?"

"No. I wasn't thinking of anything. I just..."

"Responded to me."

"Yes." It was barely a hiss of sound. His head was bending to hers and she wanted him to kiss her now, to completely blot Bobby Hewson out of anything between them.

"Then keep remembering this when he comes,

Miranda.'' A harshness in his voice now, scraped with raw emotion. ''Remember how you feel with me.''

Then he did kiss her, and it was no exploratory dip to measure her response, no trial for any special element in their tasting of each other. It was full-scale plunder, a kiss of such driving, demanding passion, Miranda was instantly consumed by the explosion of need it ignited. The hot fusion of their mouths was not enough, nowhere near enough, though as they greedily fed on every possible sensation they could find and savour…intoxicating themselves with kiss after kiss, their hands followed their own instinctive path.

Impossible to remember afterwards whether she tore at his clothes or he tore at hers. The undressing was jerky, erratic, urgent, frantic, the compulsion to be rid of everything that came between them almost violent— no stopping it—no wish to pause or think or do anything other than revel in the impact of their bodies fully touching, bare flesh meeting bare flesh, the hot exciting friction of skin against skin, his hands skimming, squeezing her soft curves, her fingers raking the taut musculature that seemed to bristle with masculinity.

She remembered thinking he was a magnificent bull of a man and she wanted to be mated with him, wanted it more than anything she'd wanted in her life, to have the strength of him inside her, to feel him moving with her…this man who called so deeply to the woman she was, whatever else either of them were.

He propelled them to the bed, hauled her onto it, took the dominant position over her, and she automatically arched her body to meet his as he sought entry. His eyes connected with hers…a fierce blaze of desire…fiercely returned…both of them throbbed with an urgency that could not brook any denial.

Her whole body quivered with elation as she felt him push forward, sheathing himself with her moist heat, her inner muscles convulsing around him in bliss, the hard fullness of him opening a passage that pulsed with wild anticipation, wanting all he could give her. She wrapped her legs around him, pressing him on, and the plunge that followed was exquisitely fulfilling, so incredibly deep it felt as though he had entered her womb, an eerie, intimate sensation that spread out in concentric circles, totally captivating in its intensity.

From that moment on, Miranda's whole being was totally focused on the rhythmic ripples set in constant motion by Nathan's powerful thrusting. She was acutely aware of their strengthening infiltration of every cell of her body, the aching sweetness accompanying their invasion, the sense of their building towards a shattering peak, of pleasure becoming too intense to sustain within the space of her being. A time came when she seemed poised on the edge of it and a cry of anguish broke from her throat.

In the very next instant all the torturous tension exploded into a sunburst of glorious ecstasy, and she was floating in some heavenly space, and the man who had brought her there was sharing it with her, cradling her in a hug that kept them bound together as he rolled to one side, removing his weight, yet still enveloping her in a cocoon of strength, caring, protective, possessive.

Their breathing slowed. The thunder of their heartbeats dropped to a barely discernible pulse. The languor that stole over them was seductive…warm, peaceful, enticing a prolonged stay of judgement on what they'd done. It couldn't be examined with words. It had gone beyond words.

Miranda was acutely aware she had never experienced anything like this before…such primitive, compelling passion…yet somehow instinctively right with this man…and being held by him now felt right, too, as though she belonged with him. While it made no rational sense, her mind stood in awe of these feelings, and the longer he held her, the more immersed she became in the blind conviction that they were meant to come together and this was how a man and woman should feel when they did, and she wished she had always known this. Then she could never have been fooled about what it was supposed to be.

Eventually Nathan spoke. He was trailing strands of her hair through his fingers as she lay with her head on his chest. She felt his intake of breath and the words he said were soft but very, very decisive.

"You don't need Bobby Hewson, Miranda."

Bobby? The part of her life he had inhabited felt so minimised she could barely bring it to mind. "No, I don't," she answered fervently.

"I'll be here tomorrow evening to make sure *he* understands you don't need him."

Here? Did Nathan mean in her bed? How would Bobby know—see—the incredible difference of what she felt with Nathan?

"I'll join you and your party of guests for dinner, but I'll come earlier," he said, his voice firm with the plans in his mind.

Miranda struggled past the fuzziness in hers. Nathan

meant to be with her publicly, showing Bobby she was not alone, very much not alone!

"In time for the Happy Hour gathering," Nathan specified.

"Happy Hour!" Miranda jack-knifed out of Nathan's embrace and looked at her watch. It was almost six o'clock. "I've got to get going. I should be out there." A flush of embarrassment poured into her face as she turned to look squarely at him. "This is my job, Nathan."

"Duty calls," he said equably.

She hurtled off the bed and raced into her ensuite bathroom, frantically turning on the taps in the shower, shoving her hair into a plastic cap and stepping under the hot spray before pausing for breath or further thought. Only then did it strike her that Nathan's mind had been locked on Bobby, before and after, and he hadn't said anything about what he felt with her.

What if it had only been a male competitive thing with him?

Instantly her whole body revolted against this thought. Nathan had wanted her before he'd ever known about Bobby. It had nothing to do with Bobby. Nothing! He was purely incidental in their coming together.

It came as another jolt to realise they hadn't used protection. Just as well she was on the pill to keep her cycle regular. And she couldn't see Nathan being a health risk, having recently been in a long monogamous relationship. All the same, there should have been questions asked.

On the other hand, obviously there had been no premeditation by either of them. Which said something about the strength of the attraction between them. The moment Nathan had started kissing her she'd forgotten Bobby, her job, everything. Such a total wipe-out had never happened to her before. Never. It had to mean something special. There was no other explanation for it.

Clean and fresh again, Miranda turned off the taps and quickly towelled herself dry. A nervous energy possessed her as she attended to her hair and make-up. Had Nathan left, having made his arrangements for tomorrow? Did those arrangements mean more than fixing the problem with Bobby?

She wrapped a towel around herself before emerging from the bathroom. Modesty, at this point, seemed rather foolish but she didn't feel comfortable flaunting her naked body with the heat of passion gone, and if Nathan was still in the apartment...this was so *new*. Her mind was torn over how he viewed the intimacy they had just shared. She wanted to be sure.

He was fully dressed and placing the parcel of diaries he'd brought her on the bedside table when she opened the bathroom door. He swung to face her, his gaze making a swift, comprehensive sweep of her appearance.

"Are you all right?" he asked, searching her eyes for any flicker of concern.

"Yes." She offered an ironic smile. "A little stunned."

He nodded. "I didn't think of protection."

Relief surged through her. It might be practical caring but it *was* caring. "I've been on the pill for quite a while. I used to have problems with..." She shrugged, realising she was gabbling and he wouldn't be interested in how heavily and haphazardly she'd menstruated without medication to give her a normal cycle.

He returned her ironic smile. "I'm usually more responsible. I'm not a health risk, Miranda."

"Neither am I."

"Then there's no problem."

Supposedly not for two healthy adult people accepting a simple case of lust gone wild, Miranda thought, needing more from him than this matter-of-fact manner. He started walking towards her and she was once again mesmerised by the overwhelming power of the man, his air of solid self-assurance.

"I'll go now. You have work to do." He put his hand on her shoulder, a light reassuring touch, and dropped a kiss on her forehead. "Just to remind you to keep *us* in the forefront of your mind tomorrow, when Bobby Hewson arrives." His eyes seared hers with the intense recollection of their intimacy. "Expect me at six o'clock. I'll be here to stand by you. Okay?"

"Yes." Was this all it was to him...blotting out Bobby? "Thank you," she added, searching his eyes for more.

He suddenly grinned. "My pleasure."

She watched him leave, too captivated by his presence to move until the door closed behind him. Then conscience pricked her again and she flew to her cupboard, discarding the towel and hastily pulling on clothes.

Nathan's words—*I'll be here to stand by you*—lingered in her mind. Bobby had never done that, not in the supportive sense Nathan meant. Her mother had never had a man she could truly lean on. It was, at least, one good feeling Nathan had left her with, being able to count on him, and Miranda had no doubt he was as good as his word.

But what about when Bobby was gone? Was she to be another Susan in Nathan's life? His ...*pleasure?*

Miranda shied away from these questions. She couldn't deal with them now. She had guests waiting for her. Everything else had to be pushed aside. Tomorrow would come soon enough...Bobby... Nathan...and hopefully some answers she could live with.

CHAPTER TWELVE

IT WAS her job to greet the incoming homestead guests, and greet them she would, but Miranda's stomach was twisted into a painful knot as she watched Bobby Hewson and his new wife arrive.

He alighted from the luggage buggy first, still looking like a sun-king as she had always thought of him—his light brown hair streaked with blonde, his skin gleaming with a perfect golden tan, a dazzling white smile flashing from a face so handsome it was guaranteed to make any woman melt. But it didn't melt Miranda today. It was a strange shaky feeling, seeing him again and knowing the brilliant facade of the man hid a corrupt heart that could never, never be trusted.

"Miranda..." he called, as though the sight of her filled him with delight. "It's a real pleasure to find a familiar face in the great beyond."

His charm washed over her, too, though once it had invariably turned her inside out, dispelling doubts and making her believe he really did love her, that she was truly the light of his life. This time, her mouth didn't automatically flash a responding smile. She had to force it.

"It's a surprise to see you out of the city, Bobby."

He still managed to look city elegant in shorts and sports shirt, colour co-ordinated in navy, red and green, expensive Reeboks on his feet. His tall, gym-trained athletic body carried all clothes well.

"A new challenge always lifts the spirit," he answered, his eyes raking Miranda from head to toe with sexual intent, even as he held out his hand to the woman now stepping out of the buggy.

Inwardly bristling at Bobby's blatant cockiness, Miranda switched her attention to his wife. Her skin was dark olive, making her look quite exotic, dressed as she was in scarlet shorts, a designer T-shirt—white, splashed with an abstract pattern of colourful poppies—and a very chic straw hat with one scarlet poppy artfully placed on the brim. She was also petite, her figure slender, almost boyish, small firm breasts clearly braless.

Miranda, dressed in her usual day uniform of khaki safari shorts and shirt, suddenly felt like a drab Amazon compared to this woman, but she quickly brushed the comparison aside. She was not in competition with Bobby Hewson's wife and never would be.

Keeping her smile in place, she said, "And you must be Celine. Welcome to King's Eden, both of you."

"Thank you. It is amazing, this outback of yours," she lilted at Miranda, her native French tongue giving her English a very attractive accent. "Very much an exciting adventure."

"I hope it continues to be so," Miranda replied, noting that Celine led the way up the path to the verandah, Bobby strolling a step behind. Detaching himself from his wife?

"Did you manage to make all the bookings I phoned through this morning?" Celine asked eagerly.

"Yes, everything has been arranged," Miranda affirmed.

"Even the boat ride down Granny Gorge this afternoon?"

"The guide will be here by the time you've checked into your suite."

She clapped her hands in glee. "I did not want these few hours wasted."

Close up, Celine was younger than Miranda had imagined. She barely looked out of her teens, her pretty face framed by short black hair styled in a pixie cut, and dominated by big dark eyes, aglow with enthusiasm.

"I think I'll give the gorge a miss, Celine," Bobby dropped casually as they mounted the steps to the verandah.

"But I've booked!" she protested, her face petulant with displeasure as she turned to him.

"You can go, pet," he answered indulgently. "I'd like to have a look around the resort. See how it works."

"Business!" She heaved a vexed sigh.

He ignored it, looking over her shoulder at Miranda, his amber eyes gleaming tigerishly. "I'd like a personal tour, Miranda."

With her, he meant, and every fighting instinct rose to the fore. He was not going to get at her. She would not let him. "As you like. I'll call a guide to come and show you what you want to see."

"Come now, Miranda," he cajoled, steering his wife onto the verandah so that he could step up for a direct confrontation, his body language emitting confident demand. "Don't I merit *you* as my guide?"

She tried to construct an apologetic smile. "I'm sorry. I'm not free this afternoon."

"Oh, I'm sure you could delegate your responsibilities."

"This isn't a big city hotel, Bobby, and doesn't run like one," she explained reasonably. "All my staff have very specific responsibilities…"

"And I have a special request which I have no doubt your employers would understand and appreciate," he cut in, his eyes as hard as gold nuggets.

The threat of blackmail had no teeth here, yet the vindictive ego behind it caused her heart to contract. The thought of Nathan standing by her gave her the courage to defy any pressure to fall in with Bobby Hewson's will.

"I can provide a guide," Miranda repeated firmly. "However, if you wish to arrange something with the King family, I believe Nathan King will be here this evening."

And he won't bend to your will, either, she thought with savage satisfaction.

"Ah! So you can leave this business until then, Bobby." Celine jumped in, curling her arm around his and pouting up at him. "I want you with me."

"Well, if it's important to you, pet…" He patted his wife's hand, smiled at her, but there was no smile in the eyes he turned back to Miranda. They glittered with the promise of getting what he wanted, one way or another. "I shall look forward to meeting Nathan King tonight."

"Guests usually gather around the bar from six o'clock onwards for pre-dinner drinks," she informed them, then stood back to make way for the porter, a cheerful American lad who was working his way around Australia. "The Shiralee Suite, Eddie. The key is in the door."

"Yes, ma'am. If you'll follow me, folks."

A Jeep zoomed up to the homestead.

"There's your guide for the gorge trip," Miranda pointed out. "When you're ready…"

"We will not be long," Celine assured her, pulling Bobby with her in her zest to be off sight-seeing.

Miranda watched them follow their luggage inside, thinking Bobby's wife had no idea what she had married. Or maybe she did and was happy to go along with what he gave her anyway. She herself might have remained indefinitely in his charm-web if this marriage hadn't come up. It was a sickening thought.

As it was, her pulse was still galloping from the stressful encounter. She took a deep breath and headed down the path to give instructions to the guide in the Jeep. He could wait inside for the Hewsons. She didn't want to see them again until she had to. Hopefully Nathan would be with her by then.

Nathan…

As the afternoon wore on into early evening, her confidence in his support started wavering. Could she really trust her instincts about the kind of man Nathan was when she'd been so fooled by Bobby for three whole years?

He was different, she argued. He *felt* different. And he didn't emit a glamorous facade. There was nothing ephemeral about him, more solid substance that wasn't going to change. Or was that hope, more than reality?

Bobby could influence and manipulate people. He would not be so blatant in showing Nathan the ruthless dismissal of anything that stood in his way. He would appeal as to a peer who understood how the world really worked, man to man. And he would slyly undermine her credibility, dressing up lies with half-truths, perhaps even suggesting she had slept her way up in the trade.

Would Nathan still take her side against such supposedly confidential and authoritative information? What did he really know of her, apart from the little she'd told him?

Even if he did take her side, how could she be sure he was doing it because he believed her, or because he wanted to keep having sex with her?

And that was the most unsettling thought of all.

CHAPTER THIRTEEN

TEN past six.

And Nathan wasn't here!

Miranda had finished introducing the Hewsons to the other new guests who had arrived before lunch, as well as suffered Bobby's smarmy hug of familiarity as he confided their former professional connection to the group. Her skin was still prickling with revulsion as she escaped his stroking fingers with the excuse of fetching a tray of hors d'oeuvres.

A mistake to have worn this dress. Its shoe-string straps left too much flesh exposed for wandering hands. She'd chosen it because it was a bright lemon colour and she had matching sandals and the outfit had always made her feel upbeat and confident. Tonight she needed all the confidence she could get.

And she had wanted to look good for Nathan!

Was it another mistake to count on him?

She was half-way to the bar to put in a call to the kitchen when she heard a vehicle pulling up outside. Not the sound of one of the resort Jeeps. A more powerful engine. Her heart did a flip and a heady mixture of hope and relief surged through her. It had to be Nathan arriving!

Forgetting the hors d'oeuvres, she did an about-turn and headed for the doors to the front verandah, her pulse skipping erratically. She wanted him. She needed him. Doubts about his motives were momentarily blotted out. The doors in front of her opened automatically to her approach. In a few blurred seconds she was at the head of the steps to the verandah, and there her swiftly moving feet came to a halt.

It *was* him.

He was rounding the bonnet of a Land Cruiser, his big solid frame silhouetted against the sunset. He paused as he caught sight of her waiting to welcome him, and her heart hammered wildly at the strong visual image of him, stamped on the vibrant colours of the outback sky—long horizontal streaks of yellow behind the black spindly trees on the flat horizon, red and purple clouds clustered above them—and this man... this man looking like a lord of it all, whom nature itself was glorifying.

Then he was striding up the path and the very same skin that had crawled at Bobby's touch started tingling as Nathan's electric energy poured towards her. A quiver ran down her thighs. Her toes curled. Her mind throbbed his name over and over...Nathan, Nathan, Nathan...

She didn't hear the doors slide open behind her.

But she heard the voice and the slimy confidence in it as it said, ''Ah! Mr King arriving?'' and her heart froze as Bobby Hewson stepped up beside her, once again hanging his arm around her shoulders in an insidious claim of ownership, right in front of Nathan!

The shock of it completely paralysed her. She saw Nathan's step slow, his gaze dart from her to Bobby and back to her, and her mind jammed in horror at what he might be reading from Bobby's action.

"Good evening, Miranda," he greeted her coolly as he came to the end of the path.

His coolness jolted her tongue loose. "I expected you earlier, Nathan," she snapped, hating the situation his tardiness had set up.

Suddenly goaded into not caring how it looked, she spun out of Bobby's hug and stepped aside, throwing out one hand in formal introduction. "This is one of our guests, Bobby Hewson...Nathan King. Bobby has expressed a wish to discuss resort business with you, Nathan. If you'll both excuse me, I have other guests to see to."

She left them to it, her whole body seething with furious emotion. Let them have their man-to-man chat, her mind raged. Let Bobby do his worst behind her back. Let Nathan believe whatever he liked of her. She'd steel herself with all the armour she could summon so that neither man could touch her. It was stupid, stupid, stupid, to count on anyone to do right by her! Especially men who just wanted to feather their beds with a woman they fancied.

Terry, one of the waiters, was serving a selection of hors d'oeuvres to the guests. Bobby's wife was gaily chatting to another couple who had been to Granny Gorge that afternoon, displaying no disturbance of mind over her straying husband, not even a questioning glance at Miranda as she rejoined the group. But Celine's gaze did snap to Nathan when Bobby escorted him inside.

"Ooooh...magnifique!" she breathed in girlish awe, and Miranda sourly thought Nathan undoubtedly had the same effect on every woman. He wasn't only special to her.

Nevertheless, despite his drawing the attention of the whole group, it was she he looked at, his gaze boring straight through her defences, shaking her up again, even as she glared back at him, telling herself she wouldn't let him mean anything to her.

Bobby was talking at him in a confidential manner. There was no discernible response on Nathan's face. As they came within easy earshot, Nathan turned to him and said very clearly, ''You have the wrong man. This resort is the business of my brother Tommy, and he's happy to leave its management in Miranda's very capable hands.''

So Bobby was already trying to go over her head, Miranda surmised, though Nathan *was* the wrong man for that, which meant he'd try Tommy next.

Bobby frowned. ''Surely you network.''

''As a family, yes. But none of us interfere with each other's areas of special interests.'' His face took on a hard arrogance as he pre-empted any reply from Bobby. ''Though perhaps I should add that the whole family would swing in to protect any of our interests should they be threatened.'' His gaze cut straight to Miranda. ''We look after our own in the Kimberly.''

She was instantly thrown into more turmoil. Did he consider her *his?* Was he promising she was safe from Bobby, regardless of anything the man said to anyone?

''You're one of the Kings?'' another male guest queried, obviously fascinated by this exchange.

Nathan swung to him with a little smile of acknowledgement. "Yes. Nathan King. The cattle station is my business. And you are…?"

A flurry of introductions and handshakes followed. A keen curiosity about the running of a cattle station prompted several questions at once.

"Well, one requisite is being ready to cope with any emergency," Nathan answered. "This afternoon one of my stockmen was thrown from his horse and it looks as though his back may be broken."

Expressions of dismay and sympathy rippled around the guests. Miranda frowned. Was this the cause of his late arrival? "Calling an ambulance is not an option out here," he went on. "Under instructions from the flying doctor service, we trucked him in to the station airstrip, loaded him into a plane and flew him off to hospital."

"Any news of him yet?" Miranda asked, guilty about her own selfish concerns when one of Nathan's men might well be fighting for his life.

"No." His vivid blue eyes targeted her. "It was five-thirty by the time we had him safely on his way. I've arranged to be called here when information comes in."

"Of course," she said quickly. "Would you like a drink?"

"Yes." He nodded towards the bar. "Shall I help myself?"

The bar attendant was on his way to the group with a tray of cocktails.

"I'll make you whatever drink you'd like," she offered, hoping to have a few private moments with him.

"Thank you," he returned drily, as though no longer expecting anything from her.

Which made Miranda burn with more uncertainties.

As they both moved towards the bar, Celine called, "Bobby, why is it called a cattle station instead of a ranch?"

Miranda silently blessed the claim for her husband's attention.

"Probably because they use huge road-trains, up to fifty metres long, to take the stock to market," someone else answered.

"Yes, and it's best to get off the road if you see one coming," another guest chimed in, proceeding to recount his experience of road-trains, which occupied everyone else's attention.

A lively distraction from the injured stockman, Miranda thought, then reflected that it might have been Nathan thrown from his horse…and how would she have felt then? Even in her current state of violent confusion, he tugged at something vital in her.

"I'm sorry…about the stockman," she blurted. *And for her rude greeting,* though she couldn't bring herself to say it.

"I'm sorry I wasn't here for you on time," he returned quietly, causing her more inner writhing.

"The injured man was more important," she asserted.

"Sometimes there are injuries that aren't so easily visible."

Miranda's heart contracted. Was he talking about her? Himself? Bobby? She shot him a questioning glance as she rounded the bar to serve him. "What would you like?"

His eyes beamed back commanding authority. "I'd like you to seat me at the end of the dinner table with Bobby and Celine Hewson on either side of me. Right now I'll have a whisky. No ice."

She reached for the bottle of whisky, her hands trembling a little, her mind filling with the kind of poison Bobby would pour into Nathan's ear. "Why do you want to be placed there?" she asked, as she managed to pour his drink.

"I'd also like *you* to be seated at the other end of the table, right away from him."

Right away from Nathan, too. She wouldn't be able to hear what was going on between the two men. Which wasn't fair! How could she defend herself? She handed him the glass of whisky, hating the sense of having no control over the situation.

"What if I don't want that?" she challenged.

His eyes glittered with what looked like contempt. "You like him pawing you?"

"No!" she cried, shrivelling under the implication.

"You want to hear how much he still wants you?"

"You know I don't!"

"Do I, Miranda?" He took a sip of his drink, his eyes savagely deriding her contention. "I know nothing of what's gone on between you since he's arrived. All I know is you cut me dead out on the verandah."

"Nothing's *gone on!*" she hissed. "And I was upset by that little tableau Bobby put on for you when you arrived."

"Running away didn't resolve anything."

"Perhaps I wasn't thinking clearly."

"Undoubtedly you weren't. I see his wife is very attractive. Are you jealous?"

"She's welcome to him."

"Then why are you objecting to the seating I've suggested?"

"Because…" Miranda clamped her mouth shut. It was madness trying to fight this. She'd been right when she'd whirled back inside. Let Bobby do his worst. Let Nathan think what he liked. She was better off out of it. "Fine!" she clipped out. "Have it your way! I hope you enjoy your dinner!"

The bar attendant was on his way back. Miranda used him as interference to avoid anything more to do with Nathan as she returned to the guests. *He* strolled back to the group and began chatting up Celine. Well, not exactly chatting up, but answering her very enthusiastic curiosity about him, and Bobby was content to stay in that little circle of charm, waiting to inject his venom when the chance came.

When it was time to usher everyone to the dining table, Miranda didn't have to do any arranging of the seating. Nathan claimed the chair at the foot of the table. Celine grabbed the seat to the right of him. Bobby naturally took the seat to his left. The others chose where they willed, leaving the chair at the head of the table for Miranda, since that was where she had sat at lunch-time.

From that moment on, it seemed to Miranda, Nathan controlled everything. He played the part of a charismatic host to perfection. He was interesting, amusing, witty, extending himself to entertain everyone, the life of the party, all the guests hanging on his words, enjoying having his company, loving every minute of his good-humoured sharing of himself and his expert knowledge of the Kimberly region.

Miranda doubted they even tasted the food they consumed. No one bothered to comment on it. They were too busy lapping up the unique experience Nathan was giving them. Occasionally he referred things to her, forcing her into the conversation, and she had to respond as a good hostess would, but she kept remembering the two dinner parties at the station homestead where he hadn't bothered to put himself out so much, and she resented this performance from him now…lording it over all of them.

It was probably sticking in Bobby's craw that Nathan was the star attraction. But so what? Did that do any good? Was this some male competition to show her he was better value than Bobby was? If this was supposed to *win* her, it was the wrong way of going about it, as far as Miranda was concerned. She would have preferred to have him sitting next to her, giving her some caring attention instead of impressing how great he was on others.

After the main course was cleared from the table, Celine took herself off to the Powder Room. A fresh coat of glossy red lipstick and a respray of perfume for Nathan's benefit, Miranda darkly surmised. One of the other women asked her about a picnic box ordered for tomorrow and the rest of the party started checking their planned activities with each other.

Miranda saw Bobby lean over to murmur something to the man who'd upstaged him all evening. Nathan's face visibly stiffened. His eyes narrowed. Then he leaned over and said something to Bobby that had her former employer straightening up in his chair.

The two men eyed each other in a long, silent duel. More inaudible words were exchanged. Nathan's expression took on a hard, ruthless cast. Whatever was going on between them was not the least bit entertaining, and Miranda had the sickening feeling she was at the centre of it.

Celine returned to her chair.

The call signal of a mobile telephone came from Nathan's shirt pocket. Conversation halted as attention swung to him, the injured stockman coming to mind again.

''Please excuse me,'' he said, standing up to move away from the table.

He went out on the verandah to take the call.

The sweets course was served, providing a timely distraction. Miranda had lost her appetite for any more food, her stomach too knotted with tension to accept even a spoonful. Whatever antagonism had just been raised and aired between Nathan and Bobby was bound to make the situation worse for her, and she had to get through two more days—and nights—with the Hewsons.

Compliments about the lemon soufflé flowed around the table. Questions were asked about the chef and what other delights could be anticipated from him. Miranda assured them they would be pleased with whatever Roberto prepared but the menu often depended on the guests themselves. She smiled at the couple going fishing tomorrow and suggested they might provide their next dinner.

"Miranda…"

Her heart jumped at Nathan's call. She turned to see him standing at the opened doors to the verandah, emanating an air of authority that was not about to brook opposition.

"May I have a word with you?"

The polite but very public request could not be turned down. "Yes, of course. Please excuse me," she said to the guests as she stood up.

Chaos tore through her again. If Nathan had received bad news he might have to go. Despite her earlier raging, she didn't want him to leave. A trembling started in her legs, and it was difficult to maintain any sense of independent pride as she crossed the room, her mind feverishly fretting over the outcome of this evening's conflicts.

He smoothly engineered her passage out onto the verandah and drew her far enough away from the doors to allow their automatic closing. His grasp on her elbow was firm, warm, and Miranda felt chilled when he dropped it. Had Bobby turned him off her, or had she done that herself? A devastating emptiness yawned inside her.

"The stockman?" she asked, unable to look Nathan in the face.

"The news was good. The spinal cord wasn't damaged."

"I'm glad to hear it."

"That's not why I called you out. Look at me, Miranda."

A steely command.

For a moment, she looked out at the dark shape of his Land Cruiser, remembering her feelings when she'd seen him arrive, silhouetted against the sunset. There had been hope in her heart then. Now despair pressed its dark fingers on her mind. She dredged up some remnants of fighting spirit and turned her gaze to his, expecting nothing good.

His eyes blazed with relentless determination. "You cannot stay here," he stated unequivocally. "I have called Tommy and apprised him of the situation. He'll fly in first thing in the morning."

Alarm streaked through Miranda. What had Bobby said about her? Why was Nathan involving Tommy? Was she being fired from her position? Summarily removed because of another person's word? Though of course it wasn't just another person. It was her previous employer!

"What did you tell Tommy?" she demanded frantically, needing to know what she had to defend herself against.

"Enough to know Hewson is a threat to his business," Nathan answered tersely. "I want you to go in now and pack a bag, ready to leave. I shall keep the Hewsons occupied while you do this."

"But where am I to go?" *What had Bobby said? How was he a threat? And why did she have to leave?* "You can't do this to me," she protested. "Not without telling me why. I'm entitled to an explanation."

"I'm not *doing* anything but safeguarding you and the good name of this resort," he retorted, frowning at her response. "As to where you're going, with me, of course. You can spend the weekend at the station homestead. Once the Hewsons are gone, you'll resume your position here.''

She wasn't being fired! ''I'm to go…*with you?*'' she repeated dazedly.

''Yes. I promise you will be safe with me, Miranda. Is my word good enough for you?''

''Safe…from Bobby, you mean,'' she said, trying to sort through her confusion.

''From me, as well…if that's concerning you,'' he said harshly.

She shook her head, knowing Nathan would not force himself upon her. But to go to such extreme measures…''I want to know what Bobby said. Why you're doing this,'' she cried.

''Later.'' He gestured an impatient dismissal of these concerns. ''Is there anything you need to organise for the guests tonight, before you leave?'' he pressed, assuming her consent to his plans.

The realisation struck she had no choice in the matter. Nathan and Tommy had already made the decisions. ''No,'' she answered slowly, trying to adjust her mind to this entirely new set of circumstances. ''Though I usually check that they're happy with everything before they retire for the night.''

''You can do that before we leave. What about the morning? Breakfast? Activities?''

Her mind raced over possible problems and saw none. ''It's all been scheduled. It should run without a hitch. There'll be a staff member on duty here.''

''Good! Then go and pack what you need. I'll hold the party together. And don't be long about it,

Miranda." His eyes flashed contempt. "I've had enough of the Hewsons to do me a lifetime."

He hadn't been enjoying himself…

Still in a state of shock over these new developments, Miranda went back inside to follow Nathan's instructions. It took considerable effort to shake her mind free of the dark, tumultuous brooding that had possessed it since his arrival earlier this evening. However, one comforting fact did emerge. Nathan *had* come to stand by her, to protect her. And now he was taking her right out of the nightmare of having to cope with Bobby any longer.

Relief mixed with a sense of humiliation that it had come to this…taking her out…bringing in Tommy… all because of her history with a man she now despised, a past she had done everything to escape from.

Did anyone ever escape from their past? she wondered.

On the other hand, perhaps she was exaggerating her part in whatever was going on. Maybe there was some threat to the resort, competition planned by the Hewson/Parmentier hotel connection. Bobby's request for her to show him how the resort worked might have another more devious motive than just getting her alone with him.

Assuring herself she'd find out soon enough from Nathan, and having reached her room, Miranda pushed herself into thinking of what clothes to take for a weekend at the station homestead. Except it wasn't just a place to go to, a place of refuge from Bobby Hewson.

She would be spending the weekend with Nathan...in his home.

Safe, he'd said, and his word could be trusted. Miranda didn't doubt that. The problem was...could she trust herself to keep safe from him? She hated the distance she had put between them tonight. Maybe it was a sensible distance. Maybe he no longer wanted to cross it.

What had Bobby said about her?

Her heart quivered in trepidation. Her life didn't feel her own any more. But she went through the motions of packing a bag. A weekend with Nathan should sort out something, she argued. Safe or not, it had to be better than staying here with Bobby Hewson.

CHAPTER FOURTEEN

NATHAN had taken her chair at the head of the table, continuing his assumed role of host in her absence. Miranda noted he was still promoting a congenial mood amongst the guests, though keeping a physical distance from the Hewsons. She dropped her bag near the doors and crossed the lounge area to the split-level dining section, nervously wondering how he intended to direct their departure.

He rose from her chair, pushing it right back so he could gather her to his side, smiling at her as he slid his arm around her waist, deliberately coupling them to face the table guests together.

"All ready?" he asked, his eyes commanding her assent.

"Yes," she murmured, acutely aware of his hand resting possessively on the curve of her hip.

He transferred his smile to the guests who were all watching this linking with speculative interest. "I must beg you to excuse us from the rest of this evening's dinner party," he said charmingly. "Duty calls me back to the station and this is Miranda's weekend off. I've persuaded her to find out firsthand what the life of a cattleman is like."

He turned an intimate grin to her and added, "I can't, in all conscience, expect her to marry me until she knows what she's committing herself to."

Marry!

Miranda was too poleaxed to say a word. Somehow she managed to maintain the smile she'd pasted on her face.

One of the male guests laughingly remarked, "Well, that's making your intentions clear, Nathan."

"One of the things we learn in the outback is always seize the day," he answered good-humouredly. "And when a woman like Miranda comes along, a man would be a fool not to."

Heat bloomed in her cheeks. She rolled her eyes at Nathan, not knowing where else to look. It amused the guests who were obviously enjoying his very open confidences.

"My brother, Tommy, will be here in the morning to manage you through the rest of the weekend," he went on. "Staff will be standing by to see you off on your activities tomorrow. Is there anything you need to check with Miranda before I sweep her away with me?"

The inquiry brought only jovial remarks.

"We're all set. Best of luck to you, Nathan!"

"Yo! We've made a note of everything. Got to say you two look well-matched."

"No problem for us. Don't let him steam-roller you, Miranda."

"Huh! Firsthand knowledge sounds good to me!"

"I would seize the night if I were you, Miranda," Celine said archly.

Everyone laughed.

Except Bobby, who remained silent. Miranda didn't look at him, but she was extremely conscious of his presence and his lack of response. This performance by Nathan was for *his* benefit. She hoped it was having the right effect, whatever that was supposed to be.

Marry!

Nathan couldn't mean it. Why go so far? *What had Bobby said to him?*

''Then we'll say goodnight to you. Enjoy yourselves.'' Nathan rolled on, saluting them with one hand and digging the fingers of the other into her hip to prompt her into appropriate speech.

''Have a great time, all of you!'' she rushed out. ''And thank you for your good advice. It's a bit hard to catch one's breath around Nathan.''

It left them laughing.

They didn't know how true it was.

All the way out to his Land Cruiser, Miranda was in a ferment over his words and actions. His arm remained lodged around her waist, and she could feel his determination to prevent any backward sliding from his stated plan. It wasn't desire for her company driving him. He had taken control and was relentlessly pushing through what he considered had to be done.

He opened the front passenger door and half-lifted her into the high seat. Her bag was stowed on the bench seat behind her. There was no time wasted in putting himself behind the steering wheel and getting the Land Cruiser into motion. His face was grim as they sped away from the resort homestead, and Miranda had to take a very deep breath to combat the throat-strangling tension he emitted.

''What did Bobby Hewson say to you?''

Jaw-clenching silence.

Her heart cramped at this evidence of damage done, but she could not let the issue rest any longer. "This is *later,* Nathan. I'm entitled to know."

"He was surprised you had been hired for such a position of trust without a thorough investigation into your background," he answered, his voice grating out the words.

Miranda clenched her hands at the implication she could not be trusted. "In all my working life, I have never once been considered unreliable. Your mother saw my references," she shot at him.

"He proceeded to tell me *your* mother was little better than a whore, a kept mistress who'd serviced several married men, one of whom had fathered you. She'd also been an alcoholic who eventually drank herself to death."

The stark facts of her mother's life sounded ghastly, stripped as they were of any mitigating circumstances or sympathetic understanding. Miranda felt sick, remembering how Bobby had wanted to know more about her life and had been sweetly comforting when she had confided the truth. But she had never, never used such brutal terms in speaking of her mother, and she had wept over the sadness of it all...the initial deceit of a married lover who had left her alone and pregnant, the inability to cope and the desperate drowning of that inability in alcohol.

She closed her eyes, savagely berating herself for having revealed such deeply personal matters to a man who had no compunction in using them against her. Pillow-talk. Intimacy she had believed was precious to both of them. Now this malicious betrayal of it.

"Did he tell you I was bent the same way?" she asked dully.

"He said you knew how to work the sexual angles to your advantage, that he himself had been pleasured by you in years gone by, and he wouldn't put it past you to fleece any male guest who fancied you."

Humiliation burned her soul. "It's not true," she whispered. "I've never...*sold* myself. He's saying these things because he thought he could buy me and I wouldn't go along with it."

"You don't have to defend yourself to me, Miranda. I don't enjoy repeating this muck-raking. It was all I could do, not to smash his face in."

Relief poured some soothing balm on her wounds. At least Nathan believed she was being slandered. In fact, the sheer savagery in his voice spurred the courage to open her eyes and really look at him. His face was taut with barely suppressed anger. His knuckles gleamed almost white where he was gripping the steering wheel.

"You had to be taken out of there," he said with biting conviction. "He would have used you to create a nasty situation. He was setting up for it. Without you as a flesh-and-blood focus, he loses his teeth. In moving you onto my ground, there's no way he can get at you."

Miranda sighed, understanding his tactics and grateful for being spared Bobby's treacherous company, but suspecting frustration would only drive the slandering further. "It won't stop him telling lies about me, Nathan. In fact, your suggestion of marriage will probably fuel his claim of my playing the sexual angles for profit.''

''No. It reinforces how serious my threat was to him.''

''Threat?'' The idea startled her. Then she remembered the hard, ruthless cast of his face when he had answered Bobby at the dinner table. ''What did you threaten him with?'' she asked, unable to think of anything that would hurt a Hewson.

''I told him if I heard so much as another word breathed against you, I would set about wrecking his marriage and the Hewson-Parmentier merger with every bit of armament at my disposal.''

Shock pummelled her. ''But how could you do it?''

''Through his wife.''

''You would hurt her?''

''Against him I would use anything.'' He slanted her a hard, cynical look. ''Don't be wasting your sympathy on the sultry Celine…a new bride, fancying a lustful dalliance with me. Hardly an expression of true love for her husband.''

It was all very well to criticise the morality of others, but if Nathan had been encouraging Celine, was he any better? Feeling very much at odds with this tactic, Miranda recalled his reaction to her own supposed position of mistress to a married man. ''You told me adultery wasn't your scene,'' she tersely reminded him.

''It's not,'' he replied without hesitation, shooting her a sardonic look as he added, ''but neither of them know that. I'm bluffing, Miranda, and a bluff only succeeds if it is credible.''

"Do you think it's credible…talking about marrying me?"

"There wasn't a person around that table who didn't believe me," he said with arrogant confidence.

A bluff…Miranda closed her eyes again, a dull weariness settling through her. Right now it was all too much…Bobby's mean and malevolent assault on her reputation, Nathan's moves to counter it. Though, of course, he did have to counter it—Tommy, as well— or the slurs on her character could very well taint the good name of the resort, most especially with the wealthy guests who invariably passed on good or bad word of mouth to their friends.

"You'd better warn Tommy that you talked about marrying me," she said tiredly. "The guests might bring it up with him."

"I've told him. He'll play along."

"They might chat with others on the resort, too. The guides…Sam…"

"A pleasant piece of gossip doesn't matter. And I made it clear it was me pursuing you, Miranda, not the other way around," he added drily.

"And eventually I'm to decide not to marry you."

He expelled a long breath. "As I've said before, most women wouldn't choose my kind of life."

"Is that what happened with Susan?"

The words slipped out, probably because she was too stressed to monitor what she said, though she didn't regret the intrusion into his private background, justifying it on the grounds that he knew all of hers now. Why not get the truth out in the open? Then maybe she could get a fix on where she actually stood with

Nathan, instead of feeling as though she was caught in another web of deceit.

"No," he answered slowly. "Marriage was never on the cards with Susan."

"You just had a mutual sex thing going," Miranda muttered bitterly, having been all too freshly reminded of how Bobby Hewson had used her.

"I suppose you could put it that way, though we were also friends and I always enjoyed her company," he said quietly. "Because of injuries from a car accident in her teens, Susan couldn't have children. She told me straight up not to ever get seriously attached to her. It was her unshakable belief that one day I would want children of my own and she'd hate not being able to give them to me."

Had he tried to shake that belief? Out of a whirl of confusion came one definite fact. "Sam told me she did marry."

"Yes. To a widower who already had two young children. Susan is a schoolteacher. One of the children was in her kindergarten class last year. She told me it was her chance to be a mother and she was taking it. I was not prepared to argue that, Miranda. It was her choice."

Never judge anything before hearing all the circumstances, Miranda silently berated herself, shamed by the full story of Nathan's relationship with the woman who had engaged his interest for two years. He hadn't said he'd loved Susan but there'd been caring in his voice, caring for her personally and respect for the needs he couldn't answer.

There had to have been a sense of loss when she'd

chosen the widower with the children, closing Nathan out of her life. The ending of any long relationship left an empty place. Even Bobby's defection had left her ravaged. For Nathan it would have been much worse, presented with a set of circumstances he couldn't fight, forced to let go by his own code of decency. And since then, he'd been alone for months, Sam had told her, not interested in picking up with anyone else.

Until she had arrived on the scene and a strong sexual chemistry had hit both of them.

Had it been that way between him and Susan?

Impossible to ask. It was wrong to make comparisons. People were different and their relationships were different. She darted a glance at him but his expression was closed to her, his concentration fixed on the road. It startled her to see they were driving through the station's community, almost at the homestead.

"I'm sorry," she blurted out. "I shouldn't have brought up Susan like that."

He shrugged. "It was on your mind."

He brought the Land Cruiser to a halt in front of the entrance to his homestead and switched off the engine. For a few moments he sat frowning, his fingers tapping the steering wheel. Then he turned to her with a look that was searing in its intensity.

"I'm not another Bobby Hewson, Miranda. I have never acted dishonourably over any woman and never would. I don't want you coming into my home, feeling at risk in any way. If you do feel…compromised in some fashion…I'll take you somewhere else…to one of the families on the station…"

"No. This is fine," she protested in an agony of

embarrassment at her own blind and bitter thoughts about him. "I do trust you, Nathan. God knows you've proved you're a decent person and I thank you, very sincerely, for all the trouble you've gone to on my behalf."

He nodded, his eyes still burning into hers, intent on scouring any doubts. "I'll put you in a guest suite. I think it best if you accompany me out on the station tomorrow. Can you be up, dressed and ready for breakfast by six-thirty in the morning?"

She was too drained to argue anything any more. "If there's an alarm clock in my room and it works."

"I'll set it for you."

Decisions firmly made, he alighted from the Land Cruiser, collected her bag and was opening her door before Miranda could collect wits enough to get out of the vehicle by herself. "Thanks," she murmured as he steadied her wobbly step onto the ground.

"Want to hang onto my arm?" he offered kindly.

"I'm okay. Just tired."

Too tired to even try to figure out what Nathan was feeling, how he saw her now. There were so many layers to him…kind, caring, ruthless in carrying through decisive action, shouldering responsibility at a moment's notice, a masterful controller of situations, yet still respectful of others' choices.

Part of her very much wanted to hang onto him. Part of her recoiled from giving him any reason to wonder if she was the kind of woman Bobby Hewson had painted…perhaps giving him sex yesterday so he would take her side today.

Though it hadn't been like that.

She hoped Nathan realised it had been some spontaneous need, triggered by the man he was, nothing else. Nevertheless, she could hardly blame him for wondering about it. If enough dirt was thrown, some of it stuck, and Bobby had certainly done his worst to hang dirt on her tonight.

Too sensitive on this point to touch Nathan even accidentally, Miranda kept a safe space between them as she accompanied him inside, down the long central hallway to another hall that ran at right angles to it. They turned into this and halfway along he opened a door, switched on a light and stood back, waving her ahead of him.

It was a very welcoming room, a pretty patchwork quilt on an old-fashioned brass bed, richly polished cedar wardrobes and chests of drawers giving a warm character to the rest of the furnishings. Following her in, Nathan placed her bag on the end of the bed and moved straight to the lamp table near the bedhead, indicating the clock radio there.

"Will five-thirty give you enough time?" he asked.

"Yes. Thank you."

He set the alarm, then pointed out the door between the two wardrobes. "Your ensuite bathroom is through there. Would you like me to fetch you a hot drink or…"

"No. I just want to drop into bed. Thanks for looking after me, Nathan. I'm sorry I've brought this trouble…"

"It's not your doing," he cut in emphatically. "Just put Hewson behind you, Miranda. You won't see him again, I promise you."

Seeing Bobby again was not really the problem. As she watched Nathan give her a wide berth as he moved towards the door, she suddenly couldn't bear the thought that tonight's nasty insinuations were simmering away in his mind, seeding doubts about her integrity.

"Nathan…"

The needful cry halted him. His shoulders squared before he turned around, and she mentally cringed at what seemed like his reluctance to face her again. He looked back at her with hooded eyes, tensely waiting for her to complete whatever she wanted to say.

Only her deeply ingrained sense of self-worth drove her on, her eyes begging his belief. "I've never used sex to—" she agonised over the right words, desperate to correct the impression he might have "—as a tool to gain some advantage for myself."

"Miranda, if that was the way you worked, you would have targeted Tommy," he said with quiet conviction. "Don't fret over what we might think. Neither Tommy nor I will be shaken from what we've seen of you and how you've conducted yourself since you've been at King's Eden."

Tears pricked her eyes.

"You have earned the right to our support and protection," he went on. "So rest easy tonight, knowing you have it and we won't fail you."

She nodded, too choked up to speak. No one had ever thrown support behind her like this, such an unstinting degree of faith and loyalty. It gave her almost a sense of belonging, as though she was accepted as *one of their own.*

Nathan moved back to where she'd stayed, near the bag at the foot of the bed, and gently touched her cheek. ''It must have been rough, growing up in such an insecure environment,'' he murmured sympathetically. ''I admire what you've made of yourself, Miranda. It shows a lot of grit…a strong drive for survival. Don't let that slimy bastard beat you down now because you're worth a million of him. He's glitter and you're gold. Believe me…I know.''

His hand dropped to her shoulder and he gave it a light squeeze. ''Tomorrow is another day. Okay?''

''Yes,'' she managed huskily.

His mouth curved into an ironic little smile. ''Who knows? We might even make a go of marriage, you and I.''

He left her with that thought. Miranda had no idea if he was even remotely serious but just the idea of the possibility served to lift a cold, leaden weight off her heart. She touched her cheek where he had touched it, treasuring the lingering sense of warmth. It felt good.

And tomorrow was another day.

CHAPTER FIFTEEN

MIRANDA had no trouble putting Bobby Hewson behind her the next day. She was literally transported to another world. From the safety of Nathan's helicopter, she watched in awe at the incredible skill of the pilots in the two bubble helicopters, swooping from side to side as they flushed cattle out from under scrubby trees and drove them from watercourses, the clatter of the blades and the roar of the motors relentlessly pressing them into a mob and moving them towards a stock-camp.

On the ground, fences were cut in front of the gathering herd as it was funnelled from paddock to paddock and the numbers kept swelling. By lunch-time several hundred head of cattle had been mustered and driven halfway to the holding yards, where the weaned calves were to be branded and the stock for sale selected.

Nathan had informed her over breakfast that the station ran about thirty-six thousand head of cattle, and six thousand were trucked away each year. The breeding program he'd instigated more than made up these numbers. In different parts of the station were Brahman and English Shorthorn breeds, but these were Africanders, handsome red beasts who could thrive in the most arid areas.

Their movement and colour looked stunning on the backdrop of the vast, beige Mitchell grass plains. There was a wild element to the mustering that added the thrill of danger, a pitting of man against the challenge of the landscape and the unpredictability of cattle that were used to going where they willed, yet there was also a marvellous orchestration to it—the men and machines on the ground supporting the men and machines in the air, gradually dominating a long practiced strategy against the seemingly indomitable.

This was what Nathan's life was about, Miranda realised, and the grand sweep of it deeply impressed her; the understanding of how it worked, the skill and experience at controlling what was controllable, the management of time and place, and at the heart of it, an environment that demanded an intimate knowledge of its unique natural harmony.

They had lunch by the river, close to where drums of fuel had been set up for the helicopters. Nathan was clearly at ease with his stockmen, welcomed into their company, Miranda accepted without any fuss. A fire had been lit and a billy of water put on to make tea. They sat under the shade of trees and ate damper and slabs of cold meat, the men chatting over the morning's progress, Miranda content to simply immerse herself in the sights and sounds around her.

Here on the ground she could hear the thunder of hooves and the bellowing of the cattle. She could taste and smell the dust of the mob, and watch the tight intricate ballet of the mustering helicopters. Somehow it made life very vivid, real and earthy in a bigger sense than Miranda had ever experienced before. It was strangely intoxicating as though something heady had seeped into her bloodstream.

The heat of the day added a shimmering haze to the

light and when Nathan stood up, marking the end of their lunch-break, an aura seemed to gleam from him, lending even more stature to the man. He turned his gaze to her and the blue magnets of his eyes drew on her soul as though he was willing her to be bonded with him and in more than a physical sense.

His outback empire was both harsh and beautiful and she had the strong feeling he was asking if she could be part of it, if she could accept it and live with it as he did…and she knew in that instant there was nowhere for them to go unless she could honestly say *yes*. Impossible to make a marriage on sexual attraction alone, if marriage really was on his mind. It was this land that had first claim on Nathan—always would—and if she couldn't share it with him, she lost what truly made him what he was.

A subtle challenge rang through his voice as he said, "Time to move on," and held out a hand to pull her up onto her feet.

He didn't ask her if she was tired, if she'd prefer to stay at the camp by the river. Taking his hand symbolised her willingness to be where he was, see what he saw, learn the enduring pattern of his life firsthand and judge if she could fit into it. Miranda understood this intuitively, yet the feel of his hand enveloping hers was far more immediate, stimulating a strong awareness of the sexuality zinging through their physical togetherness.

He kept possession of her hand as they walked back to his helicopter and Miranda felt like dancing, her heart was so joyously lightened by the prolonged link. Nathan hadn't exactly been distant towards her since last night but his manner had remained strictly on a friendly, matter-of-fact level, which she had found inhibiting.

It was almost as though he was denying they had ever shared any intimacy and she hadn't been sure if this was to reassure her of no sexual pressure intended this weekend, or if he was reserving judgement on there being any possible future in their relationship.

There would be no false promises from Nathan King. Miranda had no doubts on that score. But his hand said he did want her and that hadn't changed. She couldn't resist moving her fingers slightly, savouring the touch of rough skin and warm strength, craving the solidity of all this man emitted.

He shot her a questing glance. ''You were quiet over lunch.''

''I had nothing to contribute.''

''You could have asked questions.''

''I didn't want to intrude.''

''I don't want you to feel like an intruder, Miranda.''

''I don't. I just wanted to listen, to take everything in.''

''So what did you think?'' His eyes were more intensely probing this time.

''I think that any woman who wanted to separate you from all this would have to be deaf, dumb and blind not to realise you *are* this and inseparable from it.''

He gave her a funny little smile, something between wry acknowledgement and self-mocking resignation. ''Do you find that off-putting?''

''No. It makes me want to know it all, Nathan,'' she answered with absolute sincerity.

Another sharp glance, then a long expulsion of breath. When he spoke, his voice was dry and flat. ''Well, when your curiosity turns to boredom, I guess I'll know. I've had plenty of practice at recognising the signs.''

She had no answer to the deeply rooted scepticism seeded by previous women in his life. Only time could lend truth to whatever she felt about him…now or years from now. Yet in her heart, Miranda was certain she would never be bored with Nathan King. There was something so special in the essence of the man, she couldn't imagine its ever losing its hold on her.

And this outback world had its hold, too. At the end of the day, a thousand head of wild cattle from three huge paddocks had been mustered into stockyards and the helicopters headed for home, their flying insect-like shapes silhouetted against the red flares of the sunset. They flew over what seemed like kilometres of nothing in the gathering darkness, yet Miranda was aware this was deceptive, that life was more spaced out here than anywhere else and it moved to a beat of its own.

Then in the distant landscape there appeared pinpricks of light, a cluster of them, and Miranda's heart lifted with a sense of homecoming as she realised they were the lights of the station buildings being switched on. It was strange…feeling they were welcoming her, like a friendly beacon drawing her in to a safe harbour. Lights had never had that effect before. Somehow, between yesterday and today, it seemed more shifts had taken place in her life.

Or perhaps it simply represented the kind of home she yearned for, a place of belonging, light after dark, a long, solid reality that lasted, regardless of good times and bad, a core history of humanity that had stayed, survived, prospered, and was now embodied in Nathan who had brought her into it with such protective caring. Safety, comfort, love…

Could he love her?

The question remained almost feverishly in her mind as they returned to the homestead, then parted to wash and change into fresh clothes for dinner. Showering made her intensely conscious of her body, how it had fitted to Nathan's, how it had felt, and it was difficult to push those memories aside and concentrate on what Nathan would want from her in the long term. Sex was not enough. Yet even sternly telling herself this did nothing to lessen her state of arousal.

The need for him continued to course through her. She put on a soft wraparound dress—a little black dress that was meant to be worn braless—knowing it would make her look accessible, wanting him to know she was accessible to anything he offered her. That was the raw, bottomline truth and she wasn't going to flinch from it any more or let any fear of consequences get in the way.

When they met in the lounge room for pre-dinner drinks, she could barely stop herself from eating him up with her eyes, the sheer maleness of his magnificent physique hitting her anew. Her pulse was galloping as he handed her a glass but his fingers didn't touch hers and he took a seat away from her, signalling his intent to control whatever he felt.

Miranda wished *she* could. Reason finally came to the fore, prompting her to ply him with questions about how the station worked, the various responsibilities of the people he employed, the schedule everyone followed to accomplish what had to be accomplished. The mental challenge of taking in his replies and fitting them all together was stimulating, too.

Not once did the conversation lag over dinner. Miranda was frightened to let it because she knew any silence would fill with sexual tension and he might think this was all there was between them. She was hungry for much, much more. All of him, not just the body that called so strongly to hers.

As it was, her interest in his world acted as an aphrodisiac, because his answers filled out the kind of man he was and to Miranda he was everything a man should be, very hands-on in taking care of every part of his business, treating his people with integrity and respect, aiming for the best that could be done within the parameters of what he worked with.

After dinner he took her to his office, pressed into showing her the map of King's Eden, pointing out the location of the different breeds of cattle and how they would be mustered over the coming month, giving her a visual picture of the whole operation and a better understanding of the scale of it. To her captivated heart and mind, it was a kingdom, and it could be an Eden…with Nathan.

He was explaining more to her but she lost the thread of what he was saying, her gaze fastening on his pointing hand, running up his tautly muscled arm, over his broad shoulder to the strong brown neck laid bare by the opened collar of his shirt. She didn't hear his voice trail into silence. Her ears were filled with the drum of her own heart as she saw the pulse at the base of his throat move to the beat of his.

Slowly his chest turned towards her and the hand that had been pointing drew back and curled over her shoulder, pulling her around to face him squarely. Realising she had been caught being inattentive, Miranda lifted pleading eyes to his, a flush of guilt scorching her cheeks as she cried, ''I'm not bored. I...''

Her mouth dried up under the searing look of hunger that burned with all the urgent heat of her own. He lifted his other hand and with featherlight fingertips stroked a few wayward strands of hair from her brow, then the soft skin at the corner of her eye, her cheek, her lips, a fine tingling tracery that stirred every nerve-ending into exquisite anticipation and caught the breath in her throat.

But he didn't kiss her. His eyes didn't move from hers. Only his hands moved, a sensual caress of her neck, shoulders, softly hooking the supporting straps of her dress with his thumbs and slowly pulling them down her arms, the cross-over pattern of the bodice parting, opening wide, sliding down the slopes of her breasts, caught briefly on peaks that had hardened with tremulous excitement before dropping to her waist, baring her breasts.

Yet still his gaze held hers, the naked hunger simmering into a lustful challenge that demanded her consent to the charged desire driving his fingertips to savour every tactile sensation, the silky texture of her skin, the curve of her spine, swirling patterns of touch all over her back, her arms, arousing erogenous zones she never knew she had, the side swells of her breasts, the hollow below her rib-cage, then upwards, circling her aureoles, outwards and inwards, building a delicate web of sensual intensity that was utterly captivating.

Then his palms, softly rotating nipples that were begging for attention, and a flare of exultant pleasure in his eyes as he saw the sweetly relieving pleasure of it in hers. No rush to passion tonight. The wanting had been mounting all day, and the desire to satisfy every bit of it was a consensual current neither of them could deny now.

She undid the tie at her waist and the soft fabric of her dress slithered to the floor. The stretch lace briefs she wore provided the smallest barrier to complete nakedness yet she felt no self-consciousness about her body. Nathan wasn't even looking at it. He was touching her mind, wordlessly telling her he had craved feeling her like this, revelling in the full sensation of her femininity, determined on missing nothing, wanting her to feel him wanting all of her.

The need to reach out to him in like manner drove her hands to feel for the lowest button on his shirt. A wild glitter leapt into his eyes, then was forcibly tamed. "Later if you want," he said gruffly, "but this I must have first."

Miranda found herself swept off her feet before she could begin to read his intention. In a few breathless seconds he carried her from the office by way of a connecting door to a bedroom she had to assume was his. The bed he laid her on was wide and long, king-size, the head of it piled with thick pillows, the rest of it covered with a softly padded quilt. The only light was from the opened doorway so there was no seeing any detail even if she'd been interested in looking. At this heart-pounding moment anything beyond Nathan was irrelevant.

He removed her briefs and sandals, his hands caressing her legs, her feet, sensitising every area he touched, leaving her flesh humming with excitement. Then he stood back and undressed himself, but not once did his gaze leave her, his clothes being discarded with methodical purpose while he spoke in a low, thrumming voice that wound around her and held her tied to him.

"Countless times have I envisaged this…you lying here on my bed, waiting for me, wanting me, nothing between us but the time it takes to come together. I don't know why it's so. It just is. Like a compelling need I cannot put aside."

"Yes," she whispered, her throat tightening at the sight of his nakedness emerging, what it meant to her, what it could mean if he shared what she felt. Need…yes…but did it go beyond what he'd known with any other woman?

Please let it be so, she fiercely prayed.

He spoke again, seeming to answer her prayer. "That first evening, when you walked into my life…it was like…this woman was made for me…no sense to it…sheer instinct beating it out. And every time I see you, the same message clamours through me, regardless…"

Regardless of what? she wanted to ask, but he leaned over and claimed her mouth in a long ravishing kiss that splintered any coherent thought. She felt him stretch out beside her, one tautly muscled thigh inserting itself between hers, a hand cupping her breast, gently kneading it as his mouth devoured hers with more and more erotic passion.

"Made for me," he breathed against her lips, a husky claim, reinforced by his hand gliding down over her stomach, fingers weaving through the silky curls at the apex of her thighs, stroking intimately, making her gasp as he aroused an explosion of exquisite yearning.

"Do you know how much I want to make you mine?" he murmured, trailing hot kisses down her throat. "To taste you, to take you inside me, to be inside you…"

How could she think…answer…the questions were being swamped by feeling.

His mouth closed over her breast, drawing it into a wild rhythmic threshing that was suddenly echoed by a more invasive stroking, a circling of her vagina, an internal caress, a teasing tantalising slide and glide that had her arching for more.

He moved his mouth to her other breast, sucking harder, tugging in a crescendo of possession given and taken as she writhed to the intense pleasure of his knowing touch, mindless to anything but the fantastic sensations arcing through her. She cried out an anguished protest when he withdrew from her, heaving himself down to the foot of the bed, but almost instantly he forged an even more intimate connection, kissing her as deeply there as he had her mouth, his lips covering other pleasure-swollen lips, his tongue seeking a sweeter cavern.

A fiercer pleasure screamed through her, driving her frantic as she felt the tension of it build towards the flood of climax. "No...no...I want you...you..." she sobbed, hands grabbing his hair, pulling hard.

He rose like a dark force of shimmering energy and surged into her, filling the need and rocketing her into the first convulsive wave of ecstatic satisfaction. Her legs whipped around him, holding him deep within, exulting in the sweet tidal flow he had set in motion.

But he didn't drive it on as she expected. He maintained the full union with her, letting the awareness of it throb acutely through both of them as he propped his body over hers, his chest brushing the extended peaks of her breasts, his eyes blazing into hers with a furnace of feeling.

"Does this feel special to you, Miranda? More special than anything you've ever known?"

The question seized her mind, focused it, forced a deeply primitive retaliation. "Is it to you?"

"Would I ask if it wasn't? I want to know if what I feel is echoed in you and I need the truth."

In a sudden flash, she realised it was Bobby disturbing Nathan's trust in her response to him, Bobby who had stirred too many bad feelings for either of them to dismiss easily. Yet he didn't belong in this precious moment. He might have been the catalyst that had driven them to this acknowledgement of each other, but the truth was...Bobby Hewson was nothing and Nathan was everything.

Her eyes met the fire in his with all the open honesty he was now giving her, the answers she'd craved...and the rightness of it poured a blissful conviction into her voice as she answered him.

"It's been the same for me...all you said...from

when I first saw you.'' She lifted her hands to his face, cupping it, pressing her need for possession of him as she added, ''I don't care if it makes sense or not. If I could have a man made for me, it would be you.''

''No ifs, Miranda. I'm here with you, in you *now*. Am I the man for you?''

''Yes.'' The answer came unequivocally. ''All that you are, Nathan.''

''Then show me.''

His arms burrowed under her and he rolled, turning onto his back and carrying her so she straddled him, still with the hard fullness of him inside her, waiting for her to go beyond passive acceptance, to be as positive in action as her words had been. He was giving her the freedom to express her desire, her need for him, and the surprise spurred by his challenge of mutuality swiftly zoomed into elation.

It wasn't a matter of showing him anything. She wanted to touch him, to caress and excite and tantalise and arouse him to the same incredible pitch of pleasure that would rip all control apart and plunge them both into the same beautiful sea of ecstatic release.

She tasted, licked, kissed, stroked, wherever desire took her, all the time consciously keeping him inside her, voluptuously rolling around him, sliding forward and backwards, feeling every inch of him enveloped and squeezed, released and teased. It was a glorious, glorious feeling…Nathan, all hers.

She exulted when she heard him catch his breath, when she felt the flesh under his skin quiver, when a husky growl escaped from his throat. Her own pleasure continued to come in delicious waves with the movement she manipulated herself, but the best of it came when he could stand no more of being *taken.*

He erupted into action, heaving her back onto the pillows, gathering her to him, plunging himself hard and fast as though his survival depended upon it, a violent, primitive mating, his energy pouring into her in bursts of need—*compelling* need—no other woman made for him—not like her—none like her—and she was drawing this from him, climbing with him until they both reached a peak of fierce jubilation in their ultimate togetherness.

They hugged each other tightly, wanting the oneness to go on and on…the reality of it, the sense of it, the flow of feeling…and for a long, long time they shared the blissful harmony. Miranda was drifting into drowsiness when Nathan spoke, his voice humming softly in her ear.

"Is it too soon to hope you will be my mistress, Miranda?"

Her heart instantly contracted at his use of a word that had so many painful memories attached to it. She could barely bring herself to speak, but reason insisted he had to be thinking in more than sexual terms. Or was her own need for more than a sexual relationship colouring reason?

"What do you mean?" she asked flatly, trying to keep her emotions in check.

He wound a long tress of her hair around his hand, then let the silky strands of it slide through his fingers. "Is this ephemeral, or something we can keep?" His chest rose and fell as he expelled a long sigh. "I'm asking if there's any chance you want to be the mistress of my heart, the mistress of my bed and home, the mistress of King's Eden...for all the years ahead of us.''

Relief and joy erased the tension of wretched doubt.

"I'm not asking for a decision," he went on. "I know it's too soon. But I think you understand how it is, that this land is another kind of mistress and you'd have to tolerate its call on me. If you don't see any possibility of sharing what I'd need you to share..."

"I'd share anything with you," she cut in fervently. "Anything!" She felt him hold his breath and into her mind slipped the words Elizabeth King had spoken of her husband, Lachan, words that held the truth of her feeling for the man holding her in his arms. She hitched herself up, sliding her arms around his neck, speaking directly to the eyes questioning hers. "*You* are where I want to be. Whatever that entails, Nathan.''

His sigh whispered out through a smile that warmed her entire being. "So we have a beginning," he said, a husky contentment in his voice.

"And no end in sight," Miranda answered exultantly.

He laughed and rolled her onto her back, looming over her in a pose of wonderfully dominant maleness. "I gave you a choice," he said teasingly.

"There was no choice," she retorted. "Only you."

"No one but you," he answered softly.

And there was respect for the truths they had spoken this night in the love-making that followed. It was a good beginning, an open and honest communication of where they stood with each other, and Miranda ardently hoped that all the tomorrows would prove they were right in feeling what they did.

CHAPTER SIXTEEN

NATHAN waited in his office for the call he was expecting from Tommy. The weekend was over and he was content he'd made the most of it with Miranda, but he wanted to be sure there would be no comeback from the man who'd driven her into his life in the first place. He was certain now that Hewson was out of her heart, but he wanted her mind clear of him, as well—the past completely past.

It appalled him that he himself had briefly cast Miranda in the role Hewson had maliciously painted—a woman on the make, uncaring whom she hurt. Lies...yet that morning at Cathedral Gorge, he had let his own frustration and her choice of words weave such a false picture.

Completely false.

And he'd hated Hewson for coming up with the same sexual scenario out of spite. All too easy to target a woman who had no back-up. But, by God! there would be no lack of back-up in this instance.

The telephone rang.

He snatched up the receiver, automatically noting the time—8.41—which more or less placed the proposed Monday morning departure on schedule.

"Nathan?"

"Here."

"The Hewson charter flight is lifting off as I speak," Tommy announced smugly. "The birds have flown."

"You saw them onto the plane yourself?"

"No. I sent Sam to do that. I'm watching it from the homestead verandah."

"Dammit, Tommy, I asked you."

"Calm it, brother. No love lost between Sam and the Hewsons. She would have hog-tied them and hauled them into their seats if they'd so much as hesitated. And quite frankly, I'd had enough of them."

"Is the problem cleared?"

"Oh, I think we established a pertinent understanding and Jared will make it stick during their stay in Broome." He chuckled. "By the time Bobby-boy pays out there, I rather fancy he'll want to forget he ever came to King's Eden."

"What payment are we talking about, Tommy?"

"Now, Nathan, you got the kudos for whizzing Miranda out of harm's way. I deserve the kudos for clearing the decks. Bring her back now and I'll tell you all."

The call was disconnected before Nathan could press the point. He hoped Tommy's confidence was not misplaced. A snake had a habit of wriggling and spitting venom even when it was spiked. Still, Tommy should know his own business. It was not only a matter of protecting Miranda. The resort was his baby.

Nathan smiled to himself as he moved out of the office and headed down the hall to Miranda's room where she'd gone to pack her clothes, ready to leave. He didn't mind the resort any more, despite the occasional irritation of tourists wandering where they shouldn't. It had brought him the gold he'd thought he'd never find. True gold. And he'd staked his claim to it. His charming and gregarious brother could win as many kudos as he liked. It wouldn't win Miranda. She was his and his mind was set on keeping her his. Whatever it took.

He knocked on her door, the memory of last night's love-making fresh in his mind. Sleep had been minimal but he didn't feel tired. He'd never felt more vibrantly alive, excitement stirring through him again as she called out, "Come in," the words reminding him of her sexual openness, inviting all he wanted of her and revelling in every intimacy.

He stepped into her room, itching to hold her once more, and the anxious eyes she turned to him spurred him on.

"Is it all right? Have they gone?"

"Yes."

She sagged into his embrace, her arms winding around his neck so the full lush femininity of her was pressed against him. He couldn't resist flattening his palm across the pit of her back, fitting her even closer as he lifted his other hand to stroke away her worry lines.

"Tommy assures me Hewson won't be coming back. It's safe for you to return to the resort."

"How did he handle it?" she asked, uncertainty still clouding her eyes.

"He insists we come and find out." He smiled to reassure her. "Tommy enjoys a bit of boasting."

She sighed, her breasts heaving sensuously. He'd never been so horny in his entire life. Difficult to push temptation aside but it was time for business now and Tommy would not appreciate being kept waiting.

"I just hope there aren't any nasty repercussions," she said, still fretful.

"Not on King's Eden, Miranda," he promised with absolute confidence, and kissed her frown away. "Ready to go?"

"Yes." Trust and courage glowed in her eyes.

His heart kicked into a joyous beat at this further evidence that his instincts had been right all along. It had simply been a matter of breaking through her barriers for her real character to be revealed and everything made sense to him now. Whatever had made Miranda Wade, the result was she was made for him. There was not one response from her that didn't fit want he wanted, what he craved.

With this assurance dancing through his mind, he broke away and picked up her bag. He would take her back to the resort and this tourist season would be long enough for her to know the life she would be taking on with him, but he had little doubt about the choice she would make. It had to be.

He took her hand. She looked at him. It was more than a physical link and she knew it. The bonding was there in her eyes. However many partings there would be, Nathan told himself none of them would change what they were to each other, and his soul filled with happiness at the thought. He would not be walking alone through life. Miranda would walk with him.

The drive back to the resort reminded Miranda of the drive away from it on Friday night…the confusion and fear that had churned through her then. The weekend had certainly sorted out where she stood with Nathan and she could almost bless Bobby Hewson for having unwittingly forced an outcome she hadn't dared to believe in a few days ago. Nevertheless, anxiety still fretted at the edges of her happiness.

She had brought this trouble to King's Eden. Inadvertently, but nonetheless irrevocably. She would feel responsible if Bobby did some damage to the resort's good reputation and she couldn't bring herself to believe he wouldn't. It was impossible to trust the man or his word.

Unlike Nathan. She feasted her eyes on him as he drove, loving every aspect of him. He wasn't just big on the outside. He was big all through. Her skin prickled in sensual delight, just remembering the pleasures they'd revelled in last night, how she'd felt so wonderfully enveloped by him, safe and cossetted, belonging to him and with him.

He hadn't said he loved her, but wanting her to think of sharing his life—all the years ahead of them—and hoping she wanted to be *the mistress of his heart*…why would he crave her love, if he didn't feel love for her? The words would come—she was sure of it—when he felt the time was right. Though she didn't really need until the end of the tourist season to know what she already knew…that nothing was going to change her mind or heart. Nathan was the man for her.

Though she did owe an obligation to Tommy, to work out her contract at the resort…if he wanted her to. It might be better if she didn't, should there be any risk of Bobby spreading damaging lies about the resort because she was the manager. Were Nathan and Tommy right in believing they had fixed the problem?

She hoped so.

It would be good to lay the past to rest, knowing it could never come back to hurt her or those she cared about, and that included everyone who'd supported her at King's Eden. As Nathan drove through the resort to the homestead, she felt she had established herself as a person in her own right here. Maybe that was the effect of the outback, bringing out one's inner resources to meet the challenge of it.

Sam and Tommy were waiting on their arrival, their stances on the homestead verandah reflecting the sparring mood typical of any conversation between them. However, attention was instantly focused on Nathan and Miranda as they alighted from the Land Cruiser. All personal wrangling halted as the *new couple* were scrutinised for sexual signals.

''Well, before I skip off,'' Sam addressed them, ''you'd better tell me if I'm to damp down the rumours or let them fly. That sleazy creep, Hewson, yapped on about Miranda, having her claws into you, Nathan, and I told him flat that if she did, it was precisely where you wanted her claws to be because no one got to you unless you opened up to them.''

''How very perceptive of you, Sam!'' Nathan answered good-humouredly.

''So?'' She gave him a piercing look. ''What am I to say?''

''That I take intense pleasure in every one of Miranda's claw-marks and can't wait for more.''

"What?" Sam's eyes goggled at Miranda. "You two truly are an item?"

"Yes," she answered, casting a chiding look at the man beside her. "Though I'm not really into clawing."

"Oh, boy, this is good! This is really good!" Sam enthused, then turned an arch look to Tommy who had apparently taken the news with bland equanimity. "Looks like you'll have to make do with Celine thinking you're adorable. And that will only last until she hooks up with Jared in Broome and gets her lustful little hands on him."

"I couldn't give a damn about Celine," Tommy retorted with a bored look. "It was just part of the game."

"And you're *such* a good game player!"

Sam stepped off the verandah and pasted a brilliant smile on her face for Nathan and Miranda. "I'm glad for both of you." She clapped Nathan's shoulder in passing. "I'll try to get Miranda to let her nails grow, Nathan. If ever a man deserves what he wants, it's you."

With that final little snipe at Tommy, she walked off jauntily, leaving him glaring after her.

"One of these days when that little witch gets off her broomstick..."

"You'll beat her with it?" Nathan drily surmised.

Tommy huffed feelingly. "You couldn't even beat submission out of Sam."

"You don't want submission, Tommy," Nathan said knowingly.

It won a crooked smile. "No, but a bit of respect would go a long way." His eyes flashed satisfaction.

"Which is what I taught Hewson. As well as ramming it home that nobody does us a damage without paying a price."

"I haven't had a chance to thank you for taking over for me, Tommy," Miranda breathed, acutely aware of what she owed both brothers.

His face broke into a cheerful grin. "One of the best moments of my life…Nathan actually asking me to stand shoulder to shoulder with him against the enemy. For that alone, you're always going to be special to me, Miranda."

He stepped back and waved them onto the verandah. "Let's go inside and park your bag. Time's moving on. I'll have to be leaving myself in a minute."

"Not before you tell us the nuts and bolts," Nathan said as they entered the homestead.

"Just got to collect my stuff from the office."

"Tommy…"

"Now, Nathan, give me credit," Tommy crowed, wagging an admonishing finger as he headed them towards the hall leading to the administration wing. "I can spin a story better than most."

"True."

"And our guests love outback stories." His eyes twinkled with teasing triumph. "So over dinner on Saturday night, I regaled them with the legend of Lachlan's law."

"Lachlan's law?" Miranda queried.

Tommy waved dismissively. "Nathan can tell you."

"A marked change of attitude on Sunday?" Nathan quizzed his brother.

"Like magic it was," Tommy assured him. "Sam

had the highly questionable pleasure of being the Hewsons' guide all day Sunday, and she reported there was no further mention of Miranda and no digs about management. Of course, I did finish up my story with the reflection that you, Nathan, were made in the same mould as our father and held in the same regard by Albert's tribe.''

"Albert?'' Miranda couldn't help asking, not understanding what the Aboriginal guide and didgeridoo player had to do with this.

"A particularly vivid touch of reality to the story since they'd met him that morning,'' Tommy remarked smugly. He grinned at Nathan. "Then last night I laid the pearls on Celine, shovelling the pitch that her skin was made for them, the perfect sheen for her beguiling perfection, etcetera etcetera and offering up Jared to show her the best in the world. And that, my dear brother, is guaranteed to cost Hewson many, many thousands of dollars.''

"The price of pride!'' Nathan said, and laughed. "I salute you, Tommy. Forget the shoulder to shoulder. You can stand in front of me any time.''

"I shall take that accolade and shove it down Sam's throat on some appropriate occasion,'' Tommy said with relish. "Meanwhile—'' he lowered his brows at both of them as they turned into the administration wing "—am I going to have to rearrange management here?''

"You can count on one season, Tommy,'' Nathan answered. "The rest is up to Miranda. Her choice.''

"Right!'' he said in some relief, halting at the office

door and gesturing them on to Miranda's private quarters. "I'm off then. No playing on my time, Nathan."

"Your time is much appreciated." A pause for a warm handshake. "Thank you."

"You're welcome."

Tommy disappeared into the office and Nathan walked on with Miranda who was silently rejoicing in how clearly and openly he had declared his interest in her, both to Sam and to Tommy. One season...then the choice was hers. No backing off from him. This wasn't pillow-talk. This was real.

She unlocked her apartment door. Nathan followed her in with her bag, moving to place it on the bed, ready for her to unpack.

"What was Lachlan's law?" she asked, closing the door to seal the privacy she wanted for just a few more minutes before taking up the reins of management again.

He set the bag down and turned around, a curious, assessing look on his face as though wondering how she would react to it. "Our family has a long history of driving serpents out of Eden, Miranda," he said, eerily conjuring up the thought she'd had about Eden on her journey here.

"In the old days, there was no law in these parts, except what we instigated and practised ourselves," Nathan went on. "For any isolated community like a cattle station to work well, a harmony had to be maintained on all levels. That remains true. Always will."

She nodded. "It's true of this resort, too, maintaining a good morale amongst the staff. I appreciate how important it is, Nathan."

"Critical to holding the right balance," he agreed. "The outback strips us of easy escapes. We have to live with what's here. And from the beginning, the Kings forged a close connection to the local tribe of Aborigines. It was of mutual benefit. They were always assured of food and shelter, and having a natural affinity to the land, they were by far the best stockmen we could have working the cattle."

"This is Albert's tribe you're talking about?"

"Yes. Twenty-seven years ago, Albert's father was the foreman at the station, a highly respected tribal elder whom my father trusted to carry through any task. A drifter arrived one day, asking for a job, said he was a trained mechanic. My father set him to work repairing machinery. A few weeks later, when the men were out at the stock-camps, he broke into the supply store, stole a bottle of whisky, got himself drunk, then bashed and raped Albert's mother."

"Oh, no!" Miranda groaned, hating the thought of any woman being so brutally victimised.

"Albert, who was eight at the time, helped her up to the homestead. My mother took her in, and sent both Albert and me out riding for my father. All the men came in because justice had to be seen to be done, especially when it involved a white man against a black woman. The rapist displayed the attitude that any abuse against Aborigines was acceptable and shouldn't be punished."

"How can people think like that?" Miranda cried.

"It was not how any of us thought on the station and if a strong stand wasn't taken on it, there would have been a very serious breach of trust amongst our people. I hope you can see that, Miranda, because King's Eden runs on the understanding—forged through generations—that the Kings look after their people.''

She gave a wry smile. ''Since I've just benefited from that principle, I'm hardly likely to criticise it, Nathan.''

He returned her smile. ''Well, just remember what I'm telling you happened almost thirty years ago, and the justice meted out was for the ultimate good of the community.''

''You're warning me it was harsh?''

''More…primitive. But then the outback is primitive.''

''Go on,'' she urged.

''To teach the man respect for the race he belittled, my father ordered that he be taken out to the most barren section of the King Leopold Range in the middle of the Kimberly, where he was to be left to survive on his own, as the Aborigines had for thousands of years.''

''Did he survive?''

Nathan shrugged. ''The story goes he's still wandering around the wilderness. There have been sightings of a feral white man over the years.''

''Cast out of Eden,'' Miranda murmured.

''He'd destroyed his right to stay. There's a lot of greys we can accommodate, but once the line of respect is abused, appropriate action has to be taken.''

''So that's Lachlan's law.''

''And mine,'' he said quietly.

''I know. And Tommy's. And Jared's. Your father passed it on to all of you, didn't he?''

"As it was passed to him."

Family lore…survival built on support and integrity.

"It's good, Nathan," she said in a burst of heartfelt belief. "I like your world."

His face lit with a smile that grew in warmth as he crossed her sitting area to where she still stood by the door. "I like…*everything* about you, Miranda Wade." He lifted a hand and stroked his finger down the slight cleft in her chin. "Do you feel okay about Hewson now?"

"Yes. He can't win. He won't want to invite more defeat."

"So you feel safe again."

"Very safe."

"I'd better go and let you get on with your work."

"Yes."

"I'll call you tonight."

"Please."

"I hope you keep liking my world, Miranda."

How could she not with him in it? But he kissed her before she could speak, kissed her with slow, beguiling sensuality, with the simmering promise of much more to come…for both of them.

CHAPTER SEVENTEEN

"A WEDDING!" Elizabeth King repeated, trying to contain the delight swelling her heart.

"Yes. Seven weeks from now," Nathan instructed. "The weekend after the resort closes. Will you do it? I know Miranda wouldn't ask but I want it for her. The whole big production...a marquee on the lawn by the river..."

"Nathan, I haven't even heard of an engagement yet. Have you asked Miranda to marry you?"

"Not in so many words. I've been waiting on the ring. Jared brought it with him today."

"You're sure of her answer?"

"Absolutely."

His eyes flashed with an indomitable arrogance that was pure Lachlan, and for a moment Elizabeth was transported back to the night when her husband-to-be told her she was *his* woman, and not to give him any runaround about it because that would just be wasting time better spent together.

"I want you to stand in for her mother, since Miranda no longer has one," Nathan went on. "Do all the wedding arrangements, take her to buy the dress, make her feel like a bride planning her big day. She's had none of the family support we take for granted. I want you to offer it to her tonight, convince her it's what you want, too."

"It is!" Elizabeth laughed in a burst of elation. She'd got it right…bringing Miranda into Nathan's life. It had worked! "My first daughter-in-law…"

"So you'll do it?" Nathan pressed.

"Of course. Any dream Miranda has I'll do my best to fulfil." *Because she will fulfil mine.*

"Good!" Nathan's face lit with satisfaction. "Then what I plan is this…"

Miranda felt increasingly nervous as she drove over to the station homestead for dinner with the King family. She hadn't seen Elizabeth or Jared since the night early in May, when she'd revealed her own lack of family. That was five months ago…five months of learning everything about King's Eden, and loving every minute of it.

But they hadn't witnessed that, hadn't seen as Tommy had, how much she'd taken to this outback life. However, they surely knew of her current relationship with Nathan and Nathan was not about to hide it. Nor did she want him to. Jared's reaction didn't worry her, but Elizabeth's…

Miranda couldn't help wanting her approval. Not that it would change her feelings for Nathan. It would just be so much nicer if his mother could readily accept her as part of Nathan's life. An integral part, Miranda hoped.

He must have been listening for the Jeep to arrive. Miranda had no sooner pulled up beside the bougainvillea hedge, than Nathan was striding down the path. She simply sat and watched him, her man coming to claim her, emanating the force of energy that always entranced her. He collected her from the Jeep, swept her with him onto the verandah, but instead of taking her into the house, led her around to the west side of it.

"What are we doing? Is something wrong?" she asked, apprehension skittering through her.

"Absolutely not." He grinned, the sparkle in his eyes denying any trouble whatsoever. "Just wanted a few private minutes with you. I find that lemon dress very fetching."

She laughed, relaxing against him as he drew her over to the verandah railing. This side of the house faced the river, which was shining like a ribbon of yellow glass, reflecting the last vibrant rays of the sun as it slipped below the horizon. Nathan slid behind her, curling his arms around her waist, rubbing his cheek against her hair.

"A golden river, a golden sky, a golden woman," he murmured.

"And you said you were never romantic," Miranda teased.

"Ah, but I am, when I truly feel it in my heart. Look what I have in my hand, Miranda."

He held it out as she glanced down. It was a grey velvet jeweler's box—a ring box!

Her heart stopped, then catapulted around her chest. Was this it...the commitment of forever?

"Open it!"

The soft pulse of his words in her ear made her dizzy. Her hands trembled as they moved to obey his command. For a moment, the spring lid of the box seemed to resist the pressure of her thumbs and fingers.

Then it opened and she gasped at the splendour of the ring twinkling up at her—a huge oval yellow diamond surrounded by smaller white diamonds, set on a band of gold.

"Wear this and the sun will never set on my love for you, Miranda," Nathan murmured as he lifted the ring from its satin slot. "Will you marry me?"

"Yes," she whispered, spreading her left hand so he could slide the ring onto her third finger. It fitted perfectly. She couldn't stop gazing at it, stunned by the sheer magnificence of his choice for her.

"Do you like it?"

Her heart too full to speak, she whirled around and let her eyes speak for her as she flung her arms around his neck and pulled his head down for all her feelings to be expressed in a kiss. She loved him so much, unequivocally, had done for a long time, and for this proposal to come now, before the season was over…and such a fabulous ring would have been ordered even earlier. Nathan had to believe they were truly made for each other and nothing would ever break the bond they shared.

"I take it that means yes," he said happily, his eyes shining into hers.

"The sun will never set on my love for you, either," she promised huskily. "I'll die with your ring on my finger, Nathan."

He laughed. "I'd rather you marry me first. If it's okay with you, that will be a week after the resort closes."

"Anything you arrange is okay with me," she said blissfully.

"Then let's go and get my mother moving on it."

"Your mother?"

"She never had a daughter. You're it, Miranda. Her first bride in the family. She can hardly wait to arrange a wedding to remember."

"Really?" Miranda had never allowed hope or imagination to zoom that far. "I was worried she might not approve of us."

"*Big* wedding! *Huge* celebration to welcome in the new mistress of King's Eden. Brace yourself for the inevitable, my love! No escape from it."

She didn't want to escape from it. At long last she truly belonged somewhere…to this man, this place, this family…and their wedding would put the final seal on the sense of belonging.

Elizabeth watched them enter the sitting-room, hand in hand, their faces aglow with happiness…a very well-matched couple, she thought with satisfaction. The party of people Nathan had invited to celebrate the engagement thronged around them, showering congratulations and good wishes—all the station community and the friends Miranda had made at the resort, most of them radiating pleasure in the announcement.

Though not quite everyone…

A wistful look on Sam's face, Elizabeth noted. And a touch of envy on Tommy's. Nothing like seeing two people really getting it together to bring home one's lack of success in that area. Perhaps Nathan and Miranda's wedding could be used to promote the match that should have been made years ago, but for two very stubborn and proud personalities.

Tommy as best man.

Sam as chief bridesmaid.

The goodwill of the day rubbing off on them.

Some discreet meddling.

Oh, yes, this was going to be a *big* wedding.

Elizabeth had the next generation of Kings right in her sights!

THE PLAYBOY KING'S
WIFE

CHAPTER ONE

A KING family wedding...but it wasn't hers and Tommy's as she'd dreamed of so many times.

Even as Samantha Connelly told herself it was a terrible thing to envy people she really liked and wished well, the feeling would not go away. In another hour or so, Miranda Wade would be exchanging marriage vows with Nathan King, their love for each other would be shining out of them, and Sam just knew she was going to be sick with envy.

The worst of it was, there was no way to avoid seeing this wedding through at close quarters. As the one and only bridesmaid, she couldn't wander off and lose herself amongst the crowd of guests. She had to be on hand, performing her duties as helper of the bride, and the whole time she would have to suffer being linked to Tommy King, Nathan's brother and best man, wishing she was the bride and he was the groom.

Tommy...who still treated her like a kid sister to be petted and teased and taken for granted as a background part of his life.

Tommy...who'd probably be eyeing off every attractive woman at the wedding. But not her. Never her. And she'd end up saying something mean and bitchy to him out of sheer frustration, when what she truly wanted...

A knock on her door and Elizabeth King's call, "Are you dressed, Sam? May I come in?" forced a swift change of expression from gloom to the expected pleasurable excitement.

"Yes. I'm ready," she replied, preparing herself for the all too discerning scrutiny of Tommy's mother.

Elizabeth stepped into the room that had been allotted to Sam years ago when she'd first come to work on the great cattle station of King's Eden. Those days were long gone, but the sense of being at home here with Elizabeth filling the role of her stand-in mother still lingered. Comfortable familiarity and affection poured into both their smiles as they viewed each other in their wedding finery.

"You look wonderful, Elizabeth." Sam spoke first, admiring the graceful silvery grey tunic and long skirt the older woman wore with distinction. The outfit was made of a soft, fine knit and trimmed with satin ribbon, and it was set off with the beautiful pearls she always wore. Even in her sixties Elizabeth King was still a very handsome woman, tall, white-haired, with the brilliant dark brown eyes Tommy had inherited.

"So do you, Sam," came the warm reply. "More beautiful than I've ever seen you."

The compliment stirred a self-deprecating laugh. "The miracle of cosmetics. I hardly recognise myself. No freckles on show, my hair done up…" She turned to her reflection in the dressing-table mirror. "It's like looking at a stranger."

"That's because you've never bothered making

the most of yourself," Elizabeth commented dryly, walking over to stand behind her. Their eyes met in the mirror. "Sometimes it does a woman's heart good to see herself at her best."

Would Tommy see her as sexy and beautiful today? Sam wryly wondered. The lilac satin strapless gown certainly emphasised every curve of her figure. Not that she was lushly curved like Miranda. All the same, she was generally satisfied with the shape of her body and it was in proportion to her average height. The slim-line gown gave her an elegance she'd never attached to herself before, but sexy?

"Well, at least I can't be seen as a tomboy in this dress," she commented, trying to ease the tight, hopeless feeling in her chest.

"You shouldn't *feel* like one, either. Why not let yourself enjoy being a woman today? Don't fight it. Just let this image you see in the mirror take over and be you," Elizabeth quietly advised.

"But it's not really me. All this clever make-up..."

"Brings out the lovely blue of your eyes and highlights the fine bone structure of your face."

"I've never worn my hair like this."

Sam tentatively touched the copper curls that had been raked back and pinned into a crown around the top of her head. Usually they dangled in a mop around her face, hiding her ears and her feelings, when she needed to hide them. This style left her without any protection.

And she wasn't at all sure of the wisdom of wearing the artificial lilac rose, pushed into one side of the high nest of curls which Sam suspected would spring out and escape the pins sooner or later. However, this look was what Miranda wanted and she was the bride, so Sam had kept her mouth firmly shut while the hairdresser had done what Miranda had directed.

"Can't you see how elegant it is?" Elizabeth appealed. "Just for once your face isn't dwarfed by a riot of curls around it, and having your hair up bares the line of your neck and shoulders, showing off your milky skin."

It made Sam feel *very* bare, especially with the strapless dress, and she simply wasn't used to *elegant,* which made her very nervous about having to carry it off. What if the rose fell out and her curls tumbled down? She could just see Tommy laughing at her as the elegant sham came apart.

"It's just not me," she repeated with an apprehensive sigh, thinking she was bound to forget the eye make-up and smudge it. Probably end up looking like a clown. Especially if she wept at the wedding ceremony and the mascara ran.

"It *is* you." Elizabeth grasped her arms and looked, for a moment, as though she wanted to shake her, but she took a deep breath and contented herself by forcing Sam to hold still and keep looking in the mirror. "It's the *you* that might have been if you hadn't been brought up on an Outback cattle station, always competing with the men, trying to prove you were as good, if not better, at everything they did, from breaking in horses to mustering by helicopter."

A flush of denial scorched Sam's cheeks. "I

wasn't trying to be a man, Elizabeth. I just wanted respect from them.''

''Well, maybe you were so busy winning respect, you forgot men want that, too.'' She sighed and her mouth curled into an ironic smile. ''You were always hell-bent on proving you could beat them at their own game, even to breaking in that maverick stallion Tommy wanted to break in for himself.''

Sam frowned at the criticism which had never been levelled at her before. Her recollection of that same incident was different. She'd been eighteen at the time and desperate to win Tommy's admiration and turn their relationship into something warmer, more personal.

''He was going the wrong way about it,'' she said in mitigation of her actions, too sensitive about her unrequited feelings to lay out her motives. ''That horse didn't want to be dominated.''

''So you showed him,'' came the pointed reply.

Her flush deepened painfully as she remembered Tommy's furious reaction to her triumphant pleasure in presenting the gentled horse. ''I wasn't trying to beat him. I meant it as a gift,'' she muttered defensively. ''I thought he'd be pleased.''

Elizabeth shook her head over the lack of understanding, and with sympathy in her eyes, explained, ''Tommy has been competing against Nathan all his life. It's why he broke away from Nathan's authority over the cattle station and built up his air charter business. To become his own man. Which he demanded Nathan acknowledge and respect when he asked for a portion of King's Eden to be turned into a wilderness resort for tourists.''

She paused, then shot home the truth as she saw it. ''Tommy doesn't want a woman competing with him, Sam. He wants a woman who will partner him. A woman...''

Sam bit her lip and swallowed the fiery retort that had leapt to her tongue, blitzing Elizabeth's view of what her second son wanted.... *Tommy's taste in women ran to nothing more than male ego-pumpers, not possible partners, and if he'd wanted a real partner in all his enterprises, a helpmate, a soul mate, there was none more capable and willing than she was and he was a fool for not seeing it.*

The blistering thoughts left an awkward silence after Elizabeth had stopped saying whatever she had said. Sam didn't know if some comment was expected of her. She had none to make anyway. None Elizabeth would want to hear.

With a sigh, Elizabeth released her hold and fossicked in the silver bag hanging from her wrist. ''I've brought you Nathan's gift for being Miranda's bridesmaid.'' She lifted out a purple velvet box and set it on the dressing-table.

Sam wrenched her mind out of its dark brooding and stared down at the box. No one had ever given her jewellery. A new horse, a new saddle, a motorbike, helicopter-flying lessons...all the birthday presents she'd ever requested had been aimed at what she wanted to do with her life, not at embellishing her femininity.

''I wasn't expecting anything,'' she half protested.

"It's traditional for the groom to thank the brides-maid this way," Elizabeth explained.

"Well, never having been a bridesmaid..." She opened the box somewhat nervously, hoping Nathan hadn't spent a lot of money on her, and gasped at the beautiful pearl pendant on a fine gold chain, accompanied by matching pearl earrings. "I can't accept this!"

"Nonsense! It's the perfect complement for your dress." Elizabeth removed the delicate necklace and hung it around Sam's throat, proceeding to fasten it there.

"My ears aren't pierced." She'd tried it once in an attempt to compete with the procession of Barbie doll women Tommy favoured, but it had been a miserable failure, the holes getting badly infected, despite her taking every care.

"They're clip-ons," Elizabeth informed her. "Made especially for you. Put them on, Sam. I want to see the complete effect."

Realising argument would be futile since Elizabeth had probably chosen the set herself, Sam fumbled them onto her almost nonexistent earlobes and tried to shut her mind to what such lustrous pearls would cost a normal buyer. To the King family it wouldn't be so much, with their ownership of the pearl farm in Broome, not to mention mining interests in gold and diamonds, as well as their legendary stake in the cattle industry and Tommy's enterprises.

Their wealth had never bothered her, never really touched her...until now. She'd always earned her keep at King's Eden, working on the cattle station

and in more recent years, at Tommy's resort. Still, if
this was Nathan's idea of a gift for her, a memento
of his wedding and the part she played in it, there
really was no other option but to accept it.

"Perfect!" Elizabeth declared, her dark eyes twinkling intense satisfaction as Sam lowered her hands,
revealing this fabulous last polish to her appearance.
"You have such dainty ears. You should show them
off more."

"Pixie ears," Sam replied with a grimace, remembering the teasing she'd suffered at school. "These
earrings will probably kill me by the end of the day."

"Ah, but they set off your face and neck beautifully. Leave them on. You look absolutely perfect
now. Luminous and alluring."

She would never have attached such words to herself, yet the pearls did make a difference, adding a
glow that seemed to make the lilac satin and even
her copper hair more lustrous.

"The beautician should be finished with Miranda
in another ten minutes," Elizabeth said, checking her
watch. "Better go along to her room then. She'll
need help with her dress and veil. I'm just going to
check on Nathan and Tommy. Make sure they're on
schedule."

She was at the door before Sam found wits enough
to say, "Thank you for…for everything, Elizabeth."

Her eyes locked onto Sam's once more. "Promise
me…" She hesitated, grimaced. "I guess it's too
much to ask."

"Please…ask."

A heavy sigh. Her eyes softened, pleading for understanding. ''Don't take this unkindly. I mean it for the best, believe me. I don't think anyone enjoys the bickering that goes on between you and Tommy. He baits, you bite. You bait, he bites. Do you think you could let all that ride today? Nathan's wedding day? I know it's a habit you've got into but it's childish and I wish…''

She shook her head, pained at having to make the apologetic request. Then with an earnest look and an appealing smile, she added, ''The elegant woman I see before me doesn't have to compete with anyone. Carry that thought with you, Sam. Win respect…for being a woman.''

Childish…The accusation burned through Sam for several minutes after Elizabeth had left. The worst of it was having to acknowledge the tit-for-tat game had started in their teens, probably a childish bid on her part to gain and hold Tommy's attention. But it had been fun in those days. It hadn't developed bite until after the horse-breaking incident, his furious resentment of her action stirring resentment in her. And sickening disappointment.

Since then…ten years of bickering, with the pattern of behaviour between them so deeply set, Sam didn't know if she could stop it. In some perverse way, it had felt like a bond of intimacy between them, a running commentary on each other's lives that none of his simpering women could share because it went so far back and held so much familiarity…

But she didn't *want* to be his kid sister.

With despairing anguish clutching her heart, Sam

turned to look again at the woman in the mirror. Not one trace of a childish spitfire in that woman. Elegant, luminous, alluring…could she be *her* today? Would Tommy treat her differently, see in her a woman he wanted in his bed, making love instead of making war?

Sam took a deep breath and made a fierce resolution.

Today, no matter how hard it might be to keep it up, she would be that woman, inside and out. She would hold that image in her mind and live up to it. Not because Elizabeth had asked her to. Not because it was Nathan's wedding. Because suddenly, she saw it as her only hope to change the ground between her and Tommy, and if it didn't work…perhaps nothing ever would.

CHAPTER TWO

HAD SHE been too hard?

Elizabeth fretted over the question as she headed towards Nathan's quarters. She had never considered Sam fragile, more a fighter, a survivor against any odds, always bouncing back with a stubborn determination to win out in the end. But she was fighting the wrong fight with Tommy. And sometimes, Elizabeth firmly told herself, one had to be cruel to be kind.

All the same, it troubled her that Sam had looked so...*vulnerable*. Somehow it evoked the sense of its being make or break time for these two—the son who could always make her laugh and lift her spirits, and the child-girl-woman who'd become a thorn in his side instead of the smile in his heart. What should have turned out right for both of them had taken a wrong twist and Elizabeth wasn't sure if her interference could correct it.

After years of observing them at loggerheads, she had come to the conclusion that pride wouldn't allow them to change their attitudes. Maybe it was too late and the mutual sniping had killed what might have been. Laid it to waste. She'd tried to tell them, lecturing them on lost opportunities, time going past that could never be regained, but to no avail. If she

15

couldn't jolt them into a new awareness of each other at this wedding…well, at least she would have tried.

Ultimately, they were responsible for their own happiness. The problem was—Elizabeth no longer trusted them to make it happen themselves. Not that she could make it happen, either. All she could do was push.

Nathan wasn't in his room.

Tommy's was vacant, as well.

She found all three of her sons sitting at the bar in the billiard room, Jared, her youngest, pouring champagne into glasses. In their formal black tie wedding attire, each one of them was strikingly handsome, though quite individual in their looks; Nathan so big and tall and strong and impressively male, with the bluest of blue eyes and straight black hair, almost the image of his father; Tommy, with his endearing, untameable tight black curls, and wickedly charming brown eyes, always the flash of a mischievous devil about him; and Jared, having a less obvious strength, a quieter charm, his eyes darkly serious and always receptive, just a wave in his black hair, subtly providing a balance between the other two.

For several moments Elizabeth stood still, enjoying her pride in them. Lachlan would be proud of them, too, she thought, wishing her husband was still alive and at her side today, celebrating the wedding of his firstborn. His boys were all men now, men in their own right and pursuing their chosen paths, and it did Elizabeth's heart good to see them so happily at ease with each other, enjoying a togetherness they rarely had time to share.

"I thought you would have all had more than enough to drink at last night's buck's party," she remarked, finally drawing their attention.

"Just a last toast to the end of my bachelorhood," Nathan excused with a grin.

"Settling his nerves," Jared teased.

"I, for one, definitely need fortification," Tommy declared. "Any man who partners Sam has to be fighting fit, and since I've been elected…"

"You could give it a break, Tommy," Nathan suggested. "Treat Sam like a lady instead of a sparring partner. Then she'd have nothing to hit off."

Elizabeth flashed her eldest son a grateful look, pleased to have a ready ally.

"Sam, a lady?" Tommy's mouth curled into a mocking smile. "First, she wouldn't know how to respond. Second, she'd accuse me of sending her up. Or she'd suspect me of some nefarious motive and see everything I did and said as a trap which I'd somehow spring on her when she'd most hate it."

He swept out an arm, gesturing to Elizabeth, his eyes beaming warm admiration. "Now, there you see a real lady. And may I say you look wonderful, Mum. Doing Nathan proud today."

"Thank you, Tommy. And I happen to think Samantha will do you proud…if you let her."

"Samantha?" His eyebrows shot up. "Since when has Sam become Samantha?"

"You'll see," Elizabeth replied knowingly, piquing curiosity.

"A glass of champagne for you, Mum?" Jared asked.

"No, thank you. I just came to check that you're all ready and nothing's amiss."

"Do we pass inspection?" Nathan asked with an amused, confident smile.

For a moment, he reminded her so strongly of Lachlan on their wedding day, she choked up, nodding her approval to cover the emotional block.

"What am I going to see?" Tommy drawled, his voice laced with scepticism. "Has Miranda waved some magic wand over Sam?"

"Could I have a private word with you, Tommy?" Elizabeth asked.

"I've got the ring." He patted his trouser pocket. "I know all the duties of a best man. You can trust me to carry them out. And despite whatever barbs Sam chooses to sling at me, my speech thanking the bridesmaid will be all you'd want it to be. Does that cover it?"

"Not quite. Please…just a few minutes of your time," Elizabeth insisted, gesturing to the adjoining lounge room.

With a much put-upon roll of his eyes, he heaved himself off the bar stool, then wickedly broke into a song and dance. "'Oh, we're going to the cha-a-apel, going to get ma-a-arried…'" And to his brothers' huge merriment, swept Elizabeth into a dance hold and whirled her into the adjoining room with all the panache of the playboy image he'd cultivated.

And what did that cover? Elizabeth had often wondered. She didn't believe he had a lust for many women. To her mind, it was more a restless search for someone to answer needs that Sam wouldn't or couldn't answer. Or a pride thing, proving other women found him readily desirable. But it wasn't giving him what he truly wanted. Elizabeth was certain of that.

"So…" he said, bringing her to a halt beyond ready earshot of the others. "…what's on your mind?"

She caught her breath, wishing she didn't have to dampen the devilish twinkle in his eyes. But she loved Tommy too much to let him hide his deep-down needs behind a wall of frivolous fun.

"It's Nathan's wedding day," she started.

He made a mock frown. "I truly am aware of that fact."

"Yes…well, I'd like it to be a very happy occasion. No bickering or snide little cracks."

He raised his eyebrows in a show of innocence. "I am the very soul of pleasure on tap."

"Then show that soul to Samantha for once, Tommy. You heard Nathan. He won't ask it directly of you but I shall. Give the fighting a break. Be kind, generous…"

His face closed up.

"Tommy, I am just asking you to treat her as you would any other woman. Don't mess this up."

"Mess what up?" he demanded coldly.

"This day. You're older than she is. And God knows you've had enough experience of women to handle the situation with finesse. She's nervous. She's afraid…"

"Afraid?" His eyes flashed derision. "Sam's never been afraid of anything."

"You think I'm a fool, Tommy? You think I'm just talking to hear myself speak?"

He glanced away, breath hissing out between his teeth.

"I'm telling you she doesn't have her usual armour today," Elizabeth drove on. "I'm telling you she's vulnerable. And if you hurt her, Tommy…it would be very, very wrong."

"I have no intention of hurting Sam," he grated.

She reached out and squeezed his arm. "I hope you take very great care not to. For your sake. And hers," she said quietly.

His gaze swung back, eyes blazing a fierce challenge. "You think it's all my fault?"

The banked passion behind those words told Elizabeth more than Tommy had ever told her…the long-burning frustration of his relationship with Samantha Connelly. But there was nothing to be gained by placing blame anywhere. Raking over the past wouldn't help. She had to appeal to the man he was now, the man who still wanted what could be…if the ground was shifted.

"No," she answered, her eyes holding his with love and understanding. "I simply trust you're big enough…and I know you are, Tommy…to rise above it today. To give of yourself without asking or expecting a return or a reward. Just to give…because giving is what today is about."

His mouth twisted into a wry smile. "Okay. You have a deal. For what it's worth." His eyes gently mocked as he added, "But you must know Sam's bound to make tatters of any gift from me."

"Then the fault will indeed be all hers. Thank you, Tommy."

"Oh, I'll be having the pleasure of being a martyred saint," he rolled out in an Irish lilt, a resurgence of devilment in his eyes.

She smiled. "Have I told you lately that I love you?"

His face softened. "You don't have to. You've always been on my side when I've needed you. And to simply say thank you is totally inadequate. But thanks all the same, Mum."

Elizabeth had never had any hesitation in throwing family money behind Tommy's enterprises, the small planes and helicopter charter business which he'd called KingAir, the wilderness resort that bore the same name as the cattle station, King's Eden, since it had once been a part of it.

He'd had a great need to prove himself, away from Nathan's big shadow, Nathan who was born to be the cattle King and wear his father's shoes. Tommy had to be his own man, and he was, very much his own man now, solidly successful in his business life.

But his personal life…he envied the love Nathan had found with Miranda. Elizabeth had seen it in his eyes on the night of their engagement party and knew he craved the same kind of love…to be accepted and respected and loved for the person he was inside.

"Let's have a happy day, Tommy," she said, knowing he would respond to her appeal for peace with Samantha.

"Sure, we will. The happiest of days. Especially for Nathan."

For you, too, Elizabeth willed. "I must go back to Miranda. Everything else is in order?"

"Running like clockwork. Don't worry. We're onto the countdown now and everything will go brilliantly."

"I hope so."

He tapped her cheek in tender affection. "It's all right. You have my promise. I'll keep smiling in the face of the tiger."

"Thank you, Tommy."

It was with a lighter heart that Elizabeth returned to the bride. She'd done what she could to set up a harmonious situation. What might come out of it was up to Tommy and Samantha now.

The bridesmaid and the best man.

A wedding.

Surely they would feel what was missing from their lives and make an effort to leap over the barriers between them and grasp this chance. Pride simply wasn't worth the loss of love.

CHAPTER THREE

AT PRECISELY 3:45, as scheduled, Tommy and Nathan stepped off the homestead verandah, leaving Jared behind to escort Miranda down the aisle in place of the unknown father who'd played no part in her life. She had no family, but she was not to walk alone. Never again alone, Nathan had sworn.

They walked down the path to where a white pergola had been erected, framing the front entrance opening. On either side of it the old bougainvillea hedge was a mass of multicoloured bloom on this fine Saturday afternoon. Shade cloth had been spread over the top of the pergola to hold off the hot sun while Miranda and Sam waited there to make their entrance. Tommy and Nathan slid out past the white lattice gates which would hide the bridal procession from view until The Moment.

A long strip of red carpet had been laid across the road, bisecting the large circular lawn in front of the homestead and leading straight to the white gazebo which had been set up at the other end of it. The whole area was shaded by magnificent old trees, the wide spread of their branches interlacing, providing the best protection for the three hundred guests, most of whom had flown in from all over Australia.

Many were already seated on the white chairs which had been laid out in a church pattern, the bulk of them facing the gazebo, but with two sections parallel to it—special sections reserved for the resort and station staff with their families on one side, and on the other, the Aboriginal tribe which had been tied to King's Eden from its beginning over a hundred years ago.

This was undoubtedly the biggest Outback wedding ever held in the Kimberly, Tommy thought, smiling to himself at the idea of another King legend in the making. There were many of them from the old days, but this…this was something else and he was proud to have had a big hand in it with KingAir flying in many of the guests and his resort providing the accommodation. Nathan couldn't have managed such a gathering on his own.

As they strode down the red carpet aisle together, a buzz of anticipation ran through the crowd. Those who hadn't taken their seats moved to settle down for the long awaited ceremony. Out of the corner of his eye, Tommy noticed Janice Findlay lingering on her feet, watching him, probably wanting his attention to turn her way.

It was over between them, as far as he was concerned, so he gave her no encouragement. He hoped she wasn't going to try reviving their affair today. The problem with Janice was she drank too much, fun when she was only tiddly but no fun at all when she bombed herself out.

If she made some kind of scene in front of Sam, the fat would be in the fire. Sam would undoubtedly let fly with caustic comments and he'd have to weather them, in keeping with his promise to his mother. He willed Janice to target some other guy at the wedding. His patience and good humour were going to be tested enough, keeping Sam sweet, though he doubted that was even remotely possible. There was no honey in her nature to start with.

Vulnerable? Well, maybe Miranda had put her in high heels and she was scared of wobbling up the aisle or tripping over herself. Sam would certainly hate looking less than competent. She probably felt like a fish out of water in female finery, having prided herself on mastering a man's world from the day she was born a girl instead of a boy.

It was to be hoped she didn't fall flat on her face. He wouldn't wish that humiliation on her, not in front of this crowd and right at the beginning of the wedding, though she was damned good at dishing out humiliation herself. Not only was she a first-class expert at one-upmanship, she nitpicked everything he did, as though she always knew better. The exasperating part was that too often she proved she was right.

Which annoyed the hell out of him.

One of these days he was going to get the better of Sam Connelly. But, given his promise to his mother, today was not the day. Unless...

A smile twitched at his lips. What if he gave her the full playboy charm treatment on this auspicious occasion...bridesmaid and best man? Shower her with compliments. Keep pressing to do whatever would make her feel happy. Focus on her needs and desires. In short—bewilder, bewitch and bedazzle.

He broke into a chuckle at the thought of clipping Sam's claws, one by one.

"What's amusing you?" Nathan asked.

"You may not be the only winner today, big brother," he answered with a grin.

Nathan looked about to pursue the point, but the pastor hailed him, breaking away from a group of guests he'd been chatting to and joining them as they reached the gazebo. With any private conversation diverted, Tommy contented himself envisaging various scenarios between him and Sam, where she would be left floundering under a barrage of unquenchable charm.

The sight of his mother emerging onto the red carpet aisle jolted his mind back onto the job of getting this wedding under way. He signalled to Albert and the other tribal elder, Ernie, to take their seats on either side of the gazebo. Out they came from amongst their families, carrying their didgeridoos—the long wooden instruments highly polished for the occasion—and with great dignity, settled themselves ready to play.

His mother reached the top of the aisle and held out her arms in a gathering gesture. With great excitement, the children streamed out from their shaded seats, all the girls under twelve years old from the station families, and two boys from the Aboriginal community. They were all puffed up with self-importance as they lined up in front of the gazebo, the boys in front, their sleek brown bodies daubed in ceremonial patterns, and both of them carrying a tribal spear, six girls in pairs behind them, looking very cute in frilly lilac dresses, white socks and shoes, little white daisies circling their hair, and carrying pretty white baskets filled with rose petals.

His mother had a few quiet words with them. There was much earnest nodding. Then off they went down the aisle, the girls positioning themselves at their allotted intervals, the boys marching straight for the white lattice gates which they were to open at the first long note from the didgeridoos. As soon as the boys were in place, his mother took her seat.

"Ready?" Tommy couldn't resist shooting at Nathan.

"Ready," he replied in a heartfelt tone.

Tommy gave the nod to Albert and Ernie, and unaccountably felt a soaring anticipation himself as the ancient Aboriginal instruments started their deep, rhythmic thrum, calling up the good spirits from the Dreamtime to bless this union with longevity and fertility. It was a sound that seemed to reverberate through the heart, linking everyone to an earthbeat as old as time itself.

In unison, the boys opened the gates wide...and out stepped...Sam?

Disbelief seized Tommy's mind.

Sam...looking like some stunning model from a fashion magazine?

A shower of rose petals dotted his vision for a moment but then she walked past them without the slightest wobble in her step. She was carrying herself straight and tall, just as his mother did. Tall? Her hair was up! The mop of bouncy red ringlets wasn't a mop anymore. It was sleeked back from her face and tamed into a sophisticated arrangement on top of her head, gleaming like burnished copper, and set off with a lilac rose nestled artistically to one side.

A brilliant touch, that rose. Made Sam look elegant and seductively feminine. And the dress she was wearing was downright sexy! Looked as though she had been poured into it, the shiny fabric emphasising a very female figure, surprisingly well-rounded breasts holding up the strapless bodice—tantalising hint of cleavage there—and a waist small enough to give a man a snug handhold, a waist that highlighted perfectly curved hips that were swaying from side to side with almost mesmerising grace.

Over her stomach she held a dainty bouquet of white daisies and green leaves, and beneath that the movement of her legs, pushing rhythmically at the shiny, slippery, slim-line skirt was incredibly sensual. Tommy started to feel the pricking of desire and a strong urge to act on it. Another shower of rose petals reminded him of where he was and the dignity required of a best man. He wrenched his gaze up from the dangerously exciting skirt.

Lovely shoulders, neck…and she was wearing pearls! A pendant gleaming on her skin below her throat and droplet earrings dangling provocatively on either side of her face. And where had her freckles gone? One thing was certain. She didn't look like anyone's kid sister!

There was nothing forbidding about that face. It was pure come-hither, her mouth painted with soft lipstick, cheekbones shaded to an exotic slant, eyebrows peaking and winging, drawing his attention to the milky smoothness of a forehead he'd never seen before, and her eyes…somehow bigger and more luminous.

Eyes fastened on him…delivering a sharp kick to his heart. The sultry look she was giving him simmered with sexual promises. His skin suddenly tingled from the top of his scalp to his toes. Countless times he had told himself he didn't want Sam Connelly. A man would have to be a masochist to want her. But this wasn't the Sam he knew. This was…

Samantha!

O-o-o-oh yes! His mother had that much right.

And if ever there was a walking invitation to discover another side of Sam, this was it, and any thought of being *lumbered* with having to do right by her or even amusing himself with games, went right out of Tommy King's mind.

CHAPTER FOUR

SAM WAS NOT sick with envy during the wedding ceremony. She was sick with excitement. The way Tommy had looked at her as she'd walked up the aisle kept buzzing through her mind and churning her insides to such a pitch she wasn't even aware that the bride and groom were up to exchanging vows over the wedding ring until Miranda turned to give Sam her bouquet to hold.

In no time at all the pastor was declaring Nathan and Miranda ''Husband and Wife,'' and they were moving towards the table at the back of the gazebo to register the marriage in the official book and sign the certificate.

Sam's heart was thumping hard as she and Tommy followed. She couldn't bring herself to look directly at him, afraid she had read too much into his expression, and now that the surprise of her appearance was over, there might only be the usual teasing glint in his eyes.

''Quite a revelation,'' he murmured.

''What?'' The word tripped out before she could catch it back. Desperate to know if he was baiting her, as usual, she risked a quick glance at his face.

''You in all your glory,'' he answered, his eyes warmly caressing, not even a twinkle of mischief.

''Miranda's choice,'' she mumbled, thrown into

hot confusion by his open admiration and hopelessly inept at accepting such a personal compliment.

"You grace it with high distinction," came the smooth rejoinder, his voice sounding sincere.

"Thank you," she managed this time, grateful for a second chance to give a gracious response.

He lightly grasped her elbow to steer her around behind the now seated bride. She had never felt so conscious of a touch. Was he just being gentlemanly on this formal occasion or was he wanting physical contact with her?

"You look very dashing yourself in formal wear," she said, giving in to the urge to show she could be generous, too.

"Mmmh...may I take that as a vote of approval?"

As he brought them to a halt, ready to move in as witnesses when required, she caught his quirky smile out of the corner of her eye and instantly hissed, "I'm sure you'll have every unattached woman here slathering over you in no time flat."

Before she could regret the tart remark, he leaned over and whispered, "You have my permission to beat them off."

She flinched at the tingle of his breath on her bared ear. "Why should I do that?" snapped straight off her wayward tongue, pride blowing resolution away.

"Because I'm your partner for the day."

Provoked by this dutiful stance she flashed him an arch look. "I might fancy someone else."

His eyes simmered darkly at her. "I'll beat off anyone who comes sniffing around you."

This was a far more satisfying image than her

beating women off him. Nevertheless, she couldn't stop herself from saying, "I don't want you to feel tied to me, just because you're the best man and I'm the bridesmaid."

"Ah, but I *want* to be tied to you today, Samantha."

He accompanied his soft, seductive drawl of her full name with a look that challenged everything female in her, and that same everything started quivering with delight. She hadn't fooled herself. He *was* seeing her as a desirable woman. And if she didn't stop these stupidly self-defeating reactions, she'd spoil this new view of her. Tommy was offering what she wanted, even if it was only for today, and if she didn't take it and run with it she'd be an absolute fool.

She poured all her wild hopes into a smile, desperately needing to negate her prickliness. "Then I'll be pleased to have your company, Tommy."

"I shall hold you to that," he murmured, a triumphant twinkle lighting his eyes.

Sam's heart leapt joyously at this evidence of serious intention. So lost was she in the magical possibility of secret dreams teetering on the edge of reality, she almost jumped when Nathan called to her.

"Your turn to sign," he said, rising from the table and waving her forward. He smiled, his blue eyes brilliant with inner happiness. "You make a beautiful bridesmaid, Sam."

"Doesn't she?" Miranda chimed in, turning her radiance on both Sam and Tommy.

''Ravishing!'' Tommy roundly declared, nudging her forward.

''Thank you,'' she rushed out breathlessly, Tommy's ''Ravishing!'' ringing in her ears and dancing through her mind. He hovered beside her as she sat and wrote her signature where the pastor pointed and the pen wobbled on the page, her hand seemingly disconnected to the task required, trembling with the excitement coursing through her.

When she'd finished, Tommy took the pen from her, not bothering to sit down, his arm encircling her bare shoulders as he leaned over the table and scrawled his signature with swift and masterful confidence. She stared at his handsome profile, almost disbelieving the feather-light caress of his fingers on her upper arm. He'd never touched her like this, as though wanting to feel her skin. Despite the heat of the afternoon, the tingling caress was causing her to break out in goose bumps.

''There! All witnessed!'' he said, reminding her of where they were and why.

She jumped up, dislodging his hold, too super-conscious to let it continue. As it was, her heart was pounding erratically as she swung around to the bride and groom. There was Nathan, a strong mountain of a man, a sound and steady friend whose kindness to her at times could only have meant he knew how she felt about his brother.

Was it all right now? she wanted to ask him. Could she trust what was happening? Was this playboy stuff from Tommy or was he intent on starting a different relationship with her? No more kid sister.

Whether Nathan read the appeal right, the tormenting uncertainty in her eyes, Sam didn't know, but he gave her a reassuring smile and a nod of approval which momentarily soothed the turbulence inside her. Impulsively, she stepped over and poured her emotion into a congratulatory hug which he warmly returned.

"I hope you two have the happiest of lives together," she said with genuine fondness for the newly wedded couple, then turning to the woman who'd won his heart. "And, Miranda, you must truly be the most beautiful bride in the whole world."

"She is to me," Nathan said with such love, tears pricked Sam's eyes.

Would Tommy ever say that of her?

The photographer summoned them to stand in a group in front of the gazebo, facing the wedding guests. Remembering her bridesmaid duties, Sam checked that Miranda's veil was falling right from the single white rose fastened in the gleaming blonde chignon, and that the beaded hem of her fabulous wedding gown was displayed properly along the folds of the graceful train.

"Enough! That's perfect," Tommy murmured, scooping her with him to stand in line for the photographs.

His arm remained around her waist, coupling them very much together, and even when the photographer was satisfied with the shots he'd taken, and the pastor announced that guests could now come forward to congratulate the bride and groom, Tommy did not release his hold, drawing her aside with him, his hand applying a light pressure around the curve of her hip.

"They look great together, don't they?" he said warmly, watching his mother and Jared bestowing a kiss on Miranda and pressing Nathan's hand.

"Do you mind losing her to Nathan?" The question slipped out, voicing the long insecurity which had been fed by Tommy's interest in other women.

He frowned. "Why would you think that? I never had Miranda to lose."

Somehow Sam couldn't let it go. "You were attracted to her when she first came to manage the resort," she stated flatly.

Beautiful, elegant Miranda, with her swishing blonde hair, lushly curved body, and fascinating green eyes hiding the mystery of her private life, keeping her distance while Tommy chased…Sam had been in knots, expecting Miranda to succumb, but she never did.

He slid her a look that challenged her judgment. "Was I?"

The taunting little question spurred her to remind him, "You kept asking her out with you."

His eyes seemed to mock her knowledge of those invitations even as he sardonically replied, "Curiosity. She was in charge of my resort. I wanted to know what made her tick…a woman like that, keeping herself to herself. You were curious, too, remember? It was you who tackled her head-on about the family she never spoke about."

She flushed at the memory. "That was awful. I

was so grateful to Nathan for smoothing it over with tales of your family.''

"At the time, I backed you up, pressing the question. Simple curiosity, Samantha. I'm not attracted to cool blondes." His mouth curved into a slow, sensual smile. "I'm much more drawn to a fiery combination."

Sam's heart flipped. The flush in her cheeks deepened. She just wasn't used to Tommy turning this kind of attention on her, and as much as she had craved it, she found herself in wretched confusion as to whether it was real or not. Somehow it felt wrong that a superficial change in her appearance should spark such a difference in his behaviour towards her.

Before she could sort out her own ambivalence, her family came streaming towards her, having been close behind Elizabeth and Jared in offering their congratulations to the bride and groom. The friendship between the Kings and the Connellys went back a long way—three generations—both families running cattle stations in the Kimberly, and Sam had been the only girl born to either family in the current generation.

Three sons to Elizabeth and Lachlan.

A daughter and two sons to Robert and Theresa Connelly.

Sam reluctantly acknowledged it was true, what Elizabeth had said earlier. All her growing-up years she had wanted to be a boy—or every bit as good as a boy in her father's eyes. Until Tommy had started stirring other feelings in her, feelings that she hadn't known how to handle then. Or now.

The distraction of her family was welcome, familiar faces, people who loved her. Her father looked very distinguished in a suit, his mane of thick white hair—all red gone out of it in recent years—curling away from his still ruggedly handsome face. Strange, she had been the only one to inherit his hair and blue eyes. Her younger brothers, Greg and Pete were built like their father, but had their mother's dark colouring, and both of them looked very attractive, all brushed up for the wedding. Her mother, as always, was the essence of femininity, her dainty figure encased in a peach lace dress.

Robert Connelly's voice boomed out from his big, barrel chest. "Well, look at you!" His hands grasped Sam's arms, squaring her up for his beaming pride and admiration. "So much for your mother's accusation I was making a man of you by letting you have your head about doing what you wanted." He turned triumphantly to his wife. "My Sam can turn into a beautiful woman any time she likes."

Her mother regarded her with more whimsical bemusement. "I couldn't imagine you looking more lovely, Samantha," she said quietly. "It was like a dream, watching you walk up the aisle."

"I guess dreams can come true sometimes, Mum," Sam wryly answered, still helplessly insecure about Tommy's response to her.

They stayed chatting about the wedding for a while before spotting friends and moving away to catch up with them. Her brothers lingered to make teasing remarks to Tommy about keeping their suddenly glamorous sister under his wing. He blithely replied he was the *best man* to take care of her, and under his wing was precisely where she belonged, this claim being accompanied by a light hug, plunging her straight into more emotional and physical turmoil as the length of her body was drawn against his, her arm pressed to his chest, hip to hip, thigh to thigh.

Her brothers laughed and wished Tommy the best of luck as they drifted off in search of some luck of their own. Sam was inwardly reeling from the electric awareness of being this close to him, feeling the strong masculinity of his physique, smelling the subtly enticing cologne he must have dabbed on his neck, sensing the strong current of energy that was so much a part of his vibrant personality.

"Do you know this rose in your hair is right in line with my mouth?" he softly mused. "I have the most extraordinary urge to pluck it out with my teeth and sweep you into a wild tango."

"Don't!"

Jolted into tilting her head to look up at him, she lost the train of protest, any further words dying in her throat. His face was perilously close to hers, the smooth clear-cut line of his jaw that invited stroking, the mouth perfectly shaped for kissing, a nose that seemed to embody a flare of passion, dark eyes dancing with wickedness and fringed with thick long lashes that were sinfully seductive, eyebrows slanting into a diabolical kick and the springy black curls that made him look so dangerously rakish.

"Such appealing eyes," he murmured. "Why

have I never seen them appealing to me before, Samantha?''

Her heart was in her mouth. She couldn't answer.

''I would always have answered an appeal from you,'' he went on. ''As I will now. Your rose is safe…until you want to match me in wanting to let your hair down and…''

''Tommy!''

The sharp call of his name broke the intimate weave of his words around her heart. It was a woman's voice, claiming his attention. Sam's head jerked towards it and her stomach contracted as she saw who the woman was…Janice Findlay, Tommy's most recent flame, and flaming she was in the look she gave Sam, a scorching dismissal that left her burning.

Before today, Sam would have instantly disengaged herself and left Tommy to his playmate. Never would she have contested any woman for his attention. But it seemed to her his words had given her the right to stay at his side and how he handled this situation would tell her more of where she stood with him than anything else.

''Ah, Janice,'' he addressed her coolly, his arm hugging Sam more tightly, apparently determined on preventing her from moving away. ''Enjoying the wedding?'' he casually added, as though Janice Findlay was no more than another guest to him.

Her auburn hair came out of a bottle, Sam decided, noting the darker roots at the side parting. So much for Tommy's taste for a *fiery combination*. Nevertheless, Janice was certainly aiming to heat up the opposite sex, the low V-neckline of her slinky black dress putting her prominent breasts on a provocative display.

"It's quite unique, darling…the setting, the Outback touch with the didgeridoos…my parents thought it marvellous," she drawled in a sexy voice. "Absolutely honoured to have been invited."

"I'm glad they're having a good time." A strictly polite reply.

Undeterred, Janice offered him a smile that reeked of provocative promise. "I notice drink waiters are circulating with glasses of champers. Come and have some bubbly with me, darling. You must be dying of thirst."

"Janice, I'm sure you can find someone else to share your fondness for champagne." There was a steely note driven through the smooth suggestion, and it emphasised his stance as he added, "As you can see…I'm busy."

Even Sam caught her breath at the direct and unmistakable rejection. As much as she wanted to be put first, it seemed a cruel set-down to a woman who probably had every right to expect him to keep fancying her.

Janice's smile twisted into bitter irony. "Off with the old, on with the new, Tommy?"

"The old ended some time ago, as well you know," he retorted quietly. "Making a scene won't win you anything, Janice."

"Won't it?" Her chin tilted up belligerently, her eyes flashing fiery venom, shot straight at him, then targeting Sam. "Well, just don't think you're sitting pretty, Samantha Connelly,'' she drawled derisively. ''You won't win anything, either.''

With a scornful toss of her hair, she turned her back on them and headed straight for one of the drink waiters. She snatched a glass of champagne off his tray, held his arm to stay his progress through the milling crowd, threw the drink down her throat, replaced the empty glass and grabbed another full one.

''At that rate she'll be under a table before the reception dinner begins,'' Tommy muttered in dark vexation.

''You were...rather cutting,'' Sam commented, feeling a twinge of sympathy for the woman he'd cast aside. She knew all too well the frustration of wanting Tommy King, and not being able to reach into him.

''She was unforgiveably rude in her self-serving attempt to cut you out,'' he stated tersely.

''Perhaps she felt she had just cause.''

Tommy swung her around to face him, anger blazing from his eyes. ''Why do you always assume the worst of me?''

Did she? Maybe she did, in some kind of perverse bid to make him less desirable so she wouldn't want him so much. ''I'm sorry. I didn't mean to,'' she rushed out in guilty agitation. ''I just don't know where you're coming from, Tommy, and faced with Janice like that...''

''My involvement with Janice ended the night she did a striptease at a party, then fell on her face, dead drunk,'' he bit out in very clear distaste. ''For me it was a complete turn-off. I saw her home safely but that was it. And I told her so. She has no excuse for slighting you and no cause to malign me.''

To Sam's intense relief, his expression changed, the anger swallowed up as his eyes gathered a commanding intensity. He lifted a hand and laid its palm gently on her cheek. ''Please...don't let her spoil this.''

Sam could not tear her eyes away from his though the passionate wanting they were communicating made her head swim. She snatched at her belief that Tommy was fundamentally decent, which surely meant he wasn't playing some deceitful game with her. He was speaking the truth. She just didn't know what *this* was to him.

''Give me credit, Samantha,'' he demanded, a harsh note creeping into his voice. ''I will not be robbed of respect today.''

Respect...the word sliced through the whirling doubts with all the force of Elizabeth's earlier reading of the problem she had created with Tommy, her failure to comprehend his need for respect or even what it meant to him.

Panicked at the thought of doing more wrong, she instinctively lifted her hand and covered his in a gesture of appeasement, as well as desperately seeking a sense of togetherness with him. ''I believe you,'' she blurted out, taking the leap of faith he asked of her.

The tension eased from his face. He smiled—a brilliant, dazzling smile—and Sam felt bathed in an exhilarating radiance. Her heart lightened. Her taut nerves relaxed into a melting sense of pleasure. Her mind was filled with the sunrise of a day she had yearned for. This was it…she and Tommy…with a clean slate between them.

CHAPTER FIVE

YES!

A fierce elation burst through Tommy. She'd given in to him. For once in her life she hadn't suspected his word, flouted it, mocked it, or walked away from it. And placing her hand on top of his was more than acceptance. Much more. It was a voluntary move towards him.

"Thank you," he breathed, revelling in the appeal to him in her eyes, the appeal of a woman who didn't want to fight, a woman who was looking—hoping—for something else from him, feeling her way tentatively towards it.

"I may not have said it, but I do admire all you've achieved, Tommy," she said earnestly. "The success you've made of the air charter business and the wilderness resort. They were great ideas and you've proved how timely they were with Outback tourism gathering more and more business."

The admission was surprisingly sweet. He was beyond needing anyone's approval or admiration for his pursuit of ventures he'd believed in. His own satisfaction in making them profitable was enough. But coming from his most nagging critic…

"I never meant to sound as though I always thought the worst of you," she rushed on apologetically. "I do respect your…your judgment on these things."

Now *that* was pure grovel and he didn't believe it for a second. She'd used him as a whipping boy far too often, invariably casting him in the worst possible light. On the other hand, the attempt at conciliation was intriguing. What did *Samantha* want today?

Her earlier tart responses had denied any desire for him and she'd been tense and uncomfortable with every physical contact he'd made. But just before Janice's intrusion, he'd definitely been on a promising roll. Keep it wild, he thought, out of the ordinary.

"Shall we start over?" he suggested whimsically.

She looked confused.

He moved his hand to capture hers and carry it to his lips. "I truly am charmed to meet you, Samantha Connelly," he declared, brushing a kiss across the back of her fingers. "And I look forward to forging a closer acquaintance with you."

She laughed—surprised, relieved, delighted and slightly embarrassed by his show of gallantry. "I think you are too forward, sir," she replied in kind, revealing her eagerness to play this game of turning a new page, to be written on as they pleased.

He gave her a wounded look. "You would forbid me your hand?"

She responded with arch chiding. "If I give you an inch you may take a mile."

He grinned. "And then some."

She shook her head at him. "A dangerous man."

He lowered her hand to cover his heart. "It's true that only the strong dare tread my path with me."

She cocked her head consideringly. "Perhaps a risk must be taken for a gain to be made."

"In meeting a challenge, much can be won," he assured her.

"If you will lead, I *may* follow."

"I trust you are open to persuasion."

Her eyebrows lifted. "That depends on how convincing the persuasion is."

"I shall put my mind to it."

"Your heart, as well, sir, or I shall take my hand back."

He laughed, exhilarated at her matching his flirtatious badinage. But then she always had matched him, before topping the matching with the last word. Not this time, he promised himself. The last word would be his this time.

With slow deliberation he raised her hand to his mouth again, then turned it over and pressed a long, sensuous kiss onto her palm. He saw her eyes widen, heard a gasp escape her lips, and knew the sexual current running through him was just as electric in her.

"Too late. Your hand is mine now," he declared, interlacing his fingers with hers.

She scooped in a quick breath, and with colour high in her cheeks, asked, "Is it safe in your keeping?"

He instantly shot the challenge back at her. "As safe as you want it to be, Samantha."

There was no answer to that. Tommy knew it was

unanswerable because it left the decisions to her. Except he now knew she wanted what he did, knew she actively wanted to satisfy herself with him, and he'd give her every chance, every encouragement, every persuasion to pursue that desire. He was well and truly primed to meet her more than halfway.

Right now, he'd pressed far enough. He lowered her hand, adopting a less aggressively possessive grip to let her feel *safe,* then nodded towards the bridal couple. "I suspect it's time to rejoin the company. The photographer is going into herding mode."

She left her hand in his as he walked her back to the gazebo, a friendly companionable link which his mother immediately noticed.

"Ah, there you are!" she said, satisfaction in her voice and pleasure in her eyes. "I'm just about to collect the children for some photographs by the gate. The pergola and bougainvillea will make a lovely frame."

"Picture perfect," Tommy drawled, referring to the image he was presenting with Samantha, mocking any triumph his mother felt at the current outcome of her interference. What was happening between himself and *the scourge of his life* bore no relation whatsoever to the extracted promise. This wasn't peace. It was war of a different kind…a war shifted onto more delicate ground…an engagement that was very much in the balance, not yet won.

"I think so," his mother returned, unperturbed. "If you'll all go on down…Miranda, Nathan, Jared…" She called them to attention. "…the photographer wants us at the lattice gate."

Jared extracted himself from a group which Tommy recognised as the pearling contingent from Broome. The gap he left revealed a spectacular woman on the other side of it. A mass of black wavy hair sprang away from a centre parting. Her oval face had an exotic cast, almond-shaped eyes, prominent cheekbones, a longish nose, a wide full-lipped mouth. Big jewellery—dangling earrings and heavy necklace in copper, evoking an Aztec design. Her dress shimmered in shades of orange, red, morone, purple—dramatic and daring.

She gave him a curious, assessing look. On some other day he might have followed up that indication of interest, but he had what he wanted right in his hand, and nothing was going to distract him from seeing where it could lead.

"Sam…" Jared spoke her name in that tone of affectionate appreciation that always grated down Tommy's spine, then topped that by spreading his arms wide in a gesture of beholding a vision of beauty. "…you *did* carry it off as superbly as you look."

Tension seethed through Tommy. If Samantha broke free of his handhold and hurtled into his brother's embrace, as she usually did with Jared, he'd pay her back by heading straight for the exotic woman. She'd already snubbed his touch once today, whipping away from it to throw herself into hugging Nathan. All these years, favouring his brothers, throwing them up to him…if she didn't show good faith now, if she was simply testing her desirability out on him…

Her fingers squeezed *his!* Then she turned her gaze up to *him,* sparkling blue eyes inviting more flirtatious fun as she said, "Oh, I just kept telling myself I mustn't fall at Tommy's feet."

"That definitely isn't where I want you," he replied with feeling, delighted when she blushed again, even more delighted with her choice to stay linked to him.

"She was a bundle of nerves before heading up the aisle," Jared explained good-humouredly.

"Then I'm glad I gave her the inspiration she needed to come all the way to me." *All the way,* Tommy vowed to himself, before this day was over. Nothing less would satisfy him.

"Without so much as a tiny falter," Jared added, smiling warmly as he stepped up and curled his hands around her naked shoulders. "A class act, Sam," he purred, and dropped a kiss on her forehead.

The jealousy Tommy had stifled so many times raged through him. "Who's the striking woman in the Broome group?" he sliced at Jared, pointedly training his gaze in her direction.

It served to spring his brother from his familiar fondling. It also caused a flutter in the fingers that had previously squeezed. And so it damned well should, Tommy thought savagely, fed up with watching open affection willingly granted to his brothers. No flinching from their touch! No avoidance of it, either.

"Oh, no you don't!" Jared warned, no purr in his voice now. It was as hard as steel.

Tommy raised his brows in quizzical innocence. "Don't what?"

"Target her," came the sharp retort.

"Now why would I be doing that when Samantha is favouring me with her company?" he asked, flashing her a smile designed to show where his interest lay, while planting a seed of jealousy that would make her work harder at holding his interest. If the interest was genuine and not just a revelling in the power of being a woman who could attract any man. Even Tommy whom she'd snubbed countless times.

This is a two-way street, sweetheart, and don't you forget it! he beamed at her.

"Just let this one go, Tommy. All right?" Jared demanded, completely missing the point.

The dead-serious glint in his younger brother's eyes suggested he was well and truly smitten. "If you're out to impress her, Jared, I'd stop acting so taken by Samantha, if I were you. It gives the wrong signals."

He frowned. "That's easily explained. Sam's part of the family."

"There's no blood relationship between the Kings and the Connellys. Think again, brother."

"Damn it, Tommy! Do me a favour and stick by Sam today. That will sort it out."

"Only if Samantha sticks by me," he countered. "She does have a habit of showing how much she likes you, Jared."

"That's because..." He stopped himself, breath hissing through his teeth as he turned to Samantha. "This is important to me."

"I'll stay with Tommy as long as he stays with me," she assured him, hedging her position.

"Now there's a promise that warms my heart," Tommy rolled out, bitterly resenting the quick understanding between the other two. "And just to show who belongs to whom..." He released Samantha's hand to tuck her arm firmly around his, drawing her into very positive partnership with him. "You can walk on the other side of me, Jared, as we proceed to the gate for more photographs. That should draw the right picture."

They both fell in with this arrangement—no other choice—and Tommy relished the control it gave him. Samantha had come his way and he wasn't about to let her go. If he had to use every tactic he knew, she was going to be his today.

"So who is this new light of your life?" he asked his brother, idly stroking the hand now clinging to his arm. He slid his thumb under her wrist and felt a highly erratic pulse beat, which put a fine zing into his own heated bloodstream.

"You'll meet her in the reception line at the marquee," Jared answered.

Not exactly forthcoming, which piqued Tommy's curiosity. Jared was clearly uncertain of himself with this woman—a tantalising prospect since he readily made multimillion dollar deals in the pearl industry with hard-headed businessmen. Confidence usually oozed from him.

"Give us a name so we don't fumble over it when we do meet her."

"Christabel Valdez."

"Interesting. Where does she hail from?"

An agitated little movement on his arm, fingers curling, nails digging into the fabric of his sleeve. Jealous of his interest? Feeling threatened? How deliciously ironic that she couldn't scorn him for it, not after her promise to Jared.

"Brazil, Holland, Singapore, Australia."

Tommy sifted the information, matching it to the woman and Jared's business interests. "A jewellery designer?"

"Yes. I've just hired her."

"What does Mum think of her work?"

"A risk."

"But you're going to take it."

"Yes."

"Well, good luck to you on both fronts."

It earned a wry smile. "Thanks."

The nails stopped digging. Threat over. But it stuck in Tommy's craw that she thought he would have no conscience about competing against his brothers for a woman either one of them was taken with. To him it was an unbreakable code of honour—respecting each other's territory—no crossing lines drawn unless invited.

He'd known Miranda was Nathan's territory the first night the two of them had met. Not that Nathan had spelled it out as Jared had just done on Christabel Valdez. Nathan wouldn't. But the writing was on the wall the moment he'd offered to show Miranda the Bungle Bungle National Park. She'd gone with Nathan, more or less pressed into the outing, then after that…nothing between them, which had intrigued Tommy into asking her out with him.

Pure curiosity…a little digging in mind…but, of course, Sam had read it differently. As she'd done with the little French piece, Celine Hewson, after he'd fixed things for Nathan and Miranda. No attempt to find out the truth of that tricky encounter or even listen to it. Judged in the worst possible light and slammed for it. Every time.

Until today. And even now the same kind of thinking was undoubtedly simmering away in her mind, ready to leap out and claw him…except it was deeply at odds with the sexual simmering, which he intended to keep fanning to the point where Samantha completely overrode Sam.

The photographer shuffled them around to a pose of his liking, moving Jared to the other side of Nathan and Miranda, with their mother beside him, the children strung out to flank the central group. With Jared out of earshot, Samantha obviously felt driven to comment.

"It's nice that Jared has found someone he fancies, don't you think?"

"Oh, I daresay in his years as a jetsetter he's fancied many women," Tommy responded noncommittally.

"But this one must be special," she pressed, an anxious thread in her voice. "He said she was important to him."

"Well, it's to be hoped she wants what he wants." He slanted a sardonic smile at her. "That's not always the case, is it?"

She looked discomfited. As well she might. Having not wanted what *he* wanted for so many years, she could hardly expect him to put the scars she'd left on him out of his mind and simply take what was now on offer. Though he would take it. If and when she proved she was really serious in wanting him, and not just responding to the excitement of feeling his desire for her.

Her gaze turned back to the milling guests. They had a clear view of Christabel Valdez in profile. Her hair rippled almost to her waist. Some Spanish heritage there, he decided.

"She's very sexy," Samantha murmured.

"Who?"

She frowned at him. "Christabel Valdez."

He pretended to find her. "Do you think so?"

"Don't you?"

"She certainly has the female assets to look desirable, but I've always thought *sexy* was in how a woman responded to me. How she looked at me, acted towards me, and generally showed I was her preferred man."

It startled her into looking back at him.

He smiled, making capital of the eye contact. "I guess what it comes down to is a man wants to be wanted by the woman he wants. Exclusively. Because he's the best man for her. That's what I'd call very, very sexy."

"Yes...exclusively," she repeated, her eyes projecting that very need.

You could have had it anytime. Anytime, he thought, all his most primitive instincts aroused and humming. If you'd ever reached out to me instead of playing your one-upmanship game. If you'd ever paused to ask where I was coming from. Ever tried to understand my needs.

He dropped a kiss on her forehead, wiping out the impression of Jared's mouth on her skin. "For me, you are by far the sexiest woman here today, Samantha," he murmured.

Her breasts heaved delectably under their satin covering. A sigh from her lips feathered his neck. Her eyes sparkled clear happiness.

Which was good.

He didn't want her confused.

He wanted her to give him what he wanted. All of it. And finally concede he *was* the best man, and always would be for her.

CHAPTER SIX

SAM dutifully smiled when the photographer said, "Smile!" but her mind was whirling with what Tommy had told her about showing him he was wanted. She'd never known how to do that. The feminine wiles used by other women had always seemed gross to her. She'd felt she should be valued for her worth as a person, not as a sexpot, trading on all the bits and pieces of her anatomy that could be displayed to provoke lust.

But maybe they were the right signals to excite a man's interest. Maybe she had it all wrong. Or maybe she'd been too frightened of failure to try in case she made a hopeless fool of herself. In moments of sheer desperation she had fantasised playing up to Tommy, but she'd never dared do it until today. Even now she felt self-conscious about it, half expecting him to drop her at the sight of someone more attractive, like Christabel Valdez.

Yet he'd given her every reason to feel positive and confident about what seemed to be happening. Tommy was focusing on her, making her feel sexy and desirable, preferring her over Janice Findlay and every other woman here. All the same, she wished she could feel secure that this was real and not just another playboy game to him.

She thought the desire was real enough. The way

Miranda had dressed her had made her feel different, so she could understand Tommy feeling differently about her, too. But what if it was a novelty that would wear off? What if…

Stop it! Where had negative thinking about Tommy got her? In a pit of her own making! This was her chance to climb out of it. Probably her only chance. She had to risk it. There was no safe course to take. If she ended up hurt, what did it matter? She'd been hurting for years.

"Thank you, children," the photographer said. "You can scoot off. I only want the six adults here now."

For the next ten minutes they were grouped and regrouped in different combinations—the final one being just the three King brothers. Sam couldn't help thinking what handsome men they were as they lined up, chatting and laughing at each other. It seemed odd that neither Nathan nor Jared affected her as Tommy did.

What was it that made Nathan so compellingly special to Miranda? Why didn't Jared set either of their pulses racing? It was only ever Tommy *she* had wanted to impress, Tommy who made her nerves jangle and tied her emotions into painful knots, inevitably plunging her into doing or saying something that put him off instead of drawing him to her.

"Right, gentlemen! Face me and smile," the photographer instructed.

Tommy's gaze zoomed to Sam, and the moment he found hers concentrated on him, the half-smile hovering on his lips widened with a dazzling burst of vitality that zinged straight into her heart, setting off an explosion of joy mingled with a clamouring need for all her fantasies to be answered.

"That's it!" the photographer called when he'd finished clicking.

"I'd like some shots taken of Miranda with me on the western verandah," Nathan requested.

"Lead the way," the photographer agreed affably.

"Sam, will you come with us and make sure I'm arranged right?" Miranda asked.

"I'll come, too. Give you the benefit of my expert eye," Tommy chimed in, waving them both forward. "Clearly I'm the best man to do it."

Miranda laughed and patted him on the cheek as she passed by to join Nathan. "The best, best man. You've been wonderful, Tommy."

"To be faultless is my aim today."

Sam stopped dead, her hopes teetering on the edge of a black abyss. Tommy transferred his devil-may-care grin from Miranda to her and she stared at him, too mortified to take another step. No faults for her to pick on...no baiting...no bickering....

"Is that why you're being nice to me?" she blurted out, unable to bear it if it was.

He frowned, as though not seeing the connection.

"Did Elizabeth ask you to...to make me feel..."

"There you go again!" he broke in, his face tightening in exasperation. "Can you not accept..."

Instant panic. "Yes! Yes, I can!" she cried, frantically denying the negativity. She reached out and grabbed his arm to press her plea. "I'm sorry. I'm just not used to you being..."

"*Nice* to you?" he repeated incredulously. His hand clamped over hers, strong fingers dragging at her skin as though he'd like to dig right inside it. "Believe me! What I'm feeling for you is not an insipid little politeness."

His voice shook with a passion that rocked Sam out of any misconception about his aim where she was concerned.

"Is that how it feels to you...*nice?*" he demanded, his eyes searing hers with their dark blaze.

"Please..." Her chest was so tight she could barely breathe and her heart was thumping like a sledge-hammer. Sheer pressure to come up with something that would blot out her gaffe, stirred her mind into flashing back to the intoxicating fun of their *starting over* repartee. "I want to take this path with you, Tommy, but there are ghosts along it. You said you'd hold my hand."

"Ghosts...ah, yes!" he answered slowly, his mouth curling over the words and his thick lashes half veiling the furnace of feeling in his eyes. "I must admit there are quite a few of those flitting along on both sides of the path. Warding them off does depend on the strength of our togetherness."

He lifted her hand, hooked his arm around hers, then covered her hand again with a reassuring squeeze. "Is that better?"

"Much," she acknowledged in blessed relief.

He swept her up to the homestead verandah, energy pumping from him in such strong waves, it somehow infiltrated Sam's tremulous legs and kept her in pace with him. Her head felt dizzy. She was glad to reach the roofed verandah and get out of the direct heat of the sun.

By the time they walked around to the western side, Nathan and Miranda were already placing themselves in a trial pose for the photographer to find his best angles.

"If you centre them between the verandah posts and feature the frieze above them, it could make a stunning frame," Tommy casually advised.

Sam was amazed he could lift himself so quickly into a natural manner, showing no trace of the contretemps that had almost left her legless. But then he hadn't been at fault. It was she who had come close to shattering the precious peace between them.

Except it wasn't peace.

It was chaos for her.

She felt as though she was skipping from ecstatic elation to despairing torment. Her stomach was a churning mess, her mind a buzz of helpless agitation. It was one thing to fantasise a coming together with Tommy, quite another to experience the reality.

Miranda called her over to make adjustments to the fall of her veil and the drape of her skirt. Tommy stood behind the photographer to get the right view of the pose so he could give her direction on the most artistic arrangement. Working in a harmonious partnership to get the best possible angles and shots soothed some of Sam's inner turmoil. Tommy projected good humour with every bit of helpful advice. An aura of love shone from Miranda and Nathan. Conflict seemed absurd in such a happy atmosphere.

Whenever she stood back to be out of the way of

the photographer, it was obvious why Nathan had chosen this place for the more intimate poses with his bride. It wasn't for the frame of the verandah posts and the ornate frieze that ran around the roof-line of the grand old homestead. It was for the view behind them—the river which was the lifeblood of King's Eden, and beyond it, the vast Mitchell grass plains of the great cattle station stretching to the horizon.

This was Nathan's land, his home, and the heart of the man belonged to it and all it meant to him—his heritage—two million acres of cattle country passing from father to son for five generations—and this was what Miranda had committed herself to sharing with him, all their lives, here in the Kimberly Outback.

Nathan...the firstborn son of Lachlan.

Tommy...the second.

Elizabeth's words suddenly flashed into her mind.... *Tommy's been competing against Nathan all his life. It's why he broke away from Nathan's authority over the cattle station and built up his air charter business.*

Was this wedding conjuring up painful reminders of what could never be for Tommy because he was the second-born son? Was that what he'd meant when he'd referred to ghosts flitting along both sides of the path they were taking today?

Strange, how all these years she'd never really looked at things from Tommy's point of view. She looked at him now, but could not discern any trace of envy in the benevolent smile he was aiming at his brother and his new sister-in-law.

"You're happy for them, aren't you?" she murmured, wanting to tap into the heart he had never shown her.

"Very," he answered warmly, then raised a quizzical eyebrow. "Any reason why I shouldn't be?"

The calmly searching probe of his eyes flustered her for a moment. Was she hopelessly wrong again? "I was wondering if you minded all this...the homestead and station...being passed on to Nathan and Miranda for them to make their lives here."

Not so much as a flicker of reaction. His eyes bored steadily into hers. "As you mind the Connelly station being passed on to your brothers?" he softly answered.

She flushed at the accuracy of that knowledge. "I did at one time," she admitted. "But it doesn't matter now. I've made my own life."

"So have I, Samantha. So have I."

The cold pride on the face he turned away from her made Sam's heart sink. She'd done it again. Struck the wrong chord with him. Better not to try to reach into him. Better to wait until he chose to reveal himself. Which would probably be never if she kept on going like this.

Resolving to keep her mouth firmly shut until he spoke to her, Sam remained doggedly silent while the photography session came to a conclusion.

"I'm going to my room to freshen up before joining the guests again," Miranda announced. "Want to come, Sam?"

Would Tommy wait for her? "No... I...uh, think I'm okay."

"I'll come with you," Nathan said, grinning wickedly at Miranda as he scooped her with him to the door that gave access to one of the hallways of the huge house.

Her husky laugh at his desire to be alone with her brimmed with sexual understanding. Sam stood rooted to the spot, watching them disappear inside, fiercely wishing she could give the same uninhibited response to Tommy, wishing he would just scoop her up and carry her off to his room and...

"Do you envy Miranda?"

She almost jumped at his quiet and all too perceptive question. Heat flared into her cheeks as she tried to banish the wildly carnal thoughts that had sprung into her mind. Agitated that he would be able to read them, she swung her gaze to the photographer who had packed up his gear and was heading down the verandah, back to the main scene of activity.

"I take it your silence means yes. Which leads me to think...you would have liked to marry Nathan yourself."

Shock jolted her into facing him. "That's not true!"

He regarded her with hard scepticism. "You've always looked up to him. As you pointed out to me, he inherits all this, which would undoubtedly have been a feather in your cap since you lose out to your brothers on your own family station. And you *have* displayed considerable feeling for him, Samantha."

"He's always been a friend to me," she expostulated, sickened by the picture Tommy was drawing of her. "But I've never wanted to be his wife. And I've never coveted this place, either. If I envy Miranda, it's because…"

"Because she'll get all his hugs from now on?" His eyes glittered derisively. "Was that your farewell hug to him in the gazebo after the wedding ceremony? Do you feel on the outer now, left without a…"

"Stop it!" She stamped her foot in sheer frustration. "I don't care for Nathan that way."

"Poor Samantha," he drawled. "Do you think I didn't see you sizing the three of us up, out by the pergola? What were you thinking? Nathan married. Jared captivated by Christabel. That only leaves me, doesn't it? Me, whom you've never cared for."

She shook her head, rendered totally speechless by his venomous reading of the situation.

"Well, since you decided to try your womanly wings out on me…" he went on, hooking his arm around her waist and pulling her so hard against him, Sam's hands instinctively flew up to defend herself against his strength, slamming onto his chest.

"…and I disappoint you in every other area…" his voice rolled on, his arm keeping her relentlessly pinned to him as he used his other hand to cup her chin, tilting her face up to his.

Anguished by his angry summation of her attitude to him, Sam didn't know where to begin to refute it. And there was no giving her any time in his eyes. They burned into hers with ruthless intent as he delivered that same intention in speech.

"...I'll try not to disappoint you in the one field where you credit me as an expert. The Playboy King. That's how you refer to me, isn't it?"

Her mouth was too dry to reply.

"But there are always two sides to that game. So why don't you slide those hands up around my neck, Samantha? As you did with Nathan earlier on. As you've done with Jared so many, many times. But never with me."

The seething challenge stirred all the desires Sam had kept hidden. They screamed through her, demanding to have at least this satisfaction. It didn't matter what she said or did, she was never going to win with Tommy, so why not have what she could? He'd invited it, however furiously, and she was not about to deny herself any part of him he offered.

Hands around his neck...

She moved them slowly, her eyes clinging to his with a fierce demand of her own—*don't you dare pull away from me, Tommy King*—as her palms soaked in the strong breadth of his chest, the hard muscle of his shoulders, the tension across his back...and her breasts pressed closer, the stiff, excited peaks of them gradually squashing into the hot wall they met...and she shifted her thighs closer, too, touching, feeling, rubbing as she lifted her arms higher to curl around his neck...every nerve in her body electrically charged with awareness of this man she had wanted for so long, feeding off every bit of contact with him.

His eyes dilated then gathered pinpoints of white-hot light. The vibration of his breathing quickened, the rhythm of it coursing through her sensitised breasts, accelerating her own intake of air. The arm locking her to him shifted, slanting down from her waist, exerting pressure on her lower back, pushing her into a more intimate fit so there was no space at all between them and she could feel the growing hardness of intense arousal—ripples of sweet delight spreading through her from the feeling.

She moved her fingers over his collar, grazing bare skin, gliding up behind his ears, into the thick wealth of springy black curls that matted his scalp. How many times had he ruffled her hair in passing, a tease she'd always hated? But she didn't ruffle his. She luxuriated in the sensual feel of it, softly raking her fingers forward and backward in a slow, loving massage.

His head started bending, eyes coming closer, like black shiny velvet now, and she knew he was about to kiss her and her heart leapt and quivered in almost painful anticipation. It had to be right. It had to be good. It had to be....

His mouth claimed hers in a wild succulent tasting and a terrible greed seized her. She wanted so much, so much, so much...her hands clutching his head, holding it to hers as she responded with a wilder tasting, kisses that taunted his wanting until he proved it with such explosive passion, Sam was lost to the overwhelming excitement of sensations streaming everywhere.

It wasn't just a kiss. It was an invasion of such riveting intimacy, it affected every part of her, arousing a super-sensitivity to the pressure of his body against hers. His hand had left her chin. He held her to him with both arms, and the hard power of his desire was evoking a compelling need in her, an ache, not a sweetness, a fierce ache to have all his mouth promised and more.

"Shall we go to your room?"

His abrupt withdrawal and the hot tingle of his breath on her ear distracted her dazed mind from registering the gruff words. She dragged in a deep breath, wishing he was still kissing her. His mouth was grazing the side of her cheek.

"It's what you want, isn't it?" he murmured.

Yes rushed out of her mind until it belatedly sifted what he'd asked first...*Go to her room?*

Which had to mean...finishing what she'd started in answer to his anger. Her body still screamed *yes*. But reason frantically argued...what about afterwards? How would Tommy feel about her then if he thought she was using him as a Nathan or Jared substitute? It would be awful...awful...

His chest expanded as he lifted his head back from hers, his shoulders squaring. "Shocked to find such strong chemistry between us, Samantha?"

Embarrassed by her own urgent ardour, she slid her hands from his hair, resting them lightly on his shoulders before daring to look up at him. The dark mockery in his eyes sparked a fiery defiance.

"You know how attractive you are to women, Tommy. Why should I be any different?"

"*Nice,* was it?" he bit out.

"Hardly *an insipid little politeness,*" she threw

straight back at him. "More like a volcanic eruption."

"Still quaking?"

"I can feel one section that's rock-hard."

His mouth quirked. "Stimulation tends to do that to a man."

"Well, it *is* nice to know you're not reacting to me as a kid sister anymore."

"Oh, you're definitely all woman today. You now have all the proof you need. Any time you want to take it further…"

Pride instantly whipped out, "I don't really care to join a queue."

"A queue? You?" He threw back his head and laughed.

Sam felt a violent urge to hit him. Wasn't she good enough to line up with the women he'd had in the past? His mouth and body had answered *yes*. If he denied that now she *would* hit him.

The devil was dancing in his eyes when they zeroed in on hers again. "Don't you know you're one of a kind, Samantha Connelly?" He brought up his hand and traced her kiss-sensitised lips with feather-light fingertips as his voice dropped to a low, throaty throb. "Which makes what you just gave me…very special. Uniquely special."

Her heart contracted, then burst into a gallop that flooded wild hope through her veins. She wasn't just another bit of sexual satisfaction…or whatever he got from the women he'd bedded.

"Now come with me," he commanded, turning her to scoop her over to the verandah railing, imprisoning her there, his hands gripping the railing on either side as he stayed close behind, speaking over her shoulder with an intensity that reverberated through her brain. "You see the land out there? It's an elemental part of Nathan. His soul is tied to it. Do you understand what I'm saying?"

"Yes," she whispered, unable to find any volume for her voice, totally confused by his actions and helpless to sort them into a sense she could understand.

"And Jared is fascinated by what can be formed by the forces of earth and nature," he went on. "Gold, diamonds, pearls. Underwater and underground treasures. Remember him panning for gold in the river, back when we were all here together?"

"Yes." The memory was clear, even though nothing else was.

"Finding such things, shaping them into beautiful objects, seeing them enhanced to their most perfect potential...that's in his soul, Samantha. And as lovely as these pearls look on you today, I don't believe they mean anything to you. Do they?"

"Not really," she acknowledged.

"Now look above the land and what do you see?"

Nothing but... "Blue sky."

"That's *my* world, Samantha. I don't envy Nathan. I don't envy Jared. Because flying in that sky is what's in my soul. It has no boundaries. It has no substance. But when I'm up there I feel I own it. Or it owns me."

She sighed, realising he was expressing her own

feelings when she was in the air, piloting whatever small craft she'd taken up.

"So where's your soul?" he murmured close to her ear. "Is it bound to the land or flying free up there, Samantha?"

It felt as though he was tugging on her soul...or laying it bare. "Up there," she answered truthfully. There was just no point in lying.

"Then that's something else you share with me...apart from strong chemistry," he said softly. "Or maybe it's part of the chemistry...a soul link like that..."

She felt his lips graze down the curve of her bare neck and shoulder, a trail of warm butterfly kisses that sent little shivers through her heart...almost as though he was caressing her soul, pressing for access. She held her breath in exquisitely tense anticipation of what might come next.

Nothing.

He dropped his imprisoning stance, stepped around her, and turning his back to the view, leaned against the railing, subjecting her to a seemingly objective appraisal from hooded eyes that revealed nothing of his feelings.

"Your lipstick is smudged," he advised her. His mouth curved into a wry little smile. "Best take a visit to your room after all...to freshen up your make-up. There'll probably be more photographs to be taken down by the marquee."

For several wretched moments Sam was ravaged with disappointment. She struggled to interpret what was going on in Tommy's mind. This sexual encounter—if it could be called that—was over. What was she to expect from him now?

"Will you wait here for me?" she asked, feeling he surely must have been establishing further ground for them to tread by suggesting a soul link.

"I've waited a long time for you to join me, Samantha. I'm not about to walk away from finding out what it's worth to me. What's it worth to both of us." He made a casual, invitational gesture. "Something for you to think about, too."

It was certainly that. She *needed* to know its worth more than he could ever guess.

Was he just stringing her along, curious as to which way she'd bounce? It was difficult to know anything with Tommy. He was like quicksilver, impossible to pin down, switching from passionate intensity to blithe spirit in the twinkling of an eye.

"I'll only be a few minutes," she said, and left him, knowing only that he had to spend more hours with her.

Throughout the whole wedding reception they would be seated next to each other at the bridal table in the marquee. Surely in that time she would be able to discern what was serious and what was play in Tommy's behaviour towards her.

A soul link...one of a kind...uniquely special... Sam grasped those words from all he'd said and welded them onto the hope that wouldn't die. They had to mean what she wanted them to mean. *They had to.*

CHAPTER SEVEN

SUNSET was the given time for guests to make their way to the huge marquee which had been set up near the river. It was always a very short twilight in the Kimberly, so even as the sun was sinking below the horizon, turning the river into a gold ribbon and streaking the purpling sky with brilliant colour, the marquee was lit up by thousands of fairy lights, making it look like a magnificent tented palace.

Appreciative remarks flew around the stream of guests walking down the long lawn towards it. Tommy slanted a grin at Sam and remarked, "Trust my mother to come up with the dramatic effect. She's really quite brilliant at organisation."

"It looks very romantic," she replied, unaware of a wistful note creeping into her voice.

"That sounds very much as though you yearn for romance, Samantha. Do you?" he asked, putting her on the spot.

Not playboy stuff, she silently amended, emotionally torn by the charm of manner Tommy had been exerting ever since they'd rejoined the throng of guests. Clearly he had switched into party mode, and while he included her in the smiles and the laughter and the happy banter, he also sought to keep people around them, socialising rather than seeking any further tete-a-tetes with her. It hadn't exactly reinforced the idea she was uniquely special to him.

However, they were more or less in a twosome now, most people focused on heading for the marquee. And he was still holding her hand, though loosely, not possessively.

"I think there's a time and place for romance. Especially when two people love each other," she answered warily.

"And how do you define love?"

The light lilt in his voice turned it into a provocative question rather than a serious one. She decided to toss it back at him.

"How do you define it, Tommy?"

He shrugged. "If I knew, I wouldn't be asking you."

"Well, what do you think it is?" she pressed, secretly glad he hadn't found it with any of the women he'd been involved with.

"I've thought it could be many things, but my feeling now is that it has to be everything. It's been my experience that half-measures never do develop into everything. They just stay…half-measures. And that's not enough."

Sam hadn't expected a serious answer, yet it was one, spoken with a wry self-mockery that underlined disillusionment in the affairs he'd entered into.

"Do I take it Janice was a half-measure?"

"More like a quarter-measure," he answered dryly. "I was feeling low at the time and Janice put a bit of fun into my life for a while."

"Why were you feeling low?"

His eyes glittered briefly at her then looked ahead as he spoke. "Oh, there's this feisty little red-haired witch on my payroll who takes pleasure in cutting me down. Even when I've been acting for the greater good, she never sees it in that light. Just keeps hacking away."

Sam frowned. Was that a fair description of how she treated him? Did she really make him feel *low?*

She flushed as she remembered Elizabeth's words—men wanted to be respected, too. Probably all those women Tommy had been with had respected him and all he stood for, while she...but didn't she deserve respect from him, too?

"It could be a reflex action to the way you treat her," she put forward, trying to keep her voice quiet and reasonable. "Perhaps she feels...down-sized by you."

He threw her a sceptical glance. "Now how could she feel *down-sized* when I trust her to run an important part of my business? And I invariably implement the ideas she comes up with."

He sounded convinced he had always done right by her.

Which bewildered Sam.

Didn't he know it went back long before he'd thought of the wilderness resort, right back to his reaction to her breaking his horse for him, and the way he'd furiously criticised her tactics with the helicopter when they'd been mustering cattle together?

At the time he'd offered her the position of resident pilot for the resort, she'd hoped their relationship would move to a different basis. A more adult basis. Mutual respect. But when she'd asked him why he'd thought of her for the job, what was his answer?

Not, "I want you with me" or "I like having you around" or "I know you'll do it well" or "I trust you more than anyone else."

It was, "You're less likely to kill yourself doing this kind of work."

Maybe he didn't realise what he did to her—all the put-downs that flattened her. In any case, and whatever the truth of his view of their relationship, this was a rare opportunity to reach an understanding with him, and however vulnerable it made her feel, Sam knew she had to seize it. Another time might never come. Besides, it was easier, putting the hostility at a distance, pretending they were speaking of someone else he knew. She chose her words with care, trying to make him see.

"I guess business is one thing and people's personal feelings are another. For example… Do you praise her? Do you make her feel valued? Have you ever shown her approval?"

The ensuing silence gathered a heavy host of memories. Sam swung between surges of guilt and self-justification over her own behaviour, but mostly she felt miserable, wishing their history had been different. She had to concede he had trusted her with a responsible job, and he had taken her ideas on board, but there'd never been any reward for what she'd done. At least, not the reward she'd wanted—having him look at her as he had today, wanting her above every other woman.

''If she feels so ill-used, why hasn't she left and got a position with another charter airline?'' came the slightly abrasive reply. ''She could have made the competition more competitive.''

Sam's heart sank. He saw no blame in himself, or was not prepared to admit to it. In actual fact, she'd thought of leaving him a thousand times. She just couldn't let go.

''If *you* feel so ill-used, why don't you get rid of her?'' she countered, her nerves very much on edge now, feeling she had lost and there was nothing she could do about it. How else could she have explained?

It wasn't all her fault, was it?

Panic clutched her again as she looked ahead and saw Elizabeth and Jared already stationed at the entrance to the marquee. There wasn't much time left for private talk. Nathan and Miranda were moving into place, setting up the reception line. She and Tommy would be joining them in a matter of seconds and then they'd be busy, greeting the full complement of guests as they passed by on their way inside.

She couldn't help an anxious glance at him. He caught it and unaccountably, shot her a crooked little smile. Then, as he'd done twice before, he lifted her hand and hooked it around his arm, drawing her into a close togetherness that set her heart fluttering with wild hopes again.

''Why do you suppose neither of us can let each other go, Samantha?'' he said softly.

In the twilight his eyes were too dark for her to read, but she felt their intensity, boring into hers, touching all the raw places he'd opened up. Her mind burned with the answer... *Because I love you. I've always loved you. And my life won't be complete unless you love me right back.* But she couldn't say those words. They would lay her too unbearably unprotected if he couldn't return them.

"Something more to think about, isn't it?" he murmured, then walked her straight to their allotted position beside the bride and groom.

A stream of guests exchanging a few happy words with them precluded any thinking beyond meeting the requirements of being sociable. Most of them passed quickly by, but Janice's parents, Ron and Marta Findlay, claimed Tommy's attention for several minutes, waxing lyrical about the wedding and the setting.

They owned a string of travel agencies across the Top End—Cairns, Darwin, Wyndham, Kununurra, Broome—and had been highly promoting Outback tourism, so they were a good business connection. Sam wondered how they viewed Tommy's short-lived affair with their daughter. They showed no sign of knowing Janice had been comprehensively dumped. Undoubtedly they would favour Tommy King as a prospective son-in-law, and they were certainly currying his favour.

Not that they were short of wealth themselves, Sam thought, eyeing the obviously expensive rings on Marta Findlay's touchy-feely hand, and her classy silk dress, featuring a similar deep cleavage to her daughter's. Nevertheless, if they were into status symbols, one of the legendary Kings of the Kimberly was probably a prize scalp to bandy around.

Sam felt relieved when Marta unclutched herself from Tommy and moved on with her husband. It was probably foolish to let such women get to her, but they invariably did with their artful little mannerisms, their gushing, their confident awareness of being *female*.

She could feel herself getting prickly every time she met one, and found it extremely vexing that men were suckered in by such stuff. To her mind, it diminished them, which was why she'd been so cutting to Tommy about the women who seemed to fawn over him. Which, according to him, had sent him straight into the arms of Janice Findlay.

Perhaps she was too judgmental. All the same, she had never seen Miranda fawning over Nathan, and they had found what they wanted in each other. Why couldn't it be that way with her and Tommy?

Her parents went by with simply a smile directed at them, not holding up the queue still outside the marquee. Sam reflected her mother had never been a gusher. Nor was Elizabeth King. Though both women had an innate pride in being women. There was definitely something to be learned from them, she decided, wondering if she could reform herself enough to hold Tommy's current interest in her.

"I'm Christabel Valdez," a soft musical voice announced.

Sam, whose gaze had followed her mother, instantly switched it to the woman now standing in front of Tommy, offering her hand.

"We haven't met," she went on.

"No, but Jared has spoken of you," Tommy said warmly, taking her hand as he added, "Welcome to King's Eden, Christabel. I hope you're enjoying yourself."

"Thank you. I now understand why Jared thought a visit here might be inspiring. Your King's Eden has a heart of its own."

She was quite awesomely beautiful, Sam thought—flawless olive skin, magnificent hair and her almond-shaped eyes were not dark as they had looked from a distance—probably the effect of the thick black lashes—but a striking golden amber.

"That it does," Tommy agreed, smiling his most charming smile. "And it tends to call us all back home from time to time."

"Yes," she answered seriously. "I imagine it would do that." She retrieved her hand and gave him a rather formal nod of acknowledgment. "I am pleased to have had the chance to meet you."

"Delighted," Tommy replied, but still she didn't smile at him.

Sam got the strong impression of a very self-contained person who made absolutely no attempt to trade on her spectacular femininity, which in Sam's opinion, left Janice Findlay's for dead. She found herself warmly approving Jared's interest in Christabel Valdez, and she was even more intrigued by her manner as the woman stepped from Tommy to her and offered a smile, as well as her hand.

No smile for Tommy but a smile for her? Sam wondered if Christabel smiled for Jared, or did she keep her distance from all men. It would answer Jared's uncertainty about her response to him.

"Hello," she said far less formally. "Samantha Connelly, is it not?"

"Yes. Nice to meet you, Christabel," Sam returned, giving her hand a friendly squeeze.

Her face lit with warm animation. "May I say I have never seen that lilac colour suit anyone so well. With your blue eyes...I look at you and think of the sky. And that is where you are happy...flying. Yes?"

"Yes." Sam found herself grinning, instinctively responding positively to Christabel Valdez. "There's nothing quite like owning the sky. For me, that is."

"Whereas with me..." she gave a little shrug "...I am suited to the earth colours of Broome. Perhaps I have found my soul-home there."

"Many have. I think more people of different nationalities have settled in Broome than anywhere else. It's like a world of its own. I hope you'll be very happy in your life there."

"Thank you."

With another little nod she moved on. Sam stared after her, suddenly struck by the echo of Tommy's words to her about the sky being in their souls and the earth in Jared's...possibly Christabel's, as well. Had Jared finally found the woman who would share his life?

"What's your impression of her?" Tommy asked between more greetings.

"I liked her. What did you think?" she shot back at him, curious to know his reaction.

"I think Jared will have a tough time winning her."

"Why?"

"She's very guarded."

"She wasn't with me."

He slid her a sardonic look. "You're not a man, Samantha."

It was on the tip of her tongue to remark that *every* woman didn't have to melt at his smile. She barely caught the acid little arrow back. It wasn't a fair comment. And Tommy's was. She'd seen the change in Christabel's manner between Tommy and herself, indicating the relaxing of a guard she kept with men that she didn't find necessary with women.

Sam wondered what had happened in her life to make her like that. It wasn't really fair to keep all men at bay on the basis of past experiences. Nevertheless, wasn't she herself doing a similarly unfair thing to Tommy, all too ready to snipe at him even when he was being reasonable? If she didn't stop it, she'd drive him away again. After all, why should he take nasty barbs from her when there were so many women who'd be sweet to him?

Here she was, standing shoulder to shoulder with him, sharing a togetherness she wanted, knowing that despite everything that had gone on between them, he wasn't about to let her go. If she hung on to him and kept being a desirable woman instead of a witch, she might be a winner instead of a loser.

Sam had no sooner thought this than her stomach curdled at the sight of her brother, Greg, with Janice Findlay hanging all over him, clutching his arm, squashing her ample cleavage around it as she poured sweet sexy suggestiveness into his ear. Sam just knew it had to be sexy because Greg's face was flushed, his eyes bright with excitement, and Janice had a feline smugness written all over her face. She was creaming him and Sam hated it, certain it was a tit for tat for Tommy's defection, which meant her brother was being taken for a ride.

"Well, Sam-m-m..." she purred, completely ignoring Tommy. "I didn't know you had such a hunky brother. I do so lu-u-u-v men of the land." She accompanied this with a fingernail stroke down this chest, bisecting the space between the lapels of his suit.

Greg laughed with a kind of embarrassed pleasure. His first hot come-on, Sam thought caustically.

"Greg is a great guy, Janice. Maybe you should take the time to get really acquainted with him."

"Oh, I intend to. There's something about weddings that makes one feel..." She let the word linger, sliding a catty look at Tommy, then back at Sam. "...deliciously horny."

With a provocative little laugh, Janice snuggled up to Greg again and carried him off into the marquee.

Before she could stop herself, Sam threw a dagger-like look at Tommy. "And *that* kind of mush from Janice made you high again?"

His eyes hardened into smoking black coals. "Don't knock it, Samantha. There are times when a man simply wants to feel wanted. As Greg does right now."

She flushed and dropped her gaze, painfully aware she hadn't made Tommy feel wanted. Until today.

"And she's probably right about weddings," he drawled sardonically. "Seems to me you were very definitely turned on when you kissed me on the verandah."

That was different. Entirely different. "She's using Greg as a substitute. You know she is, Tommy," she said fiercely.

"And you weren't?"

"No!" she flared at him. "I wanted…"

"Me?" His eyes glittered at her, pinning her down.

There was nowhere to go but the truth. "Yes. I wanted to know what it might be like with you."

"And I, with you, Samantha," he returned, giving her the instant relief of knowing he wasn't about to use her admission to any mean advantage. "Do you have a mind to continue this journey of discovery with me?"

"Yes," she said recklessly.

"Good! Because that's what I'd like, too."

A dizzy sense of triumph fuzzed her mind. Everything she'd risked so far had paid off. Tommy *was* reviewing their relationship, wanting more from it, wanting to see where it might lead if they gave it a chance to move forward.

It didn't occur to her until they were on their way into the marquee that the questions he'd put to her were all related to "feeling horny."

Had she just committed herself to having sex with him?

Did he have anything more than that in mind?

Her heart started fluttering.

Then a fierce resolution kicked in.

I don't care. I'll have whatever I can have of Tommy King. At least then I'll know how much I mean to him.

CHAPTER EIGHT

ELIZABETH smiled as she watched Nathan and Miranda happily positioning themselves for the cake-cutting ceremony. What was it…ten months since she had interviewed Miranda for the position of resort manager? Something about her had stirred the hope she might be the right one for Nathan, the one to draw him out of his entrenched view that no woman could be kept happy with his kind of life.

Here they were…married…and Elizabeth had no doubt the marriage would last. The love and need they had for each other carried the same strength she knew were in their characters. They would stand together through any adversity, those two, and it gave her a deep sense of satisfaction that she had selected Miranda for King's Eden.

There would be children now…the next generation. Lachlan would have wanted the family line to go on. At least one decisive step in that direction had now been taken, but one wasn't enough. Who could read the future? Never, for one moment, had she imagined Lachlan's life being cut short…her indomitable husband…gone…and all she had left of him were their three sons.

It wasn't enough.

She wanted to see Lachlan in the children of their children. She wouldn't let it end. And while Nathan was most like his father, that was no guarantee his children would get the major share of Lachlan's genes. It could be Tommy's children, or Jared's who inherited them. Life was a lottery, no guarantees, and the best chances had to be taken, not wasted.

The five-piece band she'd hired struck up a fanfare as the cake was finally cut. A loud round of applause followed, then the announcement from the master of ceremonies, "The new Mr. and Mrs. King will now proceed to the dance floor for the bridal waltz."

"Ready to follow them on and show them how to waltz, Mum?" Jared teased, rising from the chair beside her.

She smiled at her youngest son as he assisted her onto her feet. In some ways she was closest to Jared who had taken on and expanded the business she'd inherited from her father. He had an intuitive understanding of her interest in the pearl industry, and God knew she'd needed some interest to focus on after Lachlan had died.

"You know," Jared murmured, having taken her arm for the walk to the dance floor, "Tommy and Sam seem to be getting it together for once. Not one spat that I've seen. And looking at them now, getting up to dance…"

She looked. They were sparkling at each other and the electric charge running between them was definitely positive, their body language emitting an eagerness to dance together—anticipating pleasure, no mere sufferance for the sake of good form. For the truce she had asked for to have lasted this long—

close to six hours now—was a major miracle, and Elizabeth prayed they had settled their differences.

''It's about time they got it together,'' she murmured to Jared. ''All these years of mutual frustration…''

''Well, Sam's sure got him snagged today,'' he returned laughingly. ''Miranda made a great choice with that bridesmaid outfit.''

''I hope Tommy is seeing further than that.''

And she'd make it her business to ascertain what was actually going on there. There would be a rotation of partners during the bridal waltz. It would probably be her only chance this evening to get Tommy to herself for some straight talking.

The band started up, swinging into a waltz number, and Nathan and Miranda circled the floor, transmitting the magic of their wedding to everyone watching. Jared timed their entry with smooth grace, and Tommy whirled Samantha onto the floor with his usual zestful panache. Samantha's face was lit with happy excitement. It gave Elizabeth's heart a lift. True happiness…so hard to come by at times.

She glanced up at Jared and found his gaze trained on the table where Christabel Valdez sat. He was very taken by her. She was certainly a highly creative, innovative designer, but Elizabeth felt uneasy about a relationship developing between the beautiful Brazilian and her youngest son.

Behind the practised serenity of those golden-amber eyes, Elizabeth sensed many secrets which Christabel didn't care to bring into the light of day. Widowed, she'd said, perhaps giving legitimacy to the child she had, a little girl Jared had met by accident, not by active introduction.

And why did she continue to live in the caravan at the Town Beach in Broome, despite her current, very well-paid employment? It smacked of a deliberate choice to maintain a temporary place rather than get into a fixed address. Elizabeth didn't have the answers and the younger woman never invited any intrusion into her private life.

Christabel…she had an exotic quality that appealed to Jared. Elizabeth understood the attraction but it was worrying. She didn't want to see her youngest son hurt by it. Still, there was nothing she could do to avert that outcome. Some things just had to run their course.

"On to Nathan, Mum," Jared warned, giving her a whirl towards her eldest son before turning to take Samantha as his partner.

Nathan smiled at her as he took her in his arms. "You've done a wonderful job with the wedding, Mum. It's everything I wanted for Miranda. And your speech, welcoming her into the family…" His smile turned crooked. "…it meant so much, she was moved to tears."

"She *is* everything I wanted for you in a wife, Nathan."

He sighed contentedly. "Me, too. Lucky you hired her to manage Tommy's resort, wasn't it?"

"Yes. Though I recall you weren't too pleased with my choice of a woman manager at the time," she archly reminded him.

He laughed. "I changed my opinion the moment Miranda walked into my life."

"So you revealed in your speech." She smiled, enjoying her own secret triumph over bringing them together. "It was a lovely speech, Nathan. It moved *me* to tears."

"Just as well Tommy got us all laughing when he got up to do his best man bit. He really is a brilliant raconteur. Had everyone hanging on his next line."

"It was certainly a good performance," she agreed. The question was whether it was also a performance with Samantha. Tommy was very very good at putting on a show.

"I thought what he said about Sam was nice, too," Nathan warmly added. "Did you see her glow when he praised her for being the best helpmate anyone could ask for?"

"Yes. I'm glad he was kind."

"Mmmh…" His vivid blue eyes twinkled. "Might be a bit more than kindness, Mum. You can check him out on that one. It's his turn to dance with you."

He passed her on to Tommy who put his own unique style to the waltz steps, grinning as she matched his timing. "At last…the perfect partner!"

She raised her eyebrows. "I think someone younger should fill that position for you."

He laughed, exuberant with the excess energy that always marked high spirits in Tommy. "And very shortly will. The force is with me tonight."

"What force is that?"

Wicked teasing in his eyes. "The force that turns a witch into a princess."

Samantha! But how serious was he about claiming her as his perfect partner?

"Does this force last beyond the spell of the wedding?" she asked, keeping her voice tuned to light banter.

"Who knows? Will the prince turn back into a frog?"

"I've always thought faith could work miracles."

"Only if it's strong enough and never wavers."

"You've never been weak, Tommy. You can make it strong if you want to."

"If the ghosts stay away. Many ghosts, Mother dear. Many, many ghosts."

Yes, she thought. They'd both inflicted scars that weren't easy to push into the past.

"Take care, Tommy."

His eyes glittered down at her. "No. Taking care is not what tonight is about. What's the old saying…there's a tide in the affairs of men? Tonight I ride it. I ride it for all it's worth. And if it tosses me up on a desolate island…then it's done, isn't it?"

Such fierce, reckless passion…it was in his eyes, in his voice, in his words. All or nothing. Pride. That had always been the devil in him.

"You are now invited to join the King family on the dance floor," the master of ceremonies announced.

"Back to Jared," Tommy lilted, and passed her on to his younger brother before Elizabeth could think of anything to say that might temper the course he was bent on taking.

She looked back.

He was masterfully gathering Samantha into a dance hold that pressed every intimacy that had once banned the waltz from respectable gatherings. And the princess went willingly.

Elizabeth knew in that moment there *was* nothing she could do or say to change anything.

Good or bad…they held their own destiny in their hands.

CHAPTER NINE

FOR SAM, it was definitely the best evening of her life. She'd been the main focus of Tommy's attention ever since they'd entered the marquee—warm, considerate, charming, flattering attention—with only the occasional teasing remark. But it wasn't put-down teasing, more wickedly sexy, sparking a wonderfully intimate sense of fun that was more intoxicating than the champagne they drank.

And dancing with him was more thrilling than she'd ever imagined. All these years, whenever she'd seen him dance with other women, envy had been like a knife in the heart. Quite simply, he was the best, so attuned to rhythm he could create his own version of steps, adding an exciting challenge to the sheer pleasure of moving with him.

Often she'd meanly called him a flashy show-off, though she knew it was only because he didn't ask her to partner him. There wasn't a woman alive who wouldn't love to dance with Tommy King. He made the music come alive so physically, it was as though her whole body, and his, were instruments, too, pulsing to the beat, expressing the melody, making it mean more than it ever had before.

Best of all, was the sense of being one with him, and not just in moving around the dance floor. It was marvellous not to feel inhibited by the close body contact, to revel in Tommy's strong masculinity without any fear of his pulling away or rejecting her for some other more desirable woman. For tonight, at least, he was willingly, happily hers.

As the evening wore on, the band wound up, rolling out great sets of rock numbers from each decade—Bill Haley, Elvis, the Beatles, Abba, Neil Diamond, Michael Jackson. Everyone was singing and clapping. The men discarded jackets and ties as the party really began to swing.

At first, Tommy was fairly conservative in throwing himself into the jazzier numbers, waiting to see if Sam was comfortable with where he led. When she easily matched him and started throwing in a few little innovative movements of her own, he laughed and moved into top gear, challenging her in an exhilarating mutual contest that ended up with the rest of the dancers standing back to watch and clap and urge them on to wilder feats.

Sam was barely aware of them. She was totally captivated by the sexual energy pouring from Tommy, the sense of being stalked, tantalised, his dark eyes wickedly telling her he could take her whenever he wanted, but not yet…not yet because he wanted to revel in every anticipatory move, wanted to watch her responding to him, wanted to build the excitement, to savour it, to exult in it.

And she was possessed by the same energy, her heart pumping a wild pagan beat, her body moving with provocative intent, her arms beckoning, retreating, pretending an aloof self-containment while her eyes flirted with the burning purpose in his, and her feet glided and stamped and twirled.

Finally he pounced, trapping her legs between his, bending her over his arm in a deep swoop. His face hovered above hers, a triumphant grin on his face. Then while she was helpless to prevent it, he snatched the lilac rose from her hair with his teeth. As the band brought the number to a loud drumming end, echoing the mad drumming of her heart, Tommy lifted her upright again, stepped back to sketch a gallant bow, and presented her with the rose in a chivalrous gesture of homage, to huge applause and cheers from the onlookers.

"Champagne for my lady?" Tommy twinkled at her, sweeping her off the dance floor towards the bar which had been set up near the exit from the marquee.

Sam nodded, laughing breathlessly, still exhilarated and loving him for the very playboy qualities she had told herself she despised. Which had never been true. She knew that now. It had simply been a case of wanting him to play with her.

. The barman poured their drinks. Tommy clicked his glass against hers. "To the perfect partner," he murmured, his eyes still hot from the mating ritual they'd so blatantly started.

"For me, too," she answered huskily, bubbling with an excitement that had more to do with the champagne of this night with Tommy than with the bubbly liquid she sipped.

"I didn't know you could dance like that,

Samantha," he commented quizzically. "You never have at the few parties we've both attended."

"There aren't many men who can dance like you," she answered, stating the honest truth. Then with a little shrug, denying it mattered right now, she added, "And you chose other women to partner you."

His mouth curled with irony. "I did ask you once. You told me you didn't care to make an exhibition of yourself."

She flushed, vividly remembering that one wretched occasion. It was the opening of the wilderness resort party, and Tommy had been high on the successful completion of his dream tourist venture, his exuberant spirits bursting to be expressed. He'd grabbed her hand, arrogantly commanding as he said, "Come on, Sam. Let's pound the floor. Show 'em how fantastic we feel about this."

And she'd baulked, knowing how inept she would be in matching him, lacking the confidence to try, afraid of looking awkward and foolish, spoiling his desire to express all she didn't know how to express.

"I couldn't do it then, Tommy," she confessed, grimacing at the memory of how she'd refused him, her wayward tongue tripping out that harsh defence. "I'm not a natural like you," she explained. "I had to learn."

"Learn?" he repeated, frowning at what was obviously an alien idea to him.

She nodded. "When the Big Wet came that year, I went to Darwin and took a course of dance lessons.

All the modern stuff. Jazz ballet. I had to learn to loosen up, go with the flow.''

He shook his head in bemusement. ''You could have asked me to teach you.''

She returned his ironic smile. ''I thought you'd make fun of me. Or get impatient, exasperated…''

''No,'' he cut in, his face tightening, his eyes glittering with bitter accusation. ''You couldn't bear not being competitive. That's the truth of it, isn't it?''

Her heart stopped, and all the pumped-up excitement drained away. ''Maybe it was,'' she admitted flatly. ''I don't know anymore. All I know is…you never asked me to dance with you again…until tonight…and I wasn't competing with you just now. I was…''

Despair clutched her mind. Would they never understand each other? Always be ships passing on contrary courses? Her eyes pleaded against the harsh judgment in his and she heard her voice wobbling as she begged his understanding.

''This probably sounds crazy…but I wanted to…to share things with you…to be able to do what you could…and…and have you feel proud of me.''

Tears blurred her eyes. She fumbled the glass down on the bar table. ''Excuse me,'' she gabbled, and virtually blundered her way outside, her heart aching with the burden of always getting it wrong, somehow destroying the very thing she most wanted. And it *was* her fault. She had said those miserable things to Tommy, casting him in a lesser light because of her own sense of inadequacy, of never seeming to measure up in his eyes.

Tears of hopelessness trickled down her cheeks. She turned up towards the house, forcing her tremulous legs into the necessary action to get her to a safe refuge. Impossible to face anyone right now. Her mascara was probably running. Best to pin the stupid rose back in her hair and armour herself again to see the wedding reception through as a good bridesmaid should.

She was never going to make it with Tommy. All this evening…just a fool's paradise…a bubble of fragile happiness too easily broken. Underneath the charm she'd been basking in, Tommy had such a deep store of anger against her, and rightly so. She'd never done anything to make him feel good about himself, tearing strips off him, shunning him in favour of his brothers…the sins were endless.

How could he forget them?

She kept trudging up the long lawn, dying a little with every step, knowing she couldn't turn back the clock, wishing Tommy would come after her, accepting there was no real chance with him anyway.

Vulnerable! Tommy stood in a shocked daze as that word—his mother's word for Samantha—drummed through his mind. He hadn't believed it. He'd scorned the very idea of Samantha Connelly having any soft underbelly to be ripped open…revealing such naked hurting.

He'd been wrong.

All these years he'd been wrong.

She'd been fighting to win his admiration, wanting approval, appreciation, and he'd seen it as—he shook his head—everything else but that...turning to other women to get what she didn't give...only it was never enough because he wanted it from her.

Hell hath no fury like a woman scorned... The jibes about his affairs...they were understandable if she wanted him and thought he didn't see her as good enough. Had she wanted him all along? Had they both trodden a path of misconceptions about each other?

Her eyes filling up with tears...

She'd never cried...too strong, too proud, too gritty to show any womanly weakness. But today had been different. Tonight had been different. And be damned if he was going to lose that difference now!

Gripped by the need to act, Tommy set his glass on the bar table and headed straight for the exit, determined on following Samantha, catching her, straightening things out between them. He was waylaid, his arm clutched, with a drunken Janice Findlay swinging on it, lurching around to face him and grab a handful of his shirt.

"Hold it, lover!" she slurred, leering at him as she added, "You and I need to talk."

"Not now!" he clipped out, trying to pluck her hand away without offensive force.

She dug her nails into the fabric and snarled, "Don't think you can throw me off, Tommy King."

She was dangerously drunk, he belatedly recognised, and cast a quick glance around for Greg, hoping for handy assistance in disentangling himself.

"Hot to hump Sam Connelly, aren't you?" Janice

taunted. "But she's given you the slip and I've got you. Been waiting all night for this."

No Greg in sight, but he caught Jared's eye and aimed a frown towards Janice, indicating a problem. Taking a deep breath and telling himself to calm his sense of urgency, he met his ex-playmate's venom with as much reasonableness as he could muster.

Stroking the grasping hand to relax the grip she had on him, he spoke in a gentler tone. "What is it you want, Janice? You know it's over between us. Holding me like this won't lead anywhere. What more is there to say?"

"Think you can get off scot-free, don't you?" she jeered. "One of the great Kings of the Kimberly." She released his shirt to throw off the touch of his hand in a gesture of contempt. "You're going to pay for the pleasure you took with me. I'll make your name dirt if you don't."

"I hope you'll think better of that in the morning, Janice. In the meantime…"

"Ah, there you are…" Jared smoothly scooped her aside, a strong, purposeful arm around her waist. "…Greg was worried you might get lost going to the loo. I said Christabel would accompany you, make sure…"

Tommy didn't hear the rest. He was out of the marquee and moving fast, head swivelling, looking for a lilac gleam to follow. No sight of anything likely along the riverbank. How big a start did Samantha have? What with sorting himself out and Janice delaying him, several minutes must have passed.

His heart kicked into a greater sense of urgency as he scanned the lawn leading up to the house. There, close to the bougainvillea hedge... He broke into a run, uncaring what anyone who saw him thought. It might be his life on the line here—as good as—if what he'd worked out was right.

She was heading for the front gate, in the dark shadows thrown by the trees beside the circular driveway. Was it her? Instinct insisted it had to be. His feet pounded over the grass. She obviously couldn't hear him coming. There was no pausing from her, no turning around. Was he pursuing a ghost?

Struck by an uncharacteristic stab of anxiety, he called out, ''Wait!''

Tommy's voice? Sam's heart contracted. She looked back towards the marquee. A black and white figure was pelting up the lawn, making a beeline to where she was. It had to be Tommy...having decided he should fetch her back no matter what, mend the ruction, see the night through, hold the happy family line, the dutiful best man.

Sam instantly put on a spurt, past the lattice gate, running up the path, the steps onto the verandah, panicking at the thought of facing anything with Tommy right now. It wouldn't be about caring what she felt. He would have followed her sooner if he'd really cared about her. As for the sexual thing that had been zipping between them...it was just Tommy being the way he was with other women...nothing special to her, except perhaps an extra zing of titillating interest because it was out of their usual pattern.

She rushed into the house, along the halls to her room, needing to shut Tommy out, to give herself time to get this nerve-shuddering misery under control and paste over the cracks…make-up, hair, heart. A half hour break. Excuses could easily be made to cover that.

Tommy couldn't be sure who it had been out there. She hadn't answered him and the darkness would have precluded positive identification. Hopefully he would think he'd made a mistake, wander back and get involved with other company. Then she could turn up in the marquee again and pretend nothing was amiss.

She whirled into her room, closing the door as fast as she could. Safe, she thought, and without switching on the light, tottered over to the bed and sat down to catch her breath. The ache inside her hurt so much she sagged forward, elbows on knees, head in her hands. Somehow she had to hold herself together, finish the night.

Tomorrow she would fly home with her parents and brothers. The resort had closed, the tourist season over for the year. Tommy didn't need her, not in any sense. He could manage without her services as a pilot in his KingAir charter business. She needed time away from him, away from anything to do with him. Best to go home, lick her wounds, get herself into shape to face a different future from the one she had no hope of having.

Her heart jumped as she heard footsteps thumping

along the hall. Before she had time to think, her door crashed open and the room was flooded with light. Tommy stood there, his hand still on the light-switch, his chest heaving, his face strained, his dark eyes wildly targeting her, and tension flooded from him, swirling around her, stiffening her spine and pulling her onto her feet in a fierce burst of outrage at his intrusion.

"This is my *private* room! You have no right to..."

"As I see it, we've kept too much private from each other," he sliced in, vehemently denying her protest and closing the door, punctuating his determination to confront no matter how she felt about it.

"I'm sick of arguing with you!" she cried, her hands curling into fists.

"So am I," he retorted.

"Then what are you doing here?" She barely repressed the urge to fly at him and fight him out of her room.

"I'm here because I want you. What's gone on between us in the past doesn't matter a damn! I want you, Samantha Connelly..."

The passion in his voice brought the raging turbulence inside Sam to a paralysing stop. Her mind was only capable of clutching and repeating one thought. *He meant it....he meant it...*

"...and I think you want me!"

CHAPTER TEN

SAM STARED at Tommy, all her yearning for him mixed with the panicky doubt that this might not be the real thing. His desire for her right now was real. It was burning in his eyes, making her churn with the treacherous excitement that had gripped her earlier this evening. Except she knew now that just having sex with him wouldn't be enough. She wanted it all…what Miranda had with Nathan…and if Tommy was only wanting to be satisfied on some libido level…

He took a step towards her, emanating unshakable purpose. It propelled Sam into dashing away from the bed, frantically, instinctively, needing time and space to sort out what was happening. She caught sight of herself in the dressing-table mirror and jerked to a halt, momentarily mesmerised by the reflection of a stranger to her real self—huge eyes smudged with make-up she never normally used, skin unmarred by freckles, sophisticated hairstyle, expensive jewellery, sexy dress.

"It's not me!" The words burst out of her painful confusion and gathered a hysterical momentum. She swung to face Tommy, to confront him with the *real* truth. "You never wanted me before. It's this…" She lifted her hands and flung them down in a fierce

103

dismissal of how she looked today. "…this get-up!" she finished contemptuously.

"I did want you," he declared without batting an eye. "I always wanted you."

Oh, no! She shook her head at such a terrible lie. She didn't believe it. Couldn't believe it.

He took another step towards her. Another step.

"Stop it, Tommy!" she commanded, her voice shaking in violent protest. She knew there was a box of tissues on the dressing-table. Blindly grabbing, she pulled out a bunch of them and wiped them over her painted face, savagely destroying the work of the beautician. "See? This is me!" she hurled at him. "The Sam who isn't worth a second look from you."

He kept coming at her.

She dropped the tissues and attacked the pins holding up her hair, tearing them out, throwing them away, messing up the artificial sophistication. "You never wanted this, and this is who I am…the carrot mop-top…not to be taken seriously as a woman…the pesky squirt in the background…the freckle-faced…"

He caught her wrists and dragged her hands down, forcing them to rest against his chest, holding them there. "The feisty, freckle-faced girl I wanted to impress but never seemed able to," he said, his voice like a burr in her ears, determinedly penetrating the chaos running through her.

"The fellow spirit who feels as alive in the sky as I do," he went on, the words making her temples throb. "The woman whose beautiful, burnished curls are like magnets to my fingers…and my need to touch them could only be covered by a teasing manner because I believed you didn't want to be touched by me.''

His chest expanded as he inhaled a deep breath, and his eyes seared hers of any further covering up by either of them. ''But that's not true, is it, Samantha?''

She crumpled, unable to hold up the shields she'd hidden her feelings behind for so long. ''I didn't mean to drive you away from me, Tommy. I didn't mean to…to…'' Her lips trembled. Her throat choked up. She could feel his heart thumping under her palm. Were they touching now? Was this the truth?

''Tell me you want me,'' he demanded hoarsely.

Her truth spilled out, heedlessly, compulsively, irrevocably. ''I want you.''

For a long nerve-tearing moment, their eyes locked, a fierce, primitive challenge surging between them—no holds barred—the final ripping away of years of destructive pretence and the passion for proof of the desire declared was a violent force, climbing, clawing its way past the old inhibitors, scattering the ghosts, screaming to be satisfied to the very core of absolute truth.

Then his mouth crashed onto hers, explosively invasive, demanding a response to match his driving need, and Sam poured all her craving for him right back, voraciously and exultantly feeding the deep wrenching hunger for the feel of him, the taste of him, the heart, the mind, the soul of him.

He kissed her with the same ravening appetite,

binding her to him with an ardour that drew on everything she was, and the rush to give—to give and take—was a raging wanton wildfire, racing through her entire body. This time he was hers. Absolutely hers. His mouth, his hands, the hard, hot yearning of his body were telling her so.

Fingers kneading her hair, kisses adoring her face, burning down her throat, heating her bare shoulders; her own hands revelling in the ripple of muscles on his back, her breasts peaking with almost painful excitement, her stomach and thighs quivering with pleasure under the strong, masculine pressure he exerted on them, all her senses swimming in the intoxicating delight of his desire for her.

The zipper at the back of her dress fell open, loosening the boned bodice, the tight fit around her waist and hips. Tommy lifted her up, hauling her out of the satin sheath, burying his face between her breasts as though inhaling the scent of her and savouring the softness of her flesh as he carried her over to the bed and laid her on the quilt.

His eyes glittered over her. "Look at you," he said with an intense mixture of admiration and awe.

And she realised he loved the look of her and a glorious swell of pride swallowed up any chilling nervousness about her nakedness.

He threw off her shoes, peeled down her pantihose. "Silky red curls. I knew there would be," he murmured gruffly, tossing the last garment aside and thrusting his hand through the curls, reaching into the apex of her thighs, stroking, inflaming a tumult of sensation as he bent over and kissed her breasts, leaving them throbbing with his need to possess, aching to be taken like that again and again.

"Don't move," he muttered fiercely as he drew back. "I've never seen you like this and I've wanted to…all these years…you naked on a bed, open to me, wanting me to come to you."

The heat of his words consumed any inhibitions she might have had as she lay there, her pulse racing, her stomach churning with fever-pitch anticipation as she watched him discard his clothes. Her eyes gloated over the smooth sheen of his tanned skin, the nest of black curls across his chest, arrowing down to the flat tautness of his stomach. Her heart kicked at the sheer power of his aroused sexuality. This was Tommy wanting her…the only man in her life she had ever wanted…and excitement writhed through her. Her arms lifted, welcoming, yearning, dying to hold him to her, feel him, love him.

"Samantha…" It was a low, animal growl, a deep affirmation of who and what she was to him as he came to her, gathering her to him, flesh to flesh, a glorious pagan freedom in their touching, their kissing, the feverish need to savour every inch of each other, to drown in the sheer sensuality of this magical experience, to capture every drop of knowledge to be treasured…this first time, the reality of a dream coming true…and it was wonderful, incredibly satisfying, beyond any imaginable feelings.

Tommy…her King…and when finally, frantically, she arched herself to take him inside her, urging the ultimate intimacy, the wild, tremulous anticipation that seized her was ecstatically answered. He *was* the king of all men, the fullness of his power driving forward, possessing the path she'd most wanted him to take, the path that fused them together, and from it radiated a pulsing energy so intense, Sam was lost in a chaotic internal world, a place that shimmered to the beat of his will to be one with her, onwards, inwards, a deep rhythmic giving of himself, and she receiving the bliss of it, winding herself around him, holding on to the riveting sensation of travelling with him, the blind ecstasy of feeling him taking her further and further towards some sweet pinnacle of perfection.

It burst upon her in convulsive waves, his release, her release, great molten spasms of pleasure, and she clutched him to her, hugging the sense of absolute togetherness, wanting to feel totally immersed in his life-force, belonging to him and with him. His arms burrowed under her, hugging her just as possessively, no space between them, and he kissed her, their mouths melding, fulfilling the need to feel utterly deeply united, not wanting it to end.

This was it—she and Tommy—and surely nothing could ever part them now. The frustrations of the past…what did any of them matter? This was a new beginning—a beautiful, mutually felt beginning— that would cast its power over everything else.

Passion eased into a lovely sense of peace. Yet once their breathing became less laboured, and their hearts stopped racing, some cooler sanity trickled through the beautiful buzz of basking in their togetherness, bringing with it the realisation of where they were and where they should be…in attendance at the marquee until Miranda and Nathan took their leave.

"We can't just stay here, Tommy," Sam whispered.

"Mmmh…I'm willing to move…" He trailed his lips over hers "…as long as you promise…" soft, butterfly kisses "…this will be continued…when our duty's done."

"I promise," she answered on a rush of pure happiness.

He hitched himself up on his elbows and his eyes were deep, dark whirlpools of feeling, sucking away any doubts she might have about where they were going from here. "Having you means more to me than anyone's wedding. Tell me you believe that."

She wound her arms around his neck and smiled her implicit faith in the desire they shared. "I'm not about to let you go, Tommy. It feels as though I've been waiting all my life to have you."

He grinned. "You can say that again. For me."

Somehow that claim and the flashing dazzle of his smile came too quickly, too easily, niggling at her sense of rightness. "What about…" She instantly bit her lip, stopping the criticism and pushing it into the past where it belonged.

"The other women I've wasted my time with?" he picked up, his mouth twisting into an ironic grimace. "Something was always missing. But not this time. Not with you, Samantha. You're the woman with everything. Understand?" he softly appealed.

She wanted to accept it, had to, or what she'd just

felt with him would be diminished and *it had been perfect.* "Yes," she breathed on a contented sigh.

He nodded. "So keep this memory of us shining brighter than anything else until we're free to make it all we want. Okay?"

"Okay."

He pressed a feather-light finger to her lips, as though sealing her promise. "Then I guess we'd better get dressed and show our faces again."

Faces! She jack-knifed up, clapping her hands to her cheeks in dismay as Tommy rolled off the bed. "What will I do? I must have ruined all the make-up. And my hair!"

Having landed on his feet, Tommy turned and hauled her up to stand in his embrace, his grin a mile wide and his eyes sparkling warm approval. "Your hair is glorious just as it is. All tousled and sexy. And you don't need make-up. A bit of lipstick will make you respectable enough for the rest of the party."

"Are you sure it'll be all right?"

He laughed. "If you mean…will people take one look at us and know we've been making love…so what? I'm in the mood to trumpet it to the whole world."

Making love… Such wonderful, warming words! She thought fleetingly of Janice Findlay's remark about "feeling horny." Making love was something very different, and suddenly, like Tommy, she didn't care if the whole world knew. Though they didn't have to be told.

"Don't you dare brag, Tommy King!" she cautioned.

His eyebrows rose. "Are you asking me to hide what I feel for you?"

She flushed all over with pleasure. "No. I just meant…"

"What's private to us is private to us," he interpreted, touching his finger to her nose with tender indulgence. "Don't worry, Samantha. I'm not a crass playboy who parades his prowess with women. And what I have with you, my darling, belongs to me. No one else."

Sam sighed contentedly. His darling. She knew they should be getting dressed, getting back to the marquee, but when he kissed her, she just wanted to kiss him back, revelling in belonging to him like this, feeling securely wrapped in his warm strength, their naked bodies rubbing together, nothing coming between them.

It was Tommy who stopped it, growing aroused again and warning her, "If you don't want to be back on that bed…"

"We'd best get into our clothes," she finished with reluctant resignation.

"And tempt me not," he added wickedly.

She laughed and broke away, delighted she *could* tempt him. Her whole body tingled with the pleasure of his lustful watching as she busied herself, trying to look like a bridesmaid again. It felt very intimate, dressing themselves in full view of each other. Like a husband and wife, she thought, though they were only lovers, as yet.

Fortunately the beautician had left her an array of cosmetics so she could do a fair job of repairing her make-up. The only option with her hair was to brush it out, but since Tommy stood behind her, avidly running his fingers through the riot of curls, she didn't mind at all how it looked. He loved her hair, loved *her*... So what did anything else matter?

They left the house, hand in hand, and the night sky was full of brilliant stars. Sam had never felt so happy in her life. It was as though this night was made especially for her and Tommy, and even the sky was twinkling in celebration of their coming together.

As they strolled down the lawn, rollicking music was pumping out of the marquee, the guests were clearly getting boisterous, and Sam decided she and Tommy wouldn't have been missed at all. "What time is it?" she asked, realising the party mood had definitely elevated since they'd been gone.

He checked his watch. "Half an hour to go before Miranda and Nathan take their leave." He grinned at her. "We'll make the last show, no problem."

The reception was due to end at 1:00 a.m. Tomorrow morning there would be a big buffet breakfast, after which Miranda and Nathan would fly off to their honeymoon and the guests would make their way home.

Tommy squeezed her hand. "I want you to stay on here with me tomorrow. Will you?" His dark eyes simmered with promises yet to be spoken.

"Yes," she answered simply, discarding her earlier decision to fly home with her family.

They smiled at each other, their new understanding putting a golden glow around her heart.

"Well, well, look who's here, Greggie! Your little sister with her hair all tumbled, and Tommy the tom-cat wearing a satisfied smile," came the slurred and sexily suggestive voice of Janice Findlay.

It jerked Sam's gaze towards the clump of trees some ten metres from the marquee. From amongst the shadows Tommy's ex-lover lurched from a clinch with Greg, her black dress sagging over one shoulder, baring even more of her cleavage.

"Oh! Hi, Sam!" Greg acknowledged sheepishly, catching Janice around the waist to support her against him.

Tommy exhaled between his teeth but held his tongue, choosing to avoid any altercation. He quickened his pace, pulling Sam with him, intent on not getting involved with the necking couple. Sam dragged her feet, disturbed by her brother's attachment to Tommy's ex-lover.

"Go and get us a bottle of champagne, Greggie, darling," Janice urged. "Let's have our little orgy in style."

She patted his face indulgently, making Sam cringe inwardly, then gave him a shove towards the entrance to the marquee.

"Orgy and bubbly," he said, beaming at Sam and Tommy as he rambled off to do Janice's bidding.

"He's drunk," Sam whispered in some concern.

"So's she," Tommy muttered back.

"Should we do something?"

"Like what? They're both over the age of consent."

"Not so hot to trot now, Tommy?" Janice jeered, staggering towards them.

"She'll fall," Sam worried, stopping their progress towards the marquee.

"Got her, didn't you?" Janice went on. "Get 'em all. Snap o' your fingers. Fall like ninepins for a guy like you."

Tommy heaved an exasperated sigh. "Why don't you take better care of yourself, Janice?"

She laughed derisively. "You don't care. Left me knocked up and don't give a damn! Won't even give me time of day."

Shock punched into Sam's heart, smashing the golden glow to smithereens.

"I beg your pardon," Tommy bit out tersely.

"Preggers. Bun in the oven," Janice elaborated, jabbing an accusing finger at him. "Your little bastard, Tommy King."

Was it true? Sam darted a pleading glance at Tommy, willing it to be a spiteful lie.

"Oh, no it's not!" came his swift and vehement denial. "Don't think you can tie that on me, Janice, because I won't wear it. I took better care of you than you did yourself."

"Slipped up then, didn't you?"

"Not a chance."

Janice turned her drunken venom on Sam. "See what a sleaze he is? Bet he's got little bastards he won't own up to all around the Outback. Probably planted one in you tonight."

"That's enough!" The words cracked from Tommy like a bullwhip.

Janice rocked back and forward on her feet, her eyes rolling out of any steady focus.

Sam stood chilled to the bone, not knowing what to believe and too frightened to think about what any of this meant.

"I'd advise you to think very soberly about being sued for slander if you repeat what you've just said to anyone else," Tommy threatened, his voice as hard and cold as steel.

Janice's eyes narrowed on him. "I'm gonna slap a paternity suit on you."

"If you expect to gain anything from this, you're badly mistaken. What you need is some help before you make everything worse for yourself."

"If you're telling me to get an abortion..."

"I'm telling you you need counselling to get your life straightened out. You're off your head with alcohol half the time and don't know what you're doing."

"Do so!" Her chin went up and her face took on a smug look of animal cunning. "You got *her*." She sneered at Sam. "I got her brother. And maybe I'll load him with your child. How do you like them apples?"

"You reveal yourself for what you are, Janice," Tommy answered with biting distaste. "Nothing but a lying bitch!"

It turned her ugly. "Well, you didn't mind lying with me, lover. And Greg Connelly's lining up for it." She sliced a look of contempt at Sam. "Neither

of them are any better than me, so take that on board,
little sister.''

''Got the bubbly!'' Greg called triumphantly,
drawing their attention. He was waving the bottle
over his head as he ambled towards them. ''Glasses,
too,'' he added, holding them up like trophies.

''What a good boy you are!'' Janice drooled sickeningly. Then tossing a venomous, ''Stuff, you
two!'' at Tommy and Sam, she swayed her way over
to Greg, threw her arms around his waist and fondled
him back to the cover of the trees, giggling and teasing in a pointed demonstration of how on top of the
game she was.

''I'm Greg's big sister, not his little one,'' Sam
corrected anxiously. ''I should stop this before he
gets into trouble.''

''Leave them be! He won't thank you for it,''
Tommy answered tersely.

''But...''

''He's a man.'' Angry eyes shot daggers into hers.
''Haven't you learnt anything?''

It took Sam's breath away. However faulty her
judgment about men might have been in the past,
was this fair comment when her brother was being
manipulated into a possible scandal? A very female
rage started burning, Janice's snide words beating
through her brain—*neither of them are any better
than me.*

It was Tommy who had started this, blithely falling into an ill-judged affair with Janice Findlay,
seeking satisfaction without caring about conse-

quences. Her eyes blazed back into his as her own fierce resentments erupted.

"Am I supposed to respect a man who blinds himself to what he's taking on for the sake of a bit of easy sex?"

His face stiffened. "You respect his right to make his own choices."

"So how do you like your choice now, Tommy? What if Janice is pregnant to you?"

"She's not."

"How can you be sure?"

"You heard her!" he flung back impatiently. "This is nothing but a malicious tit for tat because I chose to be with you rather than pick up with her again."

Could the whole nasty encounter be dismissed so easily?

Tommy dropped her hand and grabbed her upper arms. Sam thought he was going to shake her, but his fingers merely pressed urgently into her soft flesh. "Are you going to let her win?" he demanded. "Can't you see it's what she wants...to spoil what there is between us?"

Sam sucked in a deep breath. Doubts were swirling through her mind. A new beginning, a new beginning, she recited frantically, trying to hold on to what she had felt before Janice had injected her poison. Tommy was hers now. A dream come true. But was it ever possible to be free of past actions? They had such long tentacles, and the longest one of all would be a child Tommy had fathered with another woman.

Anguished by the possibility, she asked again, "How can you be sure she's not pregnant to you?"

He huffed his vexation with the question. "It's been over three months since I was last with her. Why wait until today to deliver the news?"

Sam frowned. The timing did seem wrong.

"Janice was peeved by my earlier brush-off and determined to do maximum damage to us," Tommy argued, anger still pumping from him. "It's as simple as that, Samantha."

Was it?

"If she's in an alcoholic fog half the time, maybe she didn't realise her condition until very recently," Sam reasoned. "She could have thought today might be a good day to approach you on it."

"My brother's wedding day?" Tommy reminded her, his voice laced with acid scepticism.

"She might have wanted to test how approachable you were," Sam argued, thinking it couldn't be an easy thing to tell a man who'd dumped you he was the father of an unplanned child.

And Tommy had cut Janice dead.

Wouldn't that give rise to vengeful impulses?

"You're worrying over nothing," he insisted dismissively. "Apart from the time factor, I always used protection with Janice. With every woman I've ever been with, in fact."

Not with me! The memory sliced straight through his argument with devastating force. He hadn't used protection with her. Hadn't thought of it. Neither of them had.

''There's absolutely no chance she's pregnant to me. I swear it, Samantha.''

But how could she believe him? Might there not have been a time with Janice when he hadn't stopped to think? When he, too, was the worse for drink after a party?

''Now put it out of your mind,'' he commanded. ''It's not worth another thought, I promise you.'' He released her arms and drew her into a hug at his side, walking her forward towards the entrance to the marquee. ''Time we made our appearance and checked in with Nathan and Miranda,'' he said with determined authority.

That, at least, was true.

Sam let herself be carried along with him but it felt as though the stars had winked out and a dark cloud had settled over their future together.

Tommy hadn't used protection tonight.

Was that a first with him...because he was with her? Because it was different from his usual playboy affairs? Because she was the one woman he really wanted to spend his life with?

Sam wanted to believe it.

She wanted to believe Janice was lying.

But what if she wasn't?

CHAPTER ELEVEN

SHE WASN'T convinced.

Tommy knew it and cursed himself for being all kinds of a fool. He could feel fine little tremors running through Samantha's body and her submission to his lead, to the closeness he pressed on her with his hug, had nothing to do with wanting to be with him, more the aftermath of shock.

Janice's malevolent spite had broken the intimate understanding between them.

No, damn it! *He* had. For having the monumental stupidity to get involved with Janice Findlay in the first place. And not being kinder to her today. The urge to protect and pursue what was developing between him and Samantha had overriden a more tactful rejection, but he sure as hell was reaping the consequences now.

Then to have lashed back at Samantha about respecting a man's choice…utter madness! In the light of what had happened tonight—how he felt with her—*he* couldn't respect any of his previous choices, so why should she? Especially his affair with Janice.

Though she wasn't—couldn't be—pregnant to him. He didn't have to give that a second thought. But how was he going to get the doubt out of Samantha's head?

The truth was he'd been a blind idiot all these

years, fooling around with women who didn't hold
a candle to Samantha Connelly, and those ghosts
were swirling with a vengeance right now. Why
should she take his word that he'd always been responsible about contraception? She was probably remembering he hadn't used anything with her tonight.
The moment had been too big to think of precautions. Did she understand how much it meant? That
it was driven by needs that went beyond the merely
physical?

How could he prove it when she'd just been
slapped in the face by his undeniable sexual intimacy
with Janice Findlay? And he'd topped that by more
or less approving Greg's pursuit of it, too. And why?
Because he'd wanted Janice out of *his* hair, wanted
to get Samantha away from her. No noble ideals
about the right to choose in that decision!

He stopped, riven by guilt. They'd reached the entrance to the marquee and the party beckoned, but he
had to show Samantha he did have some decency.
"You go on inside," he said. "I'll find Greg and
have a word with him. Sort things out."

Slowly, she turned her gaze up to his, her beautiful
blue eyes clouded with painful confusion. "You
said…"

"I was wrong. If Janice is making Greg a scape-
goat for my sins, he ought to know about it."

"He probably won't thank you," she acknowledged with a wobbly grimace.

"Better an informed choice than an uninformed
one," he conceded dryly. He reached up and stroked
her cheek in tender reassurance. "I'm sorry for let-

ting my anger at Janice's accusation spill over onto you. It is a lie, Samantha, so please…don't let it come between us.''

Relief…hope…uncertainty….

''Save the last dance for me,'' he said with persuasive force, willing her to have more trust and confidence in him by the time he returned to her side.

Sam didn't move forward as Tommy left her. She felt incapable of making any decision about what she should do. At least the worry about her brother was eased and she was grateful for that.

She stared blankly at the party scene in front of her, too churned up inside to feel drawn to it. Her mind kept jagging over what had just transpired. People did do and say mean things out of spite and frustration, she reflected, especially when pride was wounded and envy was eating away at one's heart. She was guilty of it herself with Tommy. Maybe Janice did just want to do damage and it was wrong to let her win.

Her head was beginning to ache and the noise level around her didn't help. The drummer of the band was giving a virtuoso performance. It felt as though he was beating her brain…boom, crash, rat-a-tat-tat! She wished he'd stop.

''Sam?'' A hand on her arm…Elizabeth…concern in her eyes. ''Are you all right?''

She managed a wan smile. ''Bad headache.''

''Ah…were the pins in your hair too tight?''

Sam gratefully seized on the excuse. ''I guess I

wasn't used to them. I took them out. I hope Miranda won't mind.''

Elizabeth nodded to the dance floor, dryly commenting, ''I doubt Miranda is seeing anything but Nathan right now. They'll be making their departure soon.''

''Yes, I knew I had to be here for that.''

''If you feel really ill…''

''No. It's all right.''

A searching look showed doubt but she didn't press the issue. ''I thought I saw Tommy come in with you.''

''Yes. There was a bit of trouble outside. He decided he'd better sort it out, but he'll be right back. In time for…''

''What trouble?''

''It's nothing really,'' Sam hastily assured her. ''I was worried about Greg. He's…well…under the weather…and Tommy's gone to help him. A man-to-man talk. That's all.''

''Ah!''

Elizabeth's satisfied nod was sweet relief to Sam. She quickly changed the subject. ''We met Christabel Valdez earlier. Jared seems to be very struck on her.''

The all too shrewd gaze travelled back to the dance floor, targeting the son who worked with her and the woman who was keeping her distance from him even as they danced. Jared's face was lit with warm pleasure in his partner. Christabel's expressed a lively interest. Whether the interest was polite or deeply personal was impossible to tell.

"What do you think of her?"

The question surprised Sam. Elizabeth King was the kind of person who usually kept her own counsel, though she had spoken very personally to her earlier today. Flinching away from that memory and its on-the-mark advice, Sam concentrated hard on what was being asked, flattered that her opinion might be valued by Tommy's mother.

It was on the tip of her tongue to say Christabel was definitely not of Janice Findlay's ilk, but she bit back the too revealing remark. "I think she's a very together person inside. What she does is for herself. I liked her," she simply said.

"Yes. It's as though she's deliberately limited her needs," Elizabeth mused slowly.

Or perhaps Christabel's needs were simple. She seemed to have led a complicated life, moving from country to country, possibly shedding everything but the bare essentials to her along the way. That made sense to Sam. Although being alone, far from any family seemed a strange choice. On the other hand Christabel might be like Miranda, with no family at all.

"Do *you* like her?" It was the more important question, Sam thought, if Jared was seriously attracted to the beautiful Brazilian. He was very close to his mother, in every sense, and would surely want her approval of his choice of partner.

"There's nothing not to like. Which makes me wonder why she works so hard at it." The cryptic remark was followed by a dismissive shrug. "It's up to Jared to work it out. If he wants to enough."

Respect for choices, Sam thought. Had Elizabeth drummed that into her sons? It was a fair philosophy to live by, as long as people were prepared to accept and shoulder the consequences of those choices, because there was no escape from them. There was no clean slate.

"Christabel has a child."

The quiet statement of fact hit a mountain of raw places in Sam. A child that was not Jared's, Elizabeth meant. And what might *she* be faced with—a child of Tommy's that was not hers!

She closed her eyes, unbearably pained by the thought. How could he walk away from that? A child...a little boy...or girl...carrying his genes. It would never feel right...never!

Please, God, don't let it be true, she prayed fervently.

"Is the headache worse?"

Elizabeth's anxious question jolted her eyes open again. "No," she denied before realising she would have to explain. "Just thinking," she added, her mind working feverishly to get back on track with Elizabeth's. "It must be hard being a single mother."

"Yes. Though it didn't start that way." She looked back at the dance floor, watching the woman they were discussing. "Christabel was married. She's a widow."

Widowed...maybe she was still grieving for her first love, which could explain the distance she now kept with men. Even attractive men. Christabel could be a one-man woman, like herself with Tommy— always an empty place that no one else could fill.

Poor Jared, if that was the case. He could be travelling a path to nowhere.

"Is Christabel's child a boy or a girl?" she asked, wondering how Jared was handling that situation—a child by another man. At least, the biological father was no longer physically there. Janice would be.

"A little girl." Another flat statement of fact, no expression in her voice—judgment reserved.

The child would never be a blood granddaughter to Elizabeth, Sam thought. Whereas if Janice had Tommy's child, it would be a King, and never would Elizabeth turn her back on any grandchild of Lachlan's. It would always have a place in the family. And rightly so. The next generation…

Oh, it was wrong, wrong, wrong. A child should be born of a love like Miranda's and Nathan's. Whatever Tommy had felt with Janice was gone. Yet such unplanned births did happen, and it was impossible to ignore a child's needs, if one had any conscience at all.

"Does Christabel's daughter get on with Jared?" Sam asked, not really imagining otherwise. Maybe that was one need to be filled and Jared had a naturally kind nature.

"I don't know." There was an odd distance in Elizabeth's voice. "I haven't even seen the child. Christabel keeps her personal life very private."

She's worried, Sam thought. Worried about where this might lead for Jared. And I'm worried about whether I can share Tommy's future. He cares about me, she fiercely assured herself. He cared enough to look after Greg for me. Or did he go to have a more private word with Janice, out of my hearing?

The music stopped but no one left the dance floor. The couples just chatted together, waiting for the next number to begin. "This will be the last dance," Elizabeth murmured. "I hope Tommy won't be long." She swung her gaze back to Sam, sharply inquiring. "Was it bad trouble?"

"Still here, waiting for me!" Tommy's voice seemed to explode into the highly sensitive moment, sweeping away the question just as he swept Sam away from his mother, his highly charged energy an electrifying force that nothing was going to stop. "Last dance, Mum," he tossed back at her, and as though the band heard him and took their cue from him, they started up a slow jazz waltz.

The moment they stepped on the dance floor, Tommy wrapped Sam in his arms, pressing her so close the burning heat and steel muscle of his body was stamped on hers, like a brand of ownership he was determined on maintaining, no matter what. And the painful muddle in Sam's mind melted into a pool of wanting that went so deep, her arms simply wound themselves around his neck and locked him to her. This dance was hers, she thought fiercely. Whatever came afterwards, this last dance with Tommy was *hers*.

He didn't speak. She didn't, either. Their bodies did all the talking, clinging to the sense of togetherness, silently recalling and revelling in the intimate knowledge they'd given each other, their legs interweaving with a sexual awareness that was intensely erotic. The need—the desire—to be with him again—always be with him—was overwhelming.

Her fingers stroked the back of his neck, compelled to touch. The skin was damp there. So were his curls. Had he been running to get back to her, sweating on it? She could feel his heart thumping against his chest, his cheek rubbing against her hair, yearning emanating from every part of him, yearning for her. She was sure of it.

As she snuggled her head closer to his, she caught sight of Elizabeth watching them, smiling at them, happy satisfaction written all over her face. It was as though she was beaming at them... This is right...how it should be with these two. And Sam thought of how Elizabeth had spoken to her about Christabel, like a mother to a daughter, sharing a confidence about family matters...Tommy's mother trusting her and the long link of knowledge and understanding they shared.

The realisation crept up on her...Elizabeth *wanted* the link. That's why she had spoken so bluntly before the wedding, wanting both she and Tommy to leap over the barriers they had set between themselves. Had she sensed all along they had always really wanted each other?

Both of them such fools, if what Tommy had insisted was true—that she was the one special woman for him. And it had felt true. Still felt true, now she was in his arms again. So it had to work out right, didn't it? Somehow.

Sam shut down her mind and gave herself up to the pleasure of feeling...being with Tommy...the deliciously sensual harmony of their bodies moving in unison…music driving their feet, the rhythm of it pulsing through them…and this man she loved holding her as though he wasn't whole without her, his breath in her hair.

She wanted the dance to go on and on forever, feeding the dream she had fostered all these years…a partnership welded by love, unbreakable. The music stopped, but Tommy didn't let her go. She didn't move from him, either. They remained locked together, uncaring what anyone else thought.

"Ladies and gentlemen…that was the last dance," the master of ceremonies declared. "If you'll now form a circle to wish the bride and groom farewell…"

Tommy's chest rose and fell on a long sigh. "Ready to join the hordes?"

"I guess so," she murmured, reluctant to face reality again.

It was Elizabeth's voice that forced them into action. "Sam, here's your bouquet."

Bridesmaid! *Her* duty to look after the bouquets. Sam jerked out of Tommy's embrace. Elizabeth was smiling at them, holding both her bouquet and Miranda's. "Sorry. Forgot what I should be doing," Sam rushed out as she accepted hers.

"I'll give this to Miranda," Elizabeth said indulgently, her dark eyes sparkling pleasure in Sam's forgetfulness. "You and Tommy join up with Jared near the exit. It will get the guests moving."

Tommy retained an arm around her waist as they stepped off the dance floor. Sam quickly scanned the crowd, wondering if Greg and Janice had returned to the marquee, inwardly agitated at the thought that one or other of them might cause an unpleasant scene during the leave-taking. She couldn't see either of them.

"They're not here," Tommy murmured, attuned to her concern.

She darted an anxious glance at him. "You spoke to Greg?"

He shook his head. "I couldn't find them. I went back to where we last saw them, looked around, called out. They must have slipped away somewhere else, or didn't want to be found."

In a way it was a relief. Greg's pride would have been hurt. Angry and drunk, he might have thrown a punch at Tommy. Besides, she didn't want to think about Janice and what might have been said. Easier to postpone that issue right now.

"I just hope they don't blunder back inside before Nathan and Miranda leave," she muttered.

"I doubt they'll return at all," came the dry retort.

He was probably right, given their intention of indulging themselves in a private orgy. Though it did leave things unresolved. On the other hand, how could the pregnancy question *be* resolved unless Janice had medical proof with her, and if she'd had that, she would undoubtedly have waved it under Tommy's nose.

A lie.

A spoiling lie.

Sam didn't want what she now had with Tommy spoiled. Not tonight. Not any night. Besides, it wouldn't be morally wrong to…to go back to bed with him. It wasn't as though Tommy was married to Janice or even attached to her.

Except…would she feel really good about it, with the phantom of Janice's pregnancy hovering in her mind?

Sam silently wrestled with this dilemna as the leave-taking ceremony proceeded, Nathan and Miranda circling around everyone, kissing, hugging, shaking hands. There was much merriment over comments and advice tossed at them and she smiled and laughed with everyone else, doing her best to keep up a happy, well-wishing facade.

Since the family were gathered at the exit, with Sam next to Tommy, they were the last on the farewell circuit. Nathan gave her a big-brotherly hug and whispered, "You've got Tommy lassoed. Hold him down, Sam."

She blushed as he grinned knowingly at her before passing on to his brother. She didn't hear what he said to Tommy because Miranda was kissing her cheek and murmuring, "Thanks for being my friend, Sam. And good luck with Tommy. Hang in there."

Slightly dazed by their personal comments, Sam watched them complete the full round with Elizabeth. The band struck up a jazzy rendition of "Here they go, here they go, here they go…" and the guests sang and applauded loudly as the bride and groom slipped out into the night…their wedding night.

People milled around in the marquee, continuing conversations, finishing drinks, collecting belongings. The exodus towards arranged accommodations didn't start until well after Nathan and Miranda would have reached the homestead. Sam and Tommy were continually caught up with various groups of guests who wanted to express their pleasure in the events of the day.

Sam smiled and chatted and agreed with everyone, conscious that Tommy was at his charming best in his responses. He gave no sign of being at all perturbed by the nasty contretemps with Janice. It seemed, as far as he was concerned, that page had been turned and the book was closed on it.

Hold him down…hang in there… The advice kept echoing through her mind, pushing back the doubts and fears that had so tormented her. She had the man she loved at her side. It would be terribly self-defeating to indicate in any way that she didn't trust his word. It *had* been different with her tonight with so much feeling running between them. That was why he hadn't thought to use protection.

"Samantha…" It was her mother, glancing around the marquee worriedly as she asked, "…have you seen Greg anywhere?"

"He left earlier," Tommy answered smoothly.

Her mother frowned. "He should have stayed to farewell Nathan and Miranda."

"Tommy!" The loud hail distracted them.

"Here!" Tommy called, holding up a signalling arm as he turned to see who wanted him.

Jim Hoskins, the head park ranger from The Bungle Bungles, signalled back, then shoved his way through the guests who'd gathered close to the marquee exit, his haste transmitting a sense of urgency that spelled trouble. An instant tension held them still and silent for the few moments it took for him to reach them.

"An accident," he stated quickly. "Jeep hit a tree next to the road to the resort. Doc Hawkins is there. He and his wife were in my vehicle. Sent me back for you. Says they'll have to be flown to hospital."

"How many hurt?" Tommy rapped out.

"Two. Both unconscious. Doc suspects internal injuries and it must have happened some time ago. We didn't hear the crash. We just came upon them."

"Who is it? Who's hurt?" Sam asked, knowing a lack of identification would spread anxious alarm through all the guests.

Jim had been concentrating on Tommy, but now he looked at her, his eyes pained. "It's your brother, Sam. It's Greg. And Janice Findlay."

CHAPTER TWELVE

SHOCK gripped Sam's heart. She instantly fought it away. There was no time for shock, no time for anything but doing what had to be done. There was no ambulance service to call out here in the Kimberly cattle country. Whatever action was needed had to be organised here and now.

"Mum..." She addressed her sharply, jolting her out of shock. It was her firstborn son—Sam's closest brother—but that couldn't be dwelled on. "Would you find Dad and Pete? Get them together and...Jim..." She swung back to him. "...did you drive your vehicle down to the marquee?"

He nodded.

"You'll take my family to the accident site, won't you?"

"Sure!"

"And the Findlays," Tommy instructed. "Ask my mother to break the news to them, Jim."

"Right!" he agreed.

Tommy looked at Sam, his dark eyes intensely focused. "We'll need two planes. Nathan's, where the seats can be removed for cargo. And a six-seater."

"Dad's. He parked it near the hangar. No problem. I'll go to the airstrip, get them ready."

"You'll fly?"

"It's night flying. There's no one better."

A flash of admiration. "No one. I'll collect the station foreman, organise a stretcher team and the table-top truck to transport them to the airstrip. We'll send men to take the seats out of Nathan's plane. I'll fly the injured in. You fly the families. Okay?"

"Okay."

He squeezed her arm and was gone, striding off to take charge of the most immediate transportation operation. Jim was already making a beeline for Elizabeth. Sam swung her gaze back to check on her mother. She hadn't moved.

"Mum, can you manage? Do you want me to get Dad?"

Her glazed eyes clicked into focus, anguish pouring from them. "I'll do it. It's just…Greg…"

Sam's heart contracted again. She shut off a threatening whirl of emotion. "I know. But he needs us, Mum," she said with urgent emphasis.

"Yes." Her mother visibly pulled herself together. "I'll see you at the plane, Samantha. Your father left the keys in it."

"He always does."

"Go and do what you have to."

She went, driving legs that felt like jelly into purposeful movement. Jared joined up with her as she left the marquee. "Tommy said to accompany you, lend whatever help you need," he said succinctly.

Help and authority, Sam realised. "We need to commandeer one of the catering vans. Save running up the hill to other transport."

One of the vans roared off as they raced around

to the side of the marquee. "Tommy on his way. You two think alike," Jared noted, just as a waiter met them with keys to the other van. "Thanks, mate. I'll drive, Sam."

She veered towards the passenger side. Jared was already gunning the engine as she jumped in and slammed the door. The airstrip was on the other side of the homestead, beyond the machinery sheds. Jared wasted no time in getting them there.

"I'll get Dad's plane and taxi it out to the runway," Sam instructed him. "If you'll supervise the seat removal in Nathan's..."

"Sure! Are you okay?"

"Yes," she answered with unflinching determination.

And so she was, while ever action was required—cool, calm, efficient and effective, making no mistakes. The injured couple were carefully loaded into Nathan's plane. Tommy and Doc Hawkins took off with them. The families boarded Robert Connelly's, and Sam took off with them.

There was nothing she could do about Marta Findlay's hysterical weeping and wailing over her daughter's possible injuries except block it out as best she could. She was grateful for her own family's silent forebearance and support during the flight. They understood this was a waiting time they all had to get through.

The Kununurra airport and hospital had been alerted to deal with the emergency situation. Ambulances and other vehicles were waiting. Radio contact was constant. The moment Tommy's plane cleared the lit runway, Sam landed hers. Even so, the ambulances were already gone and Doc Hawkins with them by the time her passengers had alighted. Tommy was waiting to direct them to their transport.

Sam's father gripped his arm. "How are they?"

"Alive," Tommy assured him.

Sam saw her mother sag with relief and didn't realise she was sagging herself. Tommy stepped past her parents and wrapped her in his arms. "It's okay. You did it," he murmured, stroking her back comfortingly, injecting his own powerhouse of energy into her fading strength.

He directed both families to a waiting minibus which would take them straight to the hospital, then led Sam to his own personal vehicle, parked behind the KingAir office that handled the charter services. Her legs had gone to jelly again and she was grateful for the arm hooked around her waist, holding her up, keeping her going. She felt terribly tired, all of a sudden.

Tommy opened the passenger door and lifted her onto the seat. He even did the safety belt up for her. Strange...all these years of being so fiercely independent. Now Tommy was taking care of her and she didn't mind a bit. No pride involved. It was easy to simply accept he meant her well, easy to let him be the strong one, no competition at all.

He stroked her cheek tenderly before closing the door, his dark eyes locking briefly with hers, transmitting caring concern. "You can rest, Samantha. It's all up to others now."

Yes, it was, she thought. Her part was over. Yet

as the steely control she had held on her mind slid
away, the feelings she had been holding at bay
crowded in. It was all very well to be satisfied she
had carried off the positive action needed *after* the
accident. What about *before*…when she had done
nothing to stop what should have been stopped?

Where did responsibility begin and end? She was
older than Greg. But how could she have known he'd
be stupid enough to drive a jeep when he was rolling
drunk? Or had it been Janice behind the wheel?

"Who was driving?" she asked as Tommy settled
on the seat beside her.

He looked at her, a sad gravity on his face. "I'd
say Janice," he answered quietly. "They were both
thrown out of the jeep on impact, but Janice was on
the driver's side."

She shook her head at the foolish recklessness in-
duced by too much alcohol. And Greg was no better,
going along with the ride, letting a woman who
wasn't fit to drive take control of a vehicle, especially
an open jeep that offered no protection. It was totally
reprehensible. Utter madness. And for what? The
promise of sex on tap for the rest of the night?

How highly did men rate sex, she thought bitterly.
Risking life and limb for it seemed crazy to her, but
at Greg's level of intoxication, maybe he had felt
invincible…having what he wanted virtually held out
to him on a plate. Had it been like that with
Tommy…just going with the urge wherever it led,
regardless of consequences?

She didn't realise her hands were tightly clenched
in her lap until Tommy reached across and covered

one warmly with his own. "Don't torment yourself with *if onlys,*" he gently advised. "More than likely, speaking to them would have made no difference to the course they chose. And *they* chose it, Samantha."

"Don't ask me to respect that choice, Tommy," she flashed at him. "Drinking and driving…"

"Is stupid, yes. But neither of us was there to stop it."

"I should have spoken. Should have told Greg he was nothing but a mark to Janice."

"How do you know she wasn't just a mark to him, Samantha? A one-night stand he relished having."

The quiet but pointed argument churned up all her earlier bad feelings. "Was that what she was to you?"

He grimaced. "Is that relevant? Whatever my affair with Janice was based on…it's in the past."

"*She* brought it up tonight."

He stiffened. "You want to lay blame at my door? It's all my fault? Is that what you're thinking?"

"I don't know how well the shoe fits, Tommy. Only you know that," she retorted, too worked up to monitor what she said.

"I see." He removed his hand. The warmth died, replaced by chilling pride as he added, "You don't trust my word."

He didn't wait for a reply. Grim-faced, he turned away, switched on the ignition, revved the engine, and accelerated out of the parking lot.

Sam closed her eyes, savagely berating herself for doing precisely what she'd told herself not to do. There could be no happy future with Tommy if she didn't trust him. Why was she plunging down this destructive path? How stupid could she get? He'd answered all the stuff about Janice. Raking over it again only drove this horrible wedge between them and she didn't want it there. She wanted *him* and how he'd been towards her a few minutes ago...kind, caring, supportive.

The dark tension in the Range Rover as they drove to the hospital tore at her nerves. Guilt added its painful claws. She should be thinking of Greg, willing her brother to pull through, not fighting with Tommy over blame or anything else. Besides, it wasn't his fault. He hadn't drunk himself silly. He hadn't got behind the wheel of that jeep. He hadn't smashed it into a tree.

He had, in fact, gone to try to sort things out with Greg and Janice, and they might very well have deliberately ignored his calling out to them. She had absolutely no reason to cast Tommy as the prime mover of this wretched string of events. What went on inside other people's minds was driven by many things. And her mind, at the present moment, was a mess.

At this early hour of the morning, the parking lot at the hospital was sparsely occupied. Tommy drove straight to a bay near the emergency entrance. The minibus which had come in ahead of them was empty, both families already inside the building, waiting for news. Sam's heart clenched at the prospect of that wait. Tommy was right. There was nothing more they could do, but that knowledge didn't allay the fear of what might be happening.

The Range Rover came to a halt. As Tommy switched off the engine, a great welling of urgency turned Sam towards him. "I'm sorry." She reached out to touch him, to draw his attention to her. "It was wrong of me to…to…" She shook her head in anguish over her erratic emotions. "It's not your fault. I know it's not. I'm sorry I…"

"It's okay," he broke in gruffly. "I'm sorry, too. We've come through a lot in the past twelve hours…feels like a lifetime." His mouth curved into a wry smile. "Hard to balance a whole lifetime and get a perfect outcome when the factors are confused by other things."

She released a long, tautly held breath. "I want to trust you," she whispered, pleading his understanding.

He nodded. "Give it a chance, Samantha. Give *us* a chance."

"I want that, too. I've wanted it for so long, Tommy, it scares me. Like it can't really be true. Like something's going to smash it or take it away or make it wrong."

He undid his safety belt and leaned over, cupping her face, his eyes blazing with an intensity of feeling that demanded she focus on him…only him. "Nothing can make this feel anything but right," he murmured, and kissed her…kissed her with such passionate fervour, everything else was driven out of her mind.

She responded with a desperate hunger for the dream to come true…she and Tommy bonded together by love for the rest of their lives. The heat of desire swept away the cold reality of where they were, and why. This was a life-force that needed affirmation here and now, needed nurturing and growth. For a little while the dark clouds of the night were banished and only the two of them existed, pouring positive energy into each other.

"Hold on to the thought of us, Samantha," Tommy commanded huskily, his lips lifting away from hers. "I'm here for you. Understand? Whatever else happens this night, promise me…"

He stroked the tumbled curls away from her brow. She opened her eyes, the banked passion in his voice alerting all her senses to the import of what he wanted of her. Their kiss had re-energised every nerve and flooded her with warmth and hope and faith in their feeling for each other.

"Promise me…" he repeated, his dark eyes glowing like fiery coals "…you won't *let* anything get in the way of sharing with me all we can share."

"My family might need me," she reminded him.

"Through this crisis, yes," he agreed. "And I'll support you all I can. I meant for you to keep believing there's more to what we started today, Samantha. Much more."

She sighed, her heart warmed by the reassurance that he really did see a very definite future in their relationship. "I'm here for you, Tommy," she blurted out. "I always have been."

And that was the honest truth.

He sighed, too. "That's good to hear." With a wry little smile, he asked, "Do you want to go in now?"

No, she didn't. She wanted to stay with him. But

she quelled the selfish need and answered, "They'll be expecting me."

He nodded, unfastened her seat belt, and swivelled to alight from his side of the Range Rover. Sam didn't wait for him to open her door. More conscious now that her parents would welcome the comfort of her presence, perhaps even anxious for her to join them, she swung herself out of the vehicle, closed the door and was relieved to find her legs performing as firmly as they should.

Hand in hand, she and Tommy walked into the hospital, the bouyant feeling of being harmoniously linked with him unshaken by the clinical surroundings and what had to be faced. They found her family and the Findlays in a facilities room where mobile patients could go and make a cup of tea or coffee. It contained a kitchenette, dining setting, a couple of sofas, a bookcase and a television set.

Pete and her parents were seated at the table, hunched over coffee mugs and a plate of untouched biscuits. Ron and Marta Findlay were huddled on one of the sofas, Marta's head resting limply on her husband's shoulder, both of them looking totally worn out. They were all still dressed in their wedding finery, an incongrous touch, given the grim situation.

"Heard any news?" her father asked Tommy.

"No."

"They took them for X-rays."

"We should know something soon then."

Sam sat next to her mother and Tommy moved on to speak to the Findlays. Pete got up to make both of them coffee, glad to have something to do. The waiting was oppressive. It made any attempt at conversation feel stilted, forced. Speculation was futile. Until they knew the extent of Greg's and Janice's injuries, no plans could be made. Everything hinged on hearing something definite.

Tommy mentioned that accommodation had been booked for both families at the Kununurra Lakeside Resort. This information evoked grateful murmurs. Rest would be needed, sooner or later, and returning to King's Eden was not an option tonight. Sheer fatigue was already casting its pall over the tension of waiting, eyes drooping, bodies slumping.

At last Doc Hawkins appeared, his entrance acting like an electric shock, jolting them into a hyper alertness. He was in his fifties, grey-haired, lean and rather sharp-featured, but he had kind eyes and a gentle manner that inspired confidence.

"They'll mend. Both of them," he announced, instantly relieving them of their worst fears.

The tense stillness was broken. Everyone stirred, stretching tired and aching muscles.

"So what are the problems?" Sam's father asked, rising to his feet, ready to meet them head-on.

"Well, no cranial fracture or spinal damage, but they are both badly concussed. That will need watching for a couple of days."

"Greg's left leg?"

"Broken in two places. He also has three cracked ribs. No serious internal injuries, but quite a lot of deep bruising. The scalp wound needed stitching. Other cuts and abrasions have been dressed. He'll be sore and sorry for himself for quite some time but the healing should not be complicated.''

''Thank God!'' Sam's mother whispered, her eyes welling with tears. ''Can we see him?''

''Shortly. Though don't expect to speak to him.''

''What about Janice?'' Ron Findlay demanded gruffly, also on his feet, wanting action.

Doc Hawkins turned to him with a sympathetic grimace. ''I'm sorry to say it will be a longer haul for your daughter. Apart from the superficial injuries, her right arm and hip are broken. There is some internal damage. Nothing life-threatening to her but...''

''But what?'' Marta demanded shrilly.

In a quiet, grave voice, Doc Hawkins delivered the bombshell that was to shatter the soothing effect of his previous words.

''There was nothing we could do to save it. The bleeding...'' He shook his head sadly, sighed and simply stated, ''She lost the baby.''

CHAPTER THIRTEEN

BABY!

For a moment, Tommy's mind went blank with disbelief. Shocked incredulity was swiftly followed by a violent inner surge of protest. It wasn't true. It couldn't be true. He pushed up from his chair at the table, needing to face Doc Hawkins, needing to refute what he'd claimed. His whole body was in revolt against the idea that Janice *had been pregnant.*

"What baby?" Marta Findlay cried in bewilderment.

It snapped his head towards her. Marta's face reflected his own mental turmoil as she struggled up from the sofa, pulling at her husband's arm in an agitated need for answers she could understand.

"Ron…Ron…do you know anything about this?"

"No, I don't." Having gathered his distressed wife into a comforting hug, he frowned at the doctor. "You say Janice was pregnant?"

"No doubt about it," came the firm reply.

Not to me, Tommy thought fiercely. He'd used protection. It had to be to someone else…someone careless, and probably as drunk as Janice, just as Greg had been tonight.

"She was about three months along," Doc Hawkins added.

Tommy felt as though someone had kicked him in

the stomach. *Three months!* Even as his mind fought to deny it, the spectre of Janice carrying *his* child clung, and the recollection of everything he'd said to her today hit him like a series of sickening blows. What if the protection he'd used had failed? Nothing was a hundred percent certain.

"Three months," Ron Findlay repeated, struggling to take in the fact that his daughter had not confided in him or her mother.

"She should have told us," Marta wailed.

"I'm sorry it's come as a shock," Doc Hawkins said sympathetically. "I didn't realise…" He sighed, grimaced. "She probably wanted to work things out with the father. Privately."

Why would Janice wait until today to tell him, Tommy argued to himself, still pushing away the unacceptable. He *wasn't* the father. It felt totally wrong to him. There had to be another answer. Yet…if he was wrong…

"Three months…" Ron Findlay frowned over the time span. His gaze suddenly lifted and targeted Tommy. Without a doubt, Janice had not kept their affair a secret. Awareness of the connection and calculation on it were coming straight at him. "Do you know anything about this, Tommy?"

His heart clenched. Impossible to deny knowledge. And it would damn him…damn him in everyone's eyes. Especially Samantha's. She'd heard it all from Janice's own mouth and she would no longer believe his defence, not in the face of this medical evidence.

He heard her chair scrape out from the table. He swung to face her, desperate to stave off a rift between them. She stood up and there was a terrible dignity in her stiffened, upright stance. She looked straight at him and he knew she was in retreat from what they had shared tonight. Her blue eyes were glassy, projecting a flat challenge.

Tell them or I will.

To her it was a matter of integrity. No escape from it. No excuse for ducking what she would see as *his* responsibility. He had to bear the weight of Janice's accusation now, whether it was true or not. By cutting Janice off and branding her a liar, he was probably already an irredeemable skunk in Samantha's eyes.

He turned back to the Findlays, automatically squaring his shoulders, knowing he had to deal with the situation. "Janice told me earlier tonight that she was pregnant," he stated flatly. "Quite frankly, I didn't believe her. I thought she was playing games."

"Games!" Marta repeated shrilly, her eyes sweeping him with scathing contempt. "More likely it didn't suit you to believe her."

"When was this?" Ron demanded, his gaze flicking to Samantha, the inference clear that he'd observed how closely they'd stayed together throughout the wedding. "When precisely did Janice tell you?"

The timing damned him even further, inevitably linking him to what followed, Janice going off with Greg, the accident.

"Excuse me, please," Samantha broke in. "Doc, I think this is private business between Tommy and

Mr. and Mrs. Findlay. Could you take us to Greg while they're sorting things out?''

"Yes. Yes, of course," he quickly acceded, waving the Connelly family forward.

Tommy watched her go. She skirted the other side of the table to where he stood, clearly demonstrating a disinclination to even pass by him. There was to be no standing by her man from Samantha Connelly, he thought with bitter pride, though to be scrupulously fair, could he expect her to?

He would have stood by her.

Come hell or high water he would have stood by her!

She followed her parents and brother out of the room without so much as a backward glance at him, leaving him to face the firing squad alone. Not worth listening to. Not worth defending. Not a word or a look from her to show he was still worth something to her. Just walking out of his life as though he meant absolutely nothing. Zero.

"I'll be straight back to take you to Janice," Doc Hawkins assured them before bowing out and tactfully closing the door.

Tommy tightened his jaw as he turned back to the Findlays. There was a lot he would take on the chin, but he wasn't about to be heaped with more guilt than was his due. Ron and Marta wanted truth from him. They'd get it, along with a few truths about their daughter.

Janice was not fighting for her life.

The baby....his mind sheered away from thinking

about that loss...what might have been. He didn't know—still didn't know—if it had been his child.

What he did know was he could lose more than a child tonight.

Sam didn't quite know how she made it out to the corridor. Her head was buzzing as though it had been invaded by a swarm of bees. She felt too sick to even try to drive them out. Sick and faint and stupid for believing Tommy. For wanting to believe him.

The Playboy King.

For all she knew he had fathered other children on women he'd been with, as Janice had snidely suggested. He might well have fathered one on her tonight. And that definitely gave the lie to his claim of always using protection. Would he deny their child, too, if she'd conceived? Would he treat her as he'd treated Janice when he fancied someone else?

Sam felt herself swaying and reached out to prop herself against the wall. Black dots were dancing before her eyes and her face felt clammy. Doc Hawkins had passed her, striding ahead to lead the way to wherever Greg was. If she just rested a few moments, she would be able to catch up.

"Sam!" Her father's voice, calling to her thickly.

Her vision was wavering but she saw them all stop and look back at her. "Coming," she forced out, and tried to wave them on.

It must have been a limp, inept gesture, because her father ignored it. He backtracked so fast, Sam suddenly found herself scooped off her feet and cradled against his big barrel chest, relieved of having to take any further action.

"Pete, you go with your mother and check on Greg." His voice rumbled over her. "I'll be taking Sam outside. My little girl needs a breath of fresh air."

His little girl... Tears welled into Sam's eyes. The love in those words was her total undoing. She turned her face into her father's strong shoulder and wept for the loss of her dream. Impossible to have faith in Tommy's word anymore. He just said and did whatever would get him what he wanted.

Overwhelmed by her inner misery, Sam wasn't aware of how her father got her outside or even where they were...only that he sat down and held her on his lap, patting her back as he had whenever she'd been hurt in the long-ago days of her childhood.

"Sorry, love," he murmured, resting his cheek against her hair. "Had my mind on Greg. Wasn't seeing that you got hardest hit back there. Greg's going to be all right. But you..." His big chest rose and fell in a heavy sigh. "Tommy was always the one, wasn't he?"

"Yes," she choked out, snuffling into the comforting curve of his neck and shoulder, mindlessly wanting to be a little girl again, secure in a love that was always there for her. Her father had never let her down. Never.

"Looked like you finally had him roped tonight. Your mother and I were happy for you. I guess this business with Janice...well, it's upsetting. Wouldn't be the first time a couple made a mistake, though. Maybe…''

He was trying to make it better for her and Sam couldn't bear it. ''No, Dad,'' she sobbed. ''I was there when she told him she was pregnant and he was the father. He…he called her a liar. And I…I let myself believe him. I wanted to believe him.''

She burst into fresh tears, the anguish of her earlier uncertainties coming back in full force. Worse, because now she could feel it from Janice's side, the hell of being pregnant to a man who didn't want her anymore, who refused to even admit he could be the father…the wretched desolation of being faced with such an ungiving and unsympathetic attitude.

''There…there…'' her father soothed. ''No doubt about her having been pregnant, but Tommy might not be the father, you know. Bit of a party girl it seemed to me…the way she was carrying on with Greg.''

''Oh, Dad!'' She shuddered as the fateful chain of cause and effect marched through her mind. ''Tommy was so cold and cutting when she'd tried to talk to him earlier. I think Greg was…was a pride thing to Janice…hitting back at Tommy. And me, too, for taking his attention away from her.''

''Mmmh…hardly admirable behaviour. Maybe Tommy had cause to cut her dead if she'd played up like that with other men before. When he was going out with her. You shouldn't be too quick to judge him, Sam.''

She rolled her head in a painful negative. ''I

can't...I can't excuse him anymore, Dad. There were...other things.''

''Uh-huh. Want to tell me about them? Get them off your chest?''

''Won't help.''

''Then just give it a rest. It's been a long day. A very long day. Too much to deal with in one go. Though let me say, I'm very proud of you...the way you held up and saw everything through. Very proud. Couldn't have asked more of anyone.''

He kissed her forehead and ruffled her hair. ''You're made of the right stuff, Sam. Your mother carries on about female frippery falderals but that doesn't count for much in my book. No...doesn't amount to much at all. It's what's in the heart that counts. You've got a heart as big as the Outback. And if Tommy King didn't recognise that tonight...''

Her body instinctively scrunched up, warding off the onset of more misery.

''But we won't talk about him,'' her father soothed. ''We'll talk about the good times...eh? Don't know if I've told you this, but from the day you were born, you've been a joy to me, Sam. The best daughter a man could have. Always eager to have a go at everything. A real little braveheart, right from the start...''

Tommy was churning with urgency. He had to rescue something from this disastrous night, if it was only a stay of judgment. He couldn't bear the thought of having completely lost Samantha's respect. It wasn't right. She had to understand this wasn't a black and white situation. Damn it! He did have integrity. Never in his life had he weaselled out of responsibility for anything he'd done.

It came as another severe jolt to his system when he found none of the Connellys with Greg in the recovery room. Where were they? How long had he been with the Findlays? Driven by the fear of not having the chance to clear anything with Samantha, he shot back to the corridor and headed for the exit to the car park. If she left here tonight, still thinking the worst of him...

No, his mind fiercely dictated.

She'd promised she'd always be here for him.

The ghosts couldn't win now.

He wouldn't let them.

The exit door halted his rush for a moment. Then he was past it, breaking into a run. He saw Robert Connelly stepping up into the minibus, movement inside it.

"Wait!"

The big man stopped, stepped back onto the ground, and turned to face him. Relieved at having at least delayed the family's departure, Tommy dropped his pace to a purposeful walk, his mind racing over what to say to Samantha. However, instead of waiting by the minibus, Robert Connelly came to meet him, intent on intercepting whatever message Tommy was bringing.

"It's all right," he hastily assured Greg's father. "I just want to speak to Samantha."

"It's not all right, Tommy," he bruskly retorted,

taking a blocking stance. "You leave her be for now."

The hard-spoken command pulled him up. The look on Robert Connelly's face brooked no opposition. Tommy instinctively gestured an appeal. "You don't understand…"

"Yes, I do. You want my daughter…you clean up your act."

It rocked him. He scooped in a quick breath, frantically searching for a line of argument. "I swear to you it's not how it looks," he declared vehemently.

"I hope for both your sake and Sam's, it isn't, Tommy," came the level reply. "Your father was my greatest friend, and I can't believe that the kind of person Lachlan was didn't rub off on you…his bone-deep decency, his sense of honour…"

"You can add absolutely fair justice to that," Tommy whipped back, fiercely resenting the impugning of his character.

"Yes." Robert Connelly agreed, ploughing on with pointed intent. "And fair justice seen to be done. That was Lachlan's law. Don't tell me you've forgotten it."

Seen to be done. Even as the words were spoken, they hit home. He'd failed that test in front of Samantha.

"Whatever the rights and wrongs of tonight…" her father went on, "…they're yours to deal with. Don't drag my little girl through a mess she had nothing to do with. You understand me?"

"Yes. But will Samantha give me the benefit of the doubt in the meantime?" he argued, desperate for some foothold on the future he could see slipping away from him.

"Maybe time will help put things in perspective. I'll be taking her home with me tomorrow and I'm asking you to sort yourself out before taking up with her again. My Sam isn't one for you to trifle with, Tommy. I'll be coming after you with a gun if you play her false. Understand me?"

"I was *not* trifling with her. Nor would I," Tommy shot back at him.

"Just making sure you know what you're walking into if you walk back into Sam's life." He nodded to mark the end of the conversation. "We'll be going now. I'm hoping you can sort things out as well as your father used to. Needs doing, Tommy."

Having delivered that last piece of inarguable advice, Robert Connelly returned to his family and took them away, seeking respite from the traumas that had been inflicted upon them.

Tommy watched the tail-lights of the minibus disappear into the darkness with a heavy sense of fateful resignation. No sense in chasing after it. Robert Connelly was right. One couldn't force a future. One had to build it, and a shaky foundation didn't build a strong future.

Lachlan's law...the irony was he had recently cited it himself when he'd helped Nathan sort out a nasty situation that was hurting Miranda. He hadn't really thought about his father for a long time, probably because it was Nathan following in his legendary footsteps.

Still, he was one of Lachlan King's sons, and

proud of it, proud to have the legacy of his father's blood in his veins. He might not be a cattleman but in his own way, he'd pioneered a new industry in the Outback and he had no doubt his father would have applauded both his drive and enterprise.

But his more personal affairs…would they have won Lachlan King's approval?

Tommy took a good, hard look at himself.

The Playboy King.

What had that title won him?

Nothing of any real value. Nothing that would stick by him. Nothing but grief for the woman he really wanted.

The more critical question was…what had it cost him…and could he recover the loss he'd brought upon himself tonight?

CHAPTER FOURTEEN

CHRISTMAS day....

Sam felt none of the excited anticipation that waking up to this day would have once brought. She had no urge to leap out of bed to see if the rest of the family were up yet, and no wish to stir them into activity if they weren't. Putting on a happy face took considerable effort and it was easier to delay having to do it.

She lay quietly in the old brass bed that had always been hers, her gaze idly roving over the mementos of her childhood and adolescence. All the things she'd kept remained precisely where she had placed them. In a way, coming back here was like stepping into a previous life, though she herself hadn't really changed.

On top of the chest of drawers sat the beautiful doll her mother had given her when she was four. She'd never played with it, hadn't seen what use it was. Its long auburn ringlets were still tied with green satin bows, and the matching green satin dress with its frills and coffee-lace trim was in the same pristine state as it had been when the doll was given, twenty-four Christmases ago.

Hanging on the wall facing her were the ribbons she'd won at rodeos, riding Lightning in the barrel races. He'd been a great horse, the fastest sprinter she'd ever had and so quick at turning around the barrels, it was magic the way he responded when they were competing to win. She'd wept buckets when he died from an infection the vet couldn't fix.

But life moved on. Tragedies slid into the past and other things became more important. On the dresser was a photograph of herself holding her pilot's license, one of the proudest moments of her life. Flying a plane was more exhilarating than riding a horse; taking to the air, owning the sky...like Tommy.

She sighed to ease the tension in her chest. How long had it been now...six, seven weeks? A bit over seven. The wedding had been on the sixth of November. Tommy had made no attempt at contact with her since then. Though she did know from her mother that he'd visited Janice in hospital several times, dropping in on Greg, as well.

It had actually been easier for her when her mother and brother were away, the reminders of that dreadful night at a distance. Her father let her be and Pete minded his own business. With Greg back home and having to nurse his leg, he was more or less underfoot and wanting company. Both he and her mother kept bringing up Tommy, and as much as she tried to block any conversation about him, they still dropped loaded little comments, referring to their *togetherness* at the wedding.

They also pointedly informed her that the Findlays had taken Janice home with them to Cairns, a long way from Kununurra, right across the country to the east coast. Away from Tommy was the apparent implication, not that it mattered. Tommy had made it all too brutally clear he didn't want Janice in his life, and it was that callous brutality that stuck in Sam's mind. Greg didn't seem perturbed by the loss, either. Which clearly demonstrated what casual sex was worth. Nothing that lasted beyond the moment. Unless it resulted in an unwanted pregnancy.

It didn't really help that the pregnancy was no more.

All it did was put an end to that chapter in Tommy's life. A convenient end, she thought bitterly, given his attitude towards it.

As for the rest of his life…the rest of hers…despite everything, the torment continued to linger. Had she done the right thing, walking away from that night and all it had entailed? In sheer self-survival mode, she'd wrapped herself in a mental and emotional fog, automatically taking over the running of the Connelly homestead while her mother stayed on in Kununurra to be by Greg. She'd filled the days with chores, keeping so busy she fell into bed at night, too exhausted to think.

She didn't want to think about Tommy now, either. After Christmas would be soon enough. In the new year. When she'd have to make decisions about continuing to work for him or…her mind shied away from *or*. Best to get moving—out of bed, into a shower, clothes on. She would wear a dress for Christmas. It would please her mother.

It should have been a happy Christmas day, Elizabeth King thought, but it wasn't…quite…despite

Miranda's and Nathan's announcement this morning that they were expecting a baby. It was wonderful news—Lachlan's first grandchild—and Tommy had carried on exuberantly about becoming an uncle. But she'd seen the shadow of pain on his face before he'd switched on the positive energy expected of him.

He was very good at putting on a show.

And he'd kept it up during their festive lunch, with Jared supporting him, their witty banter keeping laughter rolling around the table. Both brothers were genuinely happy for Nathan and Miranda. Elizabeth wished they could be happy for themselves, but knew they were not.

Jared had asked her if he could invite Christabel Valdez and her daughter to King's Eden for Christmas. She'd readily given her assent, hoping he had not sensed her own misgivings about the relationship he obviously wanted. In fact, it was a curious move from him. There had never been any embargo on inviting friends to the homestead for Christmas festivities. Had he been subtly probing her reaction to the idea of having Christabel in the family circle on an intimate level?

Difficult to know with Jared. He had his own quiet way of manoeuvring pieces into position—a formidable player in the business world, but he wasn't emotionally involved when it came to cutting deals. Unrequited passion could wear patience and control very thin.

She didn't know if he had actually invited Christabel. Perhaps he'd thought better of it, not ready to commit himself so far, or realising the invitation might be rejected. Putting himself in a losing situation was not Jared's way. Nevertheless, he had to be feeling disappointment that Christabel was not here.

As for Tommy, Elizabeth feared the fallout from the Janice Findlay affair cut too deeply for him and Sam to come together again. She'd flown to Kununurra herself the Monday after the wedding. Sam had already left for home with Robert, a move which had spoken volumes even before Elizabeth had managed a heart-to-heart talk with Tess Connelly.

Time, they had hopefully decided, would put things right eventually. But time could also feed the demon, pride, Elizabeth thought now. Both Tommy and Sam had let pride be a bristling sword between them before. If they saw the climax of that night as a betrayal of each other, would either of them be prepared to risk their hearts again?

If the ghosts stay away, Tommy had said when he'd danced with her at the wedding, and Janice had undoubtedly raised many ghosts. The pity of it was…truth and justice didn't repair the hurt done to the victims of a crime. Nothing could bring back what had been destroyed. Yet, was real love ever completely destroyed?

Aware that Tommy had fallen silent at the table, Elizabeth surreptitiously observed him watching Miranda and Nathan. Jared had prompted them into discussing what names they favoured for a son or daughter. Their faces glowed with love and the pleasurable anticipation of having a child to name.

Tommy's jaw suddenly tightened. He pushed back his chair and stood up. "One last Christmas toast," he said, claiming everyone's attention as he picked up his glass and held it high. "If this is a day of peace and good will, let it be. Let it be," he repeated fiercely, and drank without waiting for anyone else to echo it.

They all watched him, somewhat startled by his abrupt change of mood. He set his glass down, swept them with a look of reckless purpose and announced, "I beg to be excused. I need to be elsewhere. And who knows?" He tossed them a devil-may-care smile as he headed out of the dining room. "I may bring back the gift of a lifetime."

"Sounds like a plane coming in," Pete remarked, killing conversation as everyone paused to listen.

It *was* a plane coming in.

Sam's heart fluttered, a wild hope zinging through her as she instantly connected the sound to Tommy. Her mind was slow to override the reaction. Why would Tommy leave King's Eden to come here on Christmas day? It made no sense. There was nothing to get excited about. Most likely it was someone lost, someone in trouble, needing help.

"I'll go and see who it is," she said, pushing up from the table, needing the activity to settle her out-of-control nerves. The wall clock above her father's head showed twelve minutes to three…midafternoon. Tommy was undoubtedly still sitting with his family over their festive lunch, just as she was. Once she'd identified the pilot, she could bury Tommy in the dark recesses of her mind again and not let him out for the rest of the day.

"Might as well all go," her father said, dragging his chair back and patting his tummy. "Need some exercise after that huge meal."

"You pigged out on the pudding, Dad," Pete teased, getting up to satisfy his curiosity.

"Christmas comes but once a year," her father declared. "Got to make the most of it."

The others laughingly agreed, moving to follow Sam as she headed for the verandah overlooking the airstrip. A rise of inner tension prevented her from laughing. She couldn't even act casually over who might be landing at the Connelly homestead. The compulsion to know drove her feet faster.

The plane touched down on the rough dirt runway as she pushed open the screen door to the verandah. Sheer impetus carried her to the railing which she instinctively gripped—a steady, external support for the inner turmoil raised by the sight of the small aircraft skimming over the ground in front of her.

No mistaking the big *K* on its tail.

KingAir printed clearly underneath it.

Could it be a charter? Or was it Tommy himself? And what would she do if it was Tommy?

Her mind jagged between a helpless wanting and almost violent rejection. Her heart felt torn. Her stomach had lost any semblance of a comfort zone. And her family emerged onto the verandah, completely relaxed and ready to welcome a visitor, outback hospitality about to be extended to whomever it was.

"See any identification on the plane?" Pete asked eagerly, watching it being turned around at the end of the runway.

No point in prevaricating. Sam worked some moisture into her mouth which had gone as dry as the land before the Big Wet. *"KingAir,"* she answered, trying to keep her voice emotionless.

"Tommy," her father said in a tone of satisfaction.

Every nerve in Sam's body tensed. She never had asked what her father had said to Tommy just before they'd left the hospital in the minibus. She'd simply been grateful to be spared any further conflict with him that night.

"Why do you think so, Dad?" she blurted out.

The plane was taxiing back to park near the homestead. Still, there was no absolute certainty about the identity of the pilot at the controls.

"Oh, it just seems like a good day for him to pick."

Her head jerked around, her gaze slicing hard and fast to her father's. "A good day for what?"

He shrugged. "Peace and good will," came the bland answer.

"Tommy was great visiting me in hospital and bringing me stuff," Greg remarked happily. "Think I'll go and meet him."

He stepped off the verandah.

"No! Wait!" Both the protest and the command burst off Sam's tongue, causing her brother to pause and look quizzically at her.

"What for?" he asked when she didn't follow up with a reason.

Panic was causing a shortness of breath. She didn't know what to do, what to say. She wasn't *prepared* for this!

"I think Sam has private business with Tommy, Greg," her father explained. "Might be best if she met him first...settle things between them."

"Oh!" Enlightenment spread into an arch look as he stepped aside to give her the right of passage. "Your move, big sis."

Which meant she had to move. Gritting her teeth, Sam forced her legs into action. Her father was right. If it was Tommy in that plane, better she met him out there, beyond earshot of her family, though there was no way they weren't going to view what went on. She could feel their interest burning into her back as she left them behind.

The plane came to a halt. Its engines were switched off. *It may not be Tommy,* she kept telling herself, trudging determinedly forward, her shoulders automatically squared and her head defiantly high. The heat haze of midafternoon made everything shimmer. She wanted to shade her eyes with her hand but it seemed like a weak action so she refrained from doing it. A fierce sense of pride quelled the inner panic. If this *was* Tommy, he could do the speaking. Then she'd know what to say.

The cockpit door opened.

Tommy King stepped out onto Connelly land.

Something punched Sam's heart. Her feet stopped

dead. He had come. He'd left his family Christmas at King's Eden and flown here…to her.

He stood where he'd stepped down, staring at her. Since she'd stopped several metres from him and he wasn't coming any closer, she couldn't see what was in his eyes yet she felt the intensity of their focus on her, the impact of it spreading electric tingles, igniting nervous mayhem.

She stared back, wishing he didn't have the power to affect her so much. Did nothing change it? Would she always feel like this with Tommy, as though the very vitality of her existence depended on him? She could cope without him but…she didn't want to. She simply didn't want to. He made life bright, exciting, challenging…and dark, and miserable and conflict-ridden, she savagely reminded herself.

There he stood, his playboy handsome face framed by the riot of black curls that seemed to embody an untamed spirit, his tall athletic body radiating energy and a strong, virile maleness that was loaded with sex appeal. And she was vulnerable to it, every bit as much as any other woman who'd fallen for it, but physical magnetism wasn't going to win her to his side. Not today. Not ever.

She wanted more than that from Tommy. Much more. If he thought she was going to cross this space between them and fall at his feet, he could think again. If that was what he was waiting for, he could wait until doomsday. It wasn't enough that he'd come this far for her. Her pounding heart demanded that he show her how much she was worth to him. In every way.

* * *

Tommy stood there, feeling her pull on every part of him, and the wanting that had been so briefly satisfied the day of Nathan's wedding, became more acute than it had been that night. He needed this woman. She answered things in him that no other ever had. Or would, he thought with painful irony, aware of how nearly his past had come to wrecking any future with her. And might still, if her mind had become completely set against him.

Funny…he hadn't considered her beautiful…all those years when he'd told himself other women were much more attractive, better-looking, sexier, and of course, appreciated the man he was more than Sam Connelly did. But she *was* beautiful. More beautiful to his eyes than all the rest.

She shone. Her hair was a halo of glory in the afternoon sunshine. He loved the sky blue clarity of her eyes, and the freckles she hated were endearingly girlish, stirring some protective streak in him. There was more appeal in her face than any supposedly classical beauty could strike.

She was wearing a blue petticoat dress that fired his memory of the soft, supple femininity of her body and the fierce tensile strength in her arms and legs, winding around him, binding him to the mutual possession that had felt so right, so perfect. The desire to feel it again seized him, but he knew he had to control it. He hadn't come for the body of Samantha Connelly. He knew she wouldn't give it unless she could give her heart, as well. That was what had to be won…won and kept.

Her approach to the plane had buoyed his hope

she was ready to be receptive, might even welcome him. Her abrupt halt at the sight of him put paid to that idea. Her rigid stance encouraged nothing. Pride set in stone, he thought, and felt his own pride start to bristle.

If she couldn't believe in him now...

If she wouldn't trust him...

He'd come this far. The risk had to be taken. He scooped in a deep, calming breath and walked towards her, purpose steeled in every stride.

There was no meeting him halfway but at least she didn't turn her back on him. She stood her ground. Her hands clenched as he came closer. Her eyes flared a warning, her chin tilted aggressively, and he knew she'd fight him if he crossed whatever line she'd drawn in her mind.

He only had one weapon that could cut through that line. Talking wasn't going to do it and touching was clearly a transgression she wouldn't tolerate. He had to gamble everything on the one possibility that might restore her faith in his word.

It went against his grain, having to accept that *his* word wasn't enough. He hadn't lied to her, not once. Yet there was no denying that circumstances had let loose the ghosts they had almost dispersed that night. No doubt they had been preying on her mind ever since.

He stopped short of her, ensuring she didn't feel threatened. Without saying a word he withdrew the envelope from his pocket and held it out to her, keeping a respectful distance. Her fiercely held gaze wavered and slowly dropped to the slightly crumpled piece of stationery.

"What's this?" she demanded hoarsely.

"Just do me the courtesy of taking it and reading what's inside, Samantha. It's self-explanatory."

She unclenched her right hand, lifted it and took the envelope. The tightness in Tommy's chest did not ease at this act of co-operation. It was up to her now...whether they'd share a future or not. All he could do was wait.

Was this the end? Sam stared down at the envelope in her hand. Did it hold a severance cheque, notice of termination of her employment as a pilot with him?

There was no name and address typed on it. Surely if it was something official, that would have been done. And why deliver it to her on Christmas day? Personally?

Her mind was a mess of painful confusion. The answer was inside the envelope, she told herself, so open it. Her fingers tremulously carried out the mental order and slowly extracted the contents—thin pages from a stationery pad, handwritten in blue biro. She unfolded them, and was startled to see it was a personal letter, dated weeks ago, with Kununurra Hospital written under the date. Bewildered, and not knowing what to expect, she started to read...

Dear Samantha,

Firstly, let me say how sorry I am to have caused so much trouble and pain. My parents told me it was you who flew them to the hospital on the night of the accident, and I appreciate that very much, especially since I'd been such a bitch to you earlier.

Janice... This was from Janice Findlay! Dazedly, Sam read on....

I'm writing this because I need to get it off my chest, and I owe it to you, too. You never did anything to hurt me and how can I make a fresh start if I don't clear my conscience? So here goes, and I hope you're still reading.

The truth is I lied about Tommy being the father of my baby. I guess getting pregnant made me face up to what a shambles my life was in. No, that's wrong. I didn't really face up to it. I kind of clutched at Tommy as the one really decent man I'd ever been with and hoped he would see me through.

He tried to steer me towards help when he broke off with me, but I just resented his advice and went off on a partying binge to forget him. One night I picked up a tourist and fell into bed with him. I couldn't even remember his name afterwards. That's how bad I'd got. Then when I found out I'd fallen pregnant, I panicked. I didn't want to tell my Mum and Dad I didn't even know the father's name.

I knew it wasn't right to try to pin it on Tommy, but by the time Nathan's wedding came around, I was seeing that as the only solution, and I kept telling myself it could have been his child, so it was fair. Although he had always used protection, I argued that nothing was a hundred percent safe so I could get past that. I just didn't bargain on you, and Tommy wanting you.

It completely threw me. I rocketed straight off to drink myself silly again and latch onto a guy who fancied me. I didn't deliberately pick your brother. Didn't even know he was your brother until we'd been chatting each other up for a while. Actually I did like Greg but life on the land is not for me.

Anyhow I really burned during the reception, seeing Tommy giving you all the attention I wanted from him. I tried to corner him when you slipped out of the marquee, but he fobbed me off on his brother, Jared, and went after you, which made me even madder.

Then I saw you both coming back, so very together, and your hair was down. I knew you'd been having sex, which meant my house of cards was tumbling all around me and I just went crazy. I guess, because I'd thought about it so much, I convinced myself Tommy was the father of my baby, doing the dirty on me, and I let you both have it because it felt like you'd taken him away from me.

I realise now how terribly wrong that was. Tommy wasn't mine. I had no claim on him at all. And you were a completely innocent party. I'm deeply ashamed of all my actions that night, hurting everyone, even killing the baby because I was so drunk and reckless and off my brain.

Well, it's pulled me up with a jolt, I can tell you. Not that it mends what I've done. I hope this letter goes some way towards fixing things between you and Tommy. Incidentally, Tommy didn't ask me to do this but I did tell him I was doing it because I wanted him to know I'm really trying to put things straight now.

He's been so kind since the accident, helping to explain things to Mum and Dad, making them see me as I am—if not an alcoholic, going that way fast—and very much in need of counselling and a lot of support to see me through it. I didn't deserve this from him. He says I'm worth saving for myself. I don't know how he can see any good in me after what I did, but I'm very grateful he's been here, holding my hand when I needed it.

I'm flying home with Mum and Dad tomorrow. Out of Tommy's life. Out of your life, too, Samantha. At least, I hope so. I hope I'm not going to leave a legacy of lies, spoiling things I had no right to spoil. I would like to think of you being happy with Tommy again, as happy as you looked that night before I stepped in and wrecked what I saw happening between you.

I'm so sorry.

Please smile at Tommy. He deserves it.

Janice Findlay.

Sam couldn't smile. Her face was impossibly stiff, aching with the build up of tears that were beginning to swim into her eyes. She couldn't speak, either. The lump in her throat was so huge she could barely swallow.

Tommy had asked her to trust him. And she hadn't. She hadn't. She had believed the accusation against him, and multiplied it to even worse proportions, doing him a terrible injustice, turning him into much less than the decent man he was. How could she have got it so wrong, she who had known him all these years, most of her life, and knowing he always treated people well, knowing he was essentially fair-minded and generous of heart?

Except with her.

But hadn't that been her fault? And this was her fault, too. She'd made a habit of judging him meanly. The leaden weight on her heart grew heavier. Was it any use, asking him to forgive her? Would he give her another chance?

Her father's words slid through the dark anguish in her mind... *Christmas Day...peace and good will...* and a bare sliver of hope whispered—why would Tommy come today if he wanted to lay blame on her?

Slowly, almost blindly, she folded the pages of Janice's letter into its original creases. Please, she prayed. Please let Tommy be here because he still wants me, despite everything. She wasn't aware that the tears had overflowed and were rolling down her cheeks. She was only conscious of desperate need.

''Don't!''

The harsh command jerked her head up, fear jabbing through her that she'd done more wrong. Her vision was too blurred to see him clearly.

"Don't cry."

Not a command. A plea. Yet the difference barely had time to register before Tommy stepped forward and wrapped her in his arms, hugging her to him so tightly, there was no room left for fear. And her own arms wound around his waist, hanging on, hanging on for dear life.

Then his voice, throbbing into her ear, "Say you still want me." And the words lifting the weight off her heart, bringing such sweet relief, instantly drawing the reply, "I do. I do want you."

His kiss, his body, the pent-up passion pouring from him, left no doubt about what he felt. And Sam gave herself up to it, shedding all her fears and uncertainties, caring only that she have this…this blissful togetherness with Tommy.

Neither of them thought about ghosts.

There were none to come between them anymore.

CHAPTER FIFTEEN

"WILL YOU come with me?"

The passionate intensity of his kiss was echoed in Tommy's murmured words, and to Sam's giddy mind he was asking if she would travel with him on whatever path took them into a future together.

"Yes," she breathed fervently, not hesitating for a second.

She felt his chest heave with relief. Then in an action so swift it left her breathless and bewildered, he scooped her off her feet and had her firmly slung across that very same chest, her legs dangling over one of his arms while his other arm held her very securely to him.

"I'm taking you to a very special place," he stated, striding back towards the plane.

"You don't have to carry me," she assured him, although she happily wound her arms around his neck, loving his strength and the determined purpose that included her.

He grinned, his eyes dancing with devilish pleasure. "I like knowing I've got you."

She laughed and it was so good to laugh, to feel free and full of the joy of being alive. Over his shoulder, she caught sight of her family, still watching from the verandah, but it didn't matter what they thought. They'd be happy for her, too, if they knew how much this meant.

"You haven't said hello to my family and I haven't said goodbye," she said, reminded of this oversight.

"We'll wave," came the unabashed reply.

Sam hitched herself up a bit to smile and wave at her parents and brothers. Greg flashed her a V for victory. Pete raised his arms above his head like a champion boxer. Her father held up a salute while gathering her mother close to him, hugging her shoulders. They were smiling at each other, prompting Sam to wonder how much they had talked about her and Tommy between themselves. It was very apparent her whole family was well pleased she was going off with him, and far from spoiling their Christmas day, it seemed to have topped it off very nicely. Which added to her sense of brilliant well-being.

Tommy bundled her into the cockpit and she wriggled over into the passenger seat, smiling to herself at the novelty of not being at the controls. Today she was not flying *for* Tommy King. She was flying *with* him, up into the wide blue sky and wherever he wanted to take her.

He waved to the Connelly family before climbing in and settling himself, ready for take-off. Before switching on the engine, he shot her a sharp, searching look. "Any questions?"

"No," she promptly replied. "None at all," she added emphatically, wanting to assert her intention never to lose faith in him and his feeling for her again.

He smiled, whatever inner reservations he'd held, wiped out in a burst of elation at her decisiveness. "No going back on that, Samantha Connelly. I won't let you," he warned.

Which instantly reminded her of the promise she'd made and hadn't kept, once Janice's claim had seemed ratified. "What about you, Tommy? Do you have any questions of me?" she asked gravely, impelled to probe how much of a scar her lack of trust had left on him.

The smile tilted into wry self-mockery. "How could you know my truth, when I've given you every reason to doubt it? Right now I'm feeling very lucky that you have such a constant heart, and I hope nothing I do will ever test it again."

"I'm sorry I..."

"No!" Silencing fingers on her lips and his eyes burning with intense resolution. "We're not going to do any more of that...looking back to what we did wrong. We've got it right now, haven't we?"

She nodded.

"There's a lot of life ahead of us, Samantha. Let's start from here. Okay?"

She nodded again, grateful for his understanding and the answering of her own hopes and needs.

He relaxed, flashing her another brilliant smile. "No clouds. Come fly with me."

"Yes," she happily agreed.

They flew to Kununurra where Tommy exchanged the plane for a helicopter from the KingAir charter service fleet and quickly grabbed some picnic supplies from the office. Her curiosity piqued, Sam asked him where they were going, but Tommy would only say it was a surprise. Since there was no mistaking the undercurrent of excitement in his manner, Sam reasoned the *special* place he had in mind, was very special to him, and she hoped it would have the same appeal to her. It would add so much more to the sense of sharing if it did.

It was a very short flight. They landed on a hill overlooking Lake Argyle which always looked fantastic—the largest manmade lake in Australia covering about two thousand square kilometres, and perfect for swimming, boating and fishing. The many bays and inlets and islands added an interesting landscape to the huge expanse of water, which definitely had a cooling effect on Outback heat—very welcome to Sam when she flew tourists here.

Though not exactly *here.* She had never landed on this hill. It wasn't a tourist place, which made it all the more attractive, having this lovely view to themselves. She smiled delightedly at Tommy as he finished laying a groundsheet under a nearby stand of gum trees so they could sit in the shade.

"Did you scout all the surrounds of the lake to find this hill?"

"More or less," he admitted.

"It's glorious, Tommy. Very special."

"I'm glad you think so because I chose it specially."

"What for?"

His eyes sparkled happy anticipation as he stepped

over to her and slid his arms around her waist. "This is my land, Samantha. I set about buying it soon after I found this place. To me, it was perfect for what I wanted."

She frowned, relating his planning to business. "Another tourist lodge?"

He shook his head and lifted a hand to smooth the lines from her forehead. His eyes smiled into hers as he warmly answered, "To build a home on. A home that would be here for me and my wife and my family."

Sam's heart turned over.

His fingers stroked gently down her face. "Would you be happy to share it with me, Samantha?"

"Yes," she whispered.

"To marry me and have my children?"

"Yes."

He sighed, a deep contentment in his eyes. "I shall love you all my life."

Sam didn't doubt that promise for a moment. Her hands slid up to link around his neck as she huskily answered, "And I you, Tommy. I you…always and forever."

And the words themselves—spoken, meant, felt—put all the magical reality of the future they wanted within tangible reach as they kissed and revelled in a totally uninhibited giving of each other. Clothes were discarded, the need to satisfy every sense of absolute union sizzling through them, and for a long, blissful time they lay on their hill, on the site of the home they would build together, making love with all the tenderness of caring, the elation of knowing, the fierce urge for mutual possession, the ecstasy of fulfilment, the sweet sensual contentment of peace and harmony.

Sunset...always an hour of relaxation at King's Eden, though Elizabeth wished Tommy was with them—Tommy and Sam. Nevertheless, it was very pleasant, sitting out here on the wicker furniture spread along the western verandah, sipping cool drinks and watching the river below them turning into a stream of gold.

The sound of a helicopter coming in jarred the peace and set Elizabeth's mind and heart racing.

"Tommy," Jared murmured.

"He flew off in a plane," Elizabeth reminded him.

"Yes. Interesting that he's returning in a helicopter."

No doubt in his voice about who the pilot was, coming in at dusk on Christmas Day. It had to be Tommy, Elizabeth conceded, and fiercely willed the change to a helicopter meant something positive.

"The question is...with or without Sam," Nathan remarked, speaking what was on all their minds.

No one commented. No one moved. There was nothing they could do, either way. Impossible for any of them to direct Tommy's life. Elizabeth knew they were all hoping his quest had been successful and he was bringing home his *gift of a lifetime,* but if he'd failed...well, he certainly wouldn't appreciate any open fuss about it.

They waited. The helicopter landed. The whirling clatter of its blades stopped. The ensuing silence stretched Elizabeth's nerves. She imagined Tommy trudging up to the homestead alone. Surely he would have stayed with the Connellys if...

Voices!

"That's Sam!" Jared said with certainty, his face breaking into a delighted grin. "He's got her!"

Elizabeth heaved a huge sigh of relief. This had to mean peace and good will, if nothing else.

"We're out here on the verandah, Tommy," Nathan called out, his voice booming with a big welcome. "Come join us!"

"Be right there!" came the happy reply. *Happy!*

Then quick and eager footsteps along the verandah, approaching the corner to the western side. Elizabeth put her glass down and leaned forward in her chair, her own eagerness to see and assess the situation brimming up in her. Tommy and Sam swung into view, hand in hand, their faces beaming so much joy there was no possible doubting they were in perfect harmony.

"This is most fortuitous!" Tommy declared. "Here you are all gathered precisely where Samantha and I shared our first kiss on Nathan's and Miranda's wedding day. Isn't that right, darling?"

She laughed, both nodding and shaking her head at him.

"And before anyone says anything," he went on, bubbling with obvious exhilaration. "Let me introduce my future wife..." He halted, turned and tenderly cupped Sam's face, bringing her gaze directly in line with his. "...who will truly be to me..." his voice dropped to a warm caress of love "…the most beautiful bride in the whole world."

Tears glistened in Sam's eyes. Elizabeth sensed those words meant a great deal to the woman she had always been inside, the woman who had wanted Tommy to recognise and love her. Now the love was so evident Elizabeth found tears pricking her own eyes.

Her heart was so full, she was the last to get up to congratulate them on their forthcoming marriage. Jared, Nathan, Miranda…all of them swarmed around the newly announced couple, hugging, laughing, showing their pleasure. Finally she was on her feet, joining the others.

"Mum…" Tommy grinned at her, his eyes dancing wickedly. "…it really goes against the grain for me, at my age, to say *Mother knows best,* but I'll grant it this time."

"And I do, too," Sam agreed, her lovely blue eyes sparkling with appreciation.

Elizabeth gestured helplessly, realising they were both acknowledging her words to them before Nathan's wedding. "It was always up to you two," she reminded them. "I just can't tell you how pleased I am that you finally found each other."

That was the truth of it. She might have prodded them a little, but it had still been their choice to open their hearts and minds to each other. And thank heaven they had!

Much, much later when the homestead was quiet, Elizabeth lay in the bed she had once shared with Lachlan, counting the blessings of this Christmas and feeling very content with the way the future was shaping—two sons married to women who were surely their soul mates, one grandchild on the way.

If she could see Jared similarly settled... Was Christabel Valdez the right woman? Would the enigmatic Brazilian ever open her heart to him? Was there anything she herself could do to foster a clearer situation between them? Or should she let that relationship fly all by itself?

Elizabeth sighed and settled herself for sleep. Today, all was well at King's Eden. Lachlan would have been so pleased and proud. And Jared was the youngest son. His time would come, too, she told herself, with or without Christabel Valdez. It had been a good year. A very good year. Nathan and Miranda and the baby, Tommy and Sam. No need to worry about Jared.

The family would go on...future generations...the Kings of the Outback...Lachlan's heritage safe. She could rest in peace tonight. She no longer felt the gnawing sense of loss that had driven her from King's Eden. It wasn't just the past here now. It held a future, as well.

THE PLEASURE
KING'S BRIDE

CHAPTER ONE

A MAN in a suit!

No-one wore a suit in Broome, especially not on a Sunday afternoon.

A surge of fear shot Christabel upright from the waist-deep water she'd been swimming in. She needed a better view of the man who was crossing the park above the beach, *wearing a suit!*

Was it one of *them*?

Had they tracked her down?

Before she could get a good look at him, his path took him behind the amenities block. She waited, her heart thumping wildly from the shock of being faced with the possibility that she had been found, despite all her precautions.

Six months she'd been here...perhaps, too long...long enough for her to start feeling safe...which was always a mistake. Stupid to ever feel *safe* from them, with so much at stake. Though there had seemed a very real chance of it, being so far away from everything that mattered to them, camped in this outpost of civilisation on the coastal edge of the great Australian outback.

Broome—a raggle-taggle, multicultural township that had grown up around the pearling industry when people still dived for pearl shell and died of the bends—was at the other end of the earth from the money men in Europe. Its history and tropical location, high on the west coast of the Kimberly region, attracted tourists, but *no-one wore a suit here*, not locals nor visitors. The heat alone demanded a minimum of clothing.

There he was again—just a glimpse of him crossing the open space between the amenities block and the cafe. His head was turned back towards the car park, making it impossible to identify him, but the suit said a lot to Christabel.

This was someone unprepared for the tropical climate.

Someone in too big a hurry to change his attire.

Someone who was heading purposefully for the caravan park that adjoined the beach area.

And *Alicia* had gone back to the caravan to fetch cans of cold drinks!

Sheer panic drove Christabel's legs to wade through the water in frantic haste. She ran through the shallows and along the damp sand, which gave her firmer footing until she could reach the rocky outcrop that led up to the camping reserve. If it was *one of them*, come to get Alicia, come to snatch her back to that other life…

No-o-o-o!

Christabel's mind burnt with fierce resolution as she leapt from rock to rock, every muscle tensing as she raced to fight for her daughter, determined on keeping her free from the nightmare world the money men would insist on constructing and maintaining. She would not let them take Alicia back to Europe. Never! Her daughter was safe *here*. If they'd just leave them alone…let them lead a normal life…

Onto the grassy bank of the reserve, her heart

pumping, feet pounding, her long wet hair whipping around her. People she'd come to know from neighbouring caravans called out, startled by her hurtling haste, but she couldn't pause, couldn't reply. First and foremost she had to reach Alicia before the man in the suit found her. Did he know where to look, which caravan they lived in? She couldn't see him but he had to be here somewhere.

Close now…she put on a last spurt, jumping over tent ropes and pegs, finally rounding the back of her van and…stopping dead.

He was there—the man in the suit—talking to her daughter, but he wasn't one of them.

It was Jared—her employer here in Broome, Jared King—nothing whatsoever to do with *them*!

And if she acknowledged the deep down truth, he was the main reason she'd stayed in this place, longer than she should have.

"Is something wrong?" he asked, frowning over her obvious state of agitation.

She leant against the side of the van, shaky with relief, one hand pressed to her wildly thumping heart, the other raking back the wet tangle of hair from her face. The dark, waist-length tresses undoubtedly looked like straggling ropes, the usual flow of waves in horrible kinks. It was embarrassing, having him see her like this, ungroomed, hopelessly discomposed and too nakedly vulnerable to successfully hide what had to stay hidden.

"Why were you running, Mummy?"

Having caught her breath, Christabel aimed what she hoped was a reassuring smile at her five-year-old daughter. "I thought you'd got lost."

Alicia huffed her indignation. "As if I would."

There she was, a delightful imp of a child, her lovely little face framed by a halo of brown curls, no fear at all in the big amber eyes, no shadow of repression hanging over her. Christabel was amazed at the happy self-assurance her daughter had developed here, in this Broome caravan park, and she was deeply grateful it was still in place.

"You were gone a long time and I was dying for a drink," Christabel offered in appeasement, conscious that Jared King was studying her quizzically and wishing he hadn't witnessed her fear. He was disturbingly perceptive at times and she simply couldn't afford to give too much away. Once people knew who she was, who her daughter was, everything changed.

"I've got them, see?" Alicia held up a string bag containing two cans of drinks. "I was on my way back…"

"I guess I should apologise for delaying her," Jared chimed in, holding up the can in his hand. "Alicia very kindly got me a cold drink, too."

"Why are you wearing a suit?" The accusatory words shot out of Christabel's mouth before she could stop them.

Another quizzical, more weighing look from Jared. In fact, his coat was off now, slung over one shoulder, and he'd loosened his tie and rolled up his shirt sleeves. The strong raw maleness that seemed to emanate from all three King brothers was coming at her in waves, making her acutely aware of being a woman.

"I mean it's so hot," she gabbled. "Ridiculous to

be walking around dressed like that. No wonder you wanted a drink.''

A slow, ironic smile. ''I must admit I'd rather be in a swimsuit.'' His eyes gliding over her appreciatively.

It wasn't a leer. Jared King wasn't the leering type. But she could feel his pleasure in seeing her like this, every curve hugged and outlined by the sleek yellow maillot, still wet from her swim, and his pleasure always did funny things to her, evoking a foolish happiness that muddled her mind and stirring physical reactions that left her miserably unsettled.

Her breasts were tingling right now, a shivery excitement running up and down her spine, her stomach turning mushy. If only he wasn't so handsome, so insidiously attractive to her in so many ways...

''Actually, I was driving home from the airport,'' he went on.

Of course! He was due home from his business trip to Hong Kong. She just hadn't connected the suit to Jared, but he would wear one to deal with the Chinese, commanding their respect on all levels. The pearl King, they called him, because he headed the pearling industry his family owned, but secretly Christabel had dubbed him the pleasure King. It was something in his eyes, a warm, caressing sensuality...

''Then I remembered my mother was away...''

His mother—Elizabeth King, of the sharp intelligence and shrewd judgment, a woman who'd lived too much and seen too much for Christabel to ever feel comfortable in her company.

''...no-one to talk to, wind down with...''

Making himself sound lonely, but there was never

any need for Jared King to be lonely, not a man like him. Or was he subtly tapping at her loneliness?

"...and I wondered if you might like to share my dinner and hear about your designs, the ones I took with me to Hong Kong."

His smile held a whimsical appeal, and there was a mocking challenge in his eyes over the bait he attached to the personal invitation. He didn't believe it would make any difference, but since she'd consistently refused to be with him in anything but a business situation, he was trying that angle...just to see her response to it.

"Did they like my jewellery?" she asked, feeling a surge of pride in the designs Jared had given her a free hand to create, and unable to deny her curiosity was piqued.

"Dinner?"

So tempting...strange how a man who always moved with such graceful elegance could exude so much male animal sexuality. He was tall and beautifully proportioned. His almost black hair tended to droop in a soft endearing wave over his forehead, but there was nothing really soft about his strongly boned face, except his rather full lower lip, lending his mouth the same sensual look she often caught in his dark brown eyes...eyes that were simmering at her now with promises of pleasure.

Christabel scooped in a deep breath, wishing she could indulge the desires he stirred in her. "No doubt you'll tell me everything at work tomorrow," she answered flatly.

"I was hoping for a pleasant evening together."

The tug to accept what he offered was stronger than

ever. But he would want too much, she told herself
for the umpteenth time. Jared King was not the kind
of man who would ever settle for less than everything
he aimed for. Behind his quiet, affable demeanor was
a will of steel she'd sensed many times.

"Vikki Chan invariably cooks a splendid homecoming dinner for me," he remarked persuasively,
dropping in the fact that his Chinese housekeeper
would be in the house—the sense of a chaperone.
"I'm sure you'll enjoy it. In fact, her steamed fish is
superb, well worth tasting."

Food wasn't the point, and he knew it.

"I like Chinese cooking," Alicia piped up.

Jared instantly dropped her a charming smile.
"What's your favourite dish?"

"Honey prawns," came the decisive reply.

"Very tasty," he agreed with relish. "I'm sure
Vikki would do some for you if your mother would
like to bring you with her to my place for dinner this
evening."

That was a hit below the belt, involving her daughter directly in the invitation. He'd never done it before
and Christabel churned with resentment at the unfair
ploy as both of them turned their gaze expectantly to
her, Alicia's expression artlessly pleased at the promise of a treat.

"Can we go, Mummy?"

"I don't think so," she answered tersely.

The curt refusal bewildered her daughter, prompting the question, "Why not?"

"Yes...why not?" Jared echoed, maintaining a
pleasantly invitational tone.

Christabel glared at him, hating the dilemma he put

her in. "Alicia eats early. She's in bed at eight o'clock."

"No problem." He glanced at his watch. "It's almost five now. If you come at six…"

"Stop it, Jared!" she burst out.

Slowly he raised his gaze to hers again and there was nothing the least bit affable in his eyes. They burned with the need to rip away every barrier she put up between them. They seared her soul with a truth she could not deny, the sure knowledge of the attraction she felt…the same attraction he felt.

"Some things can't be stopped, Christabel," he said quietly.

And she had no answer to that starkly honest statement.

Tension gripped her entire body as she fought the deeply personal needs he evoked. She wanted this man. She wanted to experience all of him so badly, it was like being torn in two, the rational part of her mind insisting an intimate involvement with him would spill over to an attachment with Alicia and the money men would never allow it, not in the long run, so it could only end in wretched torment.

Jared made one of his graceful gestures, the long artistic fingers opening in a curve of giving as he softly added, "Of course, the choice is yours."

What would it be like to have those fingers caressing her, making her feel loved and cherished and precious to him? Her stomach clenched in a savage desire to know how it would be…the pleasure King making love to her…to have this, just for herself, for at least a little time. Her heart drummed a vehement plea to make *her own choice*—a choice that shut out every other factor that had ruled her life for so many years.

"I'd like to go, Mummy."

And why shouldn't she? Christabel thought fiercely, looking at her daughter with an aching well of love. Why shouldn't Alicia enjoy the company of a man who didn't see her as a pawn in a monstrous web of greed? To add something more normal to their life here in Broome...why not?

"Then we shall go," she answered decisively, defying all the gremlins that rode on her shoulders.

Alicia clapped her hands in delight and lifted a gleeful face to Jared. "Honey prawns," she archly reminded him.

He laughed at her, his whole body visibly relaxing as he assured her, "I never go back on promises. Honey prawns there shall be."

"And chocolate chip ice-cream?"

"Alicia!" Christabel chided.

"I was just asking, Mummy," came the hasty justification.

"You know it's not good manners."

A doleful sigh. "Sorry."

Christabel sighed, too, afraid she was committing an act of utter madness on an impulse she would inevitably regret, yet when she lifted her gaze to Jared's and saw the happy warmth in his eyes, she couldn't bring herself to care about the consequences of her decision.

"Six-thirty would suit us better," she said, wanting time to dry her hair, time to feel all a woman's anticipation in the indulgence of getting ready for an evening with a man who truly wanted only *her*, not her connection to obscene wealth.

"Fine by me." He smiled the words, a smile that curled Christabel's toes.

"Thank you." Her voice came out husky, furred by emotions rushing free from the strictures of years of discipline.

"My pleasure," he replied, then transferred his smile to Alicia. "Chocolate chip?"

Her hands flew up into a fervent wish grasp. "Please?"

"I'll get some on my way home."

"Oh, thank you!"

He lifted his hand in a farewell salute to both of them, then strolled away with the air of a man who had come and conquered and the world was now his oyster.

Except it wasn't, Christabel thought ruefully. Only this little bit of the world belonged to Jared King. She remembered her visit to the great outback cattle station owned by his family, a vast land holding on the other side of the Kimberly from Broome. King's Eden, it was called. She'd been amongst the contingent of the family's employees in the pearl industry, invited to Nathan King's wedding, which had been an eerily soul-stirring ceremony, initiated by Aborigines playing didgeridoos.

She was glad she'd gone, glad she'd experienced such a unique insight into the traditions of the outback and the feeling of an ancient, timeless heritage that was tied to the land. Not the wealth made from it. The land itself. King's Eden.

Would she prove to be a serpent in Jared's Eden?

The carrier of evil that would poison his piece of paradise?

Sooner or later they would come—the powerful men in suits—and they'd destroy the normality of the life she'd established here, destroy whatever natural connections she'd made with people.

Christabel shivered.

Some things can't be stopped.

Jared's words…but they applied to much more than their feelings for each other. Still, for a little while…a defiant recklessness surged over the torturous fears…she *would* have what she wanted. And so would Jared.

It was *his* choice, too.

CHAPTER TWO

FEAR...because he'd been wearing a suit.

Jared mulled over that information as he drove back to the main shopping area to buy the chocolate chip ice-cream. It was another piece of the jigsaw he'd been fitting together ever since he'd met Christabel Valdez. The more he thought about it, the more it felt like a key piece.

His unexpected apparel had represented some kind of threat to her peace of mind. Was the suit simply an image that evoked bad memories, or was there more to it than that, a fear of someone who always wore suits turning up in her life again?

Jared didn't care for this last thought. Yet perhaps it tied in with her living in a caravan, a mobile trailer home she could take with her if she felt the need to move at a moment's notice. On the other hand, many people enjoyed the sense of a nomadic life that a caravan allowed. Not everyone wanted to put down roots in one place. Impossible to really know Christabel's truth until she chose to reveal it herself.

It wasn't the done thing to pry into the background of people who came to work in the Australian outback. There could be many reasons for dropping out of more sophisticated centres of civilisation. It might be as simple as a wish for a change of lifestyle, a need for space, a desire to experience something different...in which case they usually told you so. But there were those who stayed silent, wanting to shed what they'd left behind…and that was their personal and private business, to be respected as such.

Christabel projected the first attitude but gave out so little of her past, Jared had concluded she wanted to shut the door on it. What had been tantalising, and intensely frustrating to him, was her stance of keeping everyone, including him, at arm's length, as though she couldn't bring herself to trust a close relationship, however much she might want it.

And she did want it with him.

Jared's fingers curled more tightly around the driving wheel as triumphant excitement coursed through him. At last he'd broken through her resistance. She'd given in. Though why now…he shook his head. It didn't matter.

Perhaps it was the realisation that her fear—whatever its cause—was unfounded with him. If so, all the better. He didn't want fear to play any part in their relationship. He'd sort that out soon enough, now he had the chance to get close to her, closer than he ever had before in five long months of laying subtle siege to her defences.

Christabel…

He smiled on a wave of sheer exhilaration as he rolled the lovely lilt of her name through his mind…a name he'd thought might haunt him all his days, accompanied by a vision of eyes that glittered like gold in moments of fierce emotion and darkened to a simmering, sensual amber in moments of pleasure.

A woman with the heart of a tiger, he'd often thought, imagining her stretched out on his bed, lazily slumbrous, yet with those eyes inviting dangerous play, her satin-smooth olive skin gleaming, the rich abundance of her glorious long hair spreading silkily across pillows, the soft, perfect femininity of her body calling to everything male in him, a beautiful exotic mystery.

A haunting name, a haunting image…and all this time it had seemed the reality of her might remain forever elusive.

No more.

Tonight she would be within his reach.

Tonight…

It took considerable effort to bank down the passion she stirred in him and concentrate on practical details. Even his fingers were tingling as he activated the car phone and pressed his home number.

"Vikki here," came the familiar sing-song voice.

"Visitors for dinner, Vikki. Christabel Valdez and her daughter." It gave him intense pleasure to say that.

"Ah! So you win. I said to your mother, Jared will win. He does not know how to lose, that boy. He keeps at it until he wins."

He laughed. Vikki Chan had been with the family all his life, cook and housekeeper to his widowed grandfather, staying on to maintain the old Picard home for his mother after Angus Picard's death. It wasn't the least bit surprising she knew of his interest in Christabel. Jared suspected she knew everything that went on in Broome from her many long-established grapevines. Besides, his mother was in the habit of confiding worries to her.

"I'm about to pick up the ice-cream her daughter

likes,'' he informed. ''I also promised Alicia honey prawns...''

''No problem. I shall call and have the best green prawns delivered. Also more fish. Is fish all right for your Christabel?''

His Christabel...he hoped. ''I'm sure it will be perfect. They'll be arriving early. Six-thirty. Alicia goes to bed at eight.''

''I will take care of the little one. A bedroom near mine.''

''They may not stay beyond eight, Vikki.'' He couldn't assume too much, given the hot flare of resentment from Christabel when he had used Alicia to press the invitation. In fact, the giving in may not extend anywhere near as far as he wanted.

''I shall work it so you have time alone with her, Jared,'' came the arch reply. ''I have not lost my touch with children. And I very much doubt you have lost your touch for winning.''

Her confidence set him smiling again. ''You're a wicked old woman, Vikki Chan.''

He heard her cackling with delighted amusement as she disconnected to make other calls and imagined her wizened little face creased into a myriad happy wrinkles and her black eyes asparkle with plots and plans.

Vikki Chan would never say how old she was. Probably in her eighties, Jared guessed, though still incredibly spry and full of a zest for life. She'd be on the telephone right now to her seafood supplier, demanding the very best and threatening terrible fates if it wasn't delivered. The pencil she invariably poked through the bun that kept her scraggly grey hair under tight control would be down in her hand, making notes no one else could read.

Chinese, she said, but Jared had learnt to speak and read Chinese proficiently and he could never decipher what she wrote. It gave Vikki an enormously smug pleasure to keep her little secrets, while worming out everyone else's. Though not even she had managed to learn anything about Christabel beyond what Jared had learnt himself.

Which wasn't much.

She knew Amsterdam. A conversation on diamonds had dropped that fact. Singapore was another piece of the jigsaw, perhaps simply a stopover on her way to Australia. Wherever she had learnt it, she had an extensive knowledge of jewellery and a keen appreciation of how it was valued.

He parked the car in Carnarvon Street, crossed the road to Cocos Ice Cream Parlour, bought two individual tubs of chocolate chip for good measure since Christabel might like it, too, plus several cones in case licking was preferred to spooning.

From there it was a short drive up to the bluff where the old Picard home overlooked Roebuck Bay. Prime position, Jared always thought appreciatively, though the house itself was not a particularly impressive place, just a big, rather ramshackle wooden building, surrounded on three sides by wide verandas that could be shuttered against inclement weather.

Still, it held a lot of history for his mother and it was large enough to accommodate the whole family with space to spare whenever his brothers came to Broome. Tonight it was going to accommodate Christabel Valdez and her daughter, for as long as they were willing to stay. *As long as he could make it*, Jared privately vowed as he headed inside to the kitchen with the ice-cream supplies.

Vikki was chopping vegetables at her workbench. "Everything okay?" he asked, crossing to the freezer.

"Of course." She eyed him critically. "You look very hot, shirt sticking to your back. You need a shower and a shave."

Having put the ice-cream away, he placed the cones on the bench and shot Vikki a teasing grin. "I think I can remember to brush my teeth."

Unabashed, she returned an arch look. "That cologne you have...it is very nice. Definitely a subtle come-on."

"I'm glad you approve my choice. Been sniffing it, have you?"

She humphed. "You need all the help you can get to make the most of this night."

"Not artificial help. It won't impress Christabel one bit. Nothing has...not who I am or what I am or any material advantages she could get from me."

"Maybe...maybe not. I'm thinking a clever woman doles out a long rope for a man to hang himself with. You are a prize, Jared, and it occurs to me no other woman has ever tied you up this firmly."

He shook his head. "She doesn't see me as a prize. That's not where it's at."

She raised derisive eyes. "The executive head of Picard Pearls? A man with his own custom-fitted Learjet? One of the Kings of the Kimberly?"

"It's all irrelevant to her. I'd know if it wasn't. I'm not a fool, Vikki."

"Men in love can be blind."

"Not that blind."

There was a loud rap on the back door. "Ah, the prawns and the fish!" Vikki made a shooing gesture as she moved to answer the summons. "Go off with you, Jared. And if you want my opinion, if your Christabel doesn't know you are a prize, *she* is a fool."

Not a fool, Jared thought, leaving the kitchen to go to the suite of rooms he'd made his. Christabel operated on values that had nothing to do with wealth. That had been clear to him from the beginning, and her independent stance had remained consistent ever since. This was a woman who thought for herself, acted for herself and was wary of allowing any outside influence into her life.

He dumped his briefcase in his home office, stripped off in his bedroom and moved automatically towards showering and shaving, his mind occupied with memories....

The necklace...looking up from the paperwork on his desk and seeing it around his secretary's throat...

"Where did you get that piece of jewellery?"

"Oh, sorry!" A fluster of guilty embarrassment. "I know I should be wearing pearls..."

"It's all right. I just want to know. The design is very striking." Artistic, elegant, cleverly leading the eye to the enamelled pieces it featured.

"Yes. I love it and couldn't resist buying it."

"Where from?"

"At the Town Beach markets on Friday night."

"The markets?" It was not market goods. It was class. High class!

"Yes. Usually there's only cheap, fairly tacky stuff, but there was this rather small collection of really super costume jewellery on the stall that sells velvet jewellery bags. I would have bought more but this was seventy dollars."

"Locally made?"

"Well, the person who made it is a newcomer, though she's been here a while now. Lives in the caravan park. Very exotic-looking. Comes from Brazil, someone said."

Exotic…he'd imagined some over made up woman in a multicoloured floating garment…yet that design had tugged him into reconnoitring the market stalls at Town Beach the following Friday evening.

His first sight of her…like a magnet pulling him, his heart hammering, pulse racing. She'd been chatting to her co-stall holder. Had she *felt* him coming? Her head turned sharply. Their eyes met. An instant sexual awareness. Electric. How long had it lasted? Several seconds? Then she stiffened as though suddenly alert to danger, and her lashes swept down, shutting him out.

The abrupt switch off paused Jared in his tracks. It was wrong, unnatural. He sensed a shielding that was determined on blocking him out, and the urge to fight it welled up in him. She didn't know him, he realised, and he didn't know her. He tempered his more aggressive instincts, listening to the one warning him that storming defences was not a winning move.

He slowed his approach and made a casual study of the jewellery on the trestle table she stood behind. Each piece, to his eye, was a unique design, displaying a creative artistry he found almost as exciting as the woman. Part of her, he thought, an intrinsic part of heart, soul and mind woven into patterns and fashioned with exquisite taste. He couldn't resist touching them.

"You made these?"

Her lashes lifted. "Yes." She stood very still, her eyes alert, reminding him of a cat's, watching what his next move would be.

He smiled. "Your own designs?"

"Yes." No smile in response. A waiting tension emanating from her. "Are you interested in buying?"

She wanted him gone, which seemed so perverse it intrigued Jared even more. "You must have had training," he remarked.

She shrugged. "I am now self-employed. Do you wish to buy?"

"You come from Brazil, I'm told. Perhaps you worked with H. Stern in Rio de Janeiro?"

More tension. A flat-eyed stare. "Why are you inquiring about me? Who are you?"

"Jared King. I head the Picard Pearl Company here in Broome. I've been looking for someone. Someone special. You…I think."

A flare of alarm…recoil in her eyes.

The personal element was backfiring on him. He instantly slid into business. "I want a unique range of jewellery designed, featuring our pearls. I think you might be the right person to do it."

No hesitation, not the slightest pause or flicker of interest. "I am not the person you want, Mr. King."

"I think I should be the judge of what I want," he dryly returned.

"And *I* the judge of what *I* want," came the sharp retort.

"It could be worth your while…"

"No," she cut in firmly. "I am self-employed. I like it that way. Now, if you're not interested in purchasing…"

"I'll take the lot."

That startled her. But after the initial shocked flash of disbelief came a hard-eyed challenge. "It will not buy you anything but this jewellery, Mr. King."

"I didn't imagine it would, Miss…?"

Her mouth visibly thinned, wanting to hold it back from him, but her own intelligence told her it was too easily learnt from others here. "Valdez," she answered tersely.

He fished out his wallet. "How much?"

She noted down the prices as she wrapped each piece in individual sheets of tissue paper, then added up the total and showed him so he could check it himself.

As he paid her, he also handed her a business card. "I am seriously interested in your talent as a designer," he pressed quietly. "Please…think it over. Check my credentials. My contact numbers are on that card."

"Thank you," she said stiffly and gave him nothing more than the plastic bag in which she'd placed the tissue packets.

Having been comprehensively dismissed, he knew nothing would be gained by staying, but he left determined to seek her out again if she didn't come to him.

Two weeks he gave her, more than enough time to

check him out and consider the possibilities and advantages in the situation. Not the slightest nibble of interest from her. Nothing.

He did the pursuing and every meeting he managed was fraught with tension, her determination not to form any connection with him conflicting with the pull of an attraction she struggled to deny. It took a month of persistent angling and negotiation to get her to agree to submit designs that he could buy from her as he wished. Even then she kept her involvement with him strictly professional, continually blocking any encroachment on her private life.

Dancing with her at Nathan's wedding...the intense pleasure of finally holding her in his arms, though not nearly as intimately as he wanted, her hands pressing a resistance to full body contact.

"Are you enjoying your visit to King's Eden?"

She smiled, relaxing but still maintaining a wary distance. "Very much. It is what one might call a revelation. A world unto itself."

For once, her beautiful face was lit with fascinating animation as she listed her impressions of what she'd seen and felt throughout this outback experience. The flow of glowingly positive comments fuelled Jared's hope that she could be drawn into his life, could be happy belonging to it.

"And now you've met all my family," he prompted, wanting some hint of how she felt about them.

An enigmatic smile. "Yes. Your mother must be very proud of her three sons. And pleased with Nathan's marriage."

It was more an objective observation than a personal comment, frustrating Jared's purpose again. "What of your own family, Christabel?"

A slight twist to her smile. "I do not belong to anyone but my daughter." A gleam of warning in her eyes. "It suits me that way."

"You could have brought her with you this weekend." In fact, it was strange she had not, given how watchful and protective she was of the child.

A slight shake of her head. "The family she is staying with is safe. I know them from the markets. Good people. Long-time local residents of Broome."

"So you *wanted* to come alone."

A mocking gleam. "I simply wanted my curiosity satisfied, Jared. Don't make any more of it than that."

"And is your curiosity...completely satisfied?" he challenged, acutely aware of his own burning need for all she withheld from him.

She shrugged. "How can I fully know a legend I haven't lived? The Kings of the Kimberly...a hundred years of building what you have here and in Broome. I cannot expect to grasp more than a glimmering of what it comprehends."

The evasive answer pushed him into asking, "Do you find the idea of long roots inhibiting?"

She raised her eyebrows. "Have you found it inhibiting?"

"No."

"It is very much part of you, isn't it?" More a statement than a question.

"Yes."

"So you should stay happy with your life."

The wry resignation in her voice stirred a deep well

of frustration. Why was she keeping herself separate from him? Why couldn't she let the attraction between them follow its natural course?

"Is anyone completely happy without a partner to share their life with?" he demanded tersely, nodding to the bride and groom dancing together, just a few metres away from them. "Look at Miranda. Look at Nathan. *That is happiness*, Christabel! Can you not imagine that...want that...for yourself?"

He caught a glimpse of raw yearning on her face as she looked at his brother and the woman he had just married. For several moments an air of sadness hovered around her. Then she turned her gaze back to him and her eyes were flat, hard. "I've been married, Jared. My husband is dead but I still live with him. I will always live with him."

"He's dead, Christabel. Dead is dead," he countered harshly, unable to stop himself, feeling her vibrant vitality, the pulsing sexuality that aroused his so strongly.

"Believe me..." Her eyes bitterly derided his claim. "...you would not want to live in his shadow."

He didn't believe her.

She wasn't a woman in grief.

He'd witnessed his mother's grief after his father's death. Christabel Valdez did not want her husband back. She wanted *him*, and be damned if he'd be driven away by a shadow.

Jared wiped the few remaining bits of shaving cream from his face and grimaced at the hard ruthlessness in the eyes reflected in the mirror. He'd been thinking,

Nothing was going to come between him and Christabel Valdez tonight! But, of course, she would have her daughter with her, the daughter of the man she'd married.

He'd used the child.

Christabel may very well use her, too.

But he did have Vikki Chan on his side.

He smiled as he tossed the towel aside and picked up the bottle of cologne—Platinum Egoiste by Chanel. He might as well use every bit of ammunition he had in this war, because war it was. And he was sick to death of fighting shadows. He wanted hands-on combat. Action.

His body stirred in anticipation.

Vikki was right.

He *would* keep at it until he won.

CHAPTER THREE

CHRISTABEL parked her four-wheel drive Cherokee at the end of the street that ran parallel to the old Picard property. There was no road in front of it, nothing to disturb the view it commanded over Roebuck Bay. The house itself was considered a historic landmark, built by Captain Trevor Picard in 1919, the owner of forty pearling luggers—so she'd read in the museum records.

This was where Jared lived.

He was in there waiting for her.

Christabel's fingers stayed tightly curled around the steering wheel as she tried to steady her nerves. Ever since she'd accepted his invitation she'd been defying all the things she'd forbidden herself, wanting what he wanted, wanting to show him she did. She was twenty-seven years old and she'd never had a lover, only a husband who'd only ever cared about his own pleasure, never hers. She was sure Jared would be different.

"Is this it, Mummy?"

"Yes." This was definitely *it*, Christabel decided as she answered her daughter.

"Then why aren't we getting out?"

"Getting out now," she answered.

Alighting from the driver's seat and rounding the Cherokee to the passenger side, Christabel found her gaze drawn to the house where Jared chose to live. It was a big, solid old place. Other people with the accumulated wealth of the King Picard family might have torn it down and built something grander, more modern and impressive, and it would have meant nothing but a symbol of wealth.

Like the majestic old homestead she'd seen at King's Eden, this house seemed to stand for endurance, for something lasting beyond any one person's life and death.

It had been caringly maintained—the building, the garden. Caring...everywhere she looked...the precise paintwork on the house, the neatly trimmed bougainvillea, the lustrous clumps of ferns and tropical foliage...and the sharp realisation came that what was in front of her stood for things she could never share with Jared and what she was setting out to do was wrong.

Too wrong to go on with.

She shouldn't have accepted this invitation, shouldn't be here. Jared King was too good a man to be used and left, as though he was not worth more than a strictly lustful affair. Maybe that would be enough for him...but what if it wasn't?

She stopped by the passenger door. Alicia was making an impatient face at her through the window. Should she get back in the Cherokee and drive away? How could she explain that to her daughter—such bad manners? Impossible. Yet to go ahead, dressed as she was...it was a tease, a deliberate sexual tease, meant to signal her willingness to end the torment of wanting. Jared would notice.

And she'd burn with embarrassment at the rampant wantonness that had led her into presenting such a provocative invitation to satisfy every physical desire they'd stirred in each other.

Alicia knocked on the window. "Come on, Mummy."

She'd have to minimise the effect. Somehow. And leave as soon as she decently could. It had been wrong to give in to this...this raging temptation. She must never do it again. It wasn't fair to him. He was wasting his time with her, time better spent looking for a woman who could embrace all that his life meant to him.

Best to break the connection after tonight. Or limit it more than she already had, make Jared understand it was not to be. Maybe she could lead into that this evening.

Taking a deep breath to calm the inner flood of agitation, she opened the door and released Alicia from her seat belt, glad she had her daughter to come between her and Jared and determined now not to accept any offer of a bed for Alicia when eight o'clock came. No time alone with him. She couldn't risk it.

"Big trees, aren't they, Mummy?" Alicia commented, looking up at them as Christabel lifted her out of the vehicle.

"Older than any others in Broome, I'd imagine," she replied, struggling for an air of normality as she, too, looked up at them.

The native gum trees had been planted in a row along this side of the house, just within the white picket fence that surrounded the property. The width of their huge white and grey trunks and the spread of the branches testified to the number of years they had stood, while undoubtedly other such trees had been cut down in the past to provide building materials for the township. They were also a testament to a family who looked after what they had, who valued deep roots, who were given to *long-term commitment* as naturally as they breathed.

''I like this place,'' Alicia declared, happily taking Christabel's hand for the walk around to the front gate.

Her little face beamed excited anticipation and excess energy poured into an occasional skip to her step, making Christabel smile over the uninhibited pleasure being so naturally expressed. Alicia looked very cute in a lime green shift she'd selected herself from a hanging rack at the markets, and simple little sandals with seashells sewn on the straps. To Christabel's mind, it was much better for her daughter not to be a designer-clad little miss, filled with a pompous sense of her own importance.

She wished her own appearance was as artless, acutely aware that the cotton-knit weave of her dress clung to her curves before flaring into a flirty little skirt that ended mid-thigh. It was definitely a sexy garment, sleeveless, its low round neckline dipping to the swell of her breasts. She wore no bra and only a minimal G-string, not wanting to break the slinky feel of the soft fabric. Its dark red colour hid the nakedness underneath, but the obvious shape of her breasts and the smooth line of hip and thigh suggested it.

Despite the heat, she had left her hair down, readily touchable, rippling around her shoulders in a loose fall to her waist. Her bare feet were slipped into black strappy sandals, easily slipped out of, as well. On a black leather thong around her neck hung a copper sun disk, split in two and joined by a crescent moon from which dangled uneven strings of triangles—all in copper, which had swirls of dark red through its polished surface. It was her own design and she liked the elemental nature of it.

She had been feeling very elemental as she had chosen what to wear...*and not wear*. It was what she had wanted to feel, a woman meeting a man, intent on revelling in the most basic level there was between them. Totally pagan and primitive, she'd told herself on a wave of mad exultation, indulging the wicked sense of throwing all caution to the winds and having what she wanted, regardless of consequences.

It was only too easy to fool herself into believing she had a right to this. The right of a woman. Being a mother should not mean she had to suppress her own sexuality, and she had never wanted a man as much as she wanted Jared King.

"Looks like a storm coming, Mummy."

Jolted from her intense inner reverie, Christabel looked out over Roebuck Bay. Black clouds were looming ominously above the horizon. No romantic moonrise tonight, she thought wryly. Not that she'd come for romance. In fact, a quick tropical storm was more in keeping with the kind of relationship she'd envisaged with Jared...a storm that would blow over and just be a part of the past when she moved on.

Could it be so?

Was she worrying needlessly?

Or would it leave wreckage in its wake?

"We'd better get inside before it starts," she said,

quickening her pace, aware of how swiftly storms swept in here.

"Can we watch it from the veranda?" Alicia asked eagerly, always fascinated by the lightning show that usually preceded the deluge of heavy rain. She'd seen quite a lot of it this summer, although it wasn't called summer here. It was simply the wet season and the rest of the year was the dry. The lightning was always spectacular, and Alicia found it more exciting than frightening.

"I guess so," she answered, reasoning Jared would want to please her daughter, given his ready offer of honey prawns and chocolate chip ice-cream.

They arrived at the front gate. Christabel reached over it to work the catch on the other side. To her frustration, it seemed to be stuck. She released Alicia's hand to give herself leverage for a stronger tug, even while thinking this physical obstacle was a sign she was trespassing where she shouldn't go. The gate didn't want to let her in. It was protecting the people it was built to protect.

"I'll open it for you!"

She looked up to see Jared emerging from the veranda, already descending the steps to the path leading to the gate.

"It's probably stuck, not having been opened since the fence was last painted," he explained, striding towards her. "We mostly use the side entrance."

His white shirt was unbuttoned, flapping open as he walked, revealing black curls nestled on his darkly tanned chest and a fine line of hair arrowing down, disappearing below the belt line of white shorts. Snug, sexy shorts, leaving most of his muscular legs bare.

His flagrant maleness caught the breath in Christabel's throat. She barely had wits enough to withdraw her hand and stand back from the gate for him to work the catch free for her. The urge to simply feast her eyes on him was so strong, it was difficult to think of anything else.

His thick dark hair looked soft and springy, newly washed. He had neat ears for a man, tucked close to his head. His jaw was shiny-smooth. She picked up a tantalising scent, something sharper than fresh sea air, intriguingly attractive, multi-layered in essence. Very Jared, offering sensory pleasure.

"There!" He beamed a triumphant grin at them as he swung the gate wide.

"Thank you," Alicia piped up, minding her manners.

"You're welcome," he returned, waving them forward, his eyes gathering a gleam of more personal triumph as his gaze travelled from her daughter to Christabel herself.

"Lucky you arrived before the storm," he remarked. "I was about to close the shutters on the veranda."

"We like storms," Alicia informed him.

"Well, in that case, we'll leave the shutters open unless the rain starts coming in."

Happy with this indulgence, Alicia skipped ahead along the path. Christabel waited for Jared to shut the gate behind them, inwardly churning over what he had to be thinking, given the overt provocation of her dress. She couldn't bring herself to walk ahead, knowing she would feel him watching the free movement of her buttocks with every step she took. It wouldn't be so bad, walking with him.

His shoulder muscles bunched as he realigned the catch and fastened it. Her own tautly strung nerves thrummed with the tension coming from him, causing her stomach to contract and sending little quivers down her thighs. Yet when he turned to her, it was with a warm, welcoming smile, aimed at relaxing any fears she might have over accepting his invitation.

"I like the pendant you're wearing. Very eye-catching," he remarked.

"It goes with the dress," she answered before she could catch the words back.

To her intense relief his gaze didn't wander downwards. His eyes twinkled appreciation straight into hers. "Once again you demonstrate your talent for the perfect touch."

"I'm a long way from perfect, Jared," she blurted out, guiltily conscious of raising expectations she didn't know if she could meet or not. Would he want more from her than having his desire sated? Was it just a physical craving for him?

"You gave me the kind of showcase I wanted for our pearls, Christabel. Your designs are now on display in Hong Kong, exciting far more interest in the trade than a showing of our wholesale product."

A rush of pleasure eased her sense of guilt. "Then I've given you something of value for all the time you've spent on me."

He frowned quizzically. "I do want more."

The quiet tone carried a wealth of suggestion, tapping straight into the pulsing core of why she'd come, why he'd invited her. He wanted more and so did she, and it had nothing to do with pearls and professional business. She stared at him, feeling the gathering ache of need he stirred, wishing it could be appeased, wondering if the risk would be worth taking.

"It must mean something to you, as well," Jared went on, "knowing your creative vision has excited such interest?"

It was on the tip of her tongue to say, *I only did it for you,* but that was far too revealing a truth. "I simply enjoy designing, Jared. What you do with my work…that's your business. It doesn't relate to me any more."

"But you could make a real name for yourself," he pointed out.

A kick of alarm hit her heart. "You didn't use my name, did you?"

His frown deepened. "No. As per our agreement, the jewellery was simply labelled Designs by Picard. But I do feel very strongly that you should get recognition, Christabel."

She shook her head, the anxious moment receding at his reassurance. "I truly don't want that."

"Why not?"

Because they'll find me through you. But she couldn't say that. Dragging him into her dilemma wouldn't solve anything. "I'm happier this way."

"You could make a very substantial career."

"I don't need a career. What I need is to be free, Jared. Can you understand that?" A kind of desperate panic welled up in her, forcing an explanation that warned him where she stood. "Not to be tied down. Not to be owned. Not to have my life ordered by others. So don't count on more from me. Don't ever count on more. I've tried to tell you…."

"Yes, you have," he agreed. "I'm sorry if you think I haven't respected those feelings."

The passionate outpouring broke into a ragged sigh. "Then why am I here?" she muttered defeatedly.

"Because it's where you want to be."

As simple as that. Except nothing was really as simple as that. She looked at him in anguished uncertainty.

"Let it rest for now, Christabel. Come…" He gestured towards the veranda, smiling in light whimsy. "…it's only one evening."

One evening…he was right. It involved only a short time span. Nothing need happen that she didn't want to happen. And Alicia was with her.

Her gaze automatically swung to the veranda as she fell into step beside Jared. Alicia was chatting to a little old woman who was bent over, exuding interest in what the child was saying.

"Vikki Chan," Jared elucidated. "Probably checking when and where to serve the honey prawns."

As with many of the Chinese population in Broome, she wore loose cotton trousers and an overblouse with slits on the side. Her grey hair was scraped into a bun and her much wrinkled face was creased into an indulgent smile. Clearly Alicia was at ease with her.

Christabel gratefully seized on an impersonal topic of conversation. "I find it amazing that the Chinese and Japanese people here have adopted Western society names."

"They've been here a long time. Descendants of the divers in the old days."

"Yes, but they still keep many of their customs. Like leaving money on the graves in their cemetery."

"Ah, but that has to do with beliefs, not day-to-day mixing with people. The captains of the pearling luggers gave Western names to their divers, for their own convenience in identifying them. The practice was accepted and passed on."

"A very arrogant practice, imposing one culture on another."

"Not a culture. Just a name. The Chinese culture is alive and thriving in Broome." He slid her a dry look. "I doubt you'd find Vikki critical on that point. She's quite the queen bee in the Chinese community."

Being the keeper of the Picard home probably carried a certain status, Christabel thought, and being of a venerable age undoubtedly carried weight. She wasn't really expecting the bright and shrewd intelligence that came straight at her from the old woman's eyes when she straightened up from talking to Alicia.

Christabel felt herself blushing. Nothing was escaping those eyes. They had her stripped and logged in detail, with probably a character analysis done, as well. It took staunch discipline to keep walking up the steps to the veranda, her spine automatically stiffening at feeling herself scrutinised so comprehensively.

It reminded Christabel of her first meeting with Bernhard Kruger after she'd married his son.

Was she suitable?

Would she fit into the right mould?

Would she deliver what was required of her?

She'd had no conception of what she was getting into then. But she did here, with Jared's world, and no matter what she felt with him, the conviction came very strongly that it was wrong to even touch it as she had.

"Vikki Chan...Christabel Valdez," Jared casually introduced. "And her daughter, Alicia, whose acquaintance you've obviously already made."

The old woman bowed. "An honour to meet you."

Christabel politely inclined her head. "The honour is mine. It is very kind of you to welcome me."

Vikki Chan raised a smiling face. "Your daughter tells me she'd like to eat out here so she can watch the storm. I wondered if you would prefer inside."

"No. This is fine," Christabel quickly assured her, noting that a table on the veranda had already been set and feeling she didn't want to go farther into this house. It was easier, staying outside. Easier to leave.

"As you wish. I hope you will enjoy the evening."

Only one evening, Christabel recited firmly to herself, as she watched the old woman walk back into her domain, Jared's domain.

Behind her, a clap of thunder boomed with deafening force. It sounded like the crack of doom, warning her she should not have come. But it was *only one evening.* If she kept her head, no more would come from it.

Having screwed up the necessary willpower, she turned to face Jared...and the storm.

CHAPTER FOUR

JAGGED streaks of lightning shattered the blackness of the sky, a dramatic force of nature that was awesome, accompanied as it was by the explosion of thunder that rolled on and on. Christabel had never seen such storms in Europe, but she remembered them from her childhood in Brazil, and the flash floods they'd brought, wreaking havoc.

To Alicia, this was like a magic show, and she kept pointing out the highlights, crying excitedly, "Look! Look!" and clapping her hands with glee. "Oh, that was a big one!"

Jared laughed at her, enjoying her delight, while deftly playing the role of host, pouring them drinks, offering around a bowl of mixed nuts and rice crackers. He didn't bother buttoning his shirt, and Christabel found herself disturbingly distracted by the glimpses of bare chest.

When he handed her a glass of white wine and charmingly asked, "Or would you rather have the fruit juice Vikki made for Alicia?" she took the wine rather than be faced with him serving her another drink, standing close to her, making her too physically aware of him.

Finally he sat down at the table, on the opposite side to where she had settled herself, leaving the chair between them for Alicia, who was happy darting between the table where she helped herself to crackers and juice, and the prime watching position at the top of the veranda steps.

The table was set simply with bamboo placemats, chopsticks placed on little wooden holders, as well as conventional cutlery in case she and Alicia were unskilled with chopsticks. However, the serviettes were of good linen and the glassware fine quality, adding a touch of class to the casual mood Jared was obviously intent on establishing.

He lifted his glass, his eyes brushing over her like dark sensual velvet. "It's good to have you here."

She felt her nipples hardening and leant forward defensively, toying with her glass. "You can't really be lonely, Jared."

"There are empty places in my life. Aren't there in yours?"

She shrugged. "I dare say it's impossible to fill all of them, all the time."

"Filling some of them, some of the time, would help, don't you think?"

"Temporary measures?"

"If that's how it has to be. Better than nothing."

"Maybe the empty place would feel even bigger afterwards."

"Who can count on afterwards? I might be dead tomorrow."

"Not likely," she dryly retorted.

He glanced out at the storm, still unleashing thunderbolts. "My father died when his plane was struck by lightning, flying into Broome."

The stark statement came as a shock to Christabel. "I'm sorry. I didn't know."

His gaze swung back, fastening on hers with compelling intensity. "None of us know the day or the hour, Christabel. I believe people should make the most of the time they have, while they still can."

Certainly her husband hadn't expected to die, not before his father. Laurens had been counting on inheriting all the money and all the power, having fulfilled Bernhard's demand that he marry and beget at least one child. Nevertheless, he had more than made the most of the time he had with every woman he fancied and every bit of fast living he could pack in. It was not an attitude Christabel admired. It carried no caring for others.

She wasn't aware that her face had tightened over the bitter memories until Jared asked, "What are you thinking?"

She lowered her lashes, veiling her expression as she answered, "My husband died in an accident, too. It was a speedboat crash. Human error. Not caused by a storm."

She sipped the wine, deliberately discouraging any pursuit of that topic, wishing she hadn't brought it up. It was a mistake to talk about her marriage, except in the vaguest terms. The speedboat accident had been world news. It was a connection to all she wanted to escape from.

"How long ago did this happen?"

Jared's tone was sympathetic, stirring a savage irony. She didn't mourn Laurens. He'd lost his taste for her when she'd turned into an undesirable lump and he'd killed any shred of feeling she'd had for him with his subsequent behaviour.

"I was eight months pregnant with Alicia," she said flatly, careful not to give an actual date.

He seemed to weigh that statement before slowly commenting, "So Alicia never knew her father."

"I don't believe she feels any empty place on that score, Jared," she replied tersely, her chin lifting in defiant challenge.

"You're *all* she needs?" he queried.

"We manage well together."

"And is she all *you* need, Christabel?"

"She's all I've got," she answered quickly, trying to ignore the searing look that burrowed under her skin, finding and knowing the empty places he'd talked about and promising they didn't have to stay empty.

He was here, ready, willing and able to satisfy at least some needs. Tonight, if she gave her consent. And Christabel was once again riven by the strong temptation to do just that, to take what she could while she could. It was what he'd been offering, wasn't it, with his talk of not counting on an afterwards?

This dangerous train of thought was broken by the return of Vikki Chan, wheeling a traymobile onto the veranda, calling Alicia to her chair and switching on a lantern above the table to light the meal she was about to serve. She then proceeded to set out a platter of honey prawns and a bowl of steaming rice.

"I cooked more than enough for the little one," she informed Christabel, "so you and Jared can have some as a first course if you like."

"Thank you. They look very tasty."

The old woman smiled benevolently at them all. "Help yourselves," she invited, and left them to it.

There was no doubting that Vikki Chan was a superb cook. The honey prawns were the best Christabel had ever tasted, and Alicia even forgot the storm as she consumed her share with uninhibited pleasure, picking them up with her fingers, arguing they tasted better that way, and Jared agreeing with her.

Since finger bowls were set on the table, Christabel didn't fuss. Her mind was busily sorting through the impression that Vikki Chan had not been making any judgment of her this time. She hadn't exactly sensed approval coming from the old Chinese woman, yet there had been a definite acceptance of her being with Jared like this and a warm indulgence towards her daughter.

In between feeding herself, Alicia chatted away with Jared, enjoying his good-humoured attention, and Christabel couldn't help thinking he would be a good father, kind and caring, making any child of his feel special and loved.

Laurens would have turned their daughter over to an army of nannies, conveniently forgetting she even existed.

The means to an end…that was all his child had meant to her husband…all his wife had meant to him, too.

Special and loved…the words kept drumming through her mind, evoking a fierce surge of need to have Jared make her feel special, make her feel loved.

He instantly turned his gaze to her, as though he was instinctively attuned to her feelings and he'd caught this one right at its crest. Whatever he saw in her eyes, his suddenly blazed with a heat that scorched any denial of what flowed between them.

Her breasts started to prickle with excitement, and

a sweet, melting sensation spread towards her thighs. Despite the danger signals her body was sending, she could not wrench her gaze from the hot promise of satisfaction in his. She wanted him to prove that promise, to deliver all she craved from him, making reality of the persistent fantasy that he could and would be the one to make her feel what Laurens had never made her feel, not even on their honeymoon.

Yes...

Jared didn't say the word out loud but she felt him saying it, heard it throbbing in her mind, running through her bloodstream, zinging along every nerve in her body, building a wild exultant demand that went beyond sanity or common sense.

From behind her came a sudden swirl of wind, ruffling her hair, feathering her skin, and a clap of thunder directly above them made her heart leap, yet still that look from Jared held her, burning with an elemental force that defied other elements.

Vikki Chan reappeared. Alicia kept the old woman busy with conversation. The table was cleared. Alicia had sticky hands and she was invited to the kitchen to clean them properly. Advice was tossed back as they departed.

"Better close the shutters on the south side, Jared. The rain will come in with that wind."

It all washed over Christabel.

Jared stood up, so tall and handsome and quintessentially male, he was like a magnet, drawing on all her female instincts, forcing the recognition that some things couldn't be stopped. They were as inevitable as the rain, falling now in heavy drops on the tin roof. The wind caught the loose sides of his white shirt, billowing them out. His tanned skin gleamed under the lantern light.

"The shutters," he murmured, but he didn't move and she knew that he, too, was caught in this thrall of compelling attraction, not wanting to break it.

"I'll help you." The words spilled from her lips, unbidden, and her legs pushed up from the chair so that she was standing, matching up to him.

"Come *with* me," he said.

And she did, her heart pumping wildly as they moved into action together, sharing the task, keenly aware of the mutual feelings driving them.

The shutters were held open by metal rods. These had to be unhooked, lowered, and bolts shot home to secure closure. The wind blew fat splattering raindrops at them as they worked down the southern veranda in tandem—six shutters in all—with Jared, faster than she was, helping her with the last one.

He was so close, close enough for her to smell him, touch him, and she couldn't bring herself to step away. Her breathing was fast, shallow, out of control. Jared pulled the shutter down and they were enveloped in darkness, a warm, steamy, intimate darkness—the wind and rain shut out, beating at the house but unable to reach them.

She heard the metallic scrape of the last bolt being pushed into place. Everything was fastened down now, safe, except for all the feelings she'd tried to suppress running rampant, urging that the darkness be used to find out what she wanted to know, ached to know.

She heard Jared's breath whoosh out and knew it carried unbearable, pent-up tension. Then he was turning to face her and every nerve in her body was taut with anticipation, waiting for the first touch, the first proof that it was right for this to happen. It had to be right. It had to be worth breaking all the rules she'd set. It had to be what she'd yearned for in the darkness of other nights, countless other nights that had been filled with endless loneliness.

Take me, she begged in her feverish mind. *Take me....*

And he did, his arm sweeping around her waist and scooping her against him, plastering her against him as his other hand thrust through her hair, entwining tresses around strong, determined fingers. His chest heaved against the soft squash of her breasts. His thighs felt rock-hard. Then his mouth took hers, pleasuring it with a passion that excited her beyond anything she had known.

He aroused and kept stirring explosive sensations, kiss after kiss, feeding a deep, seemingly bottomless hunger that demanded a feast, not just a taste but an intense savouring of every taste there was. It was so absorbingly wonderful, Christabel revelled in every moment of it, consumed by the sheer power of the greed that seized her, the greed to experience everything there was to be felt with this man.

Her hands were in his hair, clinging to his head, urging the intoxicating intimacy to go on and on. Her body exulted in the hard heat of his, and when he grasped her bottom to lift her into fitting closer to him, it felt so right, so good, knowing how excited he was, wanting the ultimate connection with her, yearning for it every bit as much as she was.

''Stay with me tonight.''

He breathed the words over her tingling lips, words that throbbed their passionate need past the fuzzed edges of her mind, stirring a momentary confusion at the interruption to the silent flow of more immediate needs.

"Stay…" he repeated with raw urgency. "Alicia can be put to bed here."

Alicia! Where…? Her mind worked sluggishly. Gone with Vikki Chan to clean her hands.

"You want this, too, Christabel."

His hand on her bottom, pressing recognition of how aroused they both were. There could be no denying what was so self-evident. They both knew it. She wished he hadn't spoken, wished they had just gone on to…but there wasn't time now. That was what he meant. Alicia…Vikki Chan bringing the next course of their dinner…How long had she and Jared been locked together like this?

He lifted his head back from hers. "Look at me!"

His eyes were like black coals, glowing at her. He slid his hand from its enmeshment in her hair and gently cupped her cheek. He spoke slowly, softly, using his words like seductive tentacles, winding around her, binding her to him.

"We want each other. There's nothing wrong in that so just let it be, Christabel. Time to ourselves, doing whatever pleases us, being free of everything else, taking the night and making it our night."

Being free…just for one night…

"Say yes, Christabel. Say you'll stay with me."

"Yes," she said, impelled by more than Jared would ever know to snatch this time from the life she had to lead, the life that was forever burdened by her blindly naive decision to marry Laurens Kruger. ''I want this night with you, Jared.''

One stolen night.

What harm could there be in it?

No harm…just pleasure…with the pleasure King.

And he kissed her again to show her how it would be.

CHAPTER FIVE

WHAT they had started had to be put on hold until later. They were not alone yet, not in any practical sense, but Christabel felt oddly disconnected to being a mother or a guest in the aftermath of losing her long-held guard against the desires Jared King stirred in her.

It seemed strange, sitting at the table again as though nothing momentous had happened, secretly harbouring the excitement that continued to buzz through her body while Vikki Chan wheeled out the traymobile, reloaded with the next course for dinner. Alicia followed her, holding a cone of chocolate chip ice-cream, and she skipped over to Jared to thank him for the special treat.

Christabel couldn't stop looking at Jared, imagining what they might do when they were absolutely alone together. Was *he* still aroused? Impossible to know with him sitting on the opposite side of the table. He had felt...big. She wondered what he would look like with no clothes on, how he would feel to her then. Magnificently male and completely self-assured about his sexuality, she decided, not having to prove anything, just being himself. And letting her be herself.

"That looks superb, Vikki, as usual," he complimented as the old Chinese woman served them portions of steamed fish and braised vegetables and spooned sauce over them.

"Vikki has a Chinese dish with bamboo sticks in it for cooking the fish, Mummy," Alicia informed her importantly. "She showed me lots of special things. This house has got a really big kitchen. Bigger than our whole caravan."

"That's nice," Christabel answered vaguely, watching Alicia's tongue wrapping itself around the generous scoop of ice-cream, catching the melting drops before they dribbled down the cone.

She thought of Jared's tongue, electrifying her lips, invading her mouth, the exciting intimacy it had generated. Would he kiss her breasts like that, licking in a swirl around her nipples...

"And Vikki's got a shell collection, too," Alicia rattled on. "She said she'd show me when she finished cooking."

"That's nice," Christabel heard herself say again before forcing her mind to really register what her daughter was telling her. She turned to Vikki Chan, who was still spooning sauce. "Thank you for giving Alicia your time."

"No problem. It is a joy to see her delight in things. So it should be with a child."

"Yes," Christabel agreed, happy there was no problem with Alicia. She needed to be free of problems tonight, free to revel in the joy of her own body meeting Jared King's...making love...delighting in every pleasure he promised.

"Your mother will be staying longer than your bedtime, Alicia," Jared smoothly announced, smiling at her daughter. "When you've finished looking at the shell collection, I'm sure Vikki can find a bedroom for you to sleep in.''

''A whole bedroom for me?'' Alicia's eyes rounded at the intriguing idea before a more troublesome thought struck. ''Where will you be, Mummy?''

''Here,'' she answered. ''Here with Jared,'' she added, her heart filling with the bliss of that reality. Not fantasy tonight. No restless dreaming, either. She'd have the warm, strong, flesh-and-blood man she wanted, touching her in every sense there was.

''There is a bed in the same room as my shells,'' Vikki Chan said encouragingly to Alicia. ''Perhaps you would like that one. Shall we see?''

''Yes,'' she cried eagerly, only too happy to explore more of the house with the old woman.

They went off together, leaving Christabel and Jared to eat their dinner by themselves.

Jared refilled their glasses with wine. Christabel stared at the tight little black curls on his chest. She remembered her hands ploughing through the thick springy hair on his head as he kissed her. That was different, not the kind of hair she could twirl around her finger. She wondered if the curls would feel soft or wiry.

Jared lifted his glass as he sat down again. ''To being free,'' he said, uncannily reading her feelings as he did so often.

''This one night,'' she answered, more intoxicated by all she envisaged having with him than any wine could make her, but as she sipped the fine, oaky Chardonnay, its taste brought her palate alive and its bouquet was sharply fragrant, as though all her senses were heightened.

The fish was superb, moist, tender, flavoursome. She'd never eaten better. The vegetables and the sauce complemented it perfectly. Unskilled with chopsticks, she automatically used the conventional fork supplied, but she watched Jared using the Chinese implements, the deft control of his fingers, the smooth conveying of food to his mouth, so gracefully sure, never dropping anything.

Everything about him gave her pleasure. And it was such exquisite relief not having to put up defences, to say yes instead of no, to simply let nature take its course without any outside interference. She loved all she knew of Jared King. Tonight she would know more. As much as she could. She'd store it all up in a treasure box of memories and keep it forever.

Jared put down his chopsticks and nodded to her almost empty plate. "Good?"

"Great!" she replied with spontaneous exuberance, not having to guard her words, not having to repress anything for the rest of this night.

He smiled contentedly, sitting back with his glass of wine, watching her finish the last few morsels. It made Christabel very conscious of what he might be thinking as she ate. Was he remembering how little she wore under her dress? He had to know now, having felt the unrestricted contours when he'd held her. Was he envisaging her naked?

Her pulse quickened as she set her fork down and picked up her glass, looking at him over the rim of it as she sipped the wine, seeing the dark simmer in his eyes and feeling her stomach curl in anticipation.

"Shall we leave the table and enjoy the freshness

of the rain?'' he said, surging to his feet without waiting for a reply.

The suggestion startled her. ''Do you mean...go
out in it?'' The thunder and lightning had given way
to a torrential onslaught that was still pouring down.
They'd be soaked in seconds.

''No. Just to the edge of the veranda.'' His mouth
curved into a sensual tease as he stepped away from
his chair, heading for hers. ''I can't bear having the
table between us any longer.''

''Oh!''

Her excitement soared as Jared moved to the back
of her chair. He dropped a kiss on the top of her hair,
his warm lips grazing over the waves springing from
its centre parting. ''Bring your glass of wine with
you,'' he murmured persuasively.

It was still in her hand and she stood with it, responding unthinkingly, drawn by the compelling, seductive energy of the man behind her. He whipped
away her chair, curled an arm around her waist and
moved her out of the pool of lantern light, down the
veranda to a more shadowed area and over to the
broad balustrade between the posts.

The air did smell fresh with the rain, the oppressive
heat dispelled and the dust settled. The black sky was
still unbroken, no moon, no stars. She could hear the
storm-driven waves in the bay below them roaring
and hissing. But they were outside things and she was
most conscious of Jared, his hand resting on the curve
of her waist and hip, his body half behind hers, brushing against it as he reached past her to set his glass
of wine down on the flat width of the balustrade.

Then his arms were wrapped around her midriff,

and his cheek was rubbing against her hair, and his mouth was close to her ear, his voice low and husky as he murmured, "You've held me away from you so long, I have to know this is real."

"Yes," she whispered, hearing the echo of her own need.

"I want to breathe in the scent of your hair…feel it, taste it…"

He trailed hot kisses through it, down her neck, and Christabel instinctively arched back, revelling in the sheer sensuality of his desire for her. She felt him move his thighs apart, nestling her more snugly against him, and one of his hands moved to cup the soft swell of her breast, his thumb sweeping over its peak, fanning it into hard prominence.

She closed her eyes, wanting to focus on inner sensations, unable to resist rolling her bottom against him, inciting more awareness, exulting in the thought of exciting him. She wanted him to touch her other breast. It felt as though it was swelling, aching to be held and caressed, but he abandoned the one he held, his arms sliding down, hands spreading over her stomach, pressing an acute recognition of his arousal.

"I need to touch you and it can't wait," he warned, his fingers gliding towards her thighs, gathering up the soft fabric of her dress. "Tell me now if you've changed your mind."

She had no intention of changing her mind. It was wildly urging him on. And it was impossible to make any reply. Her breath caught in her throat as her skirt was lifted and everything inside her stilled, poised in mesmerised waiting for what would come next. Fingertips grazed the bare flesh under her hips, making it pulse with quivery excitement. His thumbs reached up and hooked onto the slim elasticised waistband of the G-string. It was drawn down so swiftly, Christabel barely had time to gasp at the boldness of the move before the flimsy garment was dangling around her ankles.

"Step out of it, Christabel."

"Jared…" It was more a choked cry of shock than protest.

Instantly his arms were around her hips again, on top of her skirt now, the fabric having naturally fallen as his hands had slid her underwear down her legs. The pressure, back into the cradle of his thighs, was a provocative reminder of her own wanton actions.

"I'll put it in my pocket," he assured her. "Neither Vikki nor Alicia will see when they come back. No-one will know you're naked under that dress except you…and me. And I want to know it, Christabel. I want to know you won't change your mind when Alicia comes to say good-night. I want to know the yes is still yes."

The passion in his voice sizzled through her. "It will be," she promised.

"You were in two minds earlier this evening. Make it decisive now. Don't tease, Christabel. Show me."

Tease… A guilty flush raced up her neck. The way she'd dressed could only be interpreted as teasing, had she not come this far with him, and what he said was true—no one else would know…except them. And there was something deliciously wicked in being dressed and naked at the same time. Wicked and sexy and terribly stimulating, knowing she was so accessible to any intimate touch from him.

She stepped out of the G-string.

He swooped, unbelievably...erotically...kissing the hollows behind her knees as he picked up the scrap of material and scrunched it into his shirt pocket. Then feather-light fingertips swirled up the outside of her calves and her thighs as he slowly straightened up, moving back into position behind her. The caress circled inwards, under her dress, and her whole body went into exquisite suspension again, tremulously waiting for him to reach further... wanting him to stroke her *there*.

But the shock of voices coming down the hallway froze that tantalising progress. Jared's hands slid away and he stepped aside, picking up his wineglass and turning his back to the rain, casually propping himself against the balustrade and studying her face as they waited for the approaching intrusion on their privacy. Christabel found her hand clenched tightly around her own wineglass and was amazed she'd kept holding it all this time.

"You are more beautiful to me than any woman I've ever known," Jared murmured. "And I want this night with you more than I've wanted anything in my life."

She shivered at the passionate intensity in his voice, suddenly fearful he would press for more afterwards. "You are special to me, too," she confessed. "But please understand...."

He pressed a light finger to her lips, halting the words she felt constrained to speak.

"You have a child. And a life you won't share with me. You don't have to tell me that, Christabel. You've told me so in a thousand ways."

"I don't want it to be like this, Jared. It just is," she pleaded.

He nodded. "I want you to know I value the gift…more than I can say."

The gift…it was a lovely way of expressing what they were doing, the giving to each other of what they most wanted, the wonder of it, the pleasure, the satisfaction of finally unwrapping what had only been imagined and knowing all it was.

"Mummy…guess what?"

Christabel felt torn as she turned to face the child who could never be Jared's child. Alicia was owned by her inheritance, and not even her mother could keep that from having its effect in the long run. Both their lives were circumscribed by it, and for several moments Christabel railed against that fate, having to remind herself that her daughter was the innocent victim of it before she could rise above a fierce wave of resentment and smile at the child she loved, now circling the table, assisting the old woman who'd accompanied her in clearing it.

"What am I to guess, Alicia?" She set her wineglass down on the balustrade, ready to attend to her daughter's needs.

"You don't have to tell me a story tonight 'cause Vikki said she would. She knows about dragons."

"That sounds exciting."

"And I'm going to sleep in the shell room."

"It's all settled then?"

"Yes," Vikki Chan answered, nodding reassurance as she added, "I'll tuck the little one into bed and see that she sleeps."

"It's very good of you."

"A pleasure."

"And thank you for the delicious meal," Christabel said belatedly, wondering just how much the old woman encompassed in her understanding. Not that it mattered. She would probably never meet Vikki Chan again. One night was one night.

"There's some ice-cream left over if you want it, Mummy."

"No. I've had enough, Alicia." The only food she wanted now was food for the soul, her own private feast of memories that might make some sense of being a woman, not just a mother.

"I'll look after coffee, Vikki," Jared slid in. "Thank you for everything."

The old woman flashed him a wise look as she finished clearing the table. "Then I shall retire, too." Having loaded the last things onto the traymobile, she turned an indulgent smile to Alicia. "You'd best say good-night to your mother now. We have much to do."

"Yes. We have lots to do," came the eager agreement. "Good night, Mummy," she cried, running towards her, arms outflung for a hug and a kiss.

Christabel had an electric few moments, hoping her daughter's feet wouldn't catch the hem of her dress as she scooped her up in their usual embrace. To her intense relief, she managed to negotiate the lift safely, with Alicia perched happily against her shoulder as they exchanged good-night kisses.

"Do I get a good-night kiss, too?" Jared asked teasingly, moving into an easily accessible position beside Christabel.

Alicia giggled and slid over to plant one on his

offered cheek. It was done without the slightest hesitation, and although Jared wasn't a stranger to her daughter, it was unusual for her to be so readily familiar with a man. Was it a natural affinity, an instinctive liking and trusting?

There was no future for them with Jared King, Christabel savagely reminded herself as she lowered Alicia to her feet again. There was no point in wondering about how good he might be for a fatherless child.

"Off you go," she urged Alicia. "I'll come and get you when it's time to leave."

"It's the shell room, Mummy."

"I'll show her where it is," Jared assured her.

"Good night to both of you," Vikki Chan said, bowing benevolently before wheeling the traymobile away, back into the house, Alicia trailing after her, asking about dragons.

There were too many dragons to fight, Christabel thought, suddenly swamped by a wave of wretched misery. Money was a curse, a terrible, terrible curse, and she was powerless to make it go away. Apart from everything else, there was always the question…had the speedboat been sabotaged?

Laurens dead, Bernhard dying of cancer despite the best medical treatment in the world…no-one to question what the money men did with the Kruger fortune once Bernhard was gone. The heir was a child who could be controlled, manipulated…*disposed of if necessary*?

Christabel shivered.

A warm arm encircled her shoulders. "She's safe with Vikki."

Safe? Not even an army of bodyguards could keep them *safe*! And what kind of life was that—imprisoned in a golden cage, never knowing who could be trusted when there was so much money at stake?

Tonight was one little window of freedom.

She sighed away her angst, determined not to let it intrude on her time with Jared. It was too precious to lose, even one second of it.

"So now we're alone," she said, lifting her hands to do what she had wanted to do ever since he'd come to open the gate for her. She slid her fingers through the black curls on his chest and smiled up at him. "I want to touch you, too."

CHAPTER SIX

TIGER eyes smiling at him...

The thought crossed Jared's mind, even as his skin seemed to leap with exultation at the sheer pleasure of her touch. There was more at stake here than fulfilling fantasies, he swiftly told himself. He sensed something deeply primitive working through her, an almost savage intent flowing through the fingers curling through his chest hair, her nails lightly scraping.

She had decided.

Now she was following through.

Was it with the heart of a tiger going for its kill, taking quickly, feasting quickly, walking away with a satisfied appetite?

No!

The fierce protest ripped through Jared.

This night would go *his* way!

One night, she'd said, but one night was never going to be enough for him. He had to make her feel it wasn't enough for her, either.

Her palms slid sensuously up to his shoulders, moving his shirt off them. He had to seize control before she tipped him out of it, make the moves his, not hers, slow everything down. But before he could stop her, she leaned forward and ran her tongue over his nipple, then pressed her mouth around it and...he couldn't bring himself to make any move.

His mind slid into meltdown, fired by her desire

for him and exploding with the sensations she was evoking, tasting him so erotically, and her hands gliding down his arms, pushing the sleeves of his shirt ahead of them. His stomach was contracting, his heart beating like a drum, wanting her mouth to move to that side, too. His shirt was dropping off him. He caught one sleeve as it fell past his hand, not knowing why, only that it was something to catch, to hold on to.

Then her hands were stroking the sensitive flesh under his rib cage and she kissed him over his heart. He had no control over his erection. His body had a life of its own and he felt it straining upwards, wanting her touch, yet he knew it would be over then and there if she did reach down and...fingers sliding under the waistband of his shorts.

He had to stop her.

Now!

He grabbed her under her arms, hauled her up and kissed her, ravishing the mouth that had ravished his body. She came up on tiptoe, flinging her arms over his shoulders, raking his back with her nails, as passionately intense as he in her wanting, kissing him back with a wild fervour that almost took him past the point of no return again.

He carried her to the balustrade, shoved his shirt over the bare wood, sat her on it and lifted his head back to draw breath. Her eyes were glazed amber, her lips still parted. The realisation hit him she had acted instinctively, compulsively, driven by desires she hadn't fully recognised, let alone planned on carrying out.

''Christabel...''

The soft call of her name cleared the glaze from her eyes and she looked at him with such vulnerable appeal his heart turned over. He lifted his hand to her cheek, stroking with a tender caring he hoped she felt.

"I want to love you...not take you."

"Was I doing something wrong?" she asked anxiously.

And he knew then, knew beyond a shadow of a doubt that what she was doing with him was new to her, that her struggle all along was not only with his interest in her, but with a sexual awakening she hadn't known how to cope with, and tonight it had become a stronger force than all the other hidden forces in her life.

What manner of man had she married for her to be so unsure of herself? He shook that enigma out of his mind. The only important thing was she'd never known *this* deep an arousal with any other man. It was as unique to her as it was to him and right now she needed to be reassured.

"No. Nothing wrong. Just too fast. You would have had me coming before I could make it special for you," he gently explained.

"Oh!"

He felt her cheek warm and to nullify any embarrassment he'd stirred, he bent and ran his tongue over the inner tissue of her parted lips. Then he kissed her slowly, sensually, determined on keeping urgency at bay, wanting to show her how it could be for them, making love.

He dropped his hand to her shoulder and gradually stretched the low neckline of her dress, shifting the bodice down below one elbow so he could lift her arm out of it, effectively baring her breast. She moaned as he filled his hand with the soft, yielding fullness of her naked flesh, and to his ears it was the sound of longing.

Sensing he had done what she wanted done to her, he bent and covered the dark areola with his mouth, swirling his tongue around it, lashing the distended nipple, tugging lightly on it with his teeth, exciting himself as her breathing quickened and he gently squeezed her breast in a pumping action. She clutched at his head, urging him on, emitting sexy little cries of intense pleasure.

She wanted more, was begging for more. He dragged the rest of her bodice down, freeing her other breast, and she actually grabbed his head and moved it across, expelling a ragged sigh as he answered the raging desire, working the deep, sensual magic he knew was coursing through her, building the ache, building the need, using his hand to keep the sensations flowing through both her breasts, and when she wrapped her legs around him and arched back, he knew she was teetering on the edge of climax.

He wound his arms around her, scooped her off the balustrade and crushed her to him, loving the naked moistness between her thighs rubbing against his bare stomach as he carried her, his face buried in the deep valley between her breasts, revelling in her lush femininity.

"Jared…what…where?" She was disoriented, confused, hanging onto his head.

"Going to turn off the light above the table," he explained.

"Oh! Was it…was it like that for you when I…when I…?"

"Yes."

"I've never felt like this." She sounded dazed, disbelieving.

"Neither have I."

It was the truth. He was seized with an all-consuming desire to give her everything she'd never known, for him to be the one she would always remember, her first real lover. And the one man she'd want to keep in her life, the one she couldn't resist sharing herself with.

He closed the front door, blocking any sound from carrying through the house, switched off the pool of light thrown by the lantern and spread Christabel across the table.

"What are you doing?" she gasped in bewilderment.

"Freeing my hands so I can finish taking off your dress."

She laughed in surprise, wriggling to help him. "Your shorts, too. I want you as naked as me."

He swiftly removed his remaining clothes, then slid her dress down her legs, ridding her feet of sandals at the same time.

"Touch your breasts, Christabel," he softly advised her as he parted her legs and moved between them, stroking her inner thighs. "Feel them as I felt them. Know them as I did…beautiful, sensual, full of womanly excitement. Do it as I do this…."

Very gently he moved his caressing to her moist lower lips. "Close your eyes. Think only of feeling," he murmured, swooping down to kiss and stroke and tease into intense arousal the most intimate part of her, spreading one hand through the silky hair above it to hold her still for him, sliding the other down the softly swollen folds, deepening the caress, circling the passage inwards, feeling the convulsive clutch of her muscles as he moved his mouth over and around the peak of excitement and breathed in the musky scent of her rush of desire for him...so sweet and heady and intoxicating.

"Jared..."

His name bursting needfully from her throat as she quivered, writhed, and he was filled with a wild exultation...Christabel calling for him...her man...the only one to make her feel like this.

"Jared...please...I can't bear it.... I can't...."

"Yes, you can," he soothed, moving to answer her need. "Go with it. Let it happen."

And he kissed his way up her pulsating body, deftly replacing the caress of his hand with the extension of himself she really craved...the glorious exhilaration of feeling her convulse around him in frantic welcome as he entered, pushing slowly inwards, providing the solidity for her to shatter around.

"Oh..." She arched in ecstasy.

He paused, kissing the highly thrusted peaks of her breasts.

"Oh...oh..." Tremulous waves rolling through her. She suddenly grabbed him, fiercely pulling him upwards. "More...more, Jared."

He gave her the full length of himself, plunging hard and fast to the inner rim of her womb, and again she arched, loving all he could give, and the blissful,

"Oh!" as she felt the completion of his thrust poured a sweet elation through Jared.

He kissed her mouth, passionately reinforcing the intimate link of their bodies. Her arms wrapped around him. Her legs wrapped around him. She clung to him, greedy for every sensation of this deep and mutual possession of each other, hugging him so tightly, he knew she wanted the feeling prolonged forever.

"Jared, this is so incredibly wonderful," she breathed against his lips.

The joy of her uninhibited heart zinged through his heart, instantly compelling the urge to control his own need while giving her all the pleasure he could. "It will keep coming," he promised. "Just ride with it now."

One orgasm—even if it was her first—wasn't special enough. Wanting her to feel a rolling sequence of them, Jared moved them both into alternating rhythms—fast and slow—reading her response, her need, driving her to each quivering pinnacle, riding the crest of it, sliding to the next one, loving the voluptuous roll of her body as she flowed with him and around him, the little cries of pleasure that burst from her throat, the sheer abandonment of herself to him.

His excitement in giving her this pleasure became so intense, he could not contain it any longer, and the last shred of control left him as he drove towards answering his own urgent need. She was so hot, so welcoming, so deliciously open to him, it was impossible to slow the compelling rush towards climax. Tension gripped his body, stretching it to the inevitable burst of sweet violent spasms, and again she wrapped herself around him, revelling in the gift of himself, and she was kissing him, caressing him, loving him, and for Jared it was the most perfect moment of his life.

"You truly are the pleasure King," she murmured in husky wonderment, still pressing soft little kisses on his face. "You truly are."

The title bemused him. "Is that how you think of me?"

"It's in your eyes, the way you touch...even that very first night you came to the markets, you took pleasure in running your fingers over my jewellery display, and when you looked at me..." She sighed, her warm breath feathering his cheek.

"Looking at you gave me pleasure, Christabel, and I want more of it now, looking at you lying on my bed where I've wanted you a thousand times. And that's where I'm taking you right this minute."

She gave a gurgle of delighted laughter as he scooped her up and held her cradled across his chest, his legs purposefully striding down the veranda to the French doors that led into his bedroom. It was coming out right, he thought triumphantly. Christabel hung her arms around his neck and nestled her head on his shoulder, wanting what he wanted.

"The rain has stopped," she observed in surprise.

"So it has," he agreed carelessly.

"A storm to remember," she murmured.

He smiled, interpreting her words as proof of the feelings he'd successfully implanted in her memory.

Once inside his bedroom, he laid her down on the pillows and switched on a table lamp, driven to match the reality of her to the fantasy he'd built up in his mind. He walked around the bed to the other side, feasting his eyes on the sheer perfection of her.

Her glorious hair was just as he'd imagined, a lustrous fan of silky waves, rippling out in sensual invitation, and her skin did gleam like smooth honey. Her body was the very epitome of femininity, lush curves and long, elegant legs, but he saw not a trace of the tiger image he'd imbued her with.

There was almost an awkward self-consciousness in the way she lay there, waiting for him to join her, not shy, but acutely aware of her nakedness and his appraisal of it. Her fingers made agitated little movements, as though uncertain of whether they should cover something, at least a little.

It made him wonder why...how she could not know the power of her sexual attraction...what had undermined the pride and confidence she should have?

Her eyes were not inviting dangerous play. Her eyes were fixed on him, avidly drinking in every detail of his physique as though it was a source of intense inner marvelling. It hit Jared forcefully that everything about this situation was new to her, being with him like this, both of them freely naked, totally unrestricted intimacy with no fear of criticism.

It was oddly moving that she was delighting in him so much, like a child being showered with gifts at a surprise party. He stretched out beside her, propping himself up on his elbow so he could watch the expressions on her face. She smiled at him, no exotic mystery in her eyes, more a twinkle of happy mischief.

"Am I allowed to touch you now?" she asked.

He grinned an open invitation. "All embargoes on touch removed. Go right ahead."

"Anywhere?"

"Whatever takes your fancy."

She immediately sat up in a commanding position, her face wickedly gleeful as she challenged him. "Then you lie down, Jared. Just you lie there and let me do what I want."

"Am I allowed to touch?" he asked teasingly as he settled his head on a pillow, assuming a totally relaxed position.

She cocked her head on one side, considering the question. "No. Better not. You'll distract me and take over and this is my turn."

He was amused and intrigued by what *her turn* would entail.

It very quickly became the most incredibly erotic experience of his life. She touched him as though she was sensually absorbing all that he was—his arms, his body, his legs, every part of him—her soft, beguiling fingerpads making their own paths and patterns, emitting a tingling magic, creating a sensational artistry focused entirely on him.

Wherever she kissed him it was with a kind of fascinated concentration on his response, wanting to know what excited, what pleasured, and clearly delighting in arousing him again. She knelt between his legs, lightly running her nails up and down the taut muscles of his thighs, watching the effect on him, the stiffening swell growing to full hardness. She reached out and wrapped her fingers around him, then gently cupped him with her other hand, squeezing as she bent over and took him in her mouth, rhythmically inciting the most intense and exquisite pleasure.

Her hair was spread all around him—his stomach, groin, thighs—silkily feathering his highly sensitised flesh as she deepened and accelerated the flow of excitement. Apart from the exquisite stimulation she was imparting, the visual pleasure of her was enthralling, lifting the whole experience to levels of intensity that blew Jared's mind. He heard himself calling her name in a wild crescendo of need.

Instantly she lifted herself and moved into straddling him. Then she was taking him inside her, lowering herself slowly, feeling and making him feel the long slide into blissful chaos as he climaxed in a series of violent tremors. Her beautiful breasts brushed his chest as she leaned over, and the soft curtain of her hair enveloped them as she loved his mouth with long, avid kisses.

Jared lost all track of the questions he'd wanted answered about Christabel. For the rest of the night they wallowed in a feast of sensuality, moving around each other, exploring and discovering, indulging an ever-increasing appetite for every possible intimacy, entranced by their connections, stimulated by their almost constant capacity for arousal, their desire to *feel* all that could be felt between them.

They didn't talk. Speech seemed irrelevant. There was a deeper, more elemental communion happening between them, a bonding that was more satisfying, more fulfilling than words could possibly express. This was Jared's instinctive belief, and his instincts had not been wrong about Christabel. She *was* the woman for him, just as certainly as he was the man for her.

When languor finally overtook them, energy completely spent, Jared drifted into sleep, never doubting that the woman he held in his arms would still be there when he stirred again. It didn't occur to him that when the night ended, Christabel would leave him. What she had stipulated earlier was forgotten, overlaid by a sense of unbreakable togetherness.

He simply didn't comprehend—couldn't comprehend—had no way of even beginning to comprehend—that for her, it had to remain...

Only one night.

CHAPTER SEVEN

SOMETHING felt wrong.

Jared was barely conscious, swimming out of deep sleep, yet he was instinctively reaching out, expecting, wanting and…there was only empty space!

It jolted him awake. Daylight hit his eyes. He was alone in his bed. Had Christabel gone to check on her daughter? How late in the morning was it?

His gaze darted to the clock radio on the bedside table, already thinking it was set to switch on at seven o'clock. It showed twelve minutes short of that. Still early, but the child was probably awake. Christabel would be very conscious of Alicia waking in a strange house, probably wanting to find her mother. Maybe she had come looking.

Jared frowned at that thought, then dismissed it. Like most old people, Vikki Chan slept lightly. She would have heard Alicia stirring, would have reassured the child, looked after her. It had to be Christabel's strong protective instincts making her act.

He rolled out of bed, wanting to be with her, wanting to forge a good relationship with her daughter, as well. He was striding towards his en suite bathroom for a quick shower and shave when the thought struck him—Christabel would not have gone to her daughter naked. They'd left their clothes on the veranda. Had she retrieved them?

He turned towards the French doors, then paused, noticing his white shorts and shirt draped over the armrest of the chair nearest the doors. Christabel had tidied up. He walked over to the chair and checked his shirt pocket looking for the G-string he'd tucked into it last night. The pocket was empty. As empty as his bed.

An unease slid into his mind...an unease he couldn't shake. He strode to his wardrobe, took out a *yukata*, quickly wrapped himself in the handy cotton robe, and with his heart hammering, took the swiftest route through the house to the shell room.

No Christabel.

No Alicia.

He made straight for the kitchen. Vikki Chan was measuring coffee grounds into the percolator. "When did they leave?" he asked, not bothering with any preamble. The need to know was too urgent, too vitally important.

"At first light," she answered, looking at him with eyes that understood his frustration.

"Did you speak to her?"

"No. I'd left the door to the shell room open so I could hear the child if she woke. She didn't wake. Her mother came and took her at first light. I heard the Cherokee she drives start up and leave."

Jared expelled a long hissing breath through his teeth.

"It was not my place to stop her, Jared."

He shook his head, stating the bleak truth, "She would not have been stopped anyway."

The night was over at dawn. That was when she'd

left him. First light. Nothing had changed for her. Nothing!

"It's Monday, Jared. A school day for the child," Vikki reminded him.

"If that was all Christabel had on her mind, she would have told me."

Vikki nodded, not arguing the case, accepting he knew better. "She carries many burdens, that one. She does not know what freedom is."

She did last night. For a little while. The need to hold onto that had Jared clenching his hands.

"You cannot fight her sense of responsibility, Jared," Vikki quietly advised. "You must lift it from her shoulders if you are to win."

"I don't know what *it* is! If I did…"

"She did not talk?"

"Not of that. In all the time I've known her…"

"She remains one step removed," Vikki finished for him. "Yes, I saw that last night. I was wrong about her playing woman games with you. She wants you but…"

"But what?" Jared pushed as she paused, frowning.

She shrugged. "It is for you to find out. All I know is this. The goodness in the child comes from the mother. There is a strong wall of integrity in Christabel Valdez which will not be broken. I think she does, and will always do, what she believes is right."

It was *right* for them to be together. How could she turn her back on what they had shared last night? How could she let it go?

Maybe she hadn't. It *was* a school day. And she

was supposed to come in to the office this morning. He'd arranged the meeting with her before going to Hong Kong, ostensibly to show her photographs of the special jewellery display—her designs for the Picard pearls—and hopefully discuss a further set of designs, a career with him.

She'd vetoed any idea of a career yesterday afternoon but there were still the photographs. He hadn't brought them out last night. If Christabel was still planning to see him at work once Alicia was off at school...he could be misinterpreting her departure at first light.

He gave himself a mental shake. Last night had meant so much to him, it had been a shock finding Christabel gone. Nevertheless, there was no need to go overboard on that action as yet. Vikki Chan was a shrewd judge of character. Christabel would do what she believed was right, bypassing any fuss over taking Alicia home, keeping the child uninvolved in their relationship until more was sorted out between them.

"I'm blowing this out of proportion," he muttered.

Vikki raised her eyebrows queryingly.

He gave her an ironic smile. "You're right. It is a school day. And a workday for me."

"Breakfast as usual?"

"Yes. Thank you." He turned to go, heading for the bathroom again.

"Your mother comes back today," Vikki called after him.

"So she does," he tossed back without pausing.

He didn't care what his mother knew about Christabel. She and Vikki could speculate all they liked about the relationship. He knew his mother would keep her own counsel unless he asked for it and he had no intention of asking for it.

Vikki hadn't told him anything he hadn't known. His mother had no better information. The only person who could tell him what he needed to know was Christabel herself, and it was well past time she started talking to him about the burdens she carried.

The long shadow cast by her dead husband.

Her fear of a man in a suit.

Had either of those burdens been diminished during their long night of loving?

Surely she would be more ready to be open with him when they met this morning. He had won her trust last night. More than her trust. They had made love for hours. It had to mean more to her than one night of sex with him.

The eleven o'clock appointment time they had agreed upon came and went. The photographs were spread across his desk, ready for Christabel to see, but the minutes kept ticking past as Jared waited and waited for her to arrive, his inner tension rising with the return of his earlier thoughts.

He remembered his toast to being free.

This one night, she'd answered.

One night.

He'd been so sure he could make it more.

Somehow he had to make it more.

A knock on his office door brought a leap of hope. She'd come. A bit late but…

His mother entered.

Jared slumped back in his chair, disappointment knifing through him.

"How was the trip?" she asked.

He summoned the energy to announce an enthusiastic, "Great!" then recollected she had spent the weekend with the Connelly family, planning the wedding between Samantha Connelly and his brother Tommy—true love having finally won out for those two. A stab of envy hit him as he asked, "Got the wedding on track?"

"They've settled on having it at Kununurra." She walked over to his desk. "Photographs of Christabel's designs?"

"Yes. They were a big hit with the Hong Kong traders."

She perused the shots he'd taken of the display. "They do look splendid. You were right about her talent, Jared." Her gaze swept up, the sharp intelligence in her dark eyes nailing him. "Will she do more for us?"

He smiled with ironic whimsy. "Who can tell with Christabel?"

"She's your enterprise, Jared."

He shrugged. "I had intended negotiating a new deal with her this morning. She hasn't shown…yet."

"And if she doesn't?"

"I don't have the right to order her time. You know that. The choice is hers."

"Nothing has changed?"

He knew it was an oblique reference to last night. She would have been to the house after the flight back to Broome, probably changed clothes before coming on here. Vikki would not have held anything back from his mother.

"Not in that respect, no," he answered, denying her any more personal insight.

Her gaze wavered. The corner of her mouth almost turned down into a grimace but she checked it. Jared sensed her vexation. She didn't like the situation with Christabel Valdez. There were too many unknowns for her to feel comfortable with it. Jared well understood her feeling, but it wasn't going to stop him. Some things couldn't be stopped.

She affected a dismissive little smile. "Well, I just dropped in to say hello. I must go and check my mail. We'll discuss the Hong Kong business after lunch."

"Fine," Jared agreed.

A tactful retreat…in case Christabel did come this morning…although it was now eleven-forty and looking highly unlikely.

He watched his mother leave. She always moved with dignity and grace. Everyone in the Kimberly referred to her as a great lady—Elizabeth Picard King of Broome and King's Eden. She was sixty-two but the only giveaway to that age was her white hair, which looked quite stunning framing a relatively unlined face—still a very striking face, dominated by her eyes and the strength of character that always shone through.

He loved and admired his mother. His father may have been the major influence in his two older brothers' lives, certainly Nathan's—the oldest son—and perhaps Tommy's, as well. Lachlan King had been a legend in his time, as had the King men before him, running the great cattle station of King's Eden.

Jared had loved and respected his father but he'd never wanted to walk in his shoes or take on his territory. Whether it was because he was the youngest son of three, or because he'd been more drawn to the Picard family's pearl industry, he'd always felt closer to his mother than he had to his father. His mother was a very special person, the most special in his life before Christabel.

Now…he had to find the answers that would make sense of Christabel's decisions. He couldn't force them from her. What he needed was more time together. She had denied him that this morning. Perhaps the strength of feeling between them last night had frightened her off. She might think he'd feel justified in making demands, putting pressure on the independent stance she insisted on maintaining.

Jared was quite certain that would not be a winning move. If she was feeling vulnerable, better to let her make the next move when she wanted to. She had to *want* to be with him, Jared reasoned. As much as he wanted to be with her. So it was a matter of leaving the door open for her to enter when she chose.

At twelve noon he picked up the telephone and dialled the number for the Town Beach Caravan Park. As expected, the call was answered by the manager, Brian Galloway, an old-time Broome personality. He was a big man with a big booming voice and a big beer belly, generally liked by everyone.

"Brian, it's Jared King here."

"And what can I be doing for you?" came the jovial response.

"I was expecting Christabel Valdez here at Picard headquarters this morning. She hasn't kept her appointment. Could I leave a message with you for her to call me at her convenience, set up another business meeting?''

''Sure thing. Leave it to me. I'll make sure the little lady gets the message.''

''Thank you, Brian. It is important.''

''No problem. Do it as soon as I can.''

''I'm much obliged.''

She had shown interest in the photographs yesterday. She would surely want her curiosity about the display of her designs satisfied. A business meeting could not be threatening to her. She had always kept control over what she did for Picard pearls. If she was feeling nervous, apprehensive over what he might have assumed from last night, this assurance of strictly business should give her enough confidence to walk through his door again.

Then what?

Grab her and make love on the desk? Make her feel so much that she'd spill out *why* they couldn't be together? His hands clenched into hard fists. He had to get hold of something he could fight, and fight he would to his dying breath. Christabel was his woman, and after last night, he had every right to fight for her. If only she'd let him!

The surge of fierce aggression gradually ebbed and he settled back into accepting the mental challenge she'd always posed. Giving her time and space had worked before. He'd give it a chance to work again before going after her. But the urge to confront was so strong, it was going to be hell holding a patient line, now that he knew what they could have together.

So how long would he give her?

Until he couldn't stand it any longer.

No call came that afternoon.

No call came on Tuesday.

By the end of the second day, Jared could not contain his frustration at Christabel's silence. They did have a business arrangement. The courtesy of a call didn't cost much.

If she'd got his message.

He snatched up the telephone and called Brian Galloway again.

"Jared King here, Brian. Were you able to get my message to Christabel Valdez?" he asked, schooling his voice to a tone of pleasant inquiry.

"Yep. Gave it to her yesterday when she came back with her daughter after school."

"Ah...thank you."

"She's been out all day today, as well. Might not have been convenient to call you. But she's home now. Do you want me to give her a reminder?"

"No...no...that's fine. Just wanted to be sure she got the message. Thanks, Brian."

She was home now, he thought, as he put the telephone down, itching to drive straight over to Town Beach and...but what could be said—or done—in front of Alicia? Bad move. He had to wait for Christabel to come to him. Time alone together. That was what he needed for progress to be made.

Besides, the fact she'd been out both days until Alicia came home from school meant she'd been deliberately avoiding any personal visit from him. Maybe she needed time to think, to reappraise the situation. He could only hope she was moving towards positive decisions, not negative ones.

Wednesday...

He'd been at his office desk for an hour when he remembered Alicia chatting to him about a special school excursion to the bird observatory. He was almost sure she'd said Wednesday. Which probably meant Christabel would have accompanied the class group. Mothers were called upon to help supervise such outings.

He'd been pushing paper around his desk, keyed up for a call that wasn't about to come. Deciding on some physical activity, he got up and went to his mother's office, poking his head around her door to announce, "I'm going out to the pearl farm, see how the shell fishing is progressing. I'll be back after lunch."

She simply nodded, aware of his disinclination to talk.

Half an hour later he was on the Beagle Bay Road out of Broome, hoping for a day of distraction. He was no longer expecting any calls. When his car phone beeped, he frowned at it before leaning forward and activating the receiver. It wouldn't be Christabel. She didn't have this number.

"Jared King," he said, automatically identifying himself.

"Jared..." His mother's voice. "...I have some gentlemen in my office inquiring about Christabel Valdez."

Every nerve in his body leapt to red alert. He put his foot on the brake, slowing the four-wheel drive to a halt while his mind zipped through possibilities.

"Men in suits?" he asked.

"Yes."

"Where are they from?"

"I've been given to understand that Mr. Santiso, Mr. Vogel and Mr. Wissmann have flown all the way from Europe to talk to Christabel. At the moment they are trying to locate her. Brian Galloway of the Town Beach Caravan Park informed them of her connection with Picard Pearls and mentioned that she might have contacted you today."

Big guns from Europe. The formality in his mother's voice meant she was dealing with power. The long shadow of Christabel's dead husband?

"Yes, she did," Jared lied. "In fact, I'll be meeting her in about an hour's time."

Long before the men in suits got to her!

"At the pearl farm?" his mother smoothly inquired, knowing there was no way they could reach her before he did, even if he was speaking the truth.

"Yes. I would expect Christabel to be back in Broome in time to pick her daughter up from school this afternoon. However, if they want to pass on a message…?"

He heard his mother offer what he'd fed to her and snatches of the ensuing conversation. Finally, "No message, Jared. Thank you for your information."

They didn't need to leave a message, Jared reasoned. They thought they had Alicia as hostage to Christabel's return to Broome.

Santiso, Vogel, Wissmann…he recited their names, memorising them as he turned the four-wheel drive around and headed back to Broome as fast as he safely could. The bird observatory was eighteen kil-

ometres on the other side of the township. He prayed
Christabel was there with her daughter.

This was crunch time.

He knew it in his bones.

Christabel was frightened of men in suits.

She had to choose him.

CHAPTER EIGHT

IT WAS quite incredible, the huge flocks of waders at Crab Creek, Christabel thought, listening to the teacher identify the bird species for the children, though missing the names herself. Focusing her attention on anything external seemed beyond her. The constant mental and emotional turmoil over Jared King could not be pushed aside, and each day brought more urgency to the decision she had to face.

Stay or go…stay or go…stay or go…

It was like water torture on her brain, and her heart was so screwed up from wanting more of him, it literally ached all the time. She couldn't keep Jared dangling as she had since Sunday night. One way or another, she had to decide and act on the decision. After what they'd shared together, he had to be feeling as deeply affected as she was, and it simply wasn't fair to keep avoiding a meeting with him or even holding him at a distance as she had before.

She didn't regret her night with him. Never would, she thought fiercely. It had been the best night of her life, and she could live off the memories of it for a long, long time. Yet…it made it so hard to walk away from. She didn't want to live off memories. She desperately wanted what they'd shared to keep on going, to follow its natural course to…

Was it tempting too many fates to remain here, to fully embrace the simplicity of just being a woman in love with Jared King? Was it possible that she and Alicia could live out normal lives, untainted by an inheritance that distorted everything? If she was careful...*they* hadn't tracked her to this outback haven so far. Could she take the chance they never would?

Her whole being yearned for more time with Jared, a continuance of the intimacy he'd led her into. It had felt as though they were truly soul mates on a level nothing else could touch. If they could just journey on together, maybe the answers to her situation would somehow become clearer and the burden she carried could be moved aside to a place of less and less importance.

A flurry of beating wings drew her attention to a flock taking off behind her...birds flying free. Was it a good omen, she thought fancifully, turning to watch them. Her heart leapt into a wild flutter as she caught sight of what had disturbed them into flight...the man striding fast and purposefully towards the class group...the man she'd last seen naked...the man who had just as powerful an impact fully dressed...Jared King.

He wasn't waiting for her decision.

He'd come to claim her as his woman.

She knew it, knew it with intuitive certainty, and she stood mesmerised, feeling her stomach contract in remembered excitement. Her mind jolted through fear of the consequences and surges of dizzying pleasure. He shouldn't be here but he was...he was...he was...and even from the short distance left between them he emitted an energy that swirled around her and held her captive. She couldn't tear her eyes off him.

He wore business clothes—sports shirt, tailored shorts, long socks, lace-up shoes—not dressed for a birdwatching stroll. He'd come from work, and the grimly determined set of his face telegraphed that he would not be turned away. Not by anything. And a sense of panic started welling inside her, diffusing the pleasure of his presence. She'd stolen one night with him. Could she really keep stealing more and more time without bringing a terrible punishment on both of them?

"Christabel…"

He spoke her name in a commanding tone, just as he waved her aside from the group in a commanding gesture. The urgent intensity in his dark eyes drew her into obeying, even as her mind frantically warned of the dangers inherent in involving herself further in this relationship. She tried to gather her defences as she stepped over to where he'd halted, out of ready earshot of the children, but there was no defence that could have withstood the shock of his next words.

"What do the names Santiso, Vogel and Wissmann mean to you?"

Her heart stopped. The safety net she thought she had instantly disintegrated. They'd come. She'd stayed too long and they'd caught up with her.

"Alicia…" The name tripped off her tongue in alarm as she instinctively swung to check where her daughter was.

A hand fell on her shoulder, gripping, halting any further movement. "She's right there with her teacher," Jared assured her. "None of the men I named know where you are. They think Alicia is at school and you're at the pearl farm with me. I bought you time if time is what you want."

She looked at him, dazed by his understanding. "Where are they?" she asked, struggling to contain the full-blown panic the knowledge of their arrival had triggered.

"Last I heard they were in my mother's office at Picard headquarters. I was on my way to the pearl farm when she called me. I said you were meeting me there."

"Why did you put yourself between me and them?" she cried, anguished by his personal interference. It was the last thing she'd wanted, Jared drawing the attention of men like Rafael Santiso to him. It was what had stopped her from...too late now. Wretchedly she sought to explain the situation. "You don't know..."

"I know you're afraid of them," he cut in forcefully. "You've been running from them, Christabel. I don't know how long you've been on the run but that's why you're here, isn't it? The Australian outback seemed safe."

"There's nowhere safe," she muttered bitterly. It was over—her chance with Jared. Over before it had barely begun.

"Yes, there is."

His insistence was hollow to her, words that had no substance in the sickening reality she knew only too well. She shook her head despairingly. "They'll be more watchful this time. I won't get the chance to give them the slip again."

"We do it now. Go and collect Alicia and tell the teacher that both of you are leaving with me."

The aggressive assertiveness in his voice rattled her. "I can't let you get involved," she cried. "It's bad enough that..."

"I am involved, Christabel," he retorted vehemently.

"You don't need to be," she argued just as vehemently. "You can say I didn't turn up at the pearl farm. I won't drag you into this, Jared."

"I won't walk away. Not when you're in trouble and I can give you a way out." His eyes burned into hers with steady resolution as he reasoned, "You came here in the excursion bus. They'll have you if you go back to Broome in it. I can take you to a safe place. It will give you time to plan what you want to do."

Time...her whirling mind seized on the sliver of hope he was offering. Everything within her recoiled from going back to *them* and the dreadful life they would impose on her and Alicia. Jared had bought her time with his interference and maybe she could make good use of it. Any postponement of the inevitable was better than giving up.

"Where can we go?" she fretted. "The road only leads here and back to Broome."

"The airport." He took a mobile telephone out of his shirt pocket. "I'll ring KingAir now to get a plane ready to fly."

KingAir...the charter company owned by his brother Tommy. Of course! She and Alicia could fly anywhere. And hopefully Jared's part in their escape could be covered up. A charter service was in the public domain. Just because his brother owned it didn't necessarily mean her use of it was tied to the King family in any personal sense.

"I can pay for it. One thing I'm not short of is money," she said with savage irony.

"Fine! Get Alicia and we'll leave now."

She left him talking to someone in the KingAir office on his mobile, confident he could charter a plane for them at a moment's notice. Christabel didn't doubt he would manage it, one way or another. He was so positive about getting her and Alicia to a safe place, she let herself hope it could really happen.

As she approached the class teacher, her mind was already racing over a course of action. The emergency funds hidden behind the lining of her handbag would take her anywhere she decided to go, buy anything she and Alicia required until such time as she could get back to the safety deposit box in Sydney. The caravan and the Cherokee could be left behind. Best to completely abandon them.

The teacher was sympathetic to her apologies for leaving the group, accepting the explanation that she had to take Alicia to meet some people who'd arrived unexpectedly in Broome. Which neatly covered Jared's coming to collect her.

Alicia, of course, had more awkward questions for her to handle. "Why can't we stay, Mummy?" she half-wailed as Christabel took her hand and drew her away from her friends.

"Because we have to leave."

"But we were going to have a picnic on the beach."

"Jared is taking us somewhere better."

"Where?" she demanded truculently.

"It's a surprise."

"I don't want a surprise. I like it here."

"Don't argue with me, Alicia. We're going with Jared and that's that."

She huffed and sulked.

"Don't shame me with bad behaviour in front of Jared," Christabel tersely reproved. "He's been very kind to us."

Another more resigned sigh, then a spark of interest. "Are we going to his house again?"

"We'll have to wait and see."

Jared was replacing his mobile telephone in his pocket as they joined him. He gave Christabel a nod of confirmation, then smiled at Alicia, projecting his usual charming manner.

"Sorry to take you away from your friends, but I do have a special treat lined up for you."

She instantly brightened, her little face lighting with eager curiosity. "What is it?"

"Well…" He took her other hand, intent on hurrying the three of them along as they set off together. "…instead of watching birds, I thought you might like to zoom off into the sky like one."

"You mean in a plane?" she cried excitedly.

"Yes. A small plane. It will give you a bird's view of everything you fly over."

While Jared chatted on with Alicia, explaining how differently places looked from the sky, Christabel forced her mind off the all too distracting rapport that flowed so easily—so *appealingly*—between Jared and her daughter and concentrated on mulling over possible destinations.

Perth or Darwin were big enough cities to hide

them for a while but they'd be the first places Rafael Santiso would target, and since he'd come this far to get them under his thumb again, he'd stop at nothing in searching them out. Alice Springs was a less likely place for him to look, right in the centre of Australia.

She recollected there was a famous train—the Ghan—that ran from there to the city of Adelaide in South Australia. One didn't need identification to buy tickets for a train trip. It might throw off any investigators from picking up her track.

Having made the decision, her thoughts circled around Rafael Santiso, the formidable Argentinian who had once headed the South American branch of the Kruger network. He'd moved very fast to clinch a much higher position after Laurens's death, manoeuvring his way around the other factions to win Bernhard's trust and support, taking the reins of power the moment the old man had passed on. Christabel had never trusted him. He was the one who had benefited most from her husband's fatal *accident*.

Worriedly she glanced at Jared. He didn't realise what he was dealing with. It was a dangerous game, helping her like this, frustrating very powerful interests. Her heart was deeply torn by having to leave him, having to cut him out of her life—this beautiful, wonderful man who'd shown her how it could be when everything felt right and nothing bad intruded— yet it could never be right for them again now.

Any more stolen time with him could put all he held dear in jeopardy. No matter how strong he was, the Kruger juggernaut would run over him, uncaring what was destroyed in serving its best interests.

Somehow she had to figure out a way to keep Jared safely removed from her situation.

By the time they reached the car park and were settled in his big Range Rover, Christabel was ready to lay out her plan. With Alicia in the back seat, she had Jared more or less to herself, seated next to him at the front of the vehicle. Once he'd switched on the engine and set off towards Broome, she broached the subject of avoiding any trouble from his connection to her escape.

"The lie you told your mother about our meeting at the pearl farm…how do you intend to explain that away, Jared?"

He slanted her a wryly amused look. "I don't have to explain it, Christabel."

"You once said to me some things can't be stopped. You can count Santiso as one of those things," she warned.

His face turned grim. "Tell me why you fear him so much."

She ignored his demand for information, rushing out a scenario he could use. "You could say I called you after your mother's call and cancelled our meeting at the pearl farm, explaining about the excursion. Say I cut off the connection too quickly for you to tell me about…about the people asking for me, so you came to the bird observatory to let me know and offer us a lift back to town. I think that's a reasonable story."

"I don't need a story," he said with a hint of exasperation and a look that derided her attempt to clear his involvement with her. "What I need is the truth about these men and what part they play in your life."

"That isn't important," she shot at him anxiously. "What is important is to keep you out of it."

"Out of what, Christabel?" he persisted.

She shook her head. "Please listen to me, Jared. It's for your own good, believe me. Once we get to Broome, you can drop me and Alicia where I parked the Cherokee, near the school. I'll drive to the airport and fix things up with the KingAir office. That way you won't be personally connected to my...my getaway."

He frowned at her. "You're frightened for *me*?"

She closed her eyes at his incredulous tone. "Please...just do as I ask, Jared," she begged flatly.

He made no reply for an agonising length of time. For Christabel, the tension of waiting was so painful she could barely contain the emotions churning through her. She fiercely willed him to agree, to cut himself free of her and Alicia.

"Give me your car keys," he brusquely commanded.

Her eyes flew open in disbelief. "What?"

"Your car keys," he repeated. "I'll see that your Cherokee is parked outside the KingAir office after you're on the plane. That will cover your story, if a story eases your mind."

"But..."

"It will ease my mind to personally see you and Alicia onto a plane and know you're beyond the grasp of the men you fear." He sliced her a look of steely determination. "I'm not letting you out of this vehicle until we arrive at the airport, so just do as I say and give me your car keys."

She had to concede that his plan eliminated any

risk of running across the men she wanted to avoid. Relieved that he seemed to be accepting her cover story, she dug into her handbag for her key ring.

"Make sure it's left in the ignition," she instructed, as she handed over the set of keys she carried.

"I only need the one for the car."

"I'll never use the others again so they don't matter. I won't be coming back, Jared."

"You're prepared to leave everything behind?"

"Yes."

"Including me?"

His eyes seemed to burn into her soul. It hurt so much, more than he'd ever know, to turn her back on what they might have had together. For several moments she couldn't override the yearning that ripped through her. She wanted to reach out and hold onto him, to take whatever he'd offer her, to wallow in his caring, to lean on his strength, to tell him no-one— *no-one*—had given her what he had and she wished they could stay together.

Tears pricked her eyes. She wrenched her gaze away, took a deep breath and forced out the only answer she could give, if she was not to ruin his life in ways he wouldn't comprehend until they hit him. He would end up cursing her for involving him if she didn't finish it now.

"There is no future for us," she stated categorically. "There never was. You asked for one night. It's gone. But I'll always remember it. And I thank you for the memory."

That said it all. Pointless to expand on it even if her throat wasn't choked up. Expressing her feelings might only goad him to insist on standing by her side and she couldn't let him. If she sounded cold and heartless, so much the better. Easier for him to let her go, believing she didn't care enough to hold on.

She kept herself rigidly still, staring ahead, closing him out of her personal space, mentally sealing every crack in her composure, determined not to leave him any opening for a different ending to this final encounter. Jared King was a good man. She might not leave him feeling good about the rather curt end to their relationship, but at least she could ensure nothing worse happened to him because of her.

It should have been a relief to reach the outskirts of Broome, knowing their time together was mercifully short now. Perversely, that reality increased the painful anticipation of parting. Forever, Christabel thought, on a wave of intense misery. In a few more minutes, Jared King would only be a memory for her, and she had a terrible urge to feast her eyes on him while she still could, to stamp every detail of him on her brain. She didn't have a photograph of him. All she would have was a memory and it had to last forever.

But if she looked at him he'd see…he'd feel what she was feeling. Jared was so perceptive, so sensitive to mood changes. She couldn't risk looking. Her hands clenched in savage resistance to the urge that would undermine the attitude she had struck. For his sake, she reminded herself. For his sake she had to be content with the memory of their one night together.

The Range Rover turned onto the road to the airport. She shot a quick glance at Alicia in the back seat, realising she'd been completely quiet on the trip.

Her head was slumped in sleep. She'd nodded off, tired from the long walk at the bird observatory. A five-year-old child, Christabel thought, worrying over how long she could keep her daughter an innocent little girl, ignorant of the forces that saw only her inheritance.

Jared drove straight to the KingAir office. There was one small plane out front, ready to be taxied onto the runway. Desperate to limit any farewell scene, Christabel anxiously gabbled, "I'll take Alicia out to the plane while you notify the pilot we're here."

"She's asleep. I'll carry her. See you both strapped into your seats," he firmly countered.

"Okay," she agreed, realising his way might be easier, avoiding a spate of questions from a newly wakened Alicia.

The moment he switched off the engine, they were both out of the vehicle, Jared appearing as keen as she was to speed her on her way. There was no more talking between them. Whatever Jared thought of her decision, he was keeping it to himself and she was grateful not to have any argument from him.

They walked out to the plane in a silence that throbbed with all that remained unspoken. Having spotted them from the office window, one of the KingAir employees—the pilot?—raced out to catch up with them and be on hand to open the door and adjust the front passenger seat in the cockpit to allow access to the seats behind it. He helped Christabel into the small plane then stood back for Jared to lift Alicia into the seat beside her.

As he withdrew his arms from around her daughter, Christabel grasped his hand, wanting one last touch of him. "Thank you, she said huskily. "Thank you for everything, Jared."

His mouth took on a wry twist as he answered, "My pleasure."

But there was no pleasure in his eyes. They were hard and flat and she had the quivery feeling that they were shielding a relentless drive to accomplish what he wanted accomplished. Which was probably to cut her out of his life as ruthlessly as she was cutting him.

"Fasten your seat belts," he instructed, moving his hand from hers to lock the front seat back into place. "Take-off will be in five minutes."

He closed the door and strode back to the office with the KingAir employee. The parting was so abrupt, she'd had no time to remind him about bringing the Cherokee to the airport. He'd remember, she assured herself. Though he might not want to remember anything else.

She sat in a pall of sadness, waiting for the pilot to come. Her chest was so tight, she needed the release of tears, but knowing instructions had to be given about her destination, she held back the flood that threatened. Later, when they were in the sky, she could give way to her grief for a while.

Her heart cramped when she saw Jared walking back to the plane. Alone. Was there trouble? More delay? Wrapped in dread of last-minute complications, she didn't realise his intention, even when he walked around the other side of the plane and hauled himself into the pilot's seat and closed the door behind him.

"Do we have a problem?" she croaked out.

"None that won't get sorted," he answered, and switched on the ignition.

"Jared?" Bewilderment crashed into horror. "You can't…"

"This is my plane, Christabel, and I'm flying you to a safe place. As I promised."

"But you agreed…"

"The Cherokee will be brought to the airport to buy us more time, but when time runs out, my mother knows how to deal with your visitors."

Overwhelming panic. He was drawing his *family* into her mess! "Your mother doesn't know what she's dealing with."

"Doesn't matter. She knows I'm taking you somewhere untouchable. Where the only law is Lachlan's law," he said with grim satisfaction. "We deal from strength, Christabel, a strength that belongs uniquely to the outback."

"You don't understand their resources," she cried.

"Nor they ours," he retorted, totally unmoved by her protests, taxiing the plane towards a take-off position.

"Please, please listen," she begged. "You don't know what you're up against."

"But I will know, Christabel. Either from them or from you."

She heard the ruthless, relentless tone in his voice, knew the purpose he'd hidden behind the hard, flat eyes, and finally comprehended that Jared had no intention of letting her go before finding out everything he wanted to know.

"You might as well settle back and relax now," he instructed, facing the plane down the runway.

"Where do you think they can't get at us?" she asked in bleak resignation.

"King's Eden. We fly to King's Eden, Christabel. Tommy will monitor the airways. Nathan rules the ground. No-one can get to King's Eden without our knowing it, and if they come, it will be on our terms."

He was so sure, so confident. Maybe it was true. The Kings of the Kimberly virtually had a legendary status, having ruled their territory for over a hundred years. Were they impregnable in that majestic old homestead that had housed generation after generation of a family bonded to a hard, primitive land?

Primitive...the word stuck in her mind. For all Jared's sophisticated polish, he came from pioneering stock, people who fought for what they held, people who endured any and all adversity, people who survived and went on prospering.

She remembered the aborigines at Nathan's wedding, calling on the spirits of the Dreamtime with their didgeridoos. She remembered the timeless feel of the place, the daunting distances, the sense of a strong, unbreakable destiny embodied in Nathan King and his brothers, standing shoulder to shoulder, and the pride on their mother's face, looking at them with the bearing of a queen who knew she had given birth to kings...*kings of the outback*.

The plane lifted off, control in Jared's hands now.

Could this formidable family do it...break the chains of the Kruger juggernaut of power? She shook her head at the fanciful thought. Why should they when she and Alicia were not their responsibility? Nor did they owe her anything.

She had to tell them what they'd taken on, lay out

the whole picture for Jared to see not only what he was embroiling his family in now, but what he could expect in any future with her. Then he could decide if the fight was worth fighting.

His choice.

He'd overridden her choice.

She gave up worrying and let the blocked tears swim into her eyes. Jared might believe King's Eden was the perfect escape. He meant well. But Christabel couldn't believe it would really provide that. For her and Alicia it was the end of the road.

CHAPTER NINE

ELIZABETH KING waited for Vikki Chan's appraisal of the man who had come to her house. It was strange and rather disturbing, after all these years of widowhood, to find herself attracted—physically attracted—and excited by a man. She had believed such feelings had died in her when she'd lost Lachlan. Always to her mind, her husband had been one of a kind, unmatchable, yet Rafael Santiso had definitely put a zing in her blood.

Brilliant dark eyes zeroing in on hers, just as Lachlan's had, the power of the mind behind them reaching out, probing, challenging, so assured of commanding the situation, of dominating. Aristocratic Spanish, she'd thought this morning, taking in his elegant features and fine, upright figure. Argentinian, she knew now, and wondered if he came from a family who had owned one of the great cattle ranches in South America. There was that sense of unyielding mettle about him...but it was probably foolish to compare him to Lachlan.

A dangerous man, Jared had warned, a master of manipulation, trustee of the multimillion-dollar Kruger inheritance, and Christabel's daughter, Alicia *Kruger*, not Valdez, was the heiress. For over two years Christabel had been on the run from Rafael Santiso and the influence he wielded, and Christabel was not a fool. Her enigmatic behaviour was now answered, and given the story she had told Jared, her fears were certainly not groundless.

Yet to Elizabeth, even the sense of danger had a special exhilaration to it...the need to be on her guard, to be alert and ready to counter-challenge with her own power. She couldn't remember when she'd last felt quite so *alive*. It gave her an enormous buzz, knowing Rafael Santiso was waiting on her veranda, waiting on her pleasure, immune from any force from him.

She heard Vikki returning down the hall, and her heart lifted in anticipation of the old housekeeper's judgment. "Well?" she asked.

Vikki Chan entered the kitchen smiling, her eyes twinkling in amusement. "He is not used to being thwarted. But he is very quick, Elizabeth. In the blink of an eye he changed his intimidating manner to appealing charm."

"But he did try to walk over you initially."

"Frustration momentarily clouded his vision, but he is adept at reading people. He checked himself even as he began his demand for you, sliding it into a request."

"Your personal feeling about him?"

The shrewd black eyes didn't miss anything. "He is a mandarin."

Elizabeth frowned over the old Chinese term for a government official. The picture didn't fit for her.

"A red coral button mandarin," Vikki elaborated. "A wily governor and an efficient general."

"He's in charge of a vast financial empire," Elizabeth reminded her.

"A trustee, not an emperor."

"Christabel doesn't trust him. Such power can corrupt."

"I felt no evil in him. Neither did you, Elizabeth. You are drawn to him." Her all too wise eyes crinkled as she added, "You changed into the coral shift to match him."

Elizabeth laughed. "Does nothing escape you, Vikki?"

"He came alone. That is interesting, is it not?"

"We shall see. Bring refreshments out in about ten minutes."

"You don't wish to invite him inside?"

"No. Christabel regards him as the enemy. Until I am convinced otherwise, he will not be a guest in my home."

She was conscious of a rush of adrenalin as she walked down the hall to the front door. It *was* interesting that he had come alone. Her secretary had reported that all three men had come to her office at four o'clock, undoubtedly having discovered from Alicia's teacher that their quarry had left with Jared long before the end of the school day.

Elizabeth had deliberately gone home after she heard Jared's report from King's Eden. Let Santiso chase after her, she'd thought. How he did it would tell her more about him. He'd weighted his presence with the Swiss accountant and the German lawyer this morning, and again at four o'clock this afternoon. Now it was after five and he'd come alone. Elizabeth surmised a lot of thinking had been done in the past hour.

She opened the door. He stood well back from it, half-turned towards the view over Roebuck Bay, and he was no longer dressed in a suit. As he swivelled to face her, Elizabeth had the wild impression of a toreador, flexing his lithe muscular body and flaunting his virility.

Maybe it was the open-necked white shirt and black trousers, or the flash of sexual challenge in the magnetic dark eyes, or the sense of power tightly coiled, ready to be unleashed…whatever…the male animal impact was much stronger than before, and Elizabeth felt her stomach curl in response.

It was totally irrelevant that this was a man in his sixties, his thick black hair threaded with silver, his face lined with years of maturity. He exuded an immensely powerful sex appeal, and Elizabeth was suddenly certain he knew it and this was deliberately switched on for her.

"Mrs. King…" He offered his hand, even as she noted his voice had taken on a richer timbre, not so clipped and coolly controlled.

"Mr. Santiso," she replied, meeting his hand with hers and feeling an astonishing frisson of electricity on her skin as he fanned it with his thumb.

"Since I find that your son has flown off with Christabel and her daughter, I am at a loose end here in Broome," he went on, his eyes projecting a pleasant opportunity as he added, "I was wondering if I could persuade you to join me for dinner tonight."

Elizabeth withdrew her hand and floated it in a graceful invitation towards the table and chairs on the veranda. "An attractive suggestion, Mr. Santiso, but I shall need some persuasion. If you'd like to sit and enjoy more of the view here…"

"I've taken the Nolan Suite at the Cable Beach

Resort. It has a private dining room. I'm told the sunset from there is spectacular.''

''Indeed, it is. And I tend to think you'll be seeing many sunsets if you're waiting for Christabel and her daughter to return to Broome.'' She smiled and stepped purposefully towards the table, remarking, ''From this side of the peninsula we enjoy the moonrise.''

He laughed and followed her. ''I take it you are conceding there is more than a professional connection between your son and Christabel.''

''Jared is very dear to me, Mr. Santiso. He has been very dear to me for over thirty years.'' She settled on the chair at the far side of the table and raised an eyebrow at the man who presumed she could be won in bed. ''Do you imagine the pleasure of being in the Nolan Suite with you would make me forget that?''

He grinned, totally unabashed. ''You are, without a doubt, the most exciting woman I've ever met.''

''Then why don't you sit down and pursue my acquaintance, Mr. Santiso?'' Elizabeth replied, ignoring the absurd leap of her pulse. He had to be flattering her. Such a man could have his pick of any number of beautiful, clever and *younger* women.

He regarded her speculatively, still on his feet behind the chair at the opposite side of the table. ''Why do you not believe me?''

''Because you're here for a purpose and I am not that purpose.''

''Christabel must feel safe with your son.''

''I believe she does. But she does not feel safe with you, Mr. Santiso.''

''Rafael. My name is Rafael.''

"I know."

"May I call you Elizabeth?"

"If you wish."

"I was entrusted with the responsibility of keeping the child safe. On Alicia's eighteenth birthday, she will inherit six hundred million dollars." He paused, watching her reaction. "I see you are not surprised, Elizabeth."

"Jared informed me of that fact two hours ago."

"And he is still intent on keeping them...*safe*?"

"We are not without means," she said with dry irony, knowing full well that six hundred million dollars dwarfed the wealth the King family could lay claim to. Yet there were resources that money couldn't buy, and inadvertently Elizabeth's eyes flashed that confidence as she added, "This is not your world, Rafael. It is ours."

"The Kings of the Kimberley," he mused softly. A whimsical little smile lingered on his mouth as he moved over to the balustrade between the veranda posts and turned his back to the view, dominating her vision as he faced her.

"I came to satisfy myself about your family. That is my purpose, Elizabeth," he stated directly. "I have known about Christabel's connection to your son since it started...months ago. I knew of her visit to King's Eden for the wedding of your eldest son. And on Monday morning I received the report that suggested that an intimate relationship had developed."

Was this true? He'd had Christabel watched all this time? Or had he gathered this information since his arrival today?

"Did you come to stop it?" she probed, wanting him to reveal more.

"Do *you* want it stopped?" he countered.

"I believe Jared wants Christabel more than he's ever wanted any other woman, and none of the barriers she has raised have turned him away. Believe it or not, the child's inheritance will be totally irrelevant to him. Some things can't be stopped."

"And you will stand behind your son."

She nodded. "His brothers, as well."

"Such a fortune draws more problems than prizes," he warned.

She was well aware of the power and politics attached to the Kruger cartel, the control they exerted over the diamond and gold markets, plus virtually every precious stone in the jewellery business…except pearls. The pearl farms of Broome produced the best in the world and were owned by Australian families.

"You cannot threaten our business, Rafael," she slid at him. "We would fight any attempt at interference and I have no doubt that supply and demand would come down on our side."

He shook his head. "No threats. I simply state the reality of the situation. The inheritance is more a curse than a benefit. It's not going to go away, Elizabeth. You will be loaded with the problems it brings."

Somehow we'll deal with them, Elizabeth thought, feeling more sympathy with Christabel than she'd ever felt before. Besides, this was not Europe. If Christabel wanted to stay with Jared, the outback had a way of protecting its own. Alicia would be insulated here from those who wanted a bite of her inheritance.

The question was…where did Rafael Santiso stand in this? What were his interests?

"If the inheritance is more a curse than a benefit, why do you stay in charge of it?"

His mouth tilted self-mockingly. "I'm addicted to problem-solving."

"Yet you allowed Christabel to run in fear of you. Do you call that solving a problem?"

He cocked his head slightly to one side, deliberating over his reply, possibly assessing its believability. This was the crux of the conflict between them and both of them knew it. It had to be resolved.

"She had cause for fear…but not from me," he stated, a harsh edge to his voice. "There were those whose interests were best served by poisoning her mind against me. As a result, she was resisting my efforts to keep her and the child safe, which made the situation more difficult."

He shrugged, and his tone slid into irony. "One cannot enforce trust. I saw it would be an easier task to facilitate her escape from the Kruger network, which she viewed as a prison."

"You planned it?"

"And directed it, every step of the way. The diamonds she has used for currency, the people who bought them from her, the bodyguards she never knew were watching over her. I can prove this, Elizabeth."

"Whether you can or not, she has still lived in fear of you," she tersely reminded him.

"I could not change that, and escape was her

choice. It gave her the sense of freedom she wanted,'' he sharply retorted. ''If she had reason to fear me, do you think I would have allowed her any possible alliance with your family?''

''I don't know. You're here now.''

He visibly relaxed, leaning back against the balustrade, his eyes taking on a warm velvety glow. ''I like the connection. I'm liking it more all the time, Elizabeth.''

''I think you have more explaining to do,'' she said flatly, not allowing any softening towards him.

He made an elegant open-handed gesture. ''The reality was…Christabel's and Alicia's very carefully orchestrated disappearance served two purposes. It removed them from very real danger and left me free to deal with those who were contesting Bernhard's will.''

''Is the danger now over?''

''There will always be the danger of kidnappers, but I'm satisfied that the house of Kruger has now been cleared of…malcontents.'' There was a ruthless glitter in his eyes as he curled his mouth around that last word. ''Factions who want to shift the rules will undoubtedly form from time to time.'' He smiled. ''But I am a very good watchdog.''

And much more, Elizabeth thought, sensing the drive and commitment that took this man wherever he chose to be. There was almost a devil-may-care air in his smile, and she knew intuitively he thrived on danger, as well as problem-solving. Maybe it was that quality that made him so exciting.

''We would make good partners, Elizabeth,'' he said softly.

She lifted her gaze to his and once again was hit by the sexual challenge he threw at her. "Partners in protecting Alicia?" she tossed back, struggling to contain her response to him.

"Partners in every sense. You know it. It's in your eyes. How often in a lifetime does one look at a person and know this? It is rare, Elizabeth. It has never happened for me before today."

"I find that hard to believe, Rafael."

"I am a widower. I loved my wife with a young man's love. Much passionate emotion. But you…you I feel are my true partner. I would have fought your husband for you if he was still alive."

Lachlan…for a moment Elizabeth's heart felt torn…but Lachlan was gone.

Vikki suddenly emerged onto the veranda with a tray of refreshments. Had only ten minutes passed?

"Why don't you sit down, Rafael?" Elizabeth invited again, needing more time to think.

He looked at Vikki, accepted the inevitable delay in his purpose and moved to take the chair on the opposite side of the table.

Elizabeth thought of the long lonely years of her widowhood, thought of the years still ahead of her. Her sons didn't need her any more. They'd found partners. There would be grandchildren, but would they fill the empty places in her life? Lachlan's blood line would go on. There was really nothing left to achieve.

Rafael could be lying. A master manipulator, Jared had said. But what harm could one evening with this man do? She was not about to be seduced, not mentally nor emotionally nor physically. One evening alone with him committed her to nothing, except taking a chance she wanted to take.

"Thank you, Vikki," she said as her old friend and housekeeper unloaded the tray. "Don't prepare any dinner for me. Mr. Santiso has invited me to join him for the evening at the Cable Beach Resort. In the Nolan Suite."

She smiled into the eyes watching her from across the table, eyes gleaming with brilliant satisfaction. It isn't as easy as that, Rafael, she silently promised him.

"I daresay he'd like to show me the Sydney Nolan paintings that give the suite its name."

CHAPTER TEN

THEY were so calm, so confident they could handle anything—Jared, Nathan, even Miranda, Nathan's wife, serenely serving coffee. They weren't the least bit perturbed by the call that had come through at six o'clock, giving an update on the situation in Broome.

Christabel wanted to scream at all three of them that they didn't understand how Rafael Santiso worked. She knew how his evening with Elizabeth King would end. He'd be here tomorrow with Elizabeth's blessing and he'd walk right in to King's Eden, not having to breach any defences whatsoever.

Then he'd mastermind taking her and Alicia back out. All for the best, of course. A man who could persuade Bernhard Kruger into appointing him sole trustee of the inheritance could persuade anyone to do anything, and he had six hundred million reasons for doing so. Probably more by now, with his talent for wheeling and dealing.

The thought of returning to the prisonlike mansion in Amsterdam, or the Greek island fortress, set off a convulsive shiver, shaking the coffee cup in her hand. It clattered on the saucer as she set it down.

"Perhaps coffee isn't a good idea. Keep you awake," Jared remarked, rising from his chair at the dining table. "Would you like to go for a walk, Christabel? Some fresh air and exercise before you turn in for the night?"

"Yes. Yes, I would," she gabbled gratefully.

"I'll look in on Alicia," Miranda offered.

"Thank you," Christabel clipped out, jumping to her feet before Jared reached her chair, too agitated to remain still a moment longer. "Should she wake…"

"I'll sit with her," Miranda assured her with a warm smile. "Your daughter is a pleasure to be with, Christabel. I hope I can bring up our child as well as you have Alicia."

The tall, beautiful blonde was just visibly pregnant, and it was obvious both she and Nathan would be very loving parents. For a moment Christabel felt a savage stab of envy. Even if Laurens had lived, he would have been useless as a father. Worse than useless. Damaging. Whereas Nathan would be just as good and kind and caring as Jared…Jared, who still didn't see that Alicia's inheritance made everything abnormal, or was being stubbornly blind to the problems it encompassed.

She nodded to Miranda. "You're very kind." And she had been, ever since they'd arrived at King's Eden, taking Alicia under her wing, showing her around the homestead while Christabel had spelled out her situation to both Jared and Nathan.

Neither man had made light of it, yet she had been disturbed by the calm way they had accepted the facts, proceeding to make plans to ensure that her choices and decisions were respected. It was as though they took this outcome for granted, and Christabel was half-fooled into believing they could make it happen, until Elizabeth's call had revealed

Rafael Santiso's insidious manoeuvring, going straight for the head of the family.

Jared's hand fell lightly on her shoulder and she turned blindly into the curve of his arm as he drew her with him out of the dining room. Yet not even his physical warmth and strength could comfort her.

"It will be all right," he murmured, hugging her more tightly to him. "My mother's not a fool, Christabel."

She would never have described Elizabeth King as a fool, but Rafael Santiso could pull the wool over anyone's eyes, however shrewd and smart they were. "She doesn't know him as I do," she said flatly.

"One thing our family knows rather well is the art of survival," Jared assured her. "We don't give up. Never have."

But they could give way, Christabel thought despairingly.

It was a clear night outside. No storm today, except the one that had flown in from Europe, bringing the darkest clouds of all. She looked up at a sky full of brilliant stars and thought of the diamonds in her safety deposit box at the bank in Sydney. No chance of getting to them now. The running was over.

She had just this one last night of freedom. Santiso would come tomorrow. He and Elizabeth King would make Jared see that she and Alicia didn't belong here. A simple story leaked to the media would show the King family fast enough that their lives wouldn't be their own any more if they chose to keep the Kruger heiress under their roof. The man was ruthless and relentless in pursuing his own ends. And once he had them back under his control, would they die in an accident like Laurens?

"Let's walk down to the river where the marquee was set up for Nathan's and Miranda's wedding," she said impulsively, remembering that was where she had first felt Jared's arms around her, his body moving in tune with hers as they danced together.

"Being on the run is no kind of life for you, Christabel. Nor for Alicia," Jared said quietly. "I know you're frightened of it but a stand has to be made."

She didn't answer. What point was there in railing against the situation he'd forced upon her? It was done and couldn't be undone. She had one more night with him. That was the only consolation she had, and talking wasn't what she wanted.

She slid her arm around his waist as they strolled down the slope to the flat beside the river. He rubbed his cheek against her hair, and her heart turned over at the loving tenderness expressed. He really did care about her. Her fear had triggered all his protective instincts, and she realised his need to stand between her and her enemies had driven his actions today. She couldn't blame him for being the man he was.

"Did you think the inheritance would make a difference to what I feel for you?" Jared asked, a low throb of passionate emotion in his voice.

"It hasn't touched you yet," she answered reluctantly. "It probably seems unreal to you. But it's very real when you live with it, Jared. It...*dominates*... everything."

"You would choose to live without it."

"If I could."

"Which was why you kept running."

"Yes."

"And the longest you've stayed anywhere has been in Broome."

"Yes," she sighed, knowing she'd brought this disaster upon herself by staying too long.

He paused their walk, turning her to face him. "Because of me, Christabel?"

She reached up and laid her hand on his cheek, wanting the skin-to-skin contact with him, longing for more. This was the day of truth. There was no longer any reason to hide anything from him. In a heady rush of release, she spoke what was in her heart.

"I've never felt what I've felt with you. I shouldn't have let it...take hold of me so much...but you were there...and I couldn't put you out of my mind... couldn't resist having what I could of you."

"It's the same for me," he murmured, covering her hand with his and guiding it to his mouth, pressing a kiss on its palm, then sliding her fingers along his lips, over his chin, down his throat to the open V of his shirt, clearly craving her touch as much as she craved his.

"I can't bear not to have you," he said gruffly.

"Then have me. Here...now...all night long," she invited recklessly, both of her hands flying down the buttons of his shirt, wanting it shed, wanting all their clothes shed. "Help me," she cried. "I don't want anything between us."

She whipped off the T-shirt and shorts she wore and he was just as fast in stripping himself, incited by her urgency, her need to recapture what they'd shared before. Her heart was pumping fiercely as she revelled in the sight of his naked body emerging from the trappings of civilisation. Primal man, she thought wildly, strong and hard and vital, poised to claim her as his woman in this place of ancient earth with a universe of stars overhead.

She wanted this so much, so terribly much. It was how it should be—simple, direct, as elemental as the earth and the sky, timeless.

He reached for her, and she slammed against him, exulting in the squash of her breasts against the muscular breadth of his chest, the hard pressure of his arousal against her stomach, the rocklike steadiness of his thighs. Her arms wound around his neck as she went up on tiptoe, her mouth seeking his, and he met it with a kiss that ravaged her soul.

This was her man. It was as though every cell in her body thrummed with recognition of it, rejoicing in the miracle of having found this brilliant sense of rightness. She kissed him back with a feverish passion for all she could have of him, wanting to fill her senses with him, to absorb the whole physical wonder of him and hold it within her forever.

She strained as close as she could, rubbing her body against his, loving the exciting friction, the yielding of her soft flesh to his hard masculinity, the warm skin contact, the slight roughness of his body hair. Her hands caressed the strong column of his neck and roved over his shoulders and down his back, revelling in the smooth delineation of muscles tensed in holding her, binding her to him.

And she wanted to be bound, wanted to be taken and possessed, wanted to possess him. ''Stand here,

Jared,'' she commanded in a fever of desire. "Stand here and let me take pleasure in you.''

"Christabel...''

It was a husky whisper of longing and love and she felt his hands clench in her hair as she slid down his embrace, adoring his body with kisses, feeling his stomach contract under the softly erotic brush of her lips, rubbing his hardness between her breasts, clasping his taut buttocks as she took him in her mouth.

He groaned as she knelt between his thighs, his whole body tensing at the rhythmic caress of her mouth, and he lifted her hair, wrapping it around him like a fan of silk, taking a compulsive sensual excitement from it as the throbbing need for each other became more and more intense.

With an anguished cry, he hauled her up, then knelt himself, spreading her legs across his thighs as he rocked back on his heels, then bringing her onto him, plunging himself into her so hard and fast it was shockingly glorious, the sensation of his deep penetration and her sheathing him, holding him inside her. She wrapped her legs around his hips and arched back over his supporting arm, wanting the full length of him pushed as far as it was possible, revelling in the sheer ecstasy of encompassing the absolute extent of his male power.

Just as she sighed in blissful satisfaction, he leaned forward and began kissing her breasts, swaying her from side to side as he took each one in his mouth, drawing them into spiralling peaks of pleasure, possessing them as he reinforced the other more intimate possession, rolling her around him.

The sweet flow of climax came in exquisite waves,

the rocking from side to side accentuating every ripple of it through her body. Her limbs were going limp. She was hazily conscious of her hair brushing the ground, their bodies bared to the night, the stars overhead pulsing their myriad pinpricks of light at her.

Then Jared rose onto his knees, lifting her with him, before lowering her onto the ground and looming over her, and she knew it was time for him. She did her best to move with him and he didn't seem to mind that her body was languorous. His control amazed her and she thought he must be the best lover in the world—the pleasure King—still inciting intense rolls of blissful sensation in her as he drove towards his own climax.

She loved him—all of him—and when she felt him spilling himself inside her, it seemed like the culmination of her entire life, the fulfilment of what she was born for...to have this man, to share herself with him, to be joined like this in the deepest intimacy there could be between a man and a woman.

They hugged each other, rolling onto their sides, prolonging and extending their togetherness, savouring all the contact they could have with each other; kissing, stroking, totally absorbed in immersing themselves in the communion of touch.

It was Jared who spoke. Christabel would have been content to be with him in silence. To her, it was best, simply feeling him as a beautiful entity who belonged to her, to whom she belonged in this time and place, untouchable by anything else. But he spoke, and connected them back to a world she didn't want to think about.

"Marry me, Christabel," he softly pressed. "I can't imagine my life without you."

It stilled the whole momentum of her silent loving. A chill seeped into her bones. She couldn't bear to *start* imagining a life without him. It would happen soon enough. Couldn't they have this night without bringing the future into it?

"We were made for each other. You know it," he insisted, sliding her hand up his body and holding it over the strong beat of his heart.

She sighed, trying to ease the frozen tightness in her chest. "Ask me tomorrow night, Jared," she pleaded. "Not now."

For several moments she felt the rise and fall of his breathing and willed him to let the question pass, not wanting to face the conflict that would rob them of this all too short, peaceful idyll. But she sensed the gathering of purpose in him, even before he rolled her onto her back and propped himself over her, determined on pursuing the issue.

"Why not now?" he asked, gently raking her hair back from her face, intent on seeing all he could of her face, her expression, making evasion impossible.

She stared up at him, hating the circumstances that made accepting what he offered too heavy a burden on her conscience. "I can't tie my life to yours until I know what Rafael Santiso wants. What he's come for," she prevaricated.

"What do *you* want, Christabel?"

"I'm not a free agent, Jared. Alicia is my child and I will not give her into the care of anyone else."

He frowned. "I wouldn't expect you to. Though I'd be happy to adopt her and share the responsibility of parenthood with you. I would do everything in my power to protect her and give her a good home.''

Marriage…adoption…legal ties Rafael Santiso would undoubtedly see as possible threats to his trusteeship. And Jared was no pushover. He was demonstrating right now his will to fight for what he believed in, and he had the proven ability to run a multimillion-dollar business. Given a fair playing ground, he might even win against Santiso, but she was certain the Argentinian wouldn't play fair and Jared had too much integrity to play dirty.

''Alicia does like me, you know,'' he said persuasively. ''I'm sure I can win her acceptance to my being her dad.''

Being Alicia's *father* could very well lead to his death.

She sucked in a deep breath to calm the fearful flutter that thought evoked, then reached up to trace his lips with feather-light fingertips, desperate to recall the sensuality they had been wrapped in before. ''I think you'd make a wonderful father,'' she readily conceded.

''Then say you'll marry me, Christabel.''

''Please…let me think about it, Jared.'' She moved her hand to his ear, caressing the inner coils. ''Give me tonight to…''

''No.'' He shook his head, dislodging her touch. His voice hardened. ''This time I won't let you slip away from me as you did on Sunday night, leaving me with nothing but the memory of how it had been between us.'' His eyes blazed down at her. ''Tell me what's wrong with my proposition.''

The mood had changed. Irrevocably. Christabel

recognised there would be no more lovemaking to-night unless he got his own way, and she couldn't agree to a marriage with him.

"I'm cold, Jared." It was true enough. Her heart felt like a block of ice. "I want to get dressed. Let me up."

He hesitated, hating the evasion, wanting to maintain his dominant position over her, yet force was not his style. It never had been in all the time she'd known him. Persuasion, persistence, determination, yes…but not force. Even today he had not forced her into his plane. He had simply taken charge of flying it to a destination of his choice, doing what he believed would work best for all of them.

He rose to his feet, a proud magnificent man bristling with barely leashed aggression. He offered her his hand to help her up but she didn't take it, sensing he meant to lift her into his embrace and press her into the surrender he wanted. She rolled aside and lifted herself, springing to her feet at a safe distance from him.

"You won't trust my hand?" he challenged harshly.

"It's not a question of trust," she flashed back at him, then realising his hurt—all the hurt she had inflicted on him with her silence—she laid out the truth he refused to see. "I'm poison to you, Jared. I'm like a black widow spider. Bad enough that I've taken what I have from you. If you married me, I'd consume your life."

"I'm prepared to take that risk, Christabel."

"I'm not."

"Then why put off saying so until tomorrow?"

"Because I'm selfish and greedy, and I wanted more of you before tomorrow came."

Tears welled into her eyes and she tore her gaze from his, overwhelmed by a hopeless sense of defeat. She saw a piece of her clothing and snatched it off the ground, pulling it on in swift, jerky movements.

"Nothing is going to change tomorrow," he stated, puzzled by her time limit.

"Wait and see," she threw at him bitterly, hunting around for the rest of her clothes.

"I've done too much of that, Christabel," he retorted fiercely. "Tell me what you expect to happen."

"They'll come," she grated out, hating the inevitability that hung over her, dressing herself with a sense of savage protection against it as she told Jared what she anticipated. "Your mother will bring them. Santiso will persuade her. One way or another, he'll persuade all of you that it's better to let him take Alicia and me back into his custody."

"I'll never be persuaded of that," he declared vehemently.

Fully dressed again and feeling more armoured to face his arguments, Christabel squared her shoulders and looked straight at him. He was still carelessly naked, his entire being so focused on fighting her conviction, she was instantly caught in the tension emanating from him, her own nerves snapping at the intensity of the conflict he would not stand back from.

"It won't be your choice, Jared," she said quietly. "It will be mine."

"You'd deny me the right to choose the life I want? *With you*, Christabel, whatever it takes and wherever it takes me. It's what I want above everything else.''

His voice was furred with the passionate emotion he was pouring out to her and she felt it curling around her heart, squeezing it. ''I can't live with that sacrifice,'' she pleaded. ''Don't ask me to.''

''Even if you go with Santiso, I'll follow you. I won't give up.''

''You may kill us all if you don't, Jared,'' she cried, deeply agitated by his resolve.

''Kill?'' he echoed incredulously.

''The man I married, Alicia's father, stood in the way of Rafael Santiso's ambitions. He was blown up in a boat.''

It jolted the powerful flow of his will. ''You said it was an accident.''

''It was officially declared an accident. I don't believe it. I have no proof but I don't believe it. Don't get in Santiso's way, Jared. I'll never forgive myself if you do.''

While he was still distracted by the shock of her claim, she turned and started up the slope to the homestead, forcing her legs to move away from him and keep moving.

He had to let her go.

That was the ultimate truth.

And fighting it was fatal.

CHAPTER ELEVEN

JARED let her go.

The spectre of murder held him still, its ramifications swirling through his mind as he watched her walk away from him, trudging steadily up the slope to the homestead, a lonely figure bearing a dark knowledge, moving back into a darkness there was no escape from. Not for her.

He wanted to pluck her out of it, to promise her a different life with him, but he knew they would be empty words to her. Empty words to him, as well, until he could see a way past this final fatal barrier. As it was, he realised his continual pressing of the attraction between them must have been a torment to her all these months. It would be a gross act now to subject her to more pressure. He had no ready answers to ease her pain.

He'd forgotten her husband, dismissed him as irrelevant once he knew he'd died before Alicia was born. Five years—ancient history, he'd thought, while it had been five years of living hell for Christabel. And there was no end to it. No end to the Kruger fortune and the power behind it. That was a truth he couldn't dismiss.

He watched her until she was swallowed up by the darkness of the night. For several moments he was gripped by a haunting sense of loss, and a cold, cold loneliness pressed in on him. He looked up at the stars and felt the distance of them, unreachable yet there, twinkling their invitation to those who would dare cross space to get to them, dare anything to conquer the void.

A strong surge of determination burned through him. He would not accept that he and Christabel were ships passing in the night. He had taken it upon himself to bring her and her daughter to King's Eden, to stop her running. He would not let Santiso win. If there had been murder done, as Christabel believed, then any further threat of it had to be lifted and dealt with.

At least now he understood—why she ran; why she had tried to deny the attraction between them; why she'd given in to it, if only for a limited time; why the time—to her mind—had to be limited; the wretched weight she'd been carrying on her conscience about involving him in her life, a weight she'd wanted to put aside while having this one last night with him.

He understood that, too…the compelling need to feel all there was to feel between them while she still could. It wasn't selfish or greedy. It was as natural as breathing, the wish to extend the life of something beautiful, something he knew would never come his way again.

He believed she knew it, too, that what they shared went too deep to ever find with anyone else. It wasn't wrong to take what she could of it. She'd given him as much as she took.

But Jared had no intention of letting it end here. He set about picking up his clothes and putting them on. Christabel had her own brand of integrity. Not hurting others was high on her list. Perhaps that was a woman's way, doing her utmost to save those she loved from being harmed. But letting a predator win only put off other evil hours. The harm would come anyway. It had to be stopped.

Fully dressed again, he walked slowly up to the homestead, planning what he would do if Christabel was right in her reading of the situation. Fear might have distorted her view but he was not about to discount anything she believed. She'd acted on that belief with a determination that was stronger than her own personal desires. That said a lot to Jared.

The lights were on in the living room, Nathan and Miranda waiting in case they were needed. Jared glanced at the illumined numbers on his watch—21: 43. His mobile telephone was still in his shirt pocket. He paused by the bougainvillea hedge that surrounded the majestic old house and its immediate grounds, took out the telephone and hit the computerised code for the Picard home in Broome. He wanted to talk to his mother before he spoke to Nathan.

But it wasn't his mother who answered the call.

It was Vikki Chan.

"It's Jared, Vikki."

"She is not home yet, and she did not give me a time to be home," came the reply, cutting straight to the point of his call.

Jared frowned, impatient for another report. "Where can she be reached?"

"I think you should trust your mother, Jared, and wait for her to call you."

"Tell me, Vikki," he commanded curtly. "Don't come between us. This it too important to me."

"It may be important to your mother, as well."

"She is meeting with Santiso on my behalf," he argued.

"I do not think entirely, Jared. Rafael Santiso is a very attractive man and you may not see it as her son, but your mother is still a woman with a lot of life to live."

Jared's mind reeled over this new element. Never having met the man he had to give Vikki's judgment some credence on this point, but he found it extremely difficult to imagine his mother connecting to anyone after his father. He recoiled from the idea. Vikki had to be wrong. It might be a female pretence on his mother's part to fool Santiso into relaxing his guard with her. On the other hand, Christabel's conviction suddenly rang out loud and clear.

Santiso will persuade her. One way or another, he'll persuade all of you...

"Where are they?" he demanded grimly.

Vikki sighed. "He invited your mother to dine with him in the Nolan Suite at the Cable Beach Resort."

"She's gone with him to a private suite?" Even he could hear the edge of outrage in his voice.

"You have no right to judge what is right for your mother," came the terse reproof. "I remind you she respected your choice of Christabel, knowing very little about her."

"But we do know about Santiso, don't we?" he retorted angrily. "Christabel told us."

"Trust your mother, Jared. She is not a fool."

His own words to Christabel thrown back at him, yet his judgment of his mother was now severely shaken. *She does not know him as I do,* Christabel had replied, and those words burnt into his mind, building a belief that his mother *was* being fooled by a man who had no scruples in using anything to get what he wanted.

"I'll see what happens tomorrow," he said, ending the call, his mind already occupied with Christabel's other predictions.

He activated Tommy's telephone number, determined on building a safety net. "Jared here," he announced the moment Tommy answered.

"No news of movement yet," came the instant report.

"He's with Mum. In the Nolan Suite at the Cable Beach Resort, no less. And get this, Tommy. She finds him attractive."

"You're kidding."

"Vikki Chan's judgment. Want to knock it?"

A shocked silence. Both of them were acutely aware of the old Chinese housekeeper's closeness to their mother, and her astute summing up of any situation.

"Christabel called Santiso a master manipulator," Jared went on. "She expects him to persuade Mum to bring all three of our European visitors to King's Eden tomorrow. If that's in the wind, Tommy, I want you in Broome tomorrow morning to fly them out yourself. No charter pilot. You. We keep this in the family. Okay?"

"Right you are. I won't keep Sam out, though."

"She's family." Tommy's fiancée had been like a kid sister to Jared for most of his life. He'd trust her with anything. He was going to trust her with a vital part of his plan. "I have a job for Sam, too, Tommy," he said, and outlined the responsibility he wanted her to take on.

"No problem," his brother assured him. "Where do you expect this to end, Jared?"

"I don't know yet. I'm hoping to sort out the truth tomorrow. But the final outcome—I will not have the woman I intend to marry living in fear."

"I'm with you, Jared." Hard resolve in his voice.

"Thanks, Tommy."

Satisfied he had countered whatever persuasion Rafael Santiso was working on his mother, Jared moved forward, heading for the home that had sheltered the King family for over a hundred years. He paused at the front gate, feeling the spirit of those who had built this place and the legendary memories it embodied, the hospitality that had always been extended and the rules implicit in that hospitality.

Let Santiso come, he thought grimly. If the Kruger trustee and his cronies demonstrated any poisonous fangs, they would be cast out of Eden and left in a wilderness, the like of which they would never have experienced before.

It wouldn't be the first time a transgressor learnt at first hand the rigours of survival in the outback, gradually acquiring a new respect for life and the lives of others. All the money in the world was futile and meaningless on that journey. Lachlan's law had always delivered a punishment to fit the crime—justice not only done but seen to be done.

Jared decided he would like very much to give Rafael Santiso a taste of fear, a taste of feeling there was no way out *for him*. A couple of years of that might very well revolutionise his thinking, give him a true appreciation of what Christabel had been put through. Though he had to be certain such a course was warranted before carrying it out.

His mother's apparent vulnerability to the man was another issue. It nagged at his sense of rightness as he proceeded past the gate and on to the house. Surely her sharply honed instincts wouldn't play her false. He had never once felt out of tune with his mother. Never. Could she be so deeply deceived by Santiso?

As he'd anticipated, Nathan and Miranda were waiting for him, sitting in the big room that housed generations of choices in furniture—antiques, Asian influences, modern comfort, exotic collector pieces. Somehow they all melded together into a fascinating blend of people's pleasure.

His mother always sat in the armchair upholstered in scarlet silk brocade. He wished it wasn't empty tonight. Nathan occupied the huge black leather armchair that accommodated the length and breadth of his formidable physique. Miranda, whom Jared had walked down the aisle to his brother because she had no known father or family, eyed him worriedly from the sofa she favoured.

Was Christabel bereft of any family, as Miranda had been before marrying Nathan? There was so much he still didn't know. What of her life in Brazil, before she'd met and married Laurens Kruger?

"Christabel came back alone," Miranda remarked questioningly. "She asked about Alicia then took her leave of us for the night. She looked as though she'd been crying, Jared."

He winced at the grief he'd unwittingly caused her in cutting short the comfort of loving by demanding answers to his need. Still, better that he had a fuller picture of what had to be fought. He turned to Nathan who waited patiently to be informed, his sharp blue eyes trained on his youngest brother, aware of the complexities of the situation and what Jared wanted from it.

"There's more," Jared stated bluntly, and filled Nathan in on the latest developments, delivering a sharp summary as he paced around the room, too wrought up to sit down. "So how do you stand with this?" he finished, more belligerent in his demand than he meant to be.

"With you," Nathan answered calmly, pushing up from the leather chair, his height and solidity automatically emanating authority as he moved to clasp Jared's shoulder in a gesture of unison. "We'll take whatever action is called for."

Absolute support. Jared saw it in his eyes and felt his inner angst ease. They were one in this—all three brothers—as he had assumed they would be—their father's sons—but his strong sense of family unity had been rattled by his mother's apparent leaning towards the other side.

"What about Elizabeth?" Miranda asked anxiously, echoing Jared's own concern.

Nathan swung to answer her, his face expressing no inner conflict whatsoever. "We protect our own," he stated decisively. "That means Mum, too. If her judgment is…awry, what happiness do you think she'd find with him?"

Miranda shook her head. "It's so hard to believe. Your mother is…"

"Lonely," Nathan supplied. "Rafael Santiso heads

and holds together a financial empire. It takes a certain type of character to achieve that.''

He turned back to Jared, an ironic gleam in his eyes as he added, ''Whether she feels an echo of our father in him...or something else...who knows? There has been an empty place in her life for many years.''

For the first time an attraction made some sense to Jared...a man of unshakeable willpower, a man who challenged his mother...and he well understood *empty places*. He was grateful to Nathan for his perception. Human frailty he could accept.

''We tread carefully there, Jared,'' his big brother asserted quietly but firmly. ''Hold back any sense of humiliation if Mum has been deceived. We must leave her dignity intact. Did you make that clear to Tommy?''

''No. I was angry,'' Jared had to confess. His eyes ironically acknowledged his own human frailty as he added, ''I felt...betrayed.''

Nathan nodded his understanding. ''You've been closest to her. In the end, she'll put you first. I have no doubt about that. I'll call Tommy and talk it over with him. Okay?''

Jared was reminded of all the times in his boyhood when Nathan had *fixed* things for his little brother. He smiled in wry appreciation. ''I am grown up now.''

Nathan laughed, his eyes twinkling appreciation and acknowledgment of the fact. ''Just saving you time, Jared.'' He sobered and gestured to his wife. ''Miranda's right. Christabel had been crying on her way back from her walk with you...''

''I had to take care of business, but I would be obliged if you'll talk to Tommy. And thanks,

Nathan.'' He reached up and clasped his brother's shoulder, a lump of deep emotion welling into his throat. ''You never have let me down and it's good to know you're still here for me.''

''We're here for each other,'' he answered gruffly. ''Always.''

Jared found himself too choked up to speak. He lifted his hand in a salute to Miranda, spun on his heel and walked out of the room, carrying with him a multitude of feelings that made life all the more precious to him, feelings he wanted Christabel to experience when she joined her life to his.

When, he thought fiercely. Not *if*.

He strode down the hall to the bedroom wing where she and Alicia had adjoining rooms. He'd done all he could to cover contingencies. His brothers were on-side. King's Eden was King's Eden. Tomorrow would come, but first there was this night to get through and Christabel needed to be loved.

More than that.

He needed her to believe in his love.

And that took action, not words. Tomorrow he would show her how deep and enduring his love was, but tonight was for feeling it.

He knocked softly on her door, hoping Alicia was asleep in the next room and Christabel was not sitting with her. He waited for several long seconds. When there was no response, he knocked again.

Again no sound of movement. Was she cuddling her daughter for comfort, deliberately ignoring any intrusion on her privacy? He couldn't imagine she was asleep herself, though it was possible. He glanced at his watch. It was over an hour since she'd left him.

Then the door opened a crack. "Who is it?" came the husky whisper.

"Jared."

He heard the shaky expulsion of a long breath. "There's no more to say tonight," she said listlessly, the weary dullness of her voice transmitting the sense of everything being over, and her acceptance of it.

"I just want to be with you, Christabel," he softly pressed.

The door was held at a mere crack. Jared sensed the conflict tearing at her—to open up or close—and pushed to end it.

The door swung open. No resistance. No welcome, either. She wasn't immediately visible. A lamp on the bedside table was switched on, spreading a soft glow of light around the room. The bed was mussed, the pillow dented, evidence that she had been lying down.

He found her sagged against the wall behind the door, as though she no longer cared about anything, letting him do what he willed because it really made no difference. Her head was lowered in a beaten expression, her cheeks streaked with tears, her long hair in a tangle of disarray. She wore the white nightgown Miranda had supplied, a sexy satin slip, but there was no sexual awareness in the slump of her shoulders, and her eyes were closed, shutting him out.

He closed the door and gathered her into his arms. She seemed too drained to fight anything any more, letting him draw her body to his, dropping her head limply on his shoulder. He held her, gently stroking her hair, rubbing her back, hoping he was imparting warmth and comfort, trying to wrap her in a blanket of love that would soothe her inner anguish.

Eventually her arms slid around his waist and her body heaved in a long, ragged sigh. "I'm sorry it is…how it is," she said tiredly. "I never meant to drag you…or your family…into this."

"I know," Jared murmured. "I'm sorry you've had to bear so much alone."

"I have Alicia," she answered, resigned to the curse of the inheritance—the price of having the daughter she loved.

"Was there no other family of your own to help?" he gently probed.

She raised her head, looking at him with sad, washed-out eyes. "They did help…when I went back to Rio."

She broke out of his embrace, shrugging off his solace as she turned away and walked towards the bed, her hands waving futile little gestures as she explained further.

"Through family contacts I managed to sell some of my jewellery to get untraceable money, passports in a different name. But I knew they couldn't shelter me for long. My family was known. I had to leave them." She paused, half-turned, aiming a direct look at him. "Just as you must know…I have to leave you."

He shook his head. "Not for my sake, Christabel. And not because I might endanger your life or Alicia's, because I won't do that." He strolled towards her, holding her gaze with purposeful conviction. "Only if you want to, and I don't believe you do."

He saw the flash of naked yearning in her eyes before she veiled it with her long lashes. Even as she jerked her head forward in a negative protest, he reached her and swung her around to face him, to hold her more firmly.

"Jared…"

"No. No more talking. Say you must leave me tomorrow night if you decide that's how it has to be, but love me now, Christabel, as I love you."

He kissed her and her anguish turned into a passion that matched his. No persuasion was needed. The loving was too intense not to be believed by either of them, and for Jared, that was enough to carry them through whatever had to be done to assure them of a future together.

CHAPTER TWELVE

THE day Christabel had always dreaded through her years of running had arrived. It felt strange not running any more…just sitting, waiting, letting others take charge, trying to hold onto her belief that Jared could take care of everything when the men in suits came. The clock was ticking down. In less than two more hours they'd be landing at King's Eden.

Christabel found it difficult to keep fighting the waves of panic that knotted her stomach. She felt hopelessly distanced from the King women who emitted the same calm confidence as the men, blithely chatting over the breakfast table in the old homestead's huge country kitchen, as though there was nothing whatsoever to worry about.

Jared and Nathan had left them some time ago, intent on discussing some plan with the Aboriginal tribe members who lived on the cattle station, but still no note of anxiety crept into the cheerful conversation between Nathan's wife and Tommy's fiancée.

They talked of plans for the upcoming wedding to be held in Kununurra at the end of the wet season, progress on the house Samantha and Tommy were having built on a hill overlooking Lake Argyle—exciting things in normal lives—and while most of it floated past Christabel's tension-ridden mind, Alicia was gobbling it up.

From her five-year-old view, Miranda was a lovely

lady who reigned over a cattle kingdom, and Samantha—whom everyone called Sam—so bright and pretty with her copper curls, sky-blue eyes and friendly freckled face, was an exciting adventuress who could fly a helicopter. Both of them happily pandered to Alicia's avid interest in their activities.

Christabel wondered if the imminent visit of the men from Europe and what they represented seemed unreal to them. Though she recalled that Miranda had been in hotel management before marrying Nathan, so she'd be used to dealing with people from all walks of life, and Sam Connelly, as a charter pilot, would also be familiar with moneyed clients. Even so, Christabel doubted they'd ever met the like of Rafael Santiso, and he and Vogel and Wissmann were not coming here on a pleasure jaunt.

There was no safe place, she thought bitterly. Elizabeth King had been persuaded into bringing them to King's Eden, just as Christabel had predicted, and only the fact that Tommy was flying them in kept a measure of control in the family's hands.

"Well, I guess it's time for me to be going," Sam announced, surprising Christabel out of her assumption that the whole family was gathering to present a block of support.

"You're leaving?" It felt like a desertion, rattling what little confidence she had in what they could achieve on her and Alicia's behalf.

"Have to fly to the house to supervise some carpentry." She smiled warmly at Christabel. "Since you'll be occupied with the men today, I thought Alicia might like to come with me. I have a picnic lunch in the helicopter."

"Oh, could I please, Mummy?" Alicia cried, her eyes agog with excitement.

"You can contact me any time," Sam assured Christabel, patting the mobile telephone hanging from the belt of her jeans. "It's only a fifteen-minute flight if you want us back. But it sure would be fun having your daughter along with me."

"Yes, yes," Alicia pleaded.

It dawned on Christabel that the reason Sam was here was to take Alicia out of the Kruger equation, at least physically, until the conflict of interests was settled. For the past couple of hours she had been winning the child's trust and building her liking so the invitation would be accepted quite naturally—no frightening sense of being taken away by a stranger.

"It won't be a problem," Sam promised, her clear blue eyes shooting both sympathy and moral support as she pointedly added, "she'll be safe with me."

Safe…a weight lifted off Christabel's heart. Alicia, at least, would not be subjected to any trauma today. "Thank you," she said with deep gratitude before smiling at her daughter. "Promise you'll be good and do everything Sam says."

"I promise." She was off her chair and dancing around in wild eagerness.

Miranda held out a hand to her, laughing at the childish excitement. "Come and we'll get your hat from your room."

As soon as they were gone from the kitchen, Sam addressed the *real* issue. "I've known Nathan and Tommy and Jared all my life. You couldn't have better men on your side, Christabel. None of them will shy from doing whatever has to be done to ensure you and Jared can make a life together.''

She hadn't agreed to marrying Jared, or even sharing any more of her life with him. She tried to explain her position. ''There are…risks.''

''No risks, no prizes,'' Sam lilted back at her as though her own experience had taught her that being passive didn't get her where she wanted to go. She showed no concern whatsoever over *her* part in today's arrangements and seemed intent on soothing Christabel's fears as she chatted on.

''Tommy will be flying your visitors over the most inaccessible parts of the Kimberly—no roads, no vestige of civilisation, just ancient ranges and big, daunting, uninhabited country. He wants to impress on their minds how challenging it is to survive here, and how the sheer isolation of it can eat into one's mind and heart and soul. Amazing how quickly it can change perceptions and responses and values.''

''It won't mean anything to them,'' Christabel informed her. Money people were only interested in money, she thought cynically.

Sam cocked her head on one side, apparently considering her assertion. ''It can come to mean something in hindsight, Christabel, especially to those who underestimate what they're taking on when they come face to face with the outback. It's the land that rules, not men. It changes the terms.''

Christabel looked more sharply at her, sensing she was suggesting how Rafael Santiso might be dealt with. ''Are you saying…they may be kept here until they see things differently?'' she asked incredulously.

''Well, I expect they will learn something about

very basic values on this trip." She nodded some personal satisfaction. "I think your Mr. Santiso will be considering his decisions very carefully before this day is out."

Or he'd be abducted and given a learning experience? Christabel was still struggling with this concept. "Jared and Nathan and Tommy…"

"Won't allow you and Alicia to be victimised," Sam slid in, obviously delivering the bottom line.

"But…" Her hands fluttered in agitation. "…the repercussions."

Sam shrugged. "I tend to think it will just end up a different ball game. No repercussions at all. The Kings have their own way of protecting their territory and their people. Believe me, you're *safer* with them than you would be anywhere else."

Jared believed this. Strangely, Sam's conviction gave *his* belief more substance, probably because Sam wasn't quite so personally involved, though she was taking care of Alicia today. Maybe it was being outback bred that gave Sam Connelly this knowing confidence of how this unique part of the world worked.

Her words…*doing whatever has to be done*…kept echoing in Christabel's ears. Jared had been like that from the beginning, never accepting defeat, constantly edging forward even as she fought each of his intrusions in her life. He didn't give up. And from what Sam said, neither did Nathan or Tommy.

She had been so caught up in worrying about what Rafael Santiso might do to the King family, she simply hadn't considered what the King family might do to the man who had haunted her all these years. To use the outback itself as a weapon...a persuader...changing the terms...

She remembered very vividly the primeval feeling of the land she had flown over, the same sense of it here at King's Eden, and suddenly realised it *would* have to seep into and influence the nature of the people who lived here. She had felt it about Jared each time she'd seen him naked—a powerful primitive entity intent on claiming what he wanted.

Rafael Santiso had always seemed an unstoppable force—but the King family *were* a different breed to the men he was used to dealing with. The prospect of a head-on collision between them made her feel weirdly skittish inside and she was glad when Miranda and Alicia came back, immediately presenting the activity of seeing her daughter off in the helicopter with Sam.

It was good to listen to Alicia's excited chatter as they all strolled down to the landing strip beyond the big equipment buildings. Her little face was so wonderfully alive and carefree, untouched by the inheritance she knew nothing about. Christabel fiercely wished it could be kept that way, at least for enough years for her character to develop without the influences wrought by great wealth.

A normal happy child flew off with Sam Connelly.

Christabel couldn't help feeling apprehensive about what her daughter would fly back to and how it was going to affect her.

"It's all fixed so that Alicia will not meet the men you fear unless you decide it's okay," Miranda informed her as they watched the helicopter zoom off into the distant sky.

Christabel looked sharply at her. "How is it fixed?"

Miranda smiled reassuringly. "They won't be staying here. Tommy will fly them to his wilderness resort, which adjoins the cattle station. You were accommodated in one of the cabins for my wedding, weren't you?"

"Yes. But I thought it was closed during the wet season."

"It has resident maintenance staff. Your visitors will be housed in the resort homestead for the duration of their stay at King's Eden."

"I doubt they intend to stay long."

"Well, I expect that will depend on what happens at this morning's meeting, which, of course, will be under our control."

Christabel stared into the calm green pools of her hostess's beautiful eyes. There was not the tiniest trace of apprehension marring her serenity. The King family was arranging their chessboard for the battle ahead, holding Alicia—the queen piece—safe from any possible attack, moving the enemy king and his two rooks where *they* chose, making the opposition aware of the dominant factor of *their* ground, and Christabel suddenly wondered what kind of backup Jared and Nathan were arranging with the Aboriginal tribe.

Alarm streaked through her. So much had been arranged without any consultation with her, but what if Rafael Santiso had organised his own backup before climbing into Tommy's plane this morning?

"You don't know these men and what they're capable of, Miranda," she shot out, disturbed by a confidence that had no cracks to allow for other outcomes.

"I know *our* men," she answered feelingly. "I know what they saved me from and how effectively they did it. They are quite fearless in their strength, Christabel. That's something I don't think more *civilised* men meet with in their very *civilised* lives."

It was a different reflection of what Sam had said...the primitive element of survival running through them, taught by the harshness of an environment that demanded they be fit to endure anything. Maybe the land itself did change the terms and the King family could prevail over whatever forces Rafael Santiso mustered.

Still inwardly agitated, Christabel sought more evidence of their strength. "What did they save you from?"

Miranda grimaced ruefully. "From a man who was intent on ruining my life because I wouldn't play his game. He was the heir to an international chain of hotels, with the power of great wealth behind him. He thought he could use it to influence the King family against me." She shook her head reminiscently. "It meant nothing to them. So you see, the Kruger inheritance won't mean anything to them, either."

She hooked her arm around Christabel's, lightly pressing a sympathetic togetherness as she started them on the walk back to the homestead. "They will support you. Unequivocally. Through anything that's thrown at them."

"It's asking a terrible lot," Christabel couldn't help saying. "The inheritance won't go away and others will come."

"Jared loves you." Miranda's lovely green eyes glowed with secure knowledge as she added, "Nathan loves me. Tommy loves Sam. Each of them understands what it means to them. There is nothing in this world that would make them give up their women."

Christabel's heart quivered at the enormity of such deep, abiding love. Could she accept it, unequivocally, whatever came? She wanted to. It was what she had felt flowing from Jared last night, and her whole being yearned to love and be loved by him for the rest of her life.

No risks, no prizes.

Her gaze turned up to the homestead that had stood as an emblem of endurance for over a hundred years. It was beautifully maintained. The huge white roof glistened in the morning sunshine. The white veranda posts and the decorative iron lace that ran around the eaves lent it the image of a crown, majestically dominating the vastness of the land around it.

A crown for the Kings of the outback, Christabel thought whimsically, feeling they truly were kings of men, deserving of crowns. She hoped they would endure, that she wouldn't be the one to bring them down, that somehow something could be worked out so she and Alicia could live happily with Jared.

She loved him.

But whether the prize of love would be worth all the risks, only time would tell.

CHAPTER THIRTEEN

CHRISTABEL drew in a deep breath as the minibus from the King's Eden wilderness resort came to a halt. Jared's arm was around her waist and he gave her a quick hug, reminding her she was not alone. They were lined up along the veranda at the front entrance to the homestead, he and Nathan standing together, she and Miranda on either side of them, waiting to greet the visitors.

It was forty minutes since they'd seen Tommy's plane come in—forty very long minutes, knowing *they* were here. It was almost a relief to see the Kruger triumvirate alighting from the minibus, and something of an anticlimax that they weren't wearing suits. Their open-necked shirts and light cotton trousers made them look less intimidating but Christabel knew that was an illusion, and the black leather briefcases they carried gave the lie to any casual air they might adopt.

Rafael Santiso and Elizabeth King led the little procession through the front gate, Vogel and Wissmann following, Tommy behind them, shutting the gate with the air of a shepherd who had successfully herded his flock to the designated pen.

But he'd brought the wolf into the fold, Christabel thought, and with each step Rafael Santiso took towards her, she felt her nerves tightening and her hope for an agreeable outcome dwindling.

His black-eyed gaze skimmed the four of them

152

waiting on the veranda, pausing fractionally on Christabel before turning back to Elizabeth who was talking to him. A smile lurked on his mouth as he projected interest in what she said. A smile…was the King family a joke to him? Would he learn differently?

Her heart started fluttering as he stepped up onto the veranda. Elizabeth introduced him to Nathan and Miranda first. The Argentinian was not as tall or as big as Nathan—more a match to Jared in build—but he exhibited no sign of being the least bit intimidated by Elizabeth's oldest son, and Miranda was definitely greeted with a flash of male admiration, as though this was a social occasion.

Jared he measured with sharper eyes, and his nod as he moved on to Christabel seemed to express a satisfaction that put her more on edge. How could he be pleased about the aggression she could feel pumping through Jared? Stupid thought, Christabel railed at herself. Rafael Santiso thrived on fights. The tougher the opponent, the more pleasure in the win.

"Christabel…I'm glad to see you looking well."

His cultured, urbane voice sent a shiver down her spine. She couldn't bring herself to make a reply, glaring her contempt for his supposed caring about her well-being. She felt like spitting at him.

One devilish eyebrow arched inquiringly. "Alicia is not here with you?"

"No, she's not," Christabel snapped defiantly, and the urge to puncture this charade of normal civility bolted out of her control. "She's out of your reach, Rafael."

Her fierce claim evoked only an ironic little smile.

"I see it is well past time to address the matter of trust."

"Well past time," Jared asserted, the subtle challenge in his voice drawing Santiso's attention back to him.

The brief interchange was broken by the introduction of Hans Vogel and Pieter Wissmann. Then Nathan was ushering them all inside.

Jared held her back, turning her into his embrace, his eyes boring into hers with urgent intensity. "I know you feel cornered. I also know you have the heart of a tiger. Together we can fight our way through anything," he declared with conviction.

The heart of a tiger? Was that what was pounding inside her? Through the whirl of apprehension in her mind came the thought—if ever there was a time to claw her way to freedom, this was it!

"I will fight, Jared," she promised him, and saw the leap of satisfaction in his eyes.

The big, formal dining room had virtually been turned into a boardroom for this critical meeting. When she and Jared entered, Rafael Santiso, flanked by Hans Vogel and Pieter Wissmann, occupied the far side of the huge mahogany table, the contents of their briefcases formidably stacked in front of them.

Nathan sat at the head of the table with Miranda on his left. Elizabeth sat at the foot of it with Tommy on her right. Two vacant chairs between Tommy and Miranda stood waiting for Christabel and Jared, directly across the table from Rafael Santiso.

Jared seated her between Tommy and himself. Miranda had set out jugs of iced water, and Christabel gratefully noted that the glasses around the table had been filled. Her throat was very dry. She didn't want to look at Rafael Santiso but pride made her face him, and as Jared settled beside her and took her hand, interlacing his fingers with hers, a strong surge of rebellion poured through her *tiger* heart. She would not let the Kruger trustee take over her life. She belonged with Jared.

"What business brings you to us, Rafael?" Jared opened up, letting it be known that Christabel was not to be singled out as a separate entity.

"Many serious considerations," he answered. "First, may I say how pleased I am to have the opportunity of meeting the King family en masse like this." He swept a look of pleasure around the table, stopping at Tommy. "I presume your fiancée, Samantha Connelly, has Alicia in her safekeeping."

"Yes, she does. Sam will keep her happy," Tommy rolled back at him, not the least bit ruffled by the sharp intelligence behind the assumption.

"Alicia is unaware of her inheritance and Christabel wants it kept that way," Jared stated, purposefully drawing Rafael's attention back to him and throwing out a probing challenge.

"Impossible in the long term," Rafael countered.

"We aim to keep her free of it for as many years as we can," Jared pressed.

Christabel felt the formidable power of the mind that had manipulated the trusteeship being brought to bear on the issue raised. Whatever he said would sound reasonable. In all her dealings with him he had never sounded *unreasonable*, which had made him so impossible to fight. He spun a web that covered everything. Her skin crawled as she anticipated the first set of strands, intended to wind around her in an inescapable net.

"An interesting proposition," he said *reasonably*, even with a hint of sympathy for the task. "Part of why I'm here is to assure myself of *your* capability of delivering what is needed…to ensure a relatively safe and happy life for both Christabel and Alicia."

It was the last thing any of them expected to hear and the arrogance of the claim was breathtaking. A sense of disbelief hung in the stunned silence around the table.

Christabel's mind spun at the boldness of such a strategy—evading any accountability on his part by putting the King family on the line. She leaned forward, a welling outrage demanding to be voiced, but Jared spoke first, squeezing her hand as he did so.

"That is not your business, Rafael," he stated curtly. "It's mine and Christabel's and Alicia's. You're not their guardian."

"I promised the child's grandfather I would keep her safe," came the equable reply.

"Thereby ensuring the Kruger inheritance is kept safely in your hands," Jared fired at him point-blank.

It stung, jerking Rafael's chin into a tilt of pride. "It *is* safe in my hands. Safer than in anyone else's."

"Fine." Jared belligerently tapped the table as he went on. "But you will not hold Christabel and Alicia hostages to your personal or financial interests." His hands cut a decisive scissorlike movement. "They're free of you now and they'll stay free of you."

Rafael leaned forward, his eyes glittering scorn. "But are they free of others, Jared? Do you imagine that *I* am the only one who has a personal and financial interest in the Kruger fortune? Alicia is a hostage to anyone who wants a bite of it.''

Jared leaned forward, boring in. "You're the one Christabel fears most. You're the one she fled from.''

Rafael flung a hand out in brusque dismissal. "A misconception.''

"Then clear it up, Rafael. Now!''

Jared sat back, ostensibly prepared to listen, but he left the air between him and Rafael Santiso electric with challenge. Adrenalin was pumping through Christabel. She seethed over the word *misconception*, all primed to pounce on any clarification she knew was false.

Rafael frowned momentarily as though gathering his thoughts, then with an open-handed gesture that suggested he had nothing to hide, he said, "Let me explain to all of you that when Bernhard Kruger died, the arrangements made in his will were not to the liking of two powerful factions within the company. It was…a dangerous time.''

His gaze swung directly to Christabel. "The precautions I put in place to protect you and Alicia were necessary. I know you felt imprisoned and you saw me as your gaoler.'' He shook his head ruefully. "There was nothing I could do to alter your view. In effect, it was true. At the time, I believed it was the only way of discharging my duty as Bernhard's appointed trustee.''

If it was an appeal for *her* understanding, it fell on stony ground. Christabel stared back at him, unmoved. She was sure he had Laurens's blood on his hands, and it would only be a matter of time before he'd be planning Alicia's demise, as well.

He held her gaze, determined on getting through to her. Seeing her resistance he pressed, weighting his words with very deliberate purpose. "I was more aware than you were of how quickly, how ruthlessly, a life can be snuffed out when that life can influence what happens to a fortune."

Was he warning her? Threatening her?

He paused, looking for fear in her eyes? Christabel could feel the pulse beat in her temples but she would not bend to any pressure from him. Jared would stop it somehow. Jared and his brothers.

"Remember Laurens?" Rafael continued in a softer tone.

A taunting reminder that her husband was dead? That Jared, too, could be dead if she didn't come to heel?

"It was not an accident that killed your husband, Christabel."

The shock of that open admission jolted her into speech. "I never believed it was," she flared at him, then couldn't stop the churn of truths that had driven her to take the course she had. "To me the only question was...who was behind his removal from the Kruger power pyramid? And the answer..." She stood up, needing to fight, to force him into more admissions. "...the answer, Rafael...was written in the outcome."

Her fists pressed onto the surface of the table as she leaned over it, pouring out the line of logic that couldn't be refuted by the man who'd profited most by Laurens's death.

"His death served *your* purpose so very neatly, putting you at the head of the South American network in *his* place, which brought you directly into Bernhard's inner circle. It gave you the chance to win his confidence and you do that so well, Rafael... winning people's confidence. You got it all, didn't you? And before Alicia is eighteen, no doubt you'll find a way to eliminate her, as well.''

The blistering indictment had no visible effect on him. He sat quite still.

There was a breathless silence all around the table. A pin dropping would have been a shattering sound. Christabel realised she was trembling and abruptly sat down, breathing hard as though she'd run a long race. Jared took her hand, pressing warmth and reassurance.

Hans Vogel coughed and leaned forward, looking as though he was about to protest. He was a heavy-set man, bald and bespectacled, with a bullish authority that didn't suffer fools gladly. Christabel glared at him, refusing to be reduced to a mere cipher he could roll over.

Rafael Santiso simply raised his hand and the lawyer settled back again. ''So *I* was the bête noir all along,'' he softly mused, then looked inquiringly around the table. ''And this you all know— Christabel's belief that I had her husband murdered?''

Nathan, Miranda, Jared and Tommy all remained silent, watching him, giving him nothing to hit off.

Elizabeth spoke, shock evident in her tone. ''You didn't inform me, Jared.''

''I didn't know of it until last night,'' he answered quietly. ''And it was irrelevant to the action being taken this morning. I wanted you to bring them here. It's the best place to deal with the situation. We were all agreed on that and since you now know the score…'' He swung his gaze to the man who'd charmed his mother ''…let him answer the charge.''

To Christabel's ear, there was a relentless beat in Jared's voice that carried the message it was Rafael and his men who were cornered, not her and Alicia. She squeezed his hand, her courage lifting with having him so staunchly on her side.

Rafael Santiso shook his head, as though in disbelief at finding himself in this position. His running glance from Nathan to Tommy left him in no doubt that the King brothers were sitting in judgment on him. Christabel wondered if he was remembering the country he'd flown over to get here, whether the isolation of it was hitting him now.

Then his gaze targeted her, snapping her mind back to red alert. He thought she was the weak one to be worked upon, twisted around. Not today, she silently vowed.

''You hid your suspicion well,'' he remarked, displaying no hint of acrimony over her accusations. ''I would have corrected it, or asked Bernhard to correct it, had I realised you believed me to be behind Laurens's death.''

''As you well know, Bernhard is *beyond* speaking for you,'' Christabel retorted, showing her scepticism.

He shrugged. ''The train of events will speak for him. As it was, you were deliberately cocooned from what was going on. You were heavily pregnant. There was concern for both your health and the child's.''

Another *reasonable* stance. Christabel would have none of it. She attacked straight back. ''When I spoke of my doubts about the accident to Bernhard, he dismissed what I said out of hand, Rafael. Why should I even begin to believe what you say of that time?''

''It was men's business, Christabel. You were a young woman of twenty-two. You lived under Bernhard's wing for almost three years. From your own experience of him, do you really imagine he would discuss something so personal as the murder of his son and heir with you?''

He paused, giving her time to remember the old man's patriarchal arrogance and his limited view of his daughter-in-law, then pressed home a truth she could not deny. ''Your only function to Bernhard Kruger was to be a good mother to his grand-daughter.'' His voice softened as he added, ''In that, may I say, you have always excelled.''

Christabel instantly bridled.

''I advise you that repeating Bernhard Kruger's at-titude towards Christabel is not acceptable,'' Jared in-serted coldly. ''At this point, facts will serve you bet-ter than any sentiment which reinforces her position as Alicia's mother and ignores the respect due to her as a person in her own right.''

Once again she was surprised at how closely at-tuned Jared was to her feelings and took deep comfort in how at one they were.

Rafael raised a challenging eyebrow to Christabel. ''Have I accurately summed up your situation in the Kruger household?''

''Yes. Before and after his death when *you* took over,'' she answered bitterly, all the old resentments at being treated like a brainless chattel burning through her. ''I was very young and very naive to have ever married Laurens in the first place. But then you banked on that, didn't you?''

He actually looked surprised at her reading this much into the part he'd played. ''It was your choice, Christabel.''

''Under pressure from my parents.'' Her eyes hotly accused him of being the source of that pressure. ''You brokered a deal with my father. Don't bother denying it. He confessed it after I fled to Rio to get help from my family. A bigger better jewellery business in exchange for a daughter to beget another Kruger heir.''

There was a rustle of movement from her side of the table and she sensed more than saw the heightened interest her words had sparked. She had not spoken of this to anyone, shying from revealing her past foolishness. But it was pertinent here.

Aware she was adding more fuel to the fire she was building under him, Rafael instantly sought to cool it down. ''You know it is the way the old families arrange it in South America. I was delegated to offer the bride price. That is all I did. The choice was still yours. And you seemed taken with Laurens.''

''You've already commented on how *young* I was, Rafael. I was flattered. Overwhelmed. But you knew what kind of man Laurens was and what I was being led into.''

He shook his head. ''For all I knew of you then, you could have viewed it as an advantageous marriage. Many women would see it as a passport to a life they envied. You made the decision, Christabel.''

''And I'm sure you found it advantageous—a South American bride, approved of by Bernhard

Kruger. Another little fortuitous connection on your way up the ladder.''

He lost patience with her argument, tersely replying, ''It had no bearing on my situation, which only changed after Laurens was gone.''

''And then you came into everything. My point entirely,'' she fired at him.

''Except it's based on a false premise,'' he snapped. ''I had nothing to do with Laurens's death, Christabel.''

''Prove it!''

The demand rang through the tension in the room, seeming to bounce off the walls. Anger showed clearly on Rafael Santiso's face, an anger that laced his voice as he bitingly asked, ''Are you prepared to listen now?''

''By all means lay out your *train of events*,'' she threw back at him.

He swept a dark burning gaze around the King family. ''I understand that Christabel needed to voice the suspicions that have festered for so long, but that is all they are—suspicions. Justifiable in her situation, but unjustified by any proof. Please keep that in mind.''

He turned to the lawyer beside him. ''Hans, take them through what was done.''

The lawyer was in his seventies, a long-time aide in the Kruger camp and undoubtedly privy to many secrets. As much as Christabel disliked him, Rafael's confidence in handing his defence over to the older man did intrigue her enough to command her attention.

''Bernhard instantly suspected that the boat which

exploded and killed Laurens had been sabotaged,'' Vogel related tonelessly. ''He offered a large reward for the identity of the saboteurs. The information came in. The men directly responsible for Laurens's death volunteered the name of the man who'd hired them. He revealed a conspiracy within the Kruger network, a certain pressure group that was planning a division of interests which would be highly profitable to those involved.''

He paused, his light blue eyes zeroing in on Christabel. ''It was centred on our South African connections, nothing to do with South America.''

''The boat blew up in the Caribbean,'' Christabel swiftly reminded him.

''The Caribbean is an international playground,'' came the instant rebuff. ''A place for international gossip amongst jetsetters.''

She had to grant him that.

Hans Vogel continued with barely a pause, his eyes boring through the cynical reservations in hers. ''Laurens heard a rumour of the conspiracy at a party and asked some indiscreet questions instead of bringing what he'd picked up to his father. You were married to him. You must know he liked to pump himself up, wanting to make himself a bigger man than he was. It turned into a fatal flaw.''

Yes, she did know, Christabel silently conceded. Laurens would have exulted in telling his father something Bernhard didn't know, showing off, proving how important he could be. ''Do I know any of the conspirators?'' she asked.

Hans Vogel shrugged. ''I doubt it. I do have the entire list of names in my office safe. Not with me. I can assure you Rafael Santiso is not one of them. But I can produce the reports if you so wish. It is impossible, however, for you to speak to anyone on the list about these circumstances.''

''Why is that?''

''Regrettably, all of them have died...in accidents,'' he said very dryly. ''The hand of justice, is it not?''

The hand of an old man wreaking vengeance on those who'd agreed to the murder of his son! She should have been shocked but oddly enough it all seemed very distant to her—another life, another world, one she didn't want to return to.

Pieter Wissmann, the Swiss accountant, sat forward. He was a pale thin man in his fifties who always carried an air of precision. ''If you want objective confirmation of what occurred, following on from Bernhard's investigation ...''

He looked at Nathan, Tommy, then directly at Jared. ''As men of business, you will appreciate that financial figures tell their own story. The rearrangement of the South African operation is quite dramatic, directly related to the elimination of corrupt connections and the building of a new network. If you wish to examine the records on this, I can make them available to you.''

Christabel frowned over the sheer weight of the revelations, her mind torn at having her own long-held belief in Rafael Santiso's guilt crushed. The offering of such confidential information was extraordinary. The list of the conspirators' names, their deaths, which could be officially confirmed, the money trail...she had to be wrong about Rafael's involvement in Laurens's death. There was too much evidence pointing elsewhere. *Firm* evidence, not suspicions based on steps that could have favoured him in his rise to the trusteeship of the Kruger inheritance.

Jared stirred beside her. "Do I understand, from both of you…" he said slowly "…that everything pertaining to Laurens Kruger's death was cleared up and acted upon while Bernhard Kruger was still alive?"

"Yes. The conspiracy, once uncovered, was excised with maximum efficiency," Hans Vogel replied.

"The reorganisation took longer but it was in place and running to Bernhard's satisfaction before he died," Pieter Wissmann confirmed.

"Thank you. We appreciate your candour and co-operation in offering this sensitive information," Jared assured them respectfully, then leaned forward, resting his forearms on the table, his gaze trained on Rafael Santiso. "I have two questions," he stated in a tone that demanded satisfaction.

"Ask them," Rafael invited brusquely, emitting the attitude that he could answer anything at any time.

"Given that the conspiracy had been comprehensively dealt with…why was it so dangerous for Christabel and Alicia when you took over after Berhard's death, to the point of your becoming their *gaoler*?" He let Rafael's own word hang for a moment. "And given Christabel's obvious wish to be free of you and all you represent…why didn't you respect *her* choice, *her* decision…as you did when she married Laurens Kruger?"

Jared paused, then quietly added, "Please keep in mind that Christabel has the right to choose the life she wants, and as Alicia's mother, she has the right to choose what she feels is best for her daughter. That is *our* concern here. We are yet to understand *your* concerns...the purpose behind this uninvited and unwelcome intrusion on a life that literally has nothing to do with you.''

Again there was that relentless beat in Jared's phrasing, a quiet but very real menace underlying the words that spelled out the heart of the matter in unequivocal terms, and what had to be answered.

Even as Christabel felt a strong surge of love for this man at her side...her soul partner, her champion...she looked at Rafael Santiso and wondered if he sensed what he was facing—*no escape*.

No escape, she kept thinking, amazed that those words could now apply to the seemingly all-powerful figure she had fled from.

Maybe she and Alicia could be safe here.

Or was she assuming too much, too soon?

CHAPTER FOURTEEN

JARED knew he was facing the most testing experience in his life. He'd dealt with many a cutthroat businessman in the pearl trade, but these three men were on a different level altogether. They accepted, apparently without question, Bernhard Kruger's ruthless *elimination* of the conspirators responsible for his son's death. No weighing the degree of guilt. A complete sweep.

While Christabel had not known of these extreme measures, she had certainly picked up what these people were capable of—power that recognised only its own law of maintaining power, whatever that took.

And while Rafael Santiso did not have her husband's blood on his hands, could her instincts be right about him where Alicia was concerned? Would he acknowledge that the child was not *his* to be controlled as it suited him? Even if he did, could he be believed?

Jared watched intently as the Argentinian considered the questions put to him. His mother was attracted to this man. Vikki Chan had not given any caution against him. Both women had finely tuned instincts that would normally pick up on any shading of integrity. But Jared had too much riding on the outcome of this confrontation to have blind faith in their judgment.

"Perhaps I was overzealous in protecting

Christabel and Alicia, but I cannot regret what I did,'' he said with an air of honest assessment. ''If my precautions were extreme, it was because the responsibility of their safety sat heavily on me, knowing what had happened to Laurens, and I was very conscious that Bernhard's mantle did not fit my shoulders. Those who had respected his power were all too prepared to test mine.''

A different man at the helm—a deputy instead of the old master—yes, Jared could appreciate the pressure to perform would be on.

Hans Vogel broke in, his thin mouth curling in disgust. ''Bernhard was not even in his grave before the challenges to his will began from those who led powerful factions within the Kruger organisation. As far as they were concerned, the king was dead and the throne was for their taking, regardless of Bernhard's legal appointment of Rafael as sole trustee of the inheritance.''

His bullish face turned to Christabel. ''You owe Rafael more than you know. But for him...''

''Enough, Hans!'' The silencing hand was lifted. ''The prison Christabel found herself in was not of her making.'' Rafael turned his gaze to her, his expression slightly puzzled, searching. ''The fear you had of me must have made it worse. I saw hatred for what I stood for, resentment of what I enforced, but...'' He shook his head. ''...fear I did not read.''

''I would not give you any more leverage over me,'' Christabel replied, pride ringing loud and clear.

Rafael nodded thoughtfully and looked back at Jared. ''I've already said it was a dangerous time after Bernhard died. There were many in the organisation who believed he had become unhinged from his illness and grief for his son. They had expected him to appoint a board of trustees to manage the inheritance, not just me. Alicia was certainly perceived as a vehicle to gain more control.''

His eyes took on a mocking challenge. ''What would you have done, Jared...if you were me? Let Christabel and her daughter run loose to be snatched and ransomed? Risk Alicia's life? Her death would have instantly fractured the structure Bernhard had set up—an advantageous situation to some.''

Jared recalled that he himself had taken command yesterday, not consulting Christabel about flying them to King's Eden, simply doing it, believing he knew best how to assure their safety. This place, too, could become a prison. The difference was...Christabel did not fear him as she'd feared Rafael. She *wanted* to be with him.

''Like you, I would have thrown a blanket of protection around them,'' Jared answered slowly.

''As you have here,'' Rafael was quick to point out, his eyes lighting with satisfaction.

''But I am not the oppressor,'' Jared instantly countered. ''To Christabel, you were and are, extending a life she hated. It's a question of values, Rafael. You were looking after the inheritance, regardless of any quality of life for her.''

''At least she *had* life.''

''An intolerable one.''

His head tilted in a concessionary nod. ''I did come to realise that, Jared, when Christabel effected her escape. It was a desperate act, given she knew the dangers of being without any security around her. At first

I thought…'' He shrugged. ''Once I found her jewellery was also gone, I knew it was a personal bid for freedom, rather than running to another Kruger camp.''

He leaned back in his chair, a musing little smile on his lips. ''So what would you have done then…if you were me? Let her go? Tried to find her and bring her back? What, Jared?''

It came to him in a lightning flash what Rafael Santiso had done, and why he was here now, meeting the King Family. Relief poured through him. Christabel and Alicia *were* safe, and his mother and Vikki Chan had not been fooled.

He expelled a long breath. He looked at Christabel's long-time nemesis with a new respect for the man of integrity he actually was, a man who shouldered his responsibilities with utter commitment, yet tempering that commitment with a humanity Jared had to admire. The only thing Rafael had overlooked was Christabel's fear of him, unrecognised, partly because she had hidden it from him, partly because he hadn't known how she'd painted him in her mind.

''Do you have the reports with you?'' Jared asked.

Respect instantly flashed into Rafael's eyes.

Understanding flowed between them, man to man on equal footing.

Rafael picked up a Manila folder, thick with documents, from the pile in front of him and slid it across the table. ''Much of this contains summaries. If you want more detail, Hans will supply it.''

Jared nodded, picking up the file and rising to his feet. ''I'd appreciate it if you'd run through your protection procedure with my family while I speak to Christabel privately.''

''I shall do that and give any explanation they require.''

''Thank you.''

Rafael smiled. ''It is good to know at first-hand the mettle of the man who is taking on…whatever has to be done.''

Jared turned to help Christabel out of her chair. She came unresistingly but looked totally bewildered. ''It's all right,'' he assured her. ''We'll come back after we talk.''

''Before you go…''

It snapped their attention back to Rafael. He was looking at Christabel, a powerful intensity in the eyes trained directly on hers.

''I did not know of your fear of me, Christabel, but it did serve you well in your travels, keeping you cautious and not drawing any untoward attention to yourself and Alicia. I want you to know that in the years you've been gone, I have stamped my authority on the Kruger organisation, and I no longer see any danger coming from within. From outside is another matter, but we will discuss that later.''

She shook her head, confused by the turnaround from enemy to ally. Jared took her arm and steered her from the dining room, wanting to get her out of the highly charged atmosphere that swirled with the memories of all she'd been through. She needed to feel free, to follow her own heart without fear, and Jared knew he could give that to her now.

He took her onto the veranda that skirted the homestead—fresh air to breathe, a view that had no boundaries in sight—the vast tracts of King's Eden stretching to the horizon and beyond. *The land of my fathers,* he thought, feeling a well of pride in his heritage. Because he was who he was, and all that was imbued in him, he would have Christabel and keep her, and that was a glorious feeling.

"What are these reports?" she asked anxiously. "What are we doing out here, Jared?"

"Do you still believe Rafael Santiso caused Laurens's death?" he asked, scanning her eyes for any hint of doubt.

She expelled a heavy sigh and made a wry grimace. "No. But I still think he's dangerous."

"Yes. To anyone who crosses the line he draws. But not to you nor Alicia, Christabel," he assured her with absolute certainty.

"How can you know that?" she cried, the old fear still fluttering.

"Because he's been protecting you all along. That's what these reports are about. He let you think you were free because you wanted so badly to be free, but he watched over you all the way to here, Christabel. And he came now because of me, to see if I'm good enough to take over the watch from him."

Her feet faltered to a halt. She swung to face him, her agitation intense. "He could have plucked me and Alicia back any time? Is that what you're saying?"

He nodded. "From Rio onwards would be my guess. He would have put your family under surveillance the moment he realised you'd fled with your jewellery."

The colour drained from her face. "All this time," she said faintly.

"To ensure your safety as best he could, Christabel, while giving you the freedom you craved."

She shook her head. "I can't believe it." Her gaze dropped to the file he held. "Show me. I want to see what he did."

Jared curved an arm around her shoulders. "There's a table on the western veranda. We'll sit down and you can read all you want."

She moved with him, dazedly repeating, "All this time…he knew?"

"Yes. And I'd imagine—smoothed the path for you wherever he could."

They sat where his family usually gathered to watch the sunset—the end of the day. It was only a little past noon, yet the sense of the end to a long, long road for Christabel evoked a similar feeling of being able to relax now.

He didn't read the reports. He listened to Christabel's comments on them, her initial incredulity stretching into an awed understanding of how Rafael Santiso had facilitated her *escape*, as well as taking every precaution he could for her and Alicia's continued well-being, without any overt oppression or constriction.

The passports in the name of Valdez were not forged, as she had believed. Rafael had organised that the name of Kruger be legally changed to the one she'd chosen. Wherever she had sold her diamond jewellery, *his* people had ensured she received what it was truly worth. She and Alicia had never been without bodyguards hovering close by. Even in

Broome, the caravan next to hers had been occupied by Rafael's *watchers*.

There was also a report on the King family—their history and their holdings—and an assessment on their possible reaction to Alicia's inheritance. The judgment was that it would have little or no influence on the life paths they had taken. The Kings of the Kimberly were deeply rooted in their territory and would not shift from where they were.

"You see?" Christabel commented ruefully. "The intrusion into your life and your family's has already begun, Jared." Her eyes searched his, needing reassurance. "Do you really want to take this on?"

He nodded. "Whatever comes, Christabel." He reached across the table and took her hand, enfolding it in the secure strength of his, determined on resolving everything for her to the best of his ability. "They're here to lay out the situation with Alicia's inheritance—Wissmann to deal with the money side, Vogel to deal with the legalities, Rafael to advise on protection."

She sighed, her eyes filling with pained apology. "I had it so wrong."

"Not with me. We have it right together, Christabel." He smiled, wanting to soothe the angst she felt. "Remember Vikki Chan?"

"Yes."

"A very wise old woman, Vikki. She said of you—and I remember the words exactly—*There is a strong wall of integrity in Christabel Valdez which will not be broken. I think she does, and will always do, what she believes is right.*"

A little burst of pleasure brought a golden light to

her beautiful amber eyes. "I felt her taking stock of me but...to read so much?"

"I've never known her to be wrong about people. So I'm asking you now. Can you..." He held her gaze, pouring all his love for her into his voice. "...do you believe it's right..."

He had to hold her.

"Believe what?" she asked shakily as he stood and scooped her up into his embrace.

"I need to hear you say it's right for us to marry, Christabel," he declared with a passion he could no longer contain. "That nothing could be more right because that's what I feel and I have to hear it from you..."

It wasn't a command. It wasn't an appeal. It was a burning certainty in his heart as he spoke the words he wanted her to say.

"...because it's what you feel, too."

CHAPTER FIFTEEN

SIX months on…

"Mummy looks so-o-o beautiful," Alicia breathed on an ecstatic sigh.

Vikki Chan smiled at the child's focus on her mother, who did indeed look as beautiful as a bride should. Truly Jared's bride, Vikki thought indulgently—a tiara of pearls holding her veil, a magnificent necklace of pearls around her throat and pearls studding the diamond pattern on the guipure lace of her strapless bodice. A big silk taffeta skirt billowed out from her hips—extravagant, graceful and lustrously sensual. Altogether, Christabel presented a vision that surely had Jared's cup of pleasure running over.

She was right for him—her wonderful little boy who had become such a man. Tommy was a delight. Nathan was Lachlan all over again. But Jared had always been her favourite—so sensitive and perceptive and receptive, his mind alive to the life in everything, almost Chinese in his appreciation of how nature shaped both good and bad for reasons of its own, the unseen influences that nevertheless did influence important outcomes—winning or losing.

Jared knew how to win. Instinctively, intuitively, he got it right. He had the gift for it. And he certainly looked the winner this evening—so tall and handsome and splendid in his formal silvery grey suit. Even the high peaked white collar of his dress shirt and the silk cravat looked perfect for him. A truly magnificent man. He made her feel very proud.

And having the wedding here in Broome for the whole town to see her boy and his bride…it was an occasion to savour in the days to come, talking it over with her old friends. A touch of honour, too, having Chinese lanterns hung around the grounds. It was a fine choice having the wedding at the Mangrove Hotel, out on this big lawn overlooking Roebuck Bay. Soon the moon would rise….

"Alicia King," the child lilted, trying out the name. She looked up at Vikki, her big brown eyes sparkling with excitement. "Now that Mummy's married to Jared, I'm not going to be Alicia Valdez any more. I think King sounds better, don't you, Vikki?"

"It is a fine and honourable name, Alicia, and a great blessing to be one of the Kings of the Kimberly. They are a family to be proud of."

"I love having a family," the child declared feelingly. "Now I've got a father like all the other girls in my class at school, and when Tommy and Sam fly me back to King's Eden after the wedding, Miranda said I could help mind her baby."

Vikki nodded to herself. People, not money, gave the real riches of life.

"I hope Mummy and Jared have a baby," the child rattled on. "Then I'd have a brother or a sister. Do you think they will, Vikki?"

"In time, little one. We must always wait for good things to happen. There comes a right time and that is the best time."

*   *   *

"Let's sit down, Miranda." Sam rolled her eyes at her sister-in-law. "I *need* to sit down."

Miranda laughed and accompanied her to the closest vacant table. As Christabel's matrons of honour, they'd been standing for a long time, throughout the wedding ceremony and then the photograph session, and Sam was four months pregnant, though it barely showed. It didn't show at all in the princess line dress Christabel had chosen for them, and the midnight blue colour was definitely slimming. Flattering for her own figure, as well, since it was only a month since she'd given birth to Matthew and she wasn't yet back in shape.

"All I can say is, thank heaven the morning sickness is over. Pregnancy does not suit me," Sam declared as she sank onto a chair. "I get so tired all the time."

"This, too, will pass," Miranda advised, taking the chair beside her.

"Where's your gorgeous baby boy? I need a reminder of what's at the end of this."

"Nathan has him, parading him around the guests."

They both laughed. Nathan doted on his son.

"Tommy's going to be the same. He's so cock-a-hoop that we're having a girl."

"Well, it will be the first one born to the King family for three generations."

Sam grimaced. "I always wanted to be a boy myself. I'm not good at the female thing, Miranda."

"Nonsense. Boy or girl, I think you just have to let them follow their own nature and enjoy them for what they are. Besides, you've been marvellous with Alicia and you've said yourself she's a delightful little girl.''

They both turned their gaze to Christabel's daughter who was chatting away to Vikki Chan, her vivacious face alight with excitement. She'd been a bundle of excitement all day, being a flower girl at her mother's wedding and so happy to be getting Jared as her father.

''You're right. I do enjoy Alicia,'' Sam conceded.

''Please God we never get some nasty investigative reporter connecting her to the Kruger heiress,'' Miranda murmured. ''She's such a lovely natural child.''

''Good thing Rafael had fixed up the Valdez identity so it was legal. It made everything easier for them.'' Sam nodded to where Rafael Santiso and Elizabeth stood together, watching the bride and groom while they enjoyed a private tête-à-tête. ''He's covered his tracks here, too, with his personal interest in Elizabeth.''

''I doubt that has much to do with covering his tracks,'' Miranda said dryly. ''Rafael is seriously courting her, Sam.''

''So it would seem. What does Nathan think?''

''He thinks she should go for it. What's Tommy's reaction?''

''If it makes her happy…''

''Look at her. She's glowing.''

''Fatherhood definitely suits you,'' Tommy declared, his eyes dancing in amusement at the sight of the itty-bitty baby snuggled in the crook of his brother's arm.

Nathan's towering height and big frame made him look like a giant compared to the smallness of his newborn son, yet he was a very gentle giant with Matthew, and Tommy was actually moved by the love so clearly emanating from his older brother.

"It's great, Tommy." Nathan grinned. "And it's great you're having a daughter. Got any names picked yet?"

"Sarah heads the list at the moment."

"It's been quite a year, hasn't it? Three weddings, a son for me and a daughter for you on the way."

"Plus an adopted daughter for Jared."

Nathan laughed. "Miranda heard her practising her new name as they were getting ready for the wedding. She was reciting Alicia King in front of the mirror and looking very smug about it."

"What do you think will happen when she gets to eighteen?"

"Best thing would be to give that inheritance away. Have Rafael administer it for charities. Alicia won't need any of it with Jared as her dad."

"And Christabel doesn't want a bar of it. I'd guess her influence will soak in over the years."

"Sure to. She's one very strong lady."

Tommy shook his head over the traumatic train of events that had eventually landed Christabel in Broome. "Hell of a thing—what she went through."

Nathan looked over the milling crowd of guests to where his youngest brother stood with his bride—the woman he'd fought for and won. "She's got Jared now," he said quietly. "I think for Christabel, he more than makes up for everything she suffered in the past." His vivid blue eyes twinkled at Tommy.

"I'd have to say our kid brother wins the white knight award."

"Oh, I don't know. We did pretty good for Miranda, don't forget. Saved her from a king rat."

"True. And I'm glad Rafael Santiso didn't turn out to be another king rat. I suspect he's going to sweep our mother off with him."

They both turned to assess what was happening on that front.

"You know, Nathan, for an older guy, he's certainly got a pouncing panther air about him."

"Mmm…not unlike Dad in many ways."

Rafael Santiso felt he had been very patient. It was time for Elizabeth to decide.

"So," he said, eyeing her with mocking challenge. "We had Tommy's wedding four months ago. Nathan's son has been safely born. Miranda is handling motherhood without any panic whatsoever. The planning for Jared's wedding has reached its culmination and is currently being perfectly executed. Your youngest son is now married. Samantha's baby is not due for another five months and I shall point out that unlike Miranda, Samantha has a mother of her own to see her through to the birth."

He arched an eyebrow. "Is there any reason you cannot leave the Kimberly and fly to Greece with me?"

She affected surprise. "I thought you were returning to Europe."

He shrugged. "Athens is on the way. I hold a small Greek island in trust. Very private. Very beautiful. It is the perfect place for relaxation after such a busy six months.''

''It has been busy.''

''And frustrating,'' he said darkly.

Her magnificent eyes twinkled seductively. ''I've never been to a Greek island.''

His heart swelled with hope. ''You have only to say yes.''

I can, with a free conscience, put myself first now, Elizabeth decided. How it would be with Rafael, she didn't really know—such a different kind of life—but she wanted to try it, wanted to explore the feelings he stirred in her. It wasn't too late to take a new path, she thought. It was never too late. She had been static for too long. Life was to be lived.

She smiled at Rafael, thinking how exhilarating it was for a woman to feel desired by such a fascinating and desirable man. ''I can't think of any family need to keep me here, so yes, I will go with you.''

''You will?'' His handsome Latin face broke into a triumphant grin.

Nothing to lose and everything to gain, Elizabeth told herself, and made the decision firm. ''I will.''

Jared curved his arm around Christabel's waist as they stood at the fence edging the grounds of the hotel, facing out to where the full moon was rising, a glowing red ball pushing slowly up from the horizon beyond Roebuck Bay.

''Happy?'' he murmured.

She smiled. ''You know I am. Though I do wonder

how your mother feels about us living in Picard house. It's been hers for so long.''

"Now that I have you, she's passing it to us, Christabel. She'll be gone by the time we come back from our honeymoon."

It surprised her. "Where is she going?"

"With Rafael."

"She'll really leave all her family to be with him?" A flash of concern in her eyes. "It's such a high-intensity life he lives, Jared."

He smiled, his confidence in his mother's ability to rise to any challenge stronger than ever. "Invigorating, Vikki says. And she predicts he'll treat her like a queen."

Christabel released a long contented sigh. "I have to admit he's been good to me. Amazing in taking care of the problems with Alicia."

"You don't mind giving up your family in Rio?" he asked quietly.

She shook her head. "They want the money. When I went to them for help, they thought I was mad to leave. It was Rafael's hand behind the scenes that made them give the help I needed. It was the same when Laurens proposed marriage. They thought only of the money."

The eyes she lifted to his held no regrets. "My life is here with you. So is Alicia's. She loves *your* family, Jared. And so do I."

The last little niggle about all the decisions they'd made in the past few months was erased. He nodded towards the bay. "It's starting."

Christabel swiftly turned her attention to the unique phenomenon that was special to Broome. It was most spectacular during the equinoctial tides of March and September when the sea could rise and fall ten metres. At such an extreme low tide, and if the sky was clear as it was this evening, the pools of water stretching across the exposed mudflats reflected the light of the moon, providing the illusion of a staircase—a magical staircase opening up from the huge glowing sphere as it rose above the horizon.

The first red bars were appearing now.

A night to remember, Christabel thought, for so many wonderful reasons, and this…what she was watching now…seemed like a reflection of what Jared had done, hauling her out of darkness and setting her feet on a path with him, a path where every step was a magical experience, glowing with his love for her.

The moon turned to gold as it lifted higher, creating a flight of golden steps coming closer and closer to them. They're for us, Christabel thought—the staircase to a golden future together. And she rested her head on Jared's shoulder, and knew she didn't need anything else. She had everything she wanted in the man who held her.

"I love you so much, Jared," she whispered. "Thank you for rescuing me and making this happen. All of it. You, me, Alicia…"

"Oh, I was only thinking of my pleasure," he teased. "After all, it is my pleasure to love you."

She smiled, her heart singing at the thought of going to bed with her *husband* tonight. Her true husband in every sense. The staircase to the moon was wonderful, but nothing—her mind flitted through the exquisite memories Jared had already given her, her body instantly zinging with anticipation of so much more to come—absolutely nothing, she thought blissfully, could be more wonderful than being *the pleasure King's bride*!

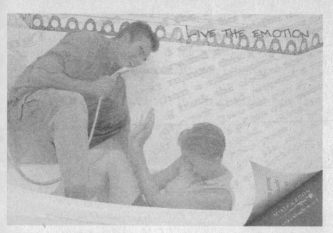

Modern Romance™
...international affairs
– seduction and
passion guaranteed

Medical Romance™
...pulse-raising
romance – heart-
racing medical drama

Tender Romance™
...sparkling, emotional,
feel-good romance

Sensual Romance™
...teasing, tempting,
provocatively playful

Historical Romance™
...rich, vivid and
passionate

Blaze Romance™
...scorching hot
sexy reads

27 new titles every month.

Live the emotion

MILLS & BOON®

MB4 V2

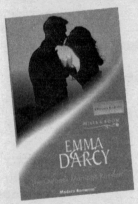

MILLS & BOON

STEPHANIE
LAURENS

*A Suitable
Marriage*

On sale 7th May 2004

*Available at most branches of WHSmith, Tesco, Martins, Borders,
Eason, Sainsbury's and all good paperback bookshops.*

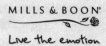

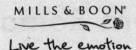

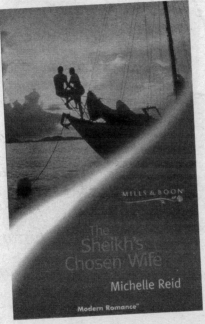

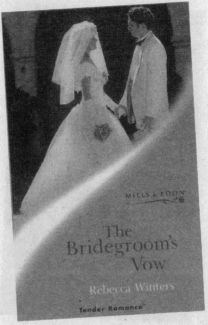

Historical Romance™
...rich, vivid and passionate

Two brand new titles each month

Take a break and find out more about Historical Romance™ on our website
www.millsandboon.co.uk

Available at most branches of WH Smith, Tesco, Martins, Borders, Eason, Sainsbury's, and all good paperback bookshops.

GEN/04/RTL8 V2

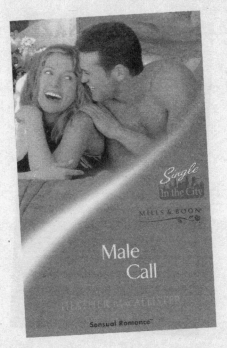

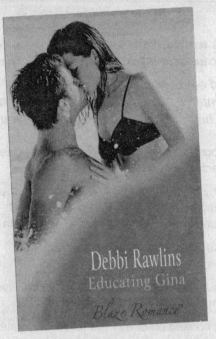